HAMMERS
IN THE
WIND

Book One of the Northern Crusade

CHRISTIAN WARREN FREED

Copyright © 2020 by Christian Warren Freed

Excerpt from *Tides of Blood and Steel* 2021 Christian Warren Freed
Cover design by Melissa Andres
Cover copyright 2021 by Warfighter Books
Author Photograph by Anicie Freed

Warfighter Books
Holly Springs, North Carolina 27540
https://www.christianwfreed.com

Second Edition: July 2021

Library of Congress Cataloging-in-Publication Data
Name: Freed, Christian Warren, 1973- author.
Title: Hammers in the Wind/ Christian Warren Freed
Description: Second Edition | Holly Springs, NC: Warfighter Books, 2021.
Identifiers: LCCN 2021911008 | ISBN 9781736804414 (trade paperback) | 9781957326191 (hardcover)
Subjects: Epic fantasy | Military fantasy | Paranormal

Printed in the United States of America

10 9 8 7 6 5 4 3 2 1

"My lord, Malweir is an ever-dangerous world. I've heard rumors of a civil war between the Dwarf clans to the east. Strange companies of Elves and Goblins have been seen wandering through the land. Some even whisper of the return of the fabled Gaimosian Knights."

Badron shook his head. He'd heard the fairy tales as well and refused to mire his thoughts in such. "For all that you name I can find no true enemy."

"That leaves Rogscroft."

The word stung, hanging in the air like a miasma of doom.

Badron sneered. "They couldn't possibly know what our plans are."

Harnin shrugged. "Perhaps not, but Prince Aurec is your daughter's lover whether you choose to accept it or not. There is a chance he might have succumbed to an act of grave stupidity."

"Or at the insistence of his father," the king finished. He smashed a fist into his palm. He regretted not invading his hated foe those many years ago. "Aurec is no fool, neither is his father. They are brash but not foolish enough to risk reprisal."

"Rogscroft will deny everything, naturally. Not that it matters much, all tracks lead back to the east. This is our chance to finally blame them. It also gives us the perfect opportunity to go to war and remove them from existence."

The prospect of no more subversion enticed Badron. "The Wolfsreik is already marshalling, but it will take time, as you pointed out, for them to actually muster the strength to march. I do not want to tip our hand to our enemies. Continue to use the Pell as an excuse. Keep our people and his spies in the dark for as long as we can and the advantage is ours. Let us catch them unaware."

The bell tolled again, deep and ominous.

"It is time, sire," Harnin grimly announced.

"Then come, let us bury my son."

"Armies of the Silver Mage was a great read...any fan of Lord of the Rings or Game of Thrones will love this book. I'm looking forward to next book."

"The book is almost an homage to the great classics like Sword of Shanara and the Lord of the Rings. The author has cleverly used his past military and combat experience to make the battle scenes more realistic."

The Northern Crusade
Hammers in the Wind
Tides of Blood and Steel
A Whisper After Midnight
Empire of Bones
The Madness of Gods and Kings
Even Gods Must Fall

The Histories of Malweir
Armies of the Silver Mage
The Dragon Hunters
Beyond the Edge of Dawn

Fractured Universe
Dreams of Winter
The Madman on the Rocks
Anguish Once Possessed
Through Darkness Besieged*

Where Have All the Elves Gone?
The Lazarus Men
Repercussions: A Lazarus Men Agenda*
Tomorrow's Demise: The Extinction Campaign
Tomorrow's Demise: Salvation
Coward's Truth*
A Long Way From Home: Memories and Observations
From Iraq and Afghanistan

Immortality Shattered
Law of the Heretic
The Bitter War of Always
Land of Wicked Shadows
Storm Upon the Dawn

Acknowledgments

Writing is a solitary endeavor but cannot be completed without the support, inspiration and contributions of our surroundings. *Hammers in the Wind* was born on a whim and evolved to become a grand adventure thanks in large part to the cadets of company F-3, United States Military Academy (2007-2009). Their encouragement and opinions proved invaluable at certain times.

I would be remiss if I didn't take the time to thank my mother and father for all they have done for me over the last forty years. (Already? Man!) My wife, Annie, who has stood by and been forced to listen to my latest creations and my pestering for her opinions on everything I wrote. Thank you all.

MALWEIR
SANKEN SWAMP
GREETH
GRIN MOT
AINGAARD
NIVEDEN PLAINS
THORN RIVER
TPN SHAL
THUNE LAKE
SHADOW GEIN
BRAEM
ELVENARA
OLD FOREST
AVERON
ANTHENEON
THED MTNS
BAIRN HILLS
BRELINOR
TWIN SPIRES OF RAGNASH
REILIN WERD
FEIST
EIST
700 LEAGUES TO OCEAN
SIBIL RIVER
GRAVEN FOREST
FEL DARRINS
JAREK MTNS
HARLEGOR
TRENNARON
JUNGLES OF BRODEN
TENG
JEBEL
JEBEL DESERT
BAY OF CURRGON
N
E
S
W

ONE

A Foul Night

High-pitched screams pierced the aged wood and stone halls of Chadra Keep. Badron, king of Delranan, sprang from his throne at the sound, his band of favored captains and counselors doing the same. His pale blue eyes turned from shock to feral rage as he quickly registered what was happening. Screams meant one thing: his family was under attack in what was supposed to be the most secure place in his kingdom. More screams and blood-choked cries mixed with the sound of clashing steel. Badron snarled grimly. The house guard, his guard, was locked in brutal struggle somewhere deep within the wooden halls of the Keep.

Badron drew his trusted sword and stormed off in search of the battle. The senior-most lords and captains of Delranan followed him. Eight in all, they comprised a most lethal band of warriors. Their deeds had forged the kingdom from a pack of warring tribes and clans into a singular monarchy that quickly became the strongest of the northern kingdoms. They wordlessly chased at the wolf skin cloak of their king as he headed towards the royal sleeping chambers.

Fear drove Badron. Long red hair, now streaked through with gray, flowed angrily down broad shoulders. Wrath commanded him, wrath so strong it could threaten the foundations of his hard-fought kingdom and make the old gods of Malweir tremble in fear. Muscles bunched under his jerkin. His bulk filled the doorway. Badron felt the old energies flow into him. His was a warrior's life and this night but an extension of it. The sound of glass breaking drew his attention. Badron bellowed and charged, heedless of any lurking dangers.

Fleeting visions of battle appeared through the flickering torchlight. The flash of a sword. A spray of blood. The ruins of a body lay in the middle of the hall, a crumpled mass of flesh. Badron knelt beside the corpse. The smell of blood kissed the stagnant air. Deep cuts and gashes immolated the young house guard. Badron tried to close the eyes, if for no other reason than to avoid staring down into the pure agony. A feathered spear, broken at the hilt, was embedded in the lad's throat.

"Pell Darga," growled Jarrik. He rubbed his bald head and spat.

The king brought his gaze up to his friend and captain. "Rouse whatever watch remains, Jarrik. I want these monsters run down and skinned alive. The rest of you with me."

Badron led them further into the Keep. The inner doors to the royal chambers were smashed to ruins. One lay in splinters across the hall while what was left of the second hung in shreds by a single hinge. Smoke curled up from within, running down the ceiling. Fresh blood stained the floor and walls in ragged patterns. More bodies. Badron grimaced. From the looks of it, his private guard had been caught unaware and slain. Their furs and spiked helmets lay stained in growing pools of blood. Badron splashed his way past.

At last they came unto the king's chambers. The doors were similarly smashed, leaving a gaping maw, dark and uninviting. Shadows leaked into the hall. Unknown fears danced around the men and threatened their resolve. Preparing his mind for the worst, Badron bunched his shoulders and surged forward. Nothing in this world meant so much to him as the memory of his late wife Rialla and the children he'd sired.

Rough hands snatched at his collar and jerked him back. "No my lord, we cannot afford to lose you," Argis whispered. Harsh tones ground from his throat.

He gestured with his head and two of the largest guards crept forward to flank the doors. Satisfied the king wasn't going to do anything rash, Argis released him and tossed his torch to the nearest man. Inion snatched it and gave his battle brother an awkward look. A hint of smile, no more than the slight curve of his lips, caressed his face. It had been too long since they'd last gone to war. Inion hefted his tulwar and threw the torch into the bedchamber. He charged, Argis immediately following with a litany of battle cries. Berserker strength churned inside them.

Badron impatiently waited. Sounds came back to him, making the hairs on his neck stand. The breaking of furniture. A crash in the dark. He forced himself to stand by and wait while others rushed to defend his honor. The idea pained him, but he must be king before warrior. That was the price for the gift he'd usurped from his brother long ago. Inion reappeared a heartbeat later. Disbelief stained his naturally dark eyes. He mouthed words that were incoherent babble.

Badron pushed forward, forgetting all restraint. "Speak man, what of my family?'

The stunned captain could only point back at the broken door.

"Is she?" he whispered.

Inion could not bear to look his king and friend in the eye. "I don't know, sire. There are traces of blood but no bodies. There was a struggle."

Emotions collided in a mass of confusion. Badron was beyond enraged and on the verge of breaking down. He'd never truthfully cared much for his daughter. In fact, he constantly blamed her for the death of his precious Rialla during childbirth. But Maleela was still his flesh and blood. He punched a massive fist into the nearest wall.

"Find my daughter or I'll have your heads on pikes by dawn. No one sleeps until the Pell Darga are found and killed. And bring me my son."

One by one they bowed and deployed throughout Chadra Keep. Only Harnin One Eye stood fast. Oldest and most loyal of the eight, Harnin watched his king with concern through his remaining eye.

"My lord, your daughter…" he whispered.

Badron shot him a cross look. "Do not remind me of what I know all too well. We shall deal with this when the time comes."

The bloodied halls of Chadra Keep felt surprisingly empty despite the flurry of activity. What remained of the decimated house guard began a room-by-room search for the royal family. Bodies were taken away and prepared for burial while servants scrubbed the blood from the walls and floor as best as they could. Many believed this night of terror was already finished. Badron knew it was only the beginning. Whatever evil the Pell had in mind would spark his final designs and begin a long-anticipated war. Badron stormed through his Keep barking orders.

It was then that he came upon the body of his only son. The young prince's head sharply drooped to the side. Pell Darga spears riddled his body. Blood wept from dozens of wounds. His sword was sheathed in blood. Badron's heart lurched. Clearly his boy had put up a good fight. Then he spied it. The gentle rise and fall the chest. His son was not yet dead. Badron quickly dropped down and cradled his son to him.

"My son," he choked.

"They…came in…through the…windo…." Blood spit through his broken lips as he talked. Soon he would journey to the halls of his ancestors, no longer a pawn to the vagaries of life. "Took… Maleela…"

A last gasp made his body shake gently. The heir to the throne of Delranan was dead, at peace. Badron shook uncontrollably. Humbled and belittled, Badron could only stop and stare. He wanted to kneel and cradle the lad one last time, to let his tears flow free. But he was king, and kings do not do such things.

"He died honorably, sire," Harnin soothed. "We should all hope for such."

Badron spun on his friend. "Honorably? He died at the hands of cowards and assassins! Do not speak to me of honor!"

"Lord Badron!"

Jarrik strode purposefully down the hallway. "Lookouts spied men on horseback riding east. They claim to have caught the wisp of a woman's gown among the riders."

Anger's edge diminished, if only slightly. The desire for revenge grew.

"How many?" he asked.

"Between thirty and forty near as they could tell."

A cold gleam twisted Badron's eyes. "Reform the council. I want blood."

Badron reentered the throne room, his unfocused eyes streaked with red. The throne seemed less. The hearth fire was cold. It was only late summer and already winter's reach struggled to find purchase. The brightest of the summer sun had already faded. It wouldn't be much longer before the snow blew in from the cruel Northern Ocean. None of that mattered of course. Badron could see only despair in the near future. The threat of winter held no danger for him. His dreams, his very life, had come crashing down this night. All the hard work he and his kind had done in building a mighty kingdom might well have died with his son. Delranan had no heir. None that is, except his unwanted daughter, Maleela. Badron snarled.

His captains entered in somber procession. Each was armed and geared for campaign. Whatever they were now, they had all been among the very best warriors in the north countries. Now was the time for sharpened steel. Words and posturing didn't belong in the future Badron envisioned for his kingdom.

"The house of the king is ruined," Badron drawled. "The Pell Darga have shamed us all this night. My son is murdered, and my *daughter* taken. How can this have happened under our noses? Chadra Keep is supposed to be the most secure building in Delranan."

His words dripped venom. All at once a chorus of rage echoed across the chamber. The call for war lifted their spirits. Frightened talk fell in hushed tones at the mention of the Pell though. Ancient hatred and superstitions cloaked the mountain dwellers. Some claimed they were nothing more than myth; one told to children to keep them in line during the long winter nights when mischief was prone to spark. No one living had ever seen one. Legend said they came from the Murdes Mountains far to the east. The Mountains of Death. No sane man volunteered to travel those dark paths.

"The Pell Darga do not exist. Surely we are missing some vital clue in all this," Jarrik cautioned. For all his great strengths, strategy was not one.

Harnin rose and cast down a blood-stained short spear. "Truly? Then explain this! Taken from the body of the king's own son as he lay dying. Mind your tongue, Jarrik. The Pell exist and it is time we confronted them."

The old man glowered at his rival but said nothing else.

"How is it they managed to sneak past our guard and slay half of the house with us unaware?" Skaning, a burly man with coal black hair man, asked.

Badron grunted. "How do giants shape the mountains, or the gods make war? You ask questions only a sorcerer might answer. This I tell you all. We have but two choices. Either we ignore this night's foul deeds." Chaotic roars swept through those assembled. Badron held his hands up for quiet, "Or we raise the Wolfsreik and march to war. To the very heart of the Murdes Mountains if need be."

"Sire, it will take a month or more to raise the full strength of the Wolfsreik," Harnin cautioned.

Ten thousand fully armed men complete with supplies and kit was no easy feat.

Badron had a familiar twinkle in his eyes. "Six weeks and we can march."

"On who exactly? The Pell Darga are not a nation. By rights we would be invading Rogscroft," Argis said.

Skaning stood. "Such an action would surely jeopardize your family more. If our goal is to retrieve the princess alive we need speed and secrecy, not the strength of arms."

"What would suggest then?" Badron asked sharply.

Clearing his throat, Skaning continued. "Send men to scour the inns and taverns. Find a stalwart band of mercenaries and adventurers willing to become heroes for a small price."

Harnin spat. "Not even a drunken fool would risk facing the Pell on their own territory. We must raise the army."

"I agree with Skaning," Jarrik seconded. "These are troubled times. Money can be a powerful motivator and the types of man we will attract are expendable at best."

"Battle against man is one thing, but these are demons from the Old Times. I for one will not waste my life so recklessly," Harnin fell silent.

"Not even at the behest of your king?" Badron asked. "We are all led to a place of dark thought. Evil must be used to combat evil if we are to succeed."

No one noticed the sudden guarded look in Harnin's eye. "My apologies sire. I have forgotten my place. But the question remains. What fool would dare enter such a realm and risk certain death?"

"Every man has a price," Argis chipped in. "All we need do is find the right ones."

Badron thoughtfully rubbed the gray stubble on his chin. "This might work. Stouds has more than enough men of lesser quality for what we need. One Eye, since you so willingly champion this idea I place you in charge. You have two days to collect the men you deem necessary. After that I sound the muster and the Wolfsreik marches."

Harnin's smile was sharp, wicked. "Yes, sire."

The king pushed away from the table. He had heard enough. He paused in the doorway to look back over his shoulder and reiterate, "You have two days."

Chadra Keep's familiar shadows offered no comfort to the lone warrior marching through. Soft winds kissed the torch in his hand. Fractured darkness covered the windows. The first hint of dawn seeped through the cold grey night. Funeral pyres were already being erected in the main courtyard. Soon the bodies would be sent to their ancestors. Servants scurried about in an almost vain attempt to return the Keep to its former glory.

He ignored it all. Gaining the top of the stair, he quickly headed down to the cellars. He eased past the dungeons and food stores. His destination was perhaps the biggest secret in the Keep. Unknown to most, there was a secret tunnel leading out into the surrounding forest, but he knew. After all, he was the one who had left the exit unsecure and allowed the attackers inside in the first place. And it was the only way he was going to be able to elude the guard without questions.

He slowly pushed the ancient door open. The sky continued to brighten. It was now a muted shade of grey; still dark but light enough for him to see where he was going. He knew that Delranan, and perhaps all Malweir, was now locked in a season of change. It was a time for myths. Trolls and Goblins, dragons and wizards. It was a season for treachery and betrayal.

He took his first step towards freedom and was met by the touch of cold steel at his throat.

TWO

Bahr

The night was no different from any other for the drunken masses in Stouds Town. The *Dragon's Bane* had just returned to port after months at sea. Perhaps the most famous vessel in the northern kingdoms, her captain and crew often inspired new heights of drunken rowdiness. Tonight was no different. Fresh from the conquest of riches and lands, her mildly depleted crew stood proud upon her decks while the harbor master finished guiding her in. Her captain was a great bear of a man with more experience at sea than many had on land. He watched with mild disinterest as flocks of gulls and pelicans trailed in the *Bane's* wake.

"A good stein of ale and a wench will do me just fine," his first mate said.

Bahr smiled. "Aye, though I doubt your wife is going to feel the same."

Bahr had a reputation throughout the northern kingdoms. Both fair and cruel, he was a hard task master who demanded the very best from himself and subordinates. He was old now, of course. Grey streaked through his hair and beard. His waistline was stretched to accommodate his love of red meats and fine ales. Despite that, he was still the bane of the Northern Ocean. Legends sprang from his deeds and inspired the young.

The first mate's mood darkened at the mention of his wife. "Doesn't mean I still can't convince her it would be in her best interests as well, Cap'n."

Bahr barked a deep laugh. He was about to reply when he spied the group of armed men awaiting them on the dock. He whistled under his breath. The axe slung over his back suddenly sat anxious. The blade was worn and in need of serious repair but Bahr had never felt more comfortable with any weapon. Bahr fought the urge to draw it, if only for the comfort of the leathered handle.

"Not the welcome I was hoping for," he said under his breath.

"I knew Badron had it out for you, but this is a bit much."

Bahr nodded. He and the king had had plenty of bad encounters through the years and there was no lack of bad blood between them. Normally they pretended the other didn't exist, which made the sight of Harnin One Eye and a handful of royal guardsmen all the more disturbing. Bahr slowly made his way down the gangplank and stood before his confronters.

"I've no business with you, One Eye," Bahr snarled.

Harnin held a staying hand up. "There is no love lost between us, Bahr, but I would have words with you on behalf of the king."

"I haven't struck you down yet have I?" Bahr asked a bit gruffer than intended. "You talk. I'll listen and you buy."

Harnin exhaled an aggravated sigh. "Agreed."

Bahr left the mooring to his first mate and the harbor master and followed the king's man to the Albatross's Nest, one of the better taverns in Stouds. They found their table and Bahr drank heartily for the first time in over two months as Harnin explained the dire aspects of the night prior. Bahr's eyebrows rose at the mention of the Pell Darga. The Shadow People. *Ha, only mad men and fools out to make a name for themselves dare go into their haunted realm.* Long moments of silence settled between them.

Bahr broke it with a deep laugh. "Harnin king's lap dog, we shall never like one another I believe, but there is an undeniable passion in your tone. I care nothing for the politics of this situation. Badron deserves what he gets. The bastard will be the ruin of this kingdom. But the Pell Darga! If what you say is true, I would not wish their evil on my worst enemy. My axe would love to drink their blood."

Harnin feigned interest by nodding. "So the king may count on your support?"

Bahr, revered around the north as the Sea Wolf, raised his hands. "Whoa now. You're putting too much into my words. I don't consign my crew on some fool's errand blindly."

Harnin shifted uncomfortably. "The king wants to put together a group of misfits and hired killers to bring his daughter back. We need your boat to take them east of the Murdes Mountains and wait for their return."

"That's it?"

"That's it."

Bahr scowled. "Why me? There are plenty of other ships."

Ah, so you suspect the trap. "Of course there are. But none of the captains have, shall we say, such strong loyalties to their convictions."

Bahr sat for a moment. The decision was almost too heavy for a singular speck of time. He had much thinking to do. "I will bring it before my crew. They have a say in this as well if they are being asked to risk their necks."

Harnin stood and gathered his bear skin cloak about him. "You have two dawns. After that the group departs, on your decks or that of another."

"Two dawns and you will have my answer. Find me here."

Nodding curtly with just a hint of condescension, Harnin took his leave.

A thunderstorm rolled in shortly after Bahr's officers and closest friends gathered in the Nest's common room. Those still sober deemed his proposal ill fortune and refused to drink more lest their opinions be forgotten to drunken stupor as the night progressed. Most knew of the bad blood between captain and king as Bahr was not one to keep his opinions private. Badron was not a man to be trusted at his word. The throne was naught but a crooked chair filled with deceit and ill will. Best they set sail now and be gone before Harnin returned to damn them all. Let Badron deal with his own problems.

Bahr listened to them all with growing interest. While it was his name at the heart of all the homespun tales and legends, it was the combined efforts of his crew that made it all work. He was nothing without them and their opinions were equally important. Many were close enough to be considered his right hand. They'd saved each other's lives countless times and were worthy of far better fates than what they prepared for. How could he tell them that he had already decided?

He sighed, forcing himself to relax. There was nothing for it. His mind was set. All that remained was for the fates to carry out their whims. He would live or die by their graces. Bahr propped a boot on the empty stool beside him. The crew didn't know it, but he was patiently awaiting the arrival of two others this night. Hopefully they would be on the same train of thought as he, making them an invaluable contribution to this quest. Hells, even if they weren't, he was still damned glad to have their talents alongside. Bahr settled back for the wait and drank deeply from his mug as the debate continued.

Skuld slipped from shadow to shadow, wraith-like as only one who was used to the streets might be. Harsh winds drove a stinging rain into his exposed flesh, soaking the young thief to the bone. He gritted his teeth and pressed on. As harsh as the weather was, Skuld knew it was the best time to catch potential victims unaware. Tonight of all nights should bring him luck considering the *Dragon's Bane* was docked.

He stole his way past the docks, avoiding the oil lamps lining the main avenues. Rain stole the smell from the corpses rotting on the central gallows. He looked into the shattered faces of those poor souls and swallowed hard. Skuld was no fool. He knew the hangman's noose waited should his luck run dry. The noose wouldn't care how young he was. Whispering a prayer for the dead, he threaded his way past the swaying bodies. A lone crow cawed at him in warning from atop the frame.

Then he stumbled upon a pair of armed men. Both were tall and built for battle. Skuld knew he'd be cut to ribbons if they caught him. Fortunately it was their conversation, not their purses that caught his attention. The teenage thief ignored the crow's warning and followed at a respectable distance, close enough to hear their words.

"I don't like it one bit," growled the large blonde brute on the left. A pair of long swords bounced seductively across his back with each step.

His partner laughed. "What's not to like? This quest seems as good as any other we've been on."

"The Shadow People are well enough left alone. They don't need us coming a stomping into their lands. Badron wants us all dead I think."

Long black braids sweeping down past his shoulders moved with his shaking head. "Badron doesn't even know your name you bonehead. I can see it now. I want Nothol Coll's head! Ha! There's a laugh. You worry too much."

"I was just saying," Nothol replied.

"We've been doing jobs together seven years and every single one starts with your same dire predictions. It does tend to get old, my friend."

Nothol Coll scowled. "You mark my words, Dorl. This will end badly for all of us. And don't go giving me that look. I'm only saying what you're thinking."

"I think I like you better when you're drunk."

"I like being drunk better than thinking about this," he snorted.

Dorl Theed rolled his eyes. "Relax already. Whatever Badron has planned is his own business. He is the king after all. All we need do is trust in Bahr. Besides, when have you ever known the Sea Wolf to go blindly into danger?"

Nothol spun on his friend, finger pointing accusingly. "Raiders and barbarians are one thing. Going off to find some fictional treasure is one thing. These are the Pell Darga. The heart of the Murdes Mountains! Is there any path more dangerous?"

"Only the road to damnation's gates," Dorl replied calmly. Much of his earlier good humor was gone. "Think of the treasure those bastards have hidden deep in their mountain haunts. We'd be rich men forever."

"Won't make a damned bit of difference if we're not alive to spend it."

Dorl slapped him on the shoulder. "That's more like it! You make me thirsty. Come on, Bahr is waiting."

"Maybe I can talk some sense into him," Nothol Coll grumbled. "You listen like my last wife."

"Not likely, I don't have the figure for it. Bahr is as headstrong as they come. Good luck changing his mind."

"Assuming he's actually going to go through with it."

"Naturally."

Nothol shook his head. "Navy men aren't very good on land."

Dorl barked a laugh. "You be the one to tell him that. I value my neck too much."

The big man tried to shake the image of the Sea Wolf rampaging into them with berserker rage. Both were highly skilled warriors with numerous years of campaigning between them, but Bahr possessed the one thing most common foot soldiers lacked: guile.

"We can still tell him no,'" Nothol finally said, his mind clear again.

Dorl was genuinely surprised. "And let Badron find some other poor fool for the task? Where's the fun in that?"

"The Pell Darga in the Mountains of Death," he snorted. "You have a sick sense of humor."

Dorl gave him a sly smile. "I know. It helps me keep life unpredictable. Now, are we just going to stand around in the damned rain all night bickering like two old ladies or can we go and enjoy some of Bahr's hospitality and hear what he has to say?"

"I already know what he has to say."

"You're impossible. Come on."

Skuld let them go. He only caught parts of the conversation but that was enough to arouse his fears and greed. Like most people, he knew scattered bits of lore about the Pell Darga. It all revolved around terror, but the very thought of hordes of untold riches sent a chill down his soaked spine. Skuld suddenly found an opportunity he never thought to have.

He had a chance to make a name for himself and rise above the filth of the gutters. To him the risk was well worth the reward.

The thief yawned, though he knew sleep was a long time in coming. Visions of demons and gold plagued the narrow corridors of his mind. He practically salivated at the idea of becoming rich. No more acts of petty pickpocketing for him. No more jeers from the adults or taunts from children. He could return rich enough to buy his own kingdom. A smile creased his thin lips. Lightning crackled in the far-off mountains. Skuld made up his mind. He had to find a way to sneak aboard the *Dragon's Bane*.

The proprietor of the Albatross's Nest wore a constant toothy grin. He always stood to make a pretty profit when the *Bane* was in port. Tonight was no different. Add the threat of the brewing thunderstorm and people practically flocked inside. He'd already gone through two kegs of ale and three roasted goats. His fat palms were greasy with greed and spilled ale. At the center of it all was the talk of Badron's quest. He wanted nothing to do with it. He'd never been the adventuring sort. Leave that to others like old Bahr conversing in his private room. Still, he found himself watching the seamen with growing interest.

A thick cloud of smoke clung to the ceiling. Most of the tables were standing room only. Men and the occasional Dwarf spoke in hurried tones. A roaring fire cackled and spit embers. The door groaned open to allow Nothol Coll and Dorl Theed entrance. They shed their rain-soaked cloaks and stretched out their shoulders. It felt good to be dry and inside. The sell swords wormed through the crowds and past the suddenly concerned proprietor. He said nothing, merely pointed towards Bahr's room. Dorl nodded and kept walking.

"You two took your sweet time in getting here," Bahr growled once they closed the door behind them.

"A philosophical discussion," Dorl said disarmingly. "It seems our friend Nothol has taken to pondering the complexities of life all a sudden."

Bahr gave a quizzical look and kicked out a stool for him to sit. "That's a dangerous thing for a fighting man."

"There's more to life than just killing," Nothol replied.

"Says the man boasting two of the most dangerous broadswords in the north strapped across his back," Bahr countered. "You're sounding like some damned cult priest. I like you better drunk."

Dorl smirked but stayed quiet.

The Sea Wolf passed them both a mug of frothy ale. He spoke while they busied quenching their thirst. "I trust you've already heard what Badron's doing? The whole damned town is buzzing with it."

Dorl set his mug down and belched. "Aye, we have. It's a risky operation."

"That's an understatement. They are the Pell Darga. It wouldn't be much fun if it weren't risky. What I need from you is your support. I need some good swords to watch my back."

Nothol tried to hide his confused look as he interrupted. "I thought Badron didn't care for his daughter?"

Bahr shrugged. "Times like this changes things. Blood comes before any differences."

"What's your honest take on the whole thing?" Dorl asked.

"I think Badron's up to something foul. It's a long way to the mountains from Chadra Keep. Our goodly king has been sticking his nose where it doesn't belong and the princess is paying for it."

"Fair enough, though I doubt his sincerity. More likely he wants her back because she's guessed some plot of his. It's not secret he's had his eyes set on Rogscroft for years now."

Bahr narrowed his eyes. "That's business for the king and his ilk. Our job is rescue, plain and simple."

"I'd almost believe that if I didn't know you."

"I wouldn't be a good captain if I didn't keep some secrets."

Dorl threw his hands up. "Have it your way, but I will say this. Nothol and I both know you've got something up your sleeve else you wouldn't have contacted us. It's our ill fortune that we were dumb enough to come when you called. If things go south, we leave."

"Are you done?" Bahr asked. His voice dropped dangerously low. He didn't like being second guessed.

"For now. Who else have you recruited?" Dorl asked.

"I never liked a man who made a habit out of using fancy words, Dorl Theed. Makes me wonder how you slipped past my guard."

"You're avoiding the question."

Bahr gave in and shrugged nonchalantly. "I heard old Thulu was interested."

"The man is a drunken washout," Nothol snorted. "You've got to have someone better in mind."

Dorl's eyes widened. "You don't have anyone do you? The great Bahr can't draw a crowd for a suicide mission."

"It's not my job to gather men. Harnin's taking care of that part. All I have to do is keep you all alive."

The Sea Wolf settled deeper into his chair. Uncomfortable with the direction of the conversation, he beckoned the crewman closest to pour him another drink. Bahr didn't like being questioned. It made him nervous. There'd been too many confrontations with Badron's cronies over the years. He vaguely wondered what kept him anchored in Delranan. Malweir was a big world and he could have his run of the seas. Deep down inside the answer was obvious, though he was unwilling to admit it.

"These are dangerous times, lads. Times when a closed mouth is worth just as much as a sharp sword. You are either in or out. I need an answer now."

Dorl gently pinched the bridge of his nose. He almost laughed. What was the use of pretending he still had reservations? Both men already knew what the other was going to say. "Deal, but don't you go risking our lives for no reason."

Bahr gave a curt nod. "Done."

Nothol Coll shook his head. "This is only going to get worse."

"Shut up Nothol. Get drunk and you'll still have all your teeth come the dawn. This ain't the time to be asking questions or complaining. You watch my back and I watch yours. Same as always."

Nothol Coll scowled and took the proffered mug.

Bahr smiled inwardly. He liked the pair, and they were damned good swordsmen, even if they were a bit off for his tastes. He wished he had more friends like them. Friends, now there was a foreign term. He was the kind of man who called few men friend, though he knew many people. Bahr was a private man with enough secrets to damn a good number of monarchs and government officials. Men like Bahr needed to remain silent, if for no other reason than self-preservation.

He quietly suspected that's why Badron offered him the job first. He was a threat to current Delranan politics and had been a target for Badron's assassins more than once. It was a game both sides played. Countless sailors and murderers alike lay at the bottom of the sea or under piles of random rocks because of it. Bahr had little doubt that Badron would make another try for his life this time as well. Natural suspicions arose from his conversation with the two sell swords and he was sorely tempted to ask if Badron had already gotten to them.

THREE

Night Visitor

Evening rains cooled the night air to a considerable chill. Bahr pulled his great overcoat closed and worked his way home from the Nest. His belly was full of a little too much to drink and his mind was troubled by the worrisome pair of Nothol Coll and Dorl Theed. They were good people, but too liberal for his liking. He wanted men who did what they were told. Combined, those two were too much to handle in large doses.

The faint patter of the last few rain drops tickled his scalp. Finally relaxed, Bahr felt the stress of the day leave. There was time enough for worry in the coming days. The sound of waves breaking comforted him. A strong desire to take to his ship and ride out to sea struggled for ascendency, but he couldn't. Not now when the stakes were so high. Bahr did his best to shake off the nagging doubt corrupting his thoughts. Oh well, he thought, there was nothing for it. He resigned himself to the lure of the softness of his bed in his expansive estate. Even he couldn't resist that. Bahr turned the final corner towards his estate and headed up the porch.

"The fabled Sea Wolf of Delranan," said a scratchy voice from the shadows in the corner before he managed another step.

Bahr's hand instinctively, albeit drunkenly, grasped the hilt of the longer dagger at his hip.

"There's no need for weapons with me. Besides, a fabled warrior such as you would only make short work of the likes of me."

Bahr seriously doubted this stranger was anything but harmless. Still, he watched him with a wary eye, desperately peering into the faint porch light for answers. Smallish in stature, the stranger wore elaborate white robes worked around a tightly trimmed beard. His face was shallow and pinched, making his nose appear slightly bigger than it was. It was the eyes Bahr found most impressive. Even in the near darkness they held several lifetimes worth of tales. Whoever he was, this man had seen his share of the world.

"You seem to know me, old man, but I don't know you. That leaves me with a disadvantage. I'm not the sort who appreciates that kind of situation," Bahr said.

The stranger smiled warmly. He bore the elegance of immense wisdom charged with a certain level of lethality. His skin was leathered from countless years in the elements and he held presence as a king.

"The answer you seek is not an easy one to give. I am old beyond measure. I am as ancient as the setting sun and the rising moons; ancient and wicked both. I am the light and the dark. I have seen gods die and dragons born. I am the wind and snow. I, who was old when this land was still submerged beneath the seas, need no introduction."

"None of that fancy talk really impresses me much, old timer," Bahr bit back.

A mischievous twinkle filled his eyes. "In the interest of simplicity my name is Anienam Keiss."

Bahr felt his muscles spasm. He'd heard the name before. Hells, practically all Malweir knew it. Murmurs and rumors abounded at the mention of his name. A wizard said some. Others cursed him as the plaything of demons. No good would come of this meeting. Regardless of what men said, Anienam Keiss was a myth, the deceptive thing of legend without a face. Yet here he was standing on Bahr's porch. The Sea Wolf suddenly felt very small.

"Ah, I can see that you have heard of me," Anienam said with a degree of smugness.

Bahr nodded. "Every man in these parts has. Damnation, a wizard on my own front porch! How is it a creature like you manages to show up during the troubled times?"

The smaller man stood quietly watching him as if assessing the quality of his character. "Mine is the will of eternity. I come and go as the world desires. Do not seek answers your mind is incapable of understanding."

Bahr rubbed his chin. His patience was gone. "Get to the point or leave. I'm in no mood for games."

Anienam continued, "The world is changing. Fate has summoned me to Delranan for a purpose I cannot yet fathom. What I do know is that you are at the center of it all. If you do not mind, I would speak with you under more, hospitable, conditions."

"Why me? They say men die when you come around."

He smiled. "You give me more credit than I deserve. Malweir would be a much different place if I had that ability. Alas, it is not so. Master Bahr, you have been chosen and only to you may I deliver my message."

Bahr weighed his options. If Fate was involved, she was fickle bitch with a mean sense of humor. His night had progressively gotten worse. Maybe he should give in, let it ride. The other options seemed less inviting. Damnation, he growled. He eyed the old wizard and said, "Okay. Let's get it over with."

He wearily stalked past the old man and opened his door. The rain began to fall again.

Torchlight flickered from the kiss of a cooling breeze shuffling through the upper rooms of the estate. Unlit candles lined the mantle in the main chamber and sat clustered in the middle of an expansive aged cherry wood table. Bahr motioned for Anienam to sit while he removed his jacket and snatched a bottle of spiced wine and poured them both a carafe.

"What makes me so special? I'm just one man, an insignificant speck in this world," Bahr asked.

"Importance is an irrelevant term when dealing with the future. There are powers at work here, ones that have long strained to escape back into the world and wreak havoc on us."

Not the answer I was looking for. "Enough of the riddles. Shoot me straight."

Anienam sipped his wine and offered the same infuriating smile. "Very well. This endeavor you have consigned yourself to is doomed to fail. King Badron's heart lies in the wrong place. He wishes the return of his daughter for the sole purpose of silencing her. Fatherly love is not part of the equation. She has knowledge that threatens his plans for the future. Indeed, it might have impact on the coming war."

"What war?"

"That is the topic of another conversation. The storm is brewing. Last night was but the catalyst," Anienam said. "The girl is the beginning."

"That girl will likely die if we don't go, yet you suggest I should just wait here, batten down the shutters and wait for the storm to blow out to sea."

"On the contrary. You must go. Your future is intricately woven into the continuation or demise of Delranan."

Bahr swirled the wine around his mouth a few times before swallowing. "You do realize this is a bit too much, even for me."

"I would like to say I empathize, but I have brought this same message to many over the years. You are but one more cog to the great design."

Bahr closed his eyes. All his long life he'd tried to be a good man. A noble man. He couldn't understand why the world was against him. In the end, his thoughts revolved around the abandoned love a father was supposed to have for his daughter.

"Badron and I have no love for each other. That much is well known. I've been suspicious of his motives for a long time. Harnin coming directly to me only served to make it worse."

"He will try to kill you before it is over if that is any comfort."

"Ha! Tell me something I don't know. Still, I don't like the direction this conversation has turned," Bahr warned.

"Honesty is often our worst of foes. It always shows us our faults when we least desire them. This is not so in your case. Yes, Badron wants you dead. You pose a legitimate threat to his power, nearly as much as his own daughter."

"Me? I know nothing of his plans or dreams for the future. Hells, he and I haven't spoken in nearly two decades."

Flames reflected sharply off the wizard's eyes. The sight provoked disturbing feelings.

"Questions. Why is it mankind feels necessary to constantly ask me questions? I cannot give you the answers you seek, Bahr. That is part of my curse. The future is yet to be written. Only you can discover the truths you seek."

"Then why go through the trouble to find me?" Bahr persisted.

Anienam finished his wine and lifted his mug. "Perhaps a little more wine first. This is a very good vintage."

Bahr refilled it and impatiently awaited at least one answer. A snarl etched across his face. "You avoid my questions. That doesn't give me much reason to place trust in you. Ten years ago I would have thrown you out on your ass. I must be getting old. Either that or you are more persuasive than I've given you credit for."

Anienam sighed. No matter how many times he'd had this conversation with men across the ages it was always the same. He would never be welcomed as a friend. His was the life of the outsider, a man never able to find a home or place to call his own. The wind, some called him. Casual indifference, others said. Regardless, Anienam Keiss did the bidding of a greater power few understood. No one bothered asking what he desired.

"Bahr of Delranan, if I could tell you the deeds you must accomplish I most certainly would. Some call what I bring a gift, others a curse. None of that is important. What is important is that your land needs you more than I can convey. Fell times ride the morning breeze. Badron's lunge for power is but the first pebble in the pond. His actions threaten coming war. You are necessary if Malweir is to avoid falling into the coming darkness."

He rose and walked over to the fire. The heat warmed his tired body. Strong flames licked up from the bricks. Bahr watched them absently. More questions plagued him. Why would the wizard mention Malweir rather than Delranan? His mind raced with visions and wicked deceptions. A hero was something he never wanted to be, but Fate seemed ever eager to push him towards exactly that.

At last he spoke. "I'm going to die, aren't I?"

"All men do. Such is the nature of this life. The gods have plans for each of us and death is but our final task."

"The gods you speak of don't exist. Men haven't had faith in several lifetimes," Bahr shot back.

"Don't they? Man may have forgotten their beginnings but the gods have not abandoned us. They are gone, yes. That much is true, but they still exist. A great war among them forced them to leave us to our own devices. All that is changing. The time of their return is fast approaching." Anienam offered a half smile, weak and thin. "Before you ask, faith is not necessary for you at this juncture. All that is required is for good men to be willing to stand up to the rising tide of tyranny. This evil must not be allowed to grow. If it does, all you know and love will end in flame and ash."

"I'm a fighting man and a damned better sailor than a husband. What I am not is a fool. For you to be in my home on this night tells me you already have good inclinations of my intentions. Very well," he turned and stared down his guest. "If it must be said, I am accepting Badron's offer, though for reasons of my own. This is not something I feel the need to explain."

"Understandable."

"Harnin ass-sniffer expects my answer tomorrow morning. He's bringing me the men needed to find the princess and bring her back home."

There was a frailty in his voice, as if he were unsure of the chance of success against so great an odd.

"A noble plan the king has chosen, though he knows it not. I have measured the worth of your character, Captain Bahr. I believe your heart is pure, though roughly calloused. That is good. Keep the princess alive. Expect the unthinkable. I will say no more on this. It is time I take my leave. Good night."

Bahr watched him go. He had no interest in following. Something about the old man screamed trouble. He wanted to laugh. Time was coming when this little bit of trouble would seem almost welcome. Earlier misgivings began to fade, though he remained unsure of how much he could trust the wizard. Blind faith was not one of Bahr's strengths. Anienam might display the best of intentions, but that carried no weight so far as the Sea Wolf was concerned. Every man had to prove himself at some point.

"Do not get off of your ship, Sea Wolf, not until the time is right."

Bahr soaked in the warmth of the fire as a stiff breeze struggled to rob him of it. The door closed behind Anienam, leaving the old captain alone in the night. His bones felt chilled. Maybe it was the night or maybe it was Anienam's parting words. Whatever the answer, Bahr was inextricably intertwined with the whims of kings and wizards.

"Shit."

FOUR

Cold Alliances

King Badron stood on his bedroom balcony watching the brewing storm with mild interest. Nothing nature offered matched the coldness of his heart. The wrath growing in him kept him warmer than any fire ever could. The pain of his son's death threatened to rip his sanity asunder. He wanted revenge. That twisted desire made demands of his soul he would gladly acquiesce to. Fists clenched behind his back, the king of Delranan plotted. That Harnin sought Bahr only compounded his anger. Of all the people in his kingdom the one-eyed fool had to choose him. Years of carefully laid plans disintegrated around him. Malweir conspired to usurp his throne.

He'd walked the blood-stained halls of Chadra Keep more than once since the night before. No matter how many times he did it or how hard he looked there was nothing new to find. Not even the ghosts of those slain remained to haunt him. His mind scoured through every thinkable scenario and he still came up short. How could the Pell Darga manage to infiltrate his most secure sanctum so effortlessly? It didn't make sense. A single idea pushed towards the front and refused to disappear. He didn't want to admit it. He couldn't. But the answer was undeniable. He had a traitor in his Keep.

"Guard!"

The tremble in his voice belied pure malevolence. A shallow-faced guard entered and saluted. He was impossibly young, even for a man of the North. Uncertainty danced in his eyes. The man he replaced had been horribly slaughtered in the attack.

Badron's gaze narrowed sharply. "Find me Lord Harnin."

"At once, sire."

The one-eyed battle lord entered shortly and bowed to his king and friend. "My lord?"

Badron kept his back to the man. Thunder played havoc with the heavens. "Have your men discovered anything?"

"Nothing as of yet."

His fists clenched tighter. "How is it the enemy so successfully managed to breach our defenses? You are charged with the security of this kingdom."

Harnin swallowed, fearful for the reasons behind his summoning.

Badron continued, "They knew exactly what they were doing, One Eye. How?"

His voice ground like stone breaking glass.

Harnin resisted the temptation to draw his sword. "We are working on that, sire. My men have only begun their investigation."

Badron finally turned. Murder reflected wildly in his blue eyes. "What promise of loyalty can you offer?"

"What are you getting at? Every last man in this keep is a loyal son."

Harnin felt the hair on the back of his neck rise. He'd been a favored son of Delranan since before Badron became king. Badron's sudden turn against him was insulting. Attacking the king offered no hope. No, that wouldn't do at all. There was no reason for this sudden suspicion. Harnin would never dream of going against his king and friend. He had nothing to hide, but Badron was a foul-tempered man with little joy in his heart.

"Loyal to you perhaps. After all, you selected every one of them personally. But how loyal are they to king and land? What reassurance can you give me that I should trust you?"

He's bordering on madness, Harnin thought. The loss of his son has pushed him too far. Harnin had to proceed cautiously from here or he would find his neck at the end of a short rope.

"Have I ever given you concern to doubt my loyalty? Everything I have done in my life has been for this kingdom. Your father shared his dreams with me and I helped achieve them. You and this kingdom are all that is important to me. I swear it on the honor of my fathers."

A wave seemed to crash in Badron's mind. The violence drained from his eyes.

"These have been dark days for us all. Forgive my insecurities but I cannot be sure whose sword still remains in my service." He took a seat on the nearest bench and wiped his forehead.

"There is nothing to forgive, sire. Had I… lost my family I would be much less of a man."

"Indeed."

Badron shifted his gaze from his most trusted captain to a wall map of the northern kingdoms. A dark glimmer clung to the corners of his eyes, a taint almost. Deep desires reflected in them. He was a man whose own world simply wasn't enough.

Suddenly emboldened by the king's softening, Harnin inched closer. "Sire, you mentioned a traitor. The idea is not farfetched, though it pains me to think so. How can we be sure who it is? All the council was assembled during the time of the attack."

"Is that the limit of your curiosity?"

"Sire?"

"This traitor could be anyone from the lowest chambermaid to my very own daughter," Badron's voice was laced with disgust.

Shock spread across Harnin's face. The relationship between king and daughter was tumultuous at best, but he'd never dreamed to accuse her of treason. "Are you saying Maleela is capable of betraying her own blood? Causing the death of her brother?"

"You and I both know she holds no loyalty to her kingdom. Our designs for the future disagree with her."

"But to sell us out to the Pell Darga? How could she even know where to find such allies?" he protested. "There must be some other force at work here."

"Few people believe the Shadow People actually exist. We know better. Both you and I have seen and fought them.

Their hatred of us is nearly as great as ours for them. I agree that if Maleela is responsible she had help from the inside."

"This takes us to a very dark place."

"No darker than the murder of my heir. Send out your spies. I want to know who did this and why."

"Yes sire."

The king nodded, satisfied for now. "Good, now on to other business. How goes the search for the men to hunt down the Pell?"

"We have more than enough willing men to go. I believe Bahr will even agree to pilot them east."

Badron's eyebrow arched. "Truly?"

"I will know for sure tomorrow at dawn. He was intrigued but doesn't want me to know."

"Perhaps his old hatreds have mellowed with age." Badron laughed. "Maybe we will get lucky and the Pell will succeed in killing him to save me the trouble."

Harnin cleared his throat. "I hate to admit it, but he is the best chance we have for success. He also has the best chance for bringing us a war."

That foul gleam returned. "Precisely. Now go. Inform me when your team is assembled. The time is fast approaching when the glory of Delranan shall be sung across all Malweir."

Heavy rains and driving winds forced the small band of riders to find shelter for the night. Outriders discovered a thick stand of firs less than a league ahead and returned to lead the rest to the relative safety. Eight horses bearing drenched and miserable riders pulled in nearly an hour later. Lightning struck the nearby hilltop as the riders dismounted.

"Tether the horses while we try to raise some tarps for shelter," Aurec shouted above the shrieking winds.

His men silently obeyed. Seasoned professionals, they knew what needed to be done. They also knew there would be no fire tonight. The prospect of a cold, wet night dampened their spirits. Aurec sighed and not for the first time. His palm caught the heavy rain drops as they fell splashing across his forearm. Doubts ate at him. He was a prince, and a damned fool of one if today was any indication. Exhausted and far from the warm halls of Rogscroft, his actions might well have pushed his kingdom to war. He shook his head ruefully. The prize stood before him, miserable and soaked to the bone. Still, her splendor was worth the risk. He only hoped she was worth the price yet to be paid.

Maleela stalked up to him and slapped him hard across the right cheek. Her eyes fumed with anger. "You idiot! Do you have any idea what would have happened if they had caught you? Do you?"

Aurec rubbed some of the sting away. "Relax my love. You know I couldn't risk leaving your safety to others. Not with so much at stake."

"My father would have fed you to the wolves and turned his army loose on your kingdom."

"I fear that is an inevitability, but your father is mad. His desires threaten to rip apart the northern kingdoms. I did what was necessary to save both our lands. War is coming and I'll not sit by while your life hangs in the balance. I had to come and get you. I… I can't imagine a world without you in my heart."

The stiffness of her stance softened. Her deep blue eyes, the same as her father's, glimmered with their own wetness. She rushed into his waiting arms and held on for dear life.

"Aurec, you shouldn't risk yourself so foolishly," she whispered through the tears. "Not even for me."

He pulled her away just far enough to look down into her face, framed so beautifully by her wet hair. "You are my everything, Maleela. For you I would risk the gates of death itself."

She hugged him like a woman who knew that she was about to lose everything. Their love remained hidden between their families. Initially endorsed by both fathers, it had become a cancer to both kingdoms. She'd long suspected Badron had used her to manipulate himself into a position to declare war. She'd even come to accept the fact that he never really loved her.

Aurec touched a fingertip softly to her lips and smiled. "Don't worry about your father, not tonight. Tonight you are safe with us."

"How did you know that is what I was thinking?"

"You think I don't know you?" he teased. "The shelter will be finished soon. Try to get what sleep you can. We've a long way to go before we reach safety. I doubt even your father's best trackers can find us in this weather."

It stopped raining sometime during in the early hours just before dawn. The ground flooded easily during the storm, turning the surrounding countryside into a marsh. Aurec's men slowly forced themselves up. Their bodies were sore from a combination of the forced ride and the weather. Their feet hurt. Wet boots and socks only made matters worse. The predawn chill dug down to the bone. Trying to start a fire was pointless. All the fuel was waterlogged. Aurec made the decision to strike camp.

Venten approached his prince wearing a haggard look. He laid out the small map and repressed a shiver. Gaunt and experienced, he rubbed his salt and pepper beard. "It is a two-day ride to the Murdes Mountains. If this weather holds Badron's hunters will catch us."

"Agreed," Aurec nodded. "But this can be turned to an advantage. Once we cross these plains the forests running the length of the foothills should give us enough cover. Badron won't know which way we went. Most of the trails leading up into the mountains are hidden."

"That's assuming he doesn't take the bait."

"What bait?" Maleela asked with a yawn.

The murder of the house guards sat ill with her. Regardless of her situation, her loyalty still lay with her kingdom and her friends. Men she'd known for the better part of her nineteen years were dead because of her. Aurec tried to assure her that they'd only killed the men that gave them no choice. Regardless, she disapproved. She and Aurec were now co-conspirators in what could only lead to war.

Venten and Aurec exchanged a cautious glance. Secrets passed silently between them.

"We didn't use any of our own weapons. Everything came from outside sources," Venten answered carefully.

Her eyes narrowed sharply. "What sources?"

Venten deferred to his prince.

He exhaled sharply. "The Pell Darga, my love."

Her heart twisted. "What! Do you have any idea they what will do to us all?"

Aurec held up his hands in mild defense. "Calm down, love. We had no choice. We couldn't allow your father to make the connection with Rogscroft. Too much is at stake."

"But the Pell Darga! They're bloodthirsty savages. My father will waste no time in marshalling the Wolfsreik."

Her face burned dark crimson. She felt betrayed. *How could he lie to me like this? Doesn't he understand what has been set in motion?* Destructive visions filled her head as she closed her eyes tightly. Maleela struggled with conflicting feelings. She loved Aurec but felt entirely helpless. He acted out of love's best interests but sometimes that wasn't right, or enough. The Pell Darga and Wolfsreik would decimate one another in a senseless struggle. Her boundaries constricted even tighter.

"The Pell are not what you believe them to be," Aurec whispered. "Our people have had dealings with them for generations. They are no more evil than you or I."

"That won't matter."

Aurec gripped her by the shoulders. "Maleela you must understand that there are grave risks each of us must undertake if this is going to be successful. I'm sorry, but those men had to die, and we had to make it look like the Pell Darga did it. Otherwise we never would have made it out of Chadra Keep. Badron will stop at nothing to take over the northern kingdoms. This was the only way. I can't ask you to understand now, just that you will forgive me for what I had to do."

Maleela relented, albeit reluctantly. She trusted Aurec enough to see them all to safety. Lingering doubts gnawed at the back of her thoughts as the band mounted up and prepared to ride. If her father was determined to attack, what difference did it matter where the hammer fell? Every man, woman, and child in the north would soon be at risk but Aurec's biggest concern was how Maleela was going to react when she learned he had killed her brother.

FIVE

The Old Ways

Age mocked the still air. Ignorance choked the stale air of the small chamber. Windowless, a single bed was the only decoration. Cobwebs clung to the shadows like secret lovers. Dust layered the cold, granite floor. Once a holy shrine to ancient gods now decayed without notice. Millennia of history slowly crumbled away for none living could remember the usefulness of the temple.

Artiss Gran strode heavily down the empty hall in deep thought. A fell dream had awakened him after nearly three thousand years of sleep. His weathered face bore no emotion, indeed little semblance to a human at all. Memories played havoc with his mind. Artiss was the last of his kind. Sworn protectors of all life on Malweir, he and his kind had stood watch against the perversions of the dark gods since time began. But now it was all gone; the gods, light and dark, his kin and friends. Artiss Gran lived a lonely life and prayed for the time when his services would no longer be required so that he might join all those who went before.

Yet such simple delights were not to be. Dark forces were rising again. It had been so long since Artiss was forced to defend the world he didn't know if he was up to it anymore. He was old. Everything about him screamed it. The darkness swirled around him, threatened to creep in and consume his soul. It called to him, beckoned him to action. Fighting the urge wasn't an option. His sole purpose was to stop the dark gods from returning to claim this world as their own. Three thousand years he had lain dormant, awaiting and dreading the day when he would be needed again. And now it was time.

He felt older, much older than his ten thousand years implied. His skin was stretched tightly over his thin frame, discolored and leathery. The marrow of his bones had long since dried to dust. His body was a shallow haunting of its former self. The dark grey cloak concealed what had become the ruin of his flesh. The gods didn't care. They demanded service and he had no choice but to accept. Artiss failed to find fairness in it. Even the gods of light had abandoned Malweir and left the races to their own devices. They left Artiss with just enough to accomplish his purpose.

"All these long years and now there is no time," Artiss muttered to himself.

Ancient torches sprang to life as he passed, as if a whisper could command such. He was a man who only thought of others. In fact, the entire scope of his existence was dedicated to the preservation of life. A normal life had been denied him ever since he accepted the task of becoming a priest. His own life came to mean little. The moment he'd been selected for ascension to priesthood had been his happiest, his most complete. He eased his way into the plain marble chamber at the heart of the temple.

No one had stood here in his lifetime. The chamber of conveyance had one task, to show the keeper of secrets what evil threatened the world. Artiss already knew the answer. His awakening was no accident. The visions of mass despair rippling through his nightmares confirmed his darkest fears. The enemies of life had somehow found a way, a breach, back into the world and were quietly planning a new campaign.

Artiss moved to the center of the chamber. A series of tightening concentric circles crafted from the precious star silver metal had been inlaid when the world was young. They guided him to his proper place. The circles flared to life at his touch. Soon the chamber glowed bright silver, bathing him in its warmth. Artiss felt the raw power surging over him. His body shuddered as it accepted the newfound strength.

All this had happened before. Malweir had almost been torn apart during the last war. Pain and suffering were visited on untold tens of thousands for hundreds of years. That's when he became the last. The dark gods moved quickly and relentlessly against his kind. All his brothers were killed in the efforts to send them back to the great abyss. Or so he chose to believe. Artiss finally won, but at a cost. He alone must remain to keep the dark gods in check. The dark gods nearly succeeded in escaping three thousand years ago and would have had it not been for a handful of Gaimosian Knights.

Artiss folded his arms across his chest as the circles of light and power opened paths into the ether. He stayed upon the chosen path, for the unknown is a terrifying thing. One misstep and he was lost. Fleeting images of fell creatures lurked just beyond reach. An ethereal breeze carried his essence into regions of time and space unknown to mortals. He traveled on the breath of time itself, ever hungering for the answers. The powers propelling him jerked suddenly, forcing Artiss to his knees. A collection of violent colors coalesced before him. This was it!

He fell, hitting the ancient floor and quickly rolled up to his knees. It had begun. The enemy was moving at last. Artiss felt sheer terror course through him, battling with the healing properties of the star silver. He hobbled over to the far wall where a map of the world hung. His eyes thoroughly scanned the combination of ancient and modern images. He never learned how, for the old masters had been killed before telling him the secrets, but the map was able to change itself. As Malweir changed so too did the map. The images Artiss Gran now looked upon had not been there three thousand years ago.

His eyes flittered over the map, desperately seeking the source. Then he found it. A tiny flame flickering far to the north; well beyond the Jebel Desert. Delranan. The doom of Malweir had begun in Delranan. Artiss tried to remember anything about the small northern kingdom but was unsuccessful. Delranan hadn't yet existed when last he awoke. Artiss hurried off to the temple library in hopes of finding the missing elements necessary to properly defend Malweir. The alarm must be raised. He only prayed the old lines were still available.

The sky remained dark, overcast and brutal as King Badron waited. He welcomed the chilled darkness for it complimented his mood. Hatred and sorrow clashed within his heart. They consumed the goodness and left a rotting shell of man bent on vengeance. It was a difficult thing to outlive his children. Now Badron was forced to embrace the torments of that fact. He prided himself on being a hard man, a strong man. That pride was often enough his closest ally. He'd seen victory on numerous battlefields yet was now humbled by a single death.

He loved his son more than any member of his family. The boy showed much potential and was being groomed for a leadership position in the Wolfsreik. The kingdom's army was a fine place to hone the skills of command. None of it mattered now. His son's broken body lay lifeless on a cold stone slab. Badron stifled back the tears even as his mind wandered back to the various conspiracy theories already suggested. He knew he shouldn't. This was a day for mourning, not plotting.

Daggers stabbed at him when he closed his eyes. Visions of torment mocked him. His son riddled with so many spears. The look of abject terror on his face. He reopened his eyes and stared down upon Delranan. Chadra Keep sprawled beneath. The old king's shoulders slumped. Once he had enjoyed this view, now it suggested the decay of his rule. Color was gone, replaced by shades of winter grey. The world had grown cruel on him. A bell tolled deep from somewhere in the city below. He sighed and turned.

Harnin One Eye patiently awaited him.

"Well?" Badron asked.

"We've had trackers scour every avenue of approach to the Keep. They determined the enemy was able to move through the eastern forest. There were a large number of tracks just outside the walls."

Badron nodded thoughtfully. That part made sense. The forest was the most vulnerable side of the Keep. He silently cursed himself for not cutting it down years ago. "So they used the cover of darkness to get close. How did they get inside though? There are no entrances on that part of the Keep."

"We are still trying to figure that out, sire. More importantly, I have come to believe that the attackers were not Pell Darga."

Badron's eyes narrowed. "Explain."

Harnin cleared his throat, uncomfortable with the hatred in his king's eyes. "The Pell are a mountain folk. As such, they have need of a sure-footed pony, not horses bred for the open steppe. No one has seen one in a lifetime, making most doubt their existence. None of our patrols have come across any signs in the last few years. What then would be their reasoning for driving down from their distant mountain kingdom to kidnap your daughter? It doesn't make sense."

The senior captain and advisor chose his words carefully, partly because he wasn't sure how Badron would react and partly because he recognized the frailty of this time. All Delranan held its breath. War was nearing, but against whom? Harnin hid his smile as Badron asked just that.

"Who then has a vested interest in seeing my house in ruins?"

"My lord, Malweir is an ever-dangerous world. I've heard rumors of a civil war between the Dwarf clans to the east. Strange companies of Elves and Goblins have been seen wandering through the land. Some even whisper of the return of the fabled Gaimosian Knights."

Badron shook his head. He'd heard the fairy tales as well and refused to mire his thoughts in such. "For all that you name I can find no true enemy."

"That leaves Rogscroft."

The word stung, hanging in the air like a miasma of doom.

Badron sneered. "They couldn't possibly know what our plans are."

Harnin shrugged. "Perhaps not, but Prince Aurec is your daughter's lover whether you choose to accept it or not. There is a chance he might have succumbed to an act of grave stupidity."

"Or at the insistence of his father," the king finished. He smashed a fist into his palm. He regretted not invading his hated foe those many years ago. "Aurec is no fool, neither is his father. They are brash but not foolish enough to risk reprisal."

"Rogscroft will deny everything, naturally. Not that it matters much, all tracks lead back to the east. This is our chance to finally blame them. It also gives us the perfect opportunity to go to war and remove them from existence."

The prospect of no more subversion enticed Badron. "The Wolfsreik is already marshalling, but it will take time, as you pointed out, for them to actually muster the strength to march. I do not want to tip our hand to our enemies. Continue to use the Pell as an excuse. Keep our people and his spies in the dark for as long as we can and the advantage is ours. Let us catch them unaware."

The bell tolled again, deep and ominous.

"It is time, sire," Harnin grimly announced.

"Then come, let us bury my son."

Somber crowds lined the main avenue from the Keep down to the shore. Most of Delranan showed to pay their respects to their prince. Mothers wept openly, for him and for all the sons who lost their lives that fell night. Fur-cloaked soldiers lined the way at specific intervals. They served as much for crowd control as for respect. Their steel helmets gleamed in the sporadic light. Spear and sword did the same. Each bore the same dour expression, as if a piece of them had been torn away. Brothers had been murdered. The guards remained perfectly still, only moving their eyes to follow the procession as it inched out from the massive gates of Chadra Keep.

King Badron led them. His robes were stately. The wolf skin cloak clasped about his shoulders shimmered in shades of black and grey. The kingdom's crown, which he seldom found cause to wear, was bejeweled and heavy upon his head. A ruby the size of baby's fist sat in the center. The king of Delranan presented the image of a hard man. His eyes, posture, the measure of his gait were all determined. To appear otherwise would invite insurrection. His face was a mask that concealed more emotion than any could have guessed. Anguish clashed with dispassion and the building thirst for revenge.

His captains and battle lords marched in step behind him. They had become the life's blood of Delranan now that his only male heir was slain. Harnin One Eye led them. Sorrow was evident on his visage, but there was more. Those who dared to look too close could see lust for power beneath all the scars. Whether that lust was focused on the throne or something much greater remained hidden.

Last of the group of captains was the young warrior Jarrik. Rumor had it that he had been born to a bear and raised in the wild. His pale blue eyes kept a feral glint. His body was large and muscled, littered with scars and hungry. He was the king's champion. He also took the funeral the hardest of all. The prince had been a good pupil and close friend over the years. Jarrik missed him sorely already. Jarrik was forced to leave his closest companion behind, the mighty double-headed battle axe sung in song and lore. The weapon had cleaved more skulls and drank more blood than any other in the kingdom and had served the champion well over the decades. The time was fast approaching when his axe would see use again.

"None of these people gave a damn about the prince," he growled in a deep baritone.

Argis called back over his shoulder. "They come to pay respect to the heir of the land."

"They come for the protection of our steel," Jarrik snapped back. "This is all a show."

"And what would the fearsome Jarrik do? Do we conscript the whole lot and send them off to the front lines?"

"I am suggesting we send them back to their homes and end this charade now so we can go off to war ourselves."

Harnin whispered, "Both of you dishonor the king like this."

The champion fumed. "I honor his son's memory by seeking rightful vengeance against his killers, One Eye."

Badron listened to every word with disgust from the head of the procession. Any other day he might have been tempted to give them a good thrashing in the training pits, but not today. This day was reserved to the honor of his son. The kingdom and his plans could wait a day.

Six men, the survivors of the house guard, marched in cadence behind the captains. Pallbearers, they bore the cleaned and prepared corpse of the prince. They'd offered their lives in return for their failure to protect the heir to the throne, but Badron waved them off with mild praise. He insisted they carry the body. Tender breeze tousled the lad's hair. The house surgeon had done his best. At least now he looked peaceful. The blood had completely drained, leaving him pale and cold. His hands were folded across his chest armor. They clutched his favorite sword and made him formidable should any foe beset him in the halls of the afterlife.

Two full companies of soldiers marched behind. Their dress was both functional for combat and ceremony. This was the color guard of the vaunted Wolfsreik, the army of the Wolf. Ten thousand strong, they were the predominant military power in the northern kingdoms. Their uniforms were a combination of black and grey, befitting the beast of their naming. Most wore beards and were the epitome of fighting strength. They had all been chosen as children and forged into a ferocious weapon wielded by the line of Delranan kings. There were no conscripts, no draftees taken from a farmer's fields. These were professional soldiers the world looked up to and feared.

Through the winding streets they marched. Cries assailed them, perhaps Badron the hardest. He struggled to maintain composure even as the honor guard broke out into song. Gulls added their song. The sea was close. The sound of waves breaking echoed the cadence. Ahead loomed the ship that would bear his son to his fathers. A pair of priests stood at the bottom of the ramp, arms folded in black robes. The smell of incense choked the air.

Badron halted. A bell rang three times. Both priests took a step forward to greet their king. Each bowed deeply.

"Why have you come upon us this day?" asked the priest on the right. He raised his head enough for Badron to see that his eyes had been cut out.

The king choked back his emotions lest they betray him now. "To commence my son into the halls of my worthy fathers."

"The way is prepared. The path is open. Are you prepared to offer his mortal host unto the flame?"

Badron bowed in return. "I am."

The words were the heaviest he'd ever spoken. The admission was forced. There was no way to decay the love between father and son. *My son*, he wept inwardly. *I have failed you*. His nose crinkled at a whiff of incense. The priests turned inward and raised their arms towards the boat.

"You may pass. Escort this man to his final resting place."

Badron boarded and immediately stepped to the side. The pallbearers came next. They gently placed the body on a constructed pyre in the center of the deck and marched off. Badron choked on his rising grief. Mastless, the boat had neither oars nor cabins. It was more of a barge than sailing vessel, but it served the purpose well. The wood smelled freshly cut. It rocked under the lapping sea. A priest boarded next and stopped at the foot of the pyre. He raised both arms to the sky and tilted his head back.

"Gods of air, water and flame, we commend the soul of this boy to your loving embrace. Guide him to his fathers so that he may take his place by their side where his sword shall make a worthy addition to their memory."

The second priest struck a heavy staff on the deck. A strong gust of wind swept through the harbor. Badron took heart from this. It was said that the old gods often showed their favor by the kiss of the wind. The priests departed and were replaced by two iron-faced men bearing torches. Badron stood beside his son. Twenty-five years were not enough. He gently laid a hand on his cheek.

"Farewell my son. The song of your vengeance shall be sung for a hundred generations."

The king turned and walked back to the pier. A bell chimed again, three somber beats that echoed down every alley and side street. The following silence was shattering. The torch bearers dropped their brands and left. Flames licked higher until the boat was ablaze. Badron stood upon the shore long into the evening. The boat had burned and sunk. Now the remaining fire burned in his eyes.

43

SIX

A Quest Begun

Nothol Coll and Dorl Theed watched the funeral procession with mild interest. Badron was the sort not known for his compassion. He was a hard and bitter man with no qualms against imposing his own sense of justice. The sell swords figured the funeral was all for show.

Dorl took a bite of a green apple. "Who could have imagined? Our good king seems to have a heart after all."

"He did just lose his only son," Nothol scolded.

"Oh I wholly sympathize with the man. The prince was the best part of the royal family, 'cept perhaps for that daughter of his. Now she was a looker!"

Nothol shook his head. The snap of teeth sinking into the apple sent a shiver down his neck. "Badron will do like any mourning father. I think he's just been made into a tyrant."

"You always find a way to dampen my day. Badron is evil. We all know that. This can only end badly."

"For whom?" Nothol asked.

"Us and them."

"You almost surprise me. There's not even a them yet," he said in disbelief.

It was Dorl's turn to shake his head. "Hopeless. Come on. We need to get back to Bahr."

Taking the last bite from his apple, Dorl tossed the core and headed off. They'd seen enough and it was time to go. The *Bane* sailed at dawn. Neither man fully understood why they agreed to help Bahr. The look in Badron's eyes as he watched the funeral boat burn scared them both. Insanity seemed to manifest in Delranan. Dorl Theed suddenly had grave reservations about tomorrow.

Nothol shifted uncomfortably, as if sensing his friend's discomfort. "Why are we doing this?"

"Doing what?"

"Putting our lives on the line for a man who could not care less if we live or die. Delranan may be our kingdom too but it's never been kind to us."

Dorl stopped midstride and nervously looked about. Thankfully they were alone. "Mind your tongue. This ain't a safe place for talk like that. And don't go getting all philosophical on me now, Nothol Coll. Keep it simple. We're going along to watch our friend's back, nothing more. All this talk isn't sitting right with me."

Nothol snorted amusement. "As if he really needs it. Bahr is more dangerous than both of us put together. I think he's up to something."

"Of course he is! He's just as hard as the damned king, which makes me feel pretty good about our chances. Besides, you don't get to live as long as him by being cautious."

Nothol's face flushed with mild anger. "What are you talking about? Bahr's one of the most cautious people I know! You talk too much sometimes."

Dorl scowled at him but kept silent. They walked on. Dark clouds rolled in, bringing the threat of more rain. Wind blew leaves from the few trees still alive in the center of town. They sounded like fingernails scratching down broken glass.

"Something else has been bothering me," Nothol finally admitted.

The older man rolled his eyes. "That being?"

"Why would the Shadow People come all the way to Chadra Keep just to kidnap the king's daughter?"

It was a valid question. It was also one no one in the kingdom had an answer for. The Pell Darga were enigmatic at best. They'd once been the scourge of the northern kingdoms. It took an alliance of nations to finally put an end to their tyranny. The cost had been terrible. Thousands lay dead on both sides. Whole cities ceased to exist. The Pell were no longer a viable threat, and nor had they been in the three hundred years that followed.

"That doesn't seem like our problem," Dorl replied after giving it some thought. "Like I said before, we're just going to watch Bahr's back."

"Dorl, the Pell haven't threatened anyone in a long time. So why now? It's doesn't make sense, not unless Badron provoked them."

Dorl choked. Those were the last words anyone needed to be caught saying, not now, not ever. "Now you listen to me, this isn't the time to go poking your nose into places it don't belong. This kingdom is gearing up for war and we're all about to get caught up in it. We need to look out for ourselves and the best way to do that is by sticking with Bahr."

"All I am saying is that the Pell couldn't have attacked."

"You're going to get us both killed."

Bahr. The Pell Darga. War. Skuld listened intently on every word. They were enough to make him rethink his brash decision from the night prior. Picking pockets was dangerous enough these days. Going off to find a war was sheer madness. In fact, it was almost enough to make him forget the mention of hidden treasure deep in the mountains. Skuld liked to think he was a simple man. All he wanted was a good life. His mother had died during a nasty bout of the flu a while back and his father was too drunk to stay on for long. He passed Skuld off to an elderly couple when the boy was five. That was the last time Skuld had seen anyone in his family.

The next few years passed quickly. Skuld ran off at ten and lived on the streets ever since. His life was hard and unfair. It had taken a soft boy and turned him into a lean man. His hair was unkempt and a greasy shade of brown. His features were hard, not quite crisp enough to be wizened. He had almost no fat on him: one of the benefits of scrounging for every meal. Lightly muscled and lanky, Skuld suffered from a war between pimples and freckles. He was never sure which one was winning on any given day. Still, he enjoyed life. And now the life he had spent countless nights dreaming about was within his grasp. All he needed to do was reach out and take it. He smiled grimly. Bahr's boat was waiting.

"You're going to get us both killed."

Damn it! He'd been caught daydreaming and missed half of what the two had been saying. He cursed his carelessness and scampered after them. Nothol Coll and Dorl Theed were too of the more well-known sell swords in the kingdom. Finding them had been a boon. It wouldn't do now for him to mess it up before sneaking aboard the boat. Closer, Skuld remained far enough back to hear what they were saying but stayed out of sight.

"Don't make light of the developing situation. Even you should appreciate what we are about to undertake."

Skuld watched Dorl shake his head again.

"Politics aren't my concern, and you don't sound right using those big words. If Badron wants a war he can have one. Look at all these people around us. Right now they will do anything he tells them."

"Because the king is manipulating them. Why can't they see it? Badron is dangerous. He has a secret too."

"Of course he does! He wouldn't be a king if he didn't," Dorl practically repeated. "What's gotten into you? You're acting spooked. I need you frosty on this one, not daydreaming about ghosts."

"I'm fine, Dorl. I am. It's just…" he paused, suddenly unsure of what to say next. That bothered Dorl more than he wanted to admit.

"Just what?" His tone was overly cautious.

"I have this feeling down in the pit of my stomach. I'm afraid, Dorl. I am really afraid for the first time in my life."

Nothol's skin turned ashen. He was genuinely spooked and if he was spooked so was Dorl. They'd come to know each other's mannerisms well over the better part of the last decade. Dorl Theed knew they were in trouble if Nothol acted like this now. They might be two of the best at what they did, but that meant nothing if karma was gone.

"What do we do?" Dorl finally asked.

Nothol shrugged. "What can we do? We've already given Bahr our word."

"Our word but not the contract. Badron doesn't know one way or the next who is going to do this. We can slip away now and find another job."

Dorl was disgusted with himself for even considering such. He'd never run from a fight and prided himself on his keen sense of honor. Soldiers were nothing without their honor, that and discipline. Right now those are the only two things keeping me in Chadra, he mused. He loved what he did, but the thought of dying for the wrong reasons ate at him.

Nothol stared at him in shock. "I've never heard you talk like this. Don't get carried away on me. I'm just telling you I'm scared."

"Yeah, well, if it's enough to raise the hair on your neck I'm smart enough to take heed. This is a crazy world, my friend."

Nothol broke out laughing.

"What's so funny?" Dorl asked.

"An hour ago you were the one trying to convince why we needed to do this. Now look at you!"

Skuld let them walk on. Their destination was no big secret. Captain Bahr frequented the same tavern each time he made port. Skuld's problem was going to be sneaking aboard the boat. The *Dragon's Bane* had to be a bustle of activity right now as she prepared for the journey. A man like Bahr was sure to have guards in place as well. This was not a friendly port. Oh well, the boy shrugged, where there's a will there's a way. Skuld went back to the crowds hoping to find enough money to buy his next meal. His stomach was already growling.

Night dropped on Chadra with the force of a hammer. Perhaps it was the pall of the funeral or perhaps it was the dying summer. The short autumn days left a harsh chill to the air. Skuld stared over at the *Bane* and wondered how in the world he was going to sneak aboard. The water was cold. It was always cold this far north. The double black sails made his heart race. Just the thought of missing his chance at glory and fortune twisted his stomach. It wasn't until then that he realized he'd entered the harbor from the wrong direction.

"Stupid," he whispered under his breath.

Now I have the whole harbor to cross. Skuld was still distracted by the conversation of the two sell swords. He didn't care for the direction their tone went. Visions of dark things crowded in on the warmth of becoming rich. Any future he chose now offered great danger. Skuld recognized this moment for what it was. He had to make a decision that would forever affect his life. He prayed he lived long enough to learn whether it was the right one.

The street thief crept through the shadows. Long years on the streets taught him how to use the environment to his advantage. Unfortunately he hadn't counted on the additional security Badron had ordered across the kingdom. The gate house, normally holding only one or two old men at the most, was filled with guards. Not the grisly old men who were more for show than anything else, but young men with fast reflexes and the desire for justice. All were heavily armed and sober. He frowned. If what Dorl and Coll said was true, nowhere was safe in Delranan.

"How am I going to do this?" he murmured.

The answer, not the one he necessarily wanted, was evident. Skuld's dark brown eyes shifted back to the cold waters lapping against the shore. He shivered. It looked really, really cold. Skuld suddenly doubted his eagerness to join this adventure. He was no soldier, no great warrior capable of bright and terrible deeds. So why was he about to crawl into freezing waters only to risk beheading by the ship's captain? Was it really all for the vague promise of money? All thoughts fled as the frigid waters swelled up past his thighs.

The cold stole his breath. His lungs constricted violently. Muscles rebelled. Skuld cleared his head and pushed on. Guard patrolled the pier but made little notice of the waters. No one in their right mind would try swimming at this time of year. So they failed to notice the smallish head floating on the surface. Skuld pushed himself faster. The cold was already getting to him. Hypothermia was already moving through his system. It took much longer than he wanted, from a combination of cold and the fear of discovery, but Skuld finally managed a handhold on the side of the *Bane*.

He couldn't stop from chattering. His body trembled. Darkness closed in around the corners of his sight. Much longer and the guards were going to find a body washing ashore at dawn. Skuld pulled himself up by the anchor chain. The sound of the incoming waves masked his climb. After what felt like hours Skuld poked his head over the edge. Relief washed through his numb body. Not a guard in sight! He used the last of his strength to climb onto the deck where he collapsed. He wished the warmth back, but it was slow in coming. He knew he was going to die if he didn't move fast. Heavy footsteps shook him from his thoughts. Rolling onto his stomach, the thief searched for the man responsible for the footsteps. A drunken deckhand stumbled up the gangway. Skuld lay directly in his path.

Using the last bit of energy, he pushed off the deck and half slid down the stairs leading to the crew quarters. The drunken mate stumbled closer. Skuld wasn't going to make it. He moved faster, until he felt the hardness of a door at his back. His heart fell. Terror and relief clashed within him. Footsteps thumped closer. Skuld reached behind, fumbled with the knob. The door swung open, surprisingly quiet for such an old ship.

Skuld ducked inside and shut the door. Darkness shrouded everything. He listened for the sound breathing. His heart pounded, threatening to give him away. Nothing happened. The deckhand stumbled back to the crew quarters and collapsed on his hammock. Skuld was safe for now. Impossibly dark, he felt his way through the room. Burlap sacks and barrels filled the floor. Skuld allowed a deep breath. He had stumbled into one of the ship's storerooms. Exhausted, he rearranged a few stacks of rice and lay down to sleep. The easy part was over.

SEVEN

Boen

Bahr strolled through the mostly empty streets of Chadra with much on his mind, forgetting the sell swords at his side. Events were moving too fast to get a good feeling for what was happening. He felt like he was being swept away in a roiling sea without a sail or oars. The old sailor knew better than to give in to these types of thoughts. He just couldn't help it. Death stalked the land openly. Ever hungry, the end of all things hungered for fresh souls. He knew it. Bahr had made the mistake of cheating death more than once and now his time was up. The reaper had come.

His thoughts turned towards tomorrow. Nothing about Badron's scheme made sense. The king had no love for his daughter, making it almost foolish to risk so many for her. Bahr began to think that the king did want a war. If that were true, whatever country caught in Badron's sights was already doomed. He'd seen the Wolfsreik unleashed before. The result still haunted his dreams. The wolf soldiers of Delranan struck hard and fierce, not stopping until the enemy was thoroughly destroyed.

Perhaps that was the reason he felt compelled to get off the boat and join the quest to bring Maleela back before leaving port. He felt guilty for lying to his friends, but they were both capable and professional men. Nothol and Dorl could take care of themselves. He hoped they did as much to take care of him. Otherwise… Bahr let the thought fade.

His mind shifted to enigmatic thoughts of Anienam Keiss. The old sorcerer selectively avoided answering his questions while sparking more. In fact, Bahr recognized the entire conversation had been manipulated at his expense. He smiled. Caught like a bear in a trap. He knew, as did Anienam, that this quest had been chosen for him. And who was he to ignore destiny?

"Why did you drag us to this part of town?" Dorl asked in a harsh whisper.

Bahr looked over his shoulder. As good as they were, he sometimes wished they were both mute.

"Because I don't trust Badron or Harnin. That one-eyed goat is pulling together the men he wants. I am simply doing the same."

Dorl didn't care for the answer. "So what you are saying is that we aren't good enough to keep you alive?'

The Sea Wolf was about to respond when Nothol cut him off.

"He's telling us he's not going to stay on the boat. Aren't you, Bahr?"

He waved it off. "We can worry about this later. Right now I need to find an old friend."

Dorl went along. "What is this friend going to be able to do for us?"

"Hopefully keep you two away from me so I can regain some measure of my sanity."

"We don't have to be here," Dorl cautioned. "Say the word and Nothol and I will be on our way to the nearest tavern."

Bahr's shoulders slumped in mock defeat. "No. That's not what I meant. You two have your special talents, and so does this man. We're going to need all the help before this comes to a head."

"Do we know him?" Nothol asked.

Bahr half smiled. "I'm sure you've heard the name."

"Are you going to tell us or do we spend the night guessing?"

Dorl knew getting Bahr mad was not a desirable outcome, but he had lost his patience.

"Very well. His name is Boen," Bahr said evenly, despite his rising anger.

Nothol and Dorl stopped in their tracks.

"Boen? The Gaimosian?" Nothol asked with disbelief.

"The mercenary?" Dorl added.

"I prefer to think of him as my friend."

The edge in his voice was sufficient to back them down.

"Bahr, Gaimosians are almost as mythical as the Pell Darga. They might exist, but no one ever sees one. Why would one be hiding here in Chadra?" Nothol pressed.

"Is your life perfect? Boen's just fallen on hard times."

They rounded a corner in front of an old, rundown two-story building. A half-rusted sign proclaimed it the Golden Lady. Dorl somehow doubted any lady, golden or otherwise, had been inside for a long, long time. The Lady was in one of the worst parts of town, the part where men went when they didn't want to attract attention. It was also the kind of place where a man's enemies came to look for him. Even Badron's night watch refused to come down this far after sunset. Bahr caught the subtle movement off in the shadows. He waved his companions back into the dark and watched. Four men in dark clothes were climbing up a trellis to the second floor.

"Looks like we're not the only ones looking for your friend," Dorl whispered and carefully unsheathed his sword.

The four assassins eased noiselessly through the partially open window at the end of the hall. Trained professionals, they'd come for the Gaimosian's head. Their employer was very specific in his request. The Gaimosian must die. He owed too much money to just suffer a broken bone or two. Only his head in a burlap sack was enough to facilitate payment in full.

The leader waited for two to slip across to the opposite side of the hall. A small candle lamp gave off a faint, haunting light. He held up three fingers. The assassins tensed. They'd gone through the drill a hundred times. The leader dropped one finger. Loud snoring filtered from under the room door. He smiled inwardly. This was going to be easier than he had hoped.

His second finger dropped. Three assassins drew their daggers. The fourth knocked a smallish, handheld crossbow. The third finger fell. A heartbeat passed. The leader drew back and kicked the door open. The snoring stopped a breath before a blackened arrow thumped into the pillow on the bed. Three charged, leaving the crossbowman alone in the hall.

The leader followed his subordinates. He only managed a few steps when he suddenly pitched forward. His startled cry was drowned out by the slamming door. The other two turned in time to see a massive figure charging from the corner of the room, blackened sword waving menacingly.

"Thought you were going to sneak up on me did you?" Boen roared.

He attacked with speed and grace a man his size shouldn't possess. A cross-body slash ripped open the first man from neck to groin. He died even before his bowels spilled onto the floor. The second managed to blow two blows before Boen beat through his guard. The Gaimosian swung his mighty broadsword clean through his would-be killer's elbow, hacking the lower arm off. Limb and blade crashed down in a spray of hot blood.

Boen finished him in the next move. He punched his sword through the assassin's heart. The blade broke through his spine. Cries of agony and the sounds of battle woke most of the occupants. Boen ignored the rising panic outside and squared on the final killer. The leader struggled to rise. Broken ribs burned in both sides. Dark blood lined the corners of his mouth. He managed a weak laugh before falling back down.

Boen dropped into a low guard. "Did I say something funny?"

Eyes narrowed, the assassin said, "Kill me all you wish. That won't change anything. More will come. You cannot win this, Gaimosian."

Boen smiled. It was the vision of death. "What makes you think you are the first to try?"

Realization set in. Boen was unlike any other he'd been paid to hunt. His gaze shifted to both of his dead men. Comrades, brothers. Pools of cooling blood grew around the bodies. The air had a metallic taint. It was a smell he knew by heart. The assassin summoned what strength he had left and surged up to meet death with courage. Boen let him come. There was no hurry. He'd already won. The assassin lunged and was rewarded by being decapitated. Boen sidestepped to avoid the rope of blood stinging the air. Head and body hit the floor. The battle was over.

He was about to wipe the blood off his sword when he remembered the arrow that narrowly missed killing him. There was one more. He dropped into a natural stance and made ready to meet his last opponent. A muffled cry came from the hallway, followed by a heavy thump. Panting, the knight waited. Time had not been kind to him. He was old and felt it. The three dead men hadn't been much of a challenge, but the fight had left him winded.

"Are you going to open the door or just stand in the damned hallway all night?" he growled. He was tired of the games.

"How about you put the sword down and open the door for me. I don't want my head taken off," replied a voice he thought he recognized.

Boen smiled. He cautiously pulled the door open. He caught a partial profile of Bahr standing off to the side. He also noticed the black clad body crumpled on the floor.

"I haven't seen you in years, Bahr." He reached out so they could clasp hands.

"Not since we hunted down those raiders up the coast," Bahr replied.

Boen lowered his sword. "Come on in. I hope you don't mind the mess. The service only comes in once a week."

Stepping over the carnage, Bahr said, "I don't think you're going to get your deposit back."

"Sign of the times." He propped up a chair that had been knocked over. "Have a seat."

The two friends sat down and were silent for a while.

"I like what you did with the man in the hallway. He was going to be trouble for me. The bastard ruined my pillow."

Bahr finally broke into smile. "Ahh, that. You're getting old. He wasn't that much trouble."

"Aside from giving me a hand tonight what brings you here?" Boen's eyes held a budding suspicion. The big man brushed his golden locks, shot through with gray, back from his face. Clean shaven, he had a scar on the corner of his right eye that ran down to his mouth. No one living knew how he got it. Despite being close to fifty, the Gaimosian was still heavily muscled and in good fighting shape.

Bahr explained everything. Naturally he omitted his personal dealings with Badron. That wasn't anyone's business and irrelevant to the mission. The Gaimosian sat back and listened intently. Much of what the Sea Wolf said was common knowledge. Badron was a temperamental man capable of terrible deeds. Of course that didn't matter. Gaimosians were a kingdomless people. They made their way across Malweir doing as they pleased. Known as Vengeance Knights, they continually searched for a future. They neither forgave nor forgot. Delranan's problems were their own. He cared little. What did matter were the needs of a friend.

Bahr settled back. His tale was finished and he knew he'd said enough to convince his friend to join him. He just wasn't sure if Boen would.

"I need you on this one," he added. The extra pressure never hurt.

Boen scraped some of the crusted blood from his chin. "How bloody are you expecting this to be?"

"Fairly. I have a hunch this isn't going to end when we bring Maleela back. Badron wants this war too much to stop there."

"What he doesn't want are loose ends. How can we be sure he's not going to double cross us the moment we succeed?"

Bahr smiled. "It wouldn't be much of an adventure if everything were guaranteed. I already have two men who can help if need be."

"Who are they?"

He almost laughed at the similarity between his friends. Everyone wanted to know who the other guy was. "A couple of local sell swords, Nothol Coll and Dorl Theed."

"Good men," Boen approved. "All right, I'm in."

They shook on it and said their goodbyes. Bahr walked away feeling much better than when he had arrived. His chances were improving.

"So, is he coming or not?" Dorl asked once the Sea Wolf returned to them.

He was still incensed at being left outside. Common sense said let the younger men take care of the assassins. What the sell sword couldn't know was that Bahr felt the need to do that just to prove that he still had it before this expedition got underway. He had to know he was still sharp enough to deal with the threats when they arose.

The Sea Wolf barely nodded. "He'll be there. This is getting better."

"If you say so," Dorl shrugged. "Nothol and I could have handled it just fine."

"I know."

The sell swords were confused by the answer. Neither had anything relevant to say so they simply fell in line behind Bahr and went back to his estate. Dawn was coming fast and they all needed a little sleep before leaving port. Bahr felt satisfied for the first time in nearly a season. Once again, the *Dragon's Bane* would set forth on a quest. He struggled to keep from smiling.

EIGHT

Departures

"We will be moving out for the docks shortly, sire." Harnin watched for any sign of hesitation or weakness.

The one-eyed captain was dressed in his old war garb. The dents had been beaten out. The tarnish replaced with a mild shine. His boots were new, as were his trousers and tunic. Only the sword strapped to his hip was ornamental. Everything else had already been tested in combat.

Badron set down the book he'd been reading. The royal library was a far cry from the fabled archives of Ipn Shal, but it sufficed for Delranan. The only books Badron was interested in were ones concerning the Pell Darga and his hated nemesis in Rogscroft. A touch of moonlight twinkled off the candelabra. The glow made him look intense, much more so than he was. Both he and Harnin understood the Pell were just a front, an excuse to wage a bigger war.

"How many men did you manage to put together?" Badron asked.

"Twenty."

"How many are loyal to Harnin One Eye and the crown?"

Harnin nervously cleared his throat. "They are loyal enough to king and kingdom."

The king knew better. "For a price, no doubt," he snorted.

"Such is the way of mercenaries these days. The honor of the past is a lost art."

"Mercenaries loyal to a king? Why does that worry me, Harnin?"

"My lord, these are all men we have been keeping an eye on. They are the dangerous ones that we won't miss once they are dealt with."

Badron thought his most trusted advisor too pensive for such a simple report. Thoughts of betrayal entertained him.

Badron had asked himself the same question time and again since the night of the attack. Was Harnin plotting against him? If so, the man was playing it close to the chest, until the proper time.

"All is going according to plan then," he finally said. "Is Bahr still agreeing to help his kingdom?"

The natural mistrust between king and captain was a bitter feud and only they knew why. No one in Delranan could have guessed the intimate secret they shared.

"He is, though I doubt his reasons mirror yours."

"Bahr is a complicated man, certainly capable of betrayal. We must keep a close watch on him."

Badron asked, "What has he done to reinforce this thought?"

"Recruited several men on his own. I don't think he trusts us."

An eyebrow peaked. "And?"

"They are not known to me, for the most part. One is rumored to be Gaimosian. My spies have followed Bahr since I met with him on the pier, but he has vanished more than once. It is entirely possible he is taking precautions."

A Gaimosian. That was news indeed. Badron was under the impression their bloodlines were extinct. Having one inside his borders sat ill with him. They had the nasty tendency to make things more dangerous than they should be. Bloodthirsty savages. Badron frowned.

"This Gaimosian is confirmed to be leaving with Bahr?" he asked. He tried to keep the worry from his voice. Where one Vengeance Knight went so went others.

"Yes. He was seen boarding the *Dragon's Bane*."

The king nodded if ever so slightly. "Is there anything else I need to be concerned about? I want to get this over with."

"Not so much. There was a strange old man seen heading to Bahr's estate two nights ago. We've seen no sign of him since. Strange, but of no concern to this quest."

"Where is he?" Badron leaned forward, the answer unacceptable.

"Disappeared. We couldn't track him. He might have been a distant relative we don't know of or a friend come calling." Harnin's voice was shaky. He didn't enjoy sounding like a fool, especially in front of his king.

"I want that ship out of my port before noon. Too much is at stake to risk delay," Badron ground out. Displeasure was evident on his hardened face.

Harnin bowed his head, waiting to see if there was more. His one eye watched Badron with interest.

"Have you learned anything else from the attack?" Badron went on to ask.

"Nothing yet. I am afraid the trail has gone cold. We are working as hard as possible, but I believe we have lost the initiative."

Badron waved him off. He wanted to be alone now. There were too many possibilities for him to get a good grasp of the situation. Badron suddenly felt the urge to kill someone. As king it was his duty and responsibility to see Delranan's would-be heroes off, but the very thought of seeing Bahr and his motley entourage sickened him. The man was a pox on the land. The sooner that damned boat sank, and with all hands, the better.

Badron threw the book he'd been reading into the corner and bellowed his frustrations to an empty room. There were too many loose ends dangling with wicked temptation. Too much could still go wrong at this delicate stage. Despite his great power and influence as king, Badron felt reduced to a mere spectator, helpless to exert his weight. He paced the length of the library, mind racing with possible conclusions.

"Pay up, I was right," Dorl elbowed Nothol in the ribs.

Nothol groaned and dug into his purse. He reluctantly handed over two gold coins. "I should have known better than to think the king would abandon us so soon."

"I told you," was the matter-of-fact answer. "Badron may be a bastard, but he knows the value of good publicity."

They watched the official party in silence as it made the winding way down through the harbor and to the pier.

Neither man was impressed, despite the quality of the guard livery.

"They don't look much for fighting, do they?" Dorl asked.

Nothol smirked. "I bet they haven't seen a battlefield in a good number of years. I still wouldn't want to fight them."

"Why not?"

"It's twenty to two," he explained.

Dorl threw a feral grin. "We could take them."

"Are you two finished?"

They looked back at Boen's aggressive face. He was clearly not amused by their banter.

"Haven't even started," Dorl shot back. He refused to be cowed, not even by a Gaimosian.

Boen grimaced. "You remind me of these two lads I had with me down in Averon a few years back. Always back and forth. Damned boys wouldn't shut up."

Nothol rolled his eyes as Dorl took the bait.

"What happened to them?"

"We ran into a nest of Trolls. Both were killed and eaten."

Boen walked back to the port side and watched the dawn break across the harbor. He hadn't wanted to scare them, but their attitude was much too carefree. They needed to know that this was for real and the worst might happen. Thinking about it, he had come off like a surly old man. Boen sighed and wondered where his youth had fled to.

Bahr watched the exchange from the wheel. His focus shifted back towards the approaching king. His face bore no emotion. The docks were lined with spectators. He understood why. This was the biggest event in recent history and they all wanted to have the memory. Bahr repressed a snarl. There were too many strangers for his liking. Naturally suspicious, Badron would feel the same. Thankfully Anienam Keiss was safely tucked away below decks so as not to arouse suspicion.

The Sea Wolf wanted to keep the wizard a secret for as long as possible. He'd already been surprised when the old man was awaiting him in the captain's cabin. Nothing from their conversation led Bahr to believe the wizard meant to travel with him. He kept a sneaking suspicion but wasn't confident enough to mention it to the others.

Harnin and his guards led the procession to the edge of the pier. A mass of mercenaries and adventurers followed. Bahr watched with casual disinterest. He'd seen their kind too much over the decades and was none impressed. He patiently waited for the One Eye to dismount and ease forward.

"That's far enough, One Eye. I can hear you from there," Bahr warned as the man's boot touched the gangplank.

Harnin's face flushed. "Captain Bahr, the king wishes your answer. Will you accept the charge of finding his daughter?"

The Sea Wolf barely shook his head. "I see no king here. If his daughter is so important then where is he?"

"King Badron has other affairs of state to attend to. He has every confidence in your abilities to see this matter through. Your success or failure will decide the future of the kingdom. War is coming."

War is coming regardless, Bahr whispered under his breath. "War against whom?"

Harnin gave a toothy grin. "Against whoever has the princess. Is your crew ready?"

"Aye, ready enough."

"I cannot stress how important speed is. Find the princess and bring her back before the Pell Darga reach the mountains," Harnin urged. "It is the only way to prevent war."

Bahr didn't believe a word said. He'd known Badron and Harnin long enough to understand their devotion to treachery. Unfortunately, most of the common citizens believed the lies. None of them would see the war until it was too late. The Wolfsreik had been roused and it wouldn't sleep again until sword and spear ran red with blood. That didn't matter to Bahr. Rescuing Princess Maleela and bringing everyone back alive were his only concerns.

"If the men you've gathered are as good as mine, we'll be back in under a month."

"Luck be with you, son of Delranan," Harnin saluted. He wrapped his cloak around himself and walked away. Further conversation was pointless and the absurdity of their exchange lessened them both.

Bahr was about to do the same, leaving the boarding to his first mate, when a single rider stormed through the crowds. Guards drew their swords as one of their own was knocked into the frigid autumn waters. The rider never slowed. Bahr began to notice distinct features. The curve of the hip. The slender shoulders. A woman, he mused. Now what could this be?

She had long silver hair that billowed in the morning breeze. Her cloak was mottled shades of grey. Her clothes were black as midnight. Her skin was a golden brown, soft yet conditioned. Whoever she was, she had drawn the attention of everyone in the harbor. Harnin fumed with outrage. Bahr almost laughed from his perch. Any excuse for the One Eye to be embarrassed suited him. Still, he couldn't begin to think of why such a slender woman would be riding hard just to reach the *Bane*.

Clearly a foreigner and smallish in stature, she held an exotic beauty unmatched by any this far north. Bahr guessed she was probably from down south of the Jebel Desert. He looked a little closer, hoping to find some clue to solve this mystery. She wore a pair of slightly curved swords, one belted to each hip. Her eyes were the softest brown and calm despite the dangers she caused. Bahr felt compelled to meet her.

Two guards blocked her way and shouted, "Halt!"

She ignored them and dismounted. Guards formed ranks behind their captain. Harnin had drawn his own sword. Only Bahr remained unaffected by the display. He waited as the woman stopped a handful of feet from the guards. She stared them down without so much as blinking.

"How dare you assault an emissary of the king?" Harnin roared at her.

"Stand aside and let me conduct my business with Captain Bahr," she replied tersely.

Now this is interesting, Bahr thought. He subconsciously inched closer towards the rail. She had a slight accent, definitely marking her as a deep southerner.

Harnin refused to back down. "Bahr is in the employ of the king and has no time to meet with foreign scum."

She grinned, savage and beautiful. "He will if your king expects to see his daughter alive again."

"Mind your tongue, woman!" Harnin snapped.

Bahr had heard enough. "Quit your posturing and let the lass by, Harnin. I doubt she came all this way just to do us harm."

The One Eye shrugged. Hidden archers waited for the signal should he give it. "It's your life."

The Sea Wolf smiled at this small victory. Unhindered, the woman brushed through the ring of guards and boarded the *Dragon's Bane*. She didn't offer them a second glance. Her eyes blazed with intent. She'd come more than a thousand leagues just to meet the man who haunted her dreams.

Dorl Theed whistled low. "She's a vision, that's for sure."

"A vision of pain," Nothol countered. "Look at the way she carries herself. She's a warrior."

"Who just backed down twenty of Badron's finest. I told you we could have taken them."

NINE

Rekka Jel

Bahr crossed his arms over his chest and waited for the newcomer. He suddenly felt overmatched. She couldn't weigh more than a hundred pounds, less than half of him but there was an undeniable lethality to her. Every inch of her warned of violence. She finally halted before him and bowed.

"Captain, my name is Rekka Jel and I have travelled far to join this quest."

Her light brown skin glowed in the breaking dawn. Bahr caught himself before he succumbed to her beauty. That didn't stop him from noticing how soft and amber her eyes were.

Bahr returned the bow, albeit awkwardly. "What would a lady from the south want with an old sea captain from the far north?"

He didn't ask the real question. How did you learn of our quest in the first place? Harnin and his men were still on the pier listening to every word. It wouldn't do to give anything away provided she truly had something important to say.

"I had a dream you were in grave danger."

He forced a smile despite the threat. "Lass, you're probably too young to understand, but I seem to always be in danger. It goes with the times."

"But I…" Rekka protested.

Bahr held up a finger and leaned forward so only she could hear him. "Say no more. There are unfriendly eyes watching us. Tell me what you will below deck."

Rekka nodded.

"Harnin, this woman has been sent to find me to offer aid. I will see what she has to say and be about the quest. You are no longer needed here," he called down.

Harnin bore a foul look. He wanted nothing more than to take every man at his disposal, storm the ship and throw everyone in irons. Doing so was not going to solve matters. And Badron would be furious.

"Very well, Captain. But keep in mind that haste is required. The king will not tolerate delay. He expects you to leave soon."

Bahr translated that to mean "leave now or else." His fingers curled around the hilt of his sword. If only, he longed. He turned his back on Harnin and led Rekka below. He politely ushered her into his cabin and offered a seat. Rekka smiled and waited for the questioning to begin.

"Now then, what's all this nonsense about a dream?" he asked. Getting to the point was the best way to deal with the problem.

"Forgive me. The dream masters of my people have long beheld visions of a terrible war begun in the north. The dreams centered on a king whose heart is laced with malice and an old seafarer past his prime. I do not mean to offend you but it is our belief that the old seafarer…"

"Is me," he finished.

She nodded, slightly embarrassed. "Yes. Each time the dream occurred there was a vessel with a black dragon on the sail. We have searched far and wide. This is the only such vessel."

Bahr remained skeptical. "I find that hard to believe. The ocean is a massive place. You could have easily missed another such as mine. Dragons are a common theme among the northern people."

"It is not the sail so much as the man."

"I don't follow."

Rekka exhaled slowly and explained. "The dragon is a symbol of power and greatness. They are revered for their wisdom and strength."

"Clearly you have never read the tales of men who have fought one," he said lightheartedly.

"Perhaps the great dragons in your legends acted aggressively because your men came to slay them," she offered back.

He had no answer.

"Your people are known as the people of the dragon in my homeland. Our texts speak of great deeds centered upon these creatures. Their age leads to a heightened awareness, revealing all their surroundings for the greater good. Kings of old once sought council in their mighty mountain lairs."

Bahr was starting to get frustrated. "You've made your point about the damned dragons. I still fail to see what this has to do with me. I put a dragon on my sail when I was a lad because I thought the image would inspire terror and make me sound hard. There are no great secrets or hidden meanings. I was young and brash. The name had already stuck by the time I grew old enough to know better."

"Captain, you must understand the convictions of my quest. Your actions may affect the fate of thousands. War is coming quickly and there is little time to prepare."

He stopped her. She was hiding something, but he knew better than to press too much too soon. "What do you mean my actions? I'm only one man. Hells, I'm not even a particularly great warrior. This world has gotten on well enough without me. Wars come and go. It is the way of things. What can I possibly do that will have such impact?"

"The dream masters say that only the brother of the evil king has the power to prevent disaster," she said after a deep breath.

Bahr's eyes widened. His face flushed, his heart thumped faster. "What did you say?"

He refused to believe his ears. No one living knew his darkest secrets, not even his best friends. How could this stranger from the south come to learn the depths of his soul without ever meeting him? He slowly began to believe parts of her story. Perhaps these dream masters did have some ethereal power. His initial impulse was to throw her off his boat, but too many questions were unanswered. This diminutive woman was much too valuable to simply discard.

"Captain Bahr, the dream tells us of two brothers driven apart by hatred. One is a king, the other a… mild pirate. One shall go through darkness and pain while the other builds on madness and seeks to bring the world to the edge of destruction. Only the brother who is forced to suffer will be able to save his people and restore order to Malweir."

He frowned, though being called a pirate was amusing. He almost liked the appellation. Still, the dilemma remained. Bahr sat down. He had too. The weight behind her words held much portent he simply wasn't willing to accept. He'd known from childhood that a day of reckoning was coming between Badron and himself. His brother was unstable, leading to rash judgments and a nasty bitter streak. Questions and scenarios overtook his thoughts. Too much. It was all too much. Bahr wasn't sure how he was going to be able to fight his own brother.

He snorted. Brother. They hadn't thought of each other as brothers in almost thirty years. Those bonds were long decayed and irreparable. It was the greatest secret in the kingdom. One he had taken extraordinary measures to keep.

Bahr finally looked into Rekka's soft brown eyes. "How did you know he was my brother? That is a truth we have kept hidden for many years. Our mother knew we would eventually come to mortal blows and made efforts to keep us apart. She died shortly thereafter."

The cabin door creaked open.

"I thought I gave orders to be left alone?"

A light chuckle followed. "You didn't really believe this young lady found her way all the way north without a little intervention did you?"

"Anienam Keiss, I should have known better," Bahr exclaimed.

The old wizard ambled into the cabin and found a chair, a crooked smile engraved on his face. Rekka Jel dropped reverently to her knees and bowed deeply.

"Come, come child. There is no call for that. As our good captain is so fond of saying, I am just a man," Anienam said. "You have done well to make it here so quickly."

Rekka slowly raised her head. "I left Teng not long after you."

"A very long journey. You deserve to rest. Where are your bags?"

"No doubt being rummaged through by Harnin's men," Bahr added. He wasn't sure, but he got the impression that Anienam was trying to divert the conversation.

"Would you be so kind as to get one of your men to retrieve them for her?" Anienam asked politely.

Bahr rose. "Sure, but I need a few answers first."

"Answers to what exactly?"

"How long have you two been working together?"

Anienam smiled. "I don't believe we have ever met."

"Then how…."

The wizard held up a staying hand. "I am a friend of many in many lands. The tribes of Brodein are well known to me. They have worked with my kind and," a pause, "others for many years. I did, however, have a hand in helping the Teng dream masters interpret the dreams."

"And the secret of my brother and I?"

"I am a wizard," he said matter-of-factly. "I have walked across Malweir for a very long time. You can't expect certain things to be beyond me. Especially now. The world is changing, Bahr. I know we spoke of some of this the other night, but there is so much more I will never be able to explain. A confluence is coming. A time when the powers of light and dark will seek to win domination over all life. I will not get into the ages old debate of whether the gods exist or not. None of that matters. What matters are your decisions during the coming days and weeks."

Bahr rubbed his chin thoughtfully. "It is a hard choice to make. I have no love for my brother, though I do not wish him ill. We are not of the same mold. Still, I would have my niece back alive even if he cares not."

He fell silent. The admission had not been an easy one. These were the childhood secrets and painful memories of a wasted family. To have a pair of complete strangers confront him so casually rattled Bahr. What else might they say? He suddenly felt uncomfortable. Bahr knew both would need a careful eye on them.

"Heed my words. I undertake the quest to find my niece freely, but I will not kill my own brother. We may hate each other, but we are still blood. If such needs doing it will be by another's hands."

Anienam replied, "No one is asking you to go to such lengths. The dreams lead us to believe you are the one to end this tyranny, but they do not say how. For that we must bear witness to history as it unfolds. There are dark times ahead, of that I am certain. We must struggle through the storm as a group before the sun will shine again."

"I have never been good with riddles. I prefer a man who talks to me straight," Bahr paused long enough to stare the old man deep in the eyes. "You two can come for the trip only on one condition."

"Name it."

"You do what I say and how. You, Rekka Jel, I expect to earn your keep while we're at sea. Don't worry lass, the voyage will be quick. No more than two or three days depending on the weather."

Rekka bowed. "It shall be as you say."

"And for me?" Anienam asked patiently.

Bahr felt irritated by the condescending look being given him. The old wizard must have done this a thousand times over, he thought.

"You stay hidden. I'm fairly certain that at least one of the men Harnin found is a spy. It makes sense. I noticed his favorite killer sneaking in with that group. Badron is no fool and Harnin's a snake. You're my ace in the hole for when things go sour."

"A fair deal. I can help in finding this spy."

"We'll find out soon enough if my suspicions are correct. Men like that act differently when they're under attack."

"Do you plan on being attacked?"

It was Bahr's turn to smile. "It wouldn't be any fun otherwise."

Boen made his way down the boarding ramp with Dorl and Nothol on his heels. Several guards blanched at the sight. They hadn't followed Harnin down to the docks with the expectations of getting into a fight. The men from the *Dragon's Bane* clearly had. They shuffled and moved back. Even Harnin found himself shifting away.

"What do you want?" he asked accusingly.

Boen flashed his teeth. It was a singular look. One that warned, "Come and test me."

"We've come for the lady's belongings," Dorl answered. "She's coming with us."

"I trust this isn't a problem?" Boen added in a deep voice.

Harnin struggled to maintain his composure. "No problem at all. I trust she will benefit the mission greatly if Bahr has deemed her worthy."

The Gaimosian shrugged. "That's his business."

Dorl and Nothol stripped the saddle bags and weapons from her horse and marched back to the Bane under Boen's watchful gaze. None of the guards so much as flinched. The last thing any of them wanted was a brawl with a handful of mercenaries on the docks. All their order and discipline meant nothing in a close fight. The men aboard the *Bane* were selected for one reason: they were dangerous. Harnin knew that all his guards, and quite possibly himself, would be dead from such an encounter.

He swallowed what little pride remained and called out, "Inform Captain Bahr he is cleared to depart at his convenience."

Boen looked back over his shoulder. "I suppose he'll leave when he's good and ready."

He boarded the *Dragon's Bane*, glad to be done with it. The sooner they were underway the better.

Dorl dropped the bags and told Nothol, "I rather enjoyed that."

"It could become habit-forming."

"Let's get her kit stored. I wouldn't mind taking another peek at her myself. Did you see that hair?"

Nothol shook his head ruefully. "Yes I did and you'd best stop thinking with your trousers. That's the quick-fire way to get killed."

Dorl grinned. "It might just be worth it."

Gulls and sea crows circled the harbor. They sensed the coming dread and grew agitated at the prospect of fresh meat. For the trials of man would affect all creatures in the world, whether they stopped to recognize it or not. What began in Delranan would consume the entirety of the world.

TEN

To the Mountains

Maleela stared down at the frost-covered ground and wondered again if she had made the right decision. Her father wasn't necessarily a bad man, or so she chose to believe. His temper was often frightening and he had a penchant for conquest, but he loved his people after a fashion. Maleela had never felt that love. All Badron wanted was sons. Rialla had given him one, but only one. The shame of going through life knowing that her mother died giving birth often caused Maleela great pain.

There was a time when a father's love was all that mattered, all she needed. It was the one thing he refused to give. He blamed her for Rialla's death and made no secret about it. Nothing she did was good enough. Every idea or thought she had was either dumb or a waste of time. He was overly critical and rarely showed good will towards her publicly. Maleela knew she was a stain upon his honor. The combination of all that was unbearable.

Then she met Aurec. The pair took an instant liking to each other. Love seemed inevitable. The kings celebrated their relationship with a grand celebration many still talked about. Joy faded quickly. Maleela learned through her own spies that her father had designs on conquering Rogscroft. That knowledge would eventually force their love underground. She and Aurec were all but forbidden to follow the paths of their hearts, leaving one alternative. The pair kept their love a secret until Aurec was finally prepared to rescue her. She waited until the night came when her prince stole her from Chadra Keep.

A twig snapping startled her. Her hand dropped, uncomfortably, to the hilt of her short dagger.

"I'm unarmed," Aurec said with a sheepish grin. His hands were held up.

She blushed. "You startled me."

"I'm sorry," he replied. "What are you doing out here all alone? It's not safe for any of us these days."

"I was just thinking." She turned back to the rolling hills stretching out before them.

Aurec moved beside her and tenderly reached for her hand. "About your father."

She nodded.

"Winter is closing in. No army is equipped to cross the mountains and wage a war a hundred leagues from home in the dead of winter, not even the Wolfsreik. We still have some time."

Maleela gave him a sad look. "You don't know my father."

"He's just one man."

"One man who will stop at nothing to keep me from warning your father. He will kill us if he catches us."

Aurec's face twisted in a stricken look. "He wouldn't hurt his own daughter."

"Oh Aurec, why can't you see? He has no love for me, none at all. He wanted sons. Strong heirs to carry on his name and ideals. I was, and am, unwanted in that house."

"And we killed his only son," he whispered.

It was more of an admission of guilt than a realization. He hadn't wanted to kill anyone at all, but there was little choice in it. The house guard responded fiercely and did their jobs well. They also paid for it dearly in lives. Telling Maleela was the hardest thing he had ever done. The decision tormented him from the moment it happened. Her anger quickly faded, though not before beating deep bruises into his chest. Aurec was surprised with how easily she put that anger aside and focused on the present. He began to doubt her sincerity towards all her family.

"Badron's vengeance will be terrible."

He looked at her and felt his heart grow weak. The woman he loved had just given up everything she'd ever known for an uncertain life with him. There was no going back and he was still unsure if he deserved it. He certainly couldn't ask for such sacrifice. Aurec winced at the fear emanating off her. Worse, he had no idea how to make it better.

"My brother was a good man. He might have been a fine king were it not for my father's influences," she quietly said.

"I promise you this will work itself out."

"At what cost?"

He had no answer. Thankfully Venten approached.

"My lord, the camp is struck. We are ready to move."

"Thank you, Venten. We'll be along shortly. Tell Mahn and Raste to push out."

The aged veteran nodded gruffly and returned to the rest of the group. He didn't say it, but he was still unsure about their present course of action, and that bothered the prince. Venten was a professional soldier with unshakable loyalties. Wherever the prince went he would follow. Still, he'd been troubled since they entered Delranan. The old veteran prayed love did not get in the way before this affair was sorted.

"How long do you think it will be before your father sends his hunters?" Aurec asked once they were alone again.

"He already has," came her reply.

He nodded glumly. "We knew it was a risk. The Pell Darga was good cover, but their kingdom lies along the same road as Rogscroft. We must hurry if we are to warn my father in time."

They rode hard. Aurec was determined to put as much ground as possible between them and Badron's hunters. Rogscroft was still far enough away to keep him comfortable. The Murdes Mountains loomed ever higher despite being far. Fortunately the road was an easy one. They could make great speed. Unfortunately their enemies could do the same. Aurec pushed them hard, driving across the grasslands and into the first foothills. All told, they rode fifteen leagues before the sun set.

Aurec decided to risk a small fire once they made camp. Satisfied that food was cooking and they could all find some warmth; he summoned his two best scouts to him. Mahn and Raste stood before their prince, awaiting their orders.

"I have a feeling we are being followed," Aurec told them. "I want you to sweep back about a league. Don't make contact though."

Mahn, a longtime sergeant and veteran of almost twenty years, cocked his head. He had shoulder-length jet black hair and a barrel chest. Tattoos decorated his cheeks just below the eyes. "If it is only one man he'll never see us coming. We should eliminate him before we lose the advantage."

"No. Killing him will only let our enemy know they are on the right path. We can't afford to take that risk."

"They might be Pell scouts," the younger Raste offered.

His golden hair and lighter frame was in sharp contrast to his counterpart. He still held a youthful lightheartedness in his pale blue eyes.

"The Pell would have made themselves known. Besides, they hardly come this far down from the mountains," Mahn countered. His natural mistrust of the Pell dripped with every word.

"Just get close enough to see who it is and report back. Nothing fancy. I'm actually going to need you two before this ends," Aurec cautioned.

"Fair enough. We will pass on the heroics for now," Mahn smiled.

The scouts left without another word and saddled their mounts, taking time to strip everything that might give them away at night. Neither was particularly enthused about their task, but they were scouts and had no room for complaints. Still, they'd been riding point for almost a month and bordered on exhaustion. Loyal sons of Rogscroft, Mahn and Raste wearily climbed back into the saddle. They slipped into the growing darkness and were lost to the evening.

"They are two of my best," Aurec told Maleela after he noticed the odd look she gave him. "If your father's men are on us, they will find out."

"What happens when they do? How much farther until we are safe?" she asked.

He lacked the nerve to tell her the truth. *Never. We will never be safe again, my love.* Badron would hound them into the grave.

"It will take us a week to cross the mountains, providing that the weather holds. Another week and we'll be at Rogscroft. My father is going to give you a warm welcome. What better way to welcome winter than with the coming of a princess?"

His smile was warm and genuine, but not enough to shake the cold feeling in her bones. Something terrible was creeping upon them and she felt helpless to prevent it. Maleela hoped nothing ill befell them before gaining the security of the city-kingdom.

Then a thought dawned on her. She gave Aurec a sly look and asked, "He doesn't know, does he?"

Aurec betrayed no emotion. "I don't know what you are talking about."

He watched her for a few moments before looking in the direction of his scouts. The world had suddenly grown more complicated.

Raste stifled a yawn. The moon was slowing, cresting the lip of the western mountains. It was already cold with temperatures dropping close to freezing. The young scout considered how good being in a goose down bed with a warm woman or two would feel then admonished himself for drifting off. That kind of thinking would get both of them killed. They'd been through the drill more times than either cared to remember. Alertness was the key to their continued success, and survival, although Raste liked to credit a little bit of good luck as well.

Mahn led them into a small copse of white birch. The site of their last encampment was only a few hundred meters away. If Aurec's suspicions were accurate, this was the perfect place to await their mystery stalker. Mahn wrapped his travelling cloak a little tighter around him and settled down for the wait. Experience taught him that it wouldn't be long. No one in their right mind wanted to be out in this weather.

He glanced over at his younger partner. Raste was almost too young to be a good scout, but the lad did have natural ability. He was good, but not quite good enough. More so, Raste was experienced. He'd been pulled from the ranks of infantry after a handful of battles to salt him. Three years ago command had assigned them together. They'd formed a tenuous bond barely days before running into a Goblin patrol. Both did their share of killing during the escape. The lesson would prove invaluable should Raste decide to pursue a career in the military. Mahn had every expectation that the lad would grow to be a fine soldier with a little time and training.

A sudden movement broke his thoughts. Mahn smiled. Their quarry moved into view with impunity. Moonlight struck the ground in mottled beams. The scouts watched unbelievably as the man rummaged through rocks and trees for signs of the princess. He was sloppy and careless, making enough noise to be heard a mile away. Mahn cursed the man for his incompetence but made no move. He could almost feel Raste's contempt rising beside him.

The younger scout thumbed the edge of his blackened dagger impatiently. He'd like nothing more than to charge in and make the kill. That wasn't his job anymore. He was being paid to sit and watch and report. So Raste sat quietly and observed his enemy. The pair had almost grown bored when the man suddenly froze. His head darted from side to side as if frantically searching for something.

"Damn," Raste barely whispered.

His first instinct was they'd been discovered and it was time to attack. If they didn't stop the spy now it was all over. He would return to his masters and report their position. That was unacceptable. He glanced over at Mahn to see if the older man's body language suggested the same intent. It didn't. Mahn sat still as a tree and watched. Raste, being the junior, resigned himself to the same.

Mahn watched their prey with extreme interest. There was nothing familiar about him. He moved like a normal man with limited field experience. His dress was non-distinct in animal furs. Weaponless, he moved without concern for his surroundings. Mahn suddenly felt as if he was wasting his time. Their stalker was definitely not from Badron's court. Mahn watched the man bolt back in the direction from which he came.

"Do we follow?" Raste immediately asked.

Mahn shook his head. "No. He's harmless."

"He might have friends."

"Then let us hope they are better at this game than this one. We don't have anything to fear from him."

Raste wasn't so sure. "I don't like it. We should at least see where he is going."

"To what purpose? I'd be willing to bet he's no more than a boy chasing an easy score. Let the wind take him. We have better things to do."

"Such as?" Raste raised an eyebrow.

They were sitting in the middle of nowhere in the middle of the night. It wasn't the worst situation Raste had been in but he could think of several better ones. Besides, it was getting too cold to be wandering through the Delranan forests by themselves. He imagined how warm Aurec's fire must be and stifled a jealous pang. The luxuries of being a prince, he guessed. *Fat and warm while all us soldiers do the dirty work. Just lovely.*

"A bit of sleep and some hot food," Mahn answered.

He'd never admit it, but he was every bit as tired and cold as Raste. Years of military service failed to immunize him to nature despite the hard edge. That edge often made it difficult to make friends or adapt in social situations very well. Mahn wasn't quite old yet. He was only a few years beyond thirty. The downside was that the military was all he knew. Part of him wished Raste never had to know the same hardships, and a little luxury was most certainly owed them.

Raste cracked a thin smile. "I like the sound of that."

"Let's head back to camp. It will be dawn in a few hours and I need some rest."

"Lead on, oh wise one."

The scouts wheeled their mounts around and headed back to their small camp. Pale moonlight bathed the ground in an eerie glow. Shadows gave the impression of foul creatures stalking the innocence of the night. Neither scout paid much attention to such. They were accustomed, if not wholly comfortable, with working in the night. Still, both remained ready in the event the darkness turned on them.

Mahn occasionally glanced behind them. He still had the sinking feeling that comes from being watched. Every time he turned he saw nothing. Mahn eventually decided the paranoia was from the lack of sleep and focused on the path ahead. So it was that he failed to see the small figure trailing them from a safe distance.

ELEVEN

Open Waters

The *Dragon's Bane* plowed through the open waters. Gulls soared along the prow. Sea spray coated those close to the rails. She made good time though Bahr felt they could do better. He paced the decks with a constant scowl. The northern ice flow had yet to encroach upon the mainland and there were simply too many variable factors to make him comfortable. A dozen different scenarios played over in his mind, none of them with appreciable endings. Weather and family. He almost felt lost.

He let his gaze settle on the wizard and the enigmatic southern girl. He didn't trust either of them for good reason. They both knew far too much about him and the king than Bahr deemed right. Things that he had long forgotten. Making matters worse, he only knew a handful of the twenty men Harnin had hired. The entire situation chafed him.

Bahr turned back to the ocean. This was where he felt safe, where he felt at home. Still, not even the troubled waters frothing against his hull managed to keep his thoughts straight. The prophetic interpretations of Rekka Jel's dream masters disturbed him. He'd never been the superstitious sort and didn't give in to the typical sailor yarn about good fortune. Bahr believed life was what you made of it, nothing more. He exhaled a long breath and rubbed his face with the palms of both hands. There was a brief moment where he felt that he was too old for this nonsense, too old to be gallivanting around Malweir's northern oceans. Then again, he hadn't a clue what else there was to do. Destiny was intent on keeping him a traveling adventurer.

"What's on your mind?" Boen asked in his rumbling voice from behind.

The big man eased alongside and offered a half-empty canteen. Bahr accepted the water and drank deeply.

"There are days when I feel like the world is stacked against me," he answered.

"You get used to it after a while," Boen answered gruffly. "This is a hard life in a hard world. We wouldn't have made it this far if we weren't good at what we do."

"Are you sure this is the right life? I almost wish there were a clear path ahead. I'm getting old, Boen."

"We all are. That doesn't mean we need to slow down or stop now. Where would the fun be if we just gave up?"

They both laughed, but without much force. Bahr knew the Gaimosian had lived a far tougher life than he could ever dream: a lifetime of warfare and change, nothing constant. Bahr doubted he'd have been able to do the same. The sad thing was Boen was more the rule than the exception. The Gaimosian people were scattered across the face of Malweir and forbidden to rebuild their kingdom. A massive army of nations combined to crush Gaimos and destroy their way of life thousands of years ago. The culture died. All that remained was a few small tribes of families and roaming mercenaries highly sought after by kings and queens. Boen had no place to call home, unlike the self-imposed exile Bahr chose.

"Can I absolutely trust you?" he finally asked.

If Boen took offense he didn't show it. "Of course you can. What kind of question is that? We've known each other for almost thirty years, you damned fool."

Bahr almost smiled. I've known my brother for longer and that hasn't turned out so well for me, he thought. "I'm not so sure about this quest anymore. It is growing more perilous by the moment."

Boen passed a quizzical look. "Getting cold feet already?"

"Nothing of the sort."

He looked around to see if anyone else was near. "You already know about the woman, Rekka Jel, but she's not our only guest."

"What do you mean? I've had suspicions that one of them is Harnin's spy but it's too early to prove who if that is what you mean."

Boen was a naturally untrusting man. It was a lesson learned early in life. One of his first partners betrayed him and tried to kill him in his sleep. Boen snapped the man's neck and never put his full faith in another soul again.

Bahr shook his head. "No. That's not what I meant. Well, I agree with you, but this is bigger. Have you ever heard the name Anienam Keiss?"

The Gaimosian's eyes widened in shock and dark recognition. "Damnation."

"He's in my cabin."

"The wizard!" he exclaimed in hushed tones. "What could possibly bring that old man among us?"

Bahr related the full story as best he could. Boen stood quietly, listening to every word said. A tactical picture began to form in his mind. Even though neither of them had a clue as to Anienam's intentions, they knew enough to find the grand scheme alarmingly disturbing. Too many forces were at work. Boen suddenly felt very small. There were too many secrets. Secrets killed people.

"This has a foul feel to it," Boen remarked once the Sea Wolf fell silent.

His eyes were darker, reflecting his foul turn of mood.

"We still have a fool's arrogance working for us, that and pride," Bahr said.

"Pride has its uses, though I doubt it can do much against a wizard should he turn on us."

Bahr shrugged. "A little late to worry about all that now. Still, I don't find the situation hopeless yet."

Boen shook his head ruefully. "Optimism doesn't suit you."

"One of us needs to try and think positively. Otherwise we might as well punch a hole in our ship and take our chances with the deep."

"That's more like it," Boen smiled. "When do I get to meet these two?"

"Tonight. Once the watch has been set and most of the crew is bedded down, I will call a few of us to my cabin."

"You're worrying too much. Right now there is no way a spy can get word back to Badron. We're already a day's sail out of Chadra."

Boen cocked his head. He tried playing the scenario out in his head again and again. All boiled down to one solidifying factor. He had an unidentified threat aboard and no idea as to who it was.

Boen read his mind. "Do you think it is this Rekka Jel? Badron could have hired her to assassinate you, us."

"I don't think so. I'm not getting any kind of ill feelings from her."

"What about the wizard?"

Again Bahr paused. He didn't really know what to think about the Anienam Keiss. There was a clear sense of danger emanating from the man but wasn't sure who it was directed against. "He doesn't seem to have any malice towards us either. I think he's really come to help."

Boen remained skeptical. "Help us or him?"

"Malweir."

"That's a vague answer."

Bahr replied, "Yes, but what can we do? We've known the dangers ever since signing on to this. It can only get harder from here."

"There's hard and then there is stupid. Anienam might be playing us for the fool, using us to achieve his own means."

Bahr scowled at the thought. The Gaimosian was going to have him seeing ghosts before much longer. "I think this conversation has run its course. Keep your ears open among the men. Let me know if there is any talk."

Boen stalked off to find a place to sit and think.

Night dropped faster than they were ready for. The *Dragon's Bane* plowed through the Northern Ocean almost ten hours that day. Each gust of wind took them that much further from Delranan and closer to the northern reaches of the Murdes Mountains and the danger beyond. A night watch was emplaced and the rest went below decks for a hot meal and a few hours of sleep. Such simple luxuries would be rare in the coming days and no sailor worth his salt passed on an opportunity.

Bahr sat at the head of the small table in his quarters and looked at each man. Dorl and Nothol were there acting bored and confused. Boen and a man selected from Harnin's chosen exchanged wary glances. Rekka Jel stood off in a corner, diminutive and deadly. Anienam Keiss was the last. He sat beside the captain as humble as possible. The Sea Wolf was almost impressed he managed to pull it off.

"Friends, let us consider this our first war council. Each day we shall meet to decide our next course of action," he began.

Harnin's emissary, Ionascu, leaned forward on his bony elbows. "Why us? Some of the boys think you're showing favorites. It don't sit well with them."

Bahr's features hardened reflexively. "Of course I am, Ionascu. I was hired to take a group of men to rescue the king's daughter. Harnin forced your group on me. Why should I give these men trust when they haven't earned it? My contract is to take you east and drop you off, nothing more. Anything else, I do of my own accord. These men you accuse of being my favorites have saved my life more times than I can recall and vice versa. They have earned my trust and confidence. So you will forgive me my indulgences until your men prove they have earned my trust."

Ionascu clearly didn't like or appreciate the answer but was experienced enough to keep his mouth shut for the time being.

Bahr gave a perfunctory look around to placate the others. "If there are no other objections, let us get down to business. Ionascu, believe me when I say that I fully intend to speak with every man before we make land. You are my responsibility so long as you remain on my ship."

"That's good enough for me," Ionascu roughly said. "I will tell them once we finish here."

Bahr sighed. The issue of new men was one of his biggest problems. Now that they were going to know he was coming he'd be able to tell who the spy was much easier. Or so he hoped. Of course the opposite might also be true. This might make the spy go deeper.

"Our first move needs to be a quick resupply when we reach the port of Dredl. We'll spend the night depending on when we arrive."

Boen grunted. "Why not push forward?"

"Into the Murdes Mountains at night? We'd be slaughtered," Dorl exclaimed.

"We'd also take the enemy off guard."

Bahr shook his head. "Dorl is right. The mountains are far too dangerous to enter at night. The Pell would eat us alive."

He failed to mention Anienam and his particular skill set. So far as Ionascu and the others were concerned Anienam was just another old man hired to oversee the daily operation of the ship. Exactly the way Bahr wanted it kept. He also failed to mention that he silently hoped Maleela was well beyond the Mountains of Death when they caught up to her.

"What better way to surprise the enemy? They'll never expect us to act so brashly," Boen insisted. "Strike fast and the advantage remains ours."

Bahr personally thought the big man was crazy, even for a Gaimosian. His suggestion was pure suicide.

"Have you ever been in those mountains?" Dorl asked. "We'll be slaughtered before dawn."

Boen laughed hard. "Give me a handful more of my blood and your barbarians wouldn't stand a chance."

"Unfortunately killing the Pell Darga is not our objective. We must rescue Badron's daughter before the enemy gets her back into their camp," Bahr answered with finality. He was growing weary with all Boen's posturing.

Nothol Coll decided to change the conversation. "Are the Pell really our enemy?"

"Harnin said it was Pell Darga spears and short swords found in the bodies of the house guard," Bahr replied. "I don't see why he'd lie about that. It would only lead us away from the kidnappers."

"You said it yourself that Badron has no love for this girl. It might all be a deception."

Ionascu scoffed. "Kidnap his own daughter? What point does that make? Why waste time and money on a bunch of mercenaries if he knows where she is?"

"No one is suggesting the king had anything to do with this," Bahr said.

"Then what?" Ionascu asked indignantly.

Dorl's eyes widened with sudden realization. "The spears were a plant!"

Nothol grinned. "Who in their right mind would want to cross the Pell?"

"That would mean the Pell are working with another kingdom. Who has Badron angered lately?" Boen asked.

None of them had the answer, except perhaps Anienam Keiss, and he was loath to admit the truth of things. The wizard was content with his secrets.

Bahr briefly closed his eyes. "This is a dark train of thought. If what you suggest is true, we have no idea who to go after."

"Not true," Dorl said.

He waited until they all stared at him. "Doesn't Maleela have a love interest? Some prince from an eastern kingdom if I remember right."

"She does!" Bahr agreed. "Then it only makes sense he came and stole her. The prince is from Rogscroft."

"Why kidnap the woman you love?" Boen asked.

"Easy," Ionascu answered, "ransom."

Nothol agreed. "This also gives us a direction to move in. Not only us, but the whole damned Wolfsreik."

"It also means our lives are about to get more dangerous," Boen added. "The future darkens."

"Could it be a coup attempt?" Bahr asked.

The idea unsettled him. He'd enlisted to rescue his niece, not aid his deranged brother in starting an unjustified war.

Dorl Theed threw up his hands in protest. "I didn't sign on for that. We're here for rescue, nothing more."

"I agree. This is not an assassin's quest," Nothol said.

"Gentlemen, I think we are getting carried away. Shadows chasing us in the night and all. The danger is not inherent to our quest. Northern Malweir is about to go to war. We stay the course and complete our mission. Agreed?" Bahr asked.

His frustrations were compounding. Night was getting on and Bahr felt that they had reached the end of any meaningful conversation. Anything else said would only be subjective and filled with conspiracy. Their arguments were valid enough, but it was practically impossible for any to guess the depths of their involvement in the grand scheme. He liked to think of himself as a quiet man with a practical approach to life. Recent complications were changing his mind. The others were fooling themselves. That much he could say for certain. Treachery and his brother seemed like perfect bedfellows. However this affair ended, Bahr knew it was could only end in bloodshed.

"Let us leave the war gaming until we have more to go off. Does anyone have anything they need to discuss before we retire?" he asked.

Rekka Jel eased forward. "Failure is not an option. The princess must be rescued."

Bahr felt his heart lurch. He was sure she was about to give away many of his closely guarded secrets and ruin it all. Success and failure were still too unsteady to be declared. Bahr had to keep them a team until they at least reached Dredl. Sudden heavy pounding on the cabin door interrupted his thoughts. He rolled his eyes. The last thing he needed was another distraction.

"Enter."

One of the younger sailors poked his head in just enough to show his face and still retreat again should the captain grow too angry. "Captain, I think you need to come and look at this. We've found a stowaway."

What now, Bahr groaned.

TWELVE

An Unwanted Mystery

Bahr led the group onto the deck. An angry glint clung to his dark eyes. Tired and slightly frustrated, he struggled to maintain composure.

"What's this?" he demanded once they stopped.

Two crewmen stood over a young boy of less than twenty. He was disgustingly filthy. His clothes were ragged and torn in more places than decent folk found acceptable. He smelled of filth and urine. His hair was unkempt, giving him a generously devious appearance. Bahr sighed. He was thankful there was no serious emergency to contend with this night.

The sailor on the left, sword drawn and pointed menacingly at the boy, leaned forward and said, "We found him hiding down in the stores with the rats."

Bahr was more worried over the lad's choice of ships to stowaway on than the fact that he had committed a crime. Looking down at the bedraggled boy he suddenly felt sympathy. Twenty years ago he wouldn't have had any problems with throwing the lad overboard and sailing on. Times continued to change.

Instead of responding, the Sea Wolf knelt and asked, "What's your name boy?"

Deep eyes stared back at him, as if measuring if Bahr could be trusted. Bahr almost laughed. He felt a grin starting despite himself. The boy sat indignant, looking up through his tangled mass of hair. He was tired and uncertain. Still, he remained silent.

"Look boy, you have two choices here. Cooperate or get fed to the ocean. Make your choice now."

The boy flinched. It was a good sign that he wasn't a fool; at least not so much of one as his actions portrayed.

"Skuld," he finally said.

Bahr nodded. "Skuld. A fitting name for someone found hiding in the dark places of my vessel. Do you know who I am?"

Skuld nodded hesitantly. "You are the most famous captain sailing the northern oceans. They sing your tales in every tavern in Chadra."

"I dare say much further than just Chadra. Why are you on the *Dragon's Bane*?"

"I...." he paused as if he'd been about to unveil some great secret. He refused to mention the treasure that filled his dreams and haunted his desires.

Bahr doubted it was that important if he remained so quiet about it. "Out with it or it's overboard for you."

The sailor covered in tattoos and deeply tanned moved closer.

Skuld hung his head in resignation. He wouldn't last more than a few minutes in the frigid waters. He also had no doubts that Bahr was as good as his words. "I overheard two of your men talking about the Mountains of Death and treasure."

You have got to be kidding me. Maybe this boy is a damned fool. Anger flashed in his eyes. "This is a contract ship in the name of the king. We are not petty treasure seekers nor is this a happy errand. Look around you boy. Some of these men may be dead before the end." Bahr stood. "Does anyone know him?"

Dorl and Nothol reluctantly slipped forward. Bahr frowned. *Of course it was you.*

"Take him and make him presentable. We're dropping him off in Dredl and that will be the end of it. Until then he earns his keep. Put him to work in the galley."

Bahr walked off. The sense of dread grew. He wondered if Skuld could be the spy. The idea made sense. Who would suspect a mere street urchin? The thought troubled him more than he wanted to accept.

"You are a foolish boy," Nothol admonished as they led Skuld down to a small washing chamber in the aft of the boat.

Skuld knew better than to defend himself.

Dorl added, "What were you thinking? Treasure? We're going to fight the Pell Darga, not visit some wayward school for troubled youth."

"I came because I heard both of you speak of treasure," he finally burst out.

Nothol pointed a stern finger. "You should know better than to eavesdrop on grown men going about their business. That's a promised way to the noose."

"How old are you?"

Skuld lifted his chin. "Old enough to take care of myself."

"Drop the tough kid act, we aren't impressed," Dorl scolded.

Despite his indignation, Dorl found a bit of himself in the boy. He might even have taken a liking to him if circumstances were different.

"I'm almost eighteen."

Dorl nodded. "Good. You're old enough to know better but dumb enough to try."

"How do you mean?"

"You've committed a crime," Nothol told him. "The captain can do whatever he sees fit to you for it. Consider yourself fortunate he didn't toss you overboard. Wash up and come back on deck. Dorl and I will see if we can find some clean clothes your size. These rags aren't fit to clean the deck."

The sell swords walked off, content in the knowledge that he posed no risk. Besides, neither of them felt the need to watch him so closely this far out to sea.

"Thank you," Skuld humbly called to them. "I...I didn't mean any trouble. I was just trying to make a better life for myself."

Dorl stopped and gave a flashing smile. "Don't thank us yet, boy. You've got to earn your keep. There is no free ride on the *Dragon's Bane*."

Rekka Jel slept lightly. She did not dream. She never did. Hers was the warrior life. The dream caste of her people was the vast minority, sparing the rest from suffering the endless cycle of joy and torment of dreams. That left the defense of their kingdom to ones like Rekka. Less than thirty years old, she was already an accomplished warrior. And now she had a worthy task. Arms folded across her chest, Rekka slept. Her hammock swayed with the motion of the waves. Dawn wasn't far off.

She awoke with a start. The noise was subtle, and decidedly wrong. Instinct immediately took over. Rekka slipped from the hammock and drew her sword even before she was conscious of her actions. Her lithe body slipped to the deck. Dressed in only a dark undershirt and trousers, she moved from the sleeping area and into the main passage of the hold. Her dark eyes sifted through the near perfect darkness of the ship.

Rekka wasn't certain, but she imagined she'd heard a cutoff scream. The sound, slight as it was, was more than enough to rouse her. She doubted many others would have done the same. Barefoot, she eased closer to the stairs. Rekka moved like one of the great cats of the Brodein Jungle. Silent and deadly. Whoever screamed was most certainly dead. Her blackened sword waved dangerously in front of her, making her the vision of death.

Talk of spies and treachery filled her mind. The idea of a killer being on board was unsettling. She reached the base of the stairs and paused. The killer might well be awaiting others to come on deck. Caution was required if she expected to catch her prey off guard.

"Hsst."

She froze. Her eyes narrowed, searching deep into the shadows. She saw nothing. Rekka loosened her muscles, preparing for a fight. Two figures took shape as her eyes grew more accustomed to the dark.

"Show yourselves," she ordered.

"Drop your sword," a familiar voice called.

Dorl Theed and Nothol Coll eased into the sliver of moonlight shining down from the hatch. Both were armed and ready to fight.

"I could have killed you both." Rekka was mad. She was also wary. Either one of these two might be the killer. Until the culprit was found, there was no way to tell.

"What are you doing up?" Dorl asked.

She replied, "You first."

He shrugged as if it were no big deal. "We heard a noise neither of us liked and decided to have a look. Your turn."

"The same."

Nothol had heard enough. They'd all arrived at the stairs at almost the same time. That was enough for him. "We can stand here and silently accuse each other all night or we can go on deck and find out what happened."

"I like the first answer better. Sounds safer at any rate," Dorl chimed.

Rekka scowled and headed up. She was in no mood for games. It was clear nothing was going to happen unless she led the way. These two talked too much. She'd noticed that the moment she came on board. This was no time for talk. Oddly, the two sell swords followed her without so much as a whisper.

Rekka reached the top of the steps and halted. This would be the perfect place for an ambush if one were to happen. The killer would have the advantage of dropping an arrow into her the moment she poked her head up. She was trapped in a funnel. Rekka had a split second to decide her next move. She could either charge onto the deck and alert everyone or she could creep a little higher and scout the area first. The decision was simple.

Rekka held a staying hand back toward the sell swords and eased up slowly. The last thing they needed was male bravado. That would only get her, possibly all three, killed. Stealth and speed were her primary skills. They'd saved her neck several times in the past and she hoped for the same here.

She eased as close to the edge as she dared. Her heart raced. The adrenaline pumping through her veins wanted more. In stark contrast her nerves were calm. She wasn't the sort to get nervous before a fight. If anything, she was anxious. Rekka took a slow breath and poked her head up enough for her to see. There was just enough moonlight for her to make out the immediate surroundings. Rekka twisted in a full circle. Her immediate line of sight was clear. So far so good.

She finished her scan, finding it slightly odd, but not disturbingly so, that there was nothing to see. Impossible. She'd reacted as soon as she heard the muffled scream. There hadn't been another sound until she ran into Nothol and Dorl. Her suspicions raised, yet she gestured them to follow. If they were the killers she might as well confront them now and get it over with.

"It is clear. Follow me," she whispered.

They slipped onto the deck like wraiths bent on mischief. Nothol brought up the rear. Rekka gestured them to fan out. The killer must be on deck still. There was nowhere else for him to go. Rekka was in her element. This was the kind of work her people excelled in. She smiled fiercely, praying that she was the one who found their prey.

Dorl was the first to stumble on the corpse. It lay crumpled and broken at the base of the main mast. A pool of blood cooled around it.

"Who is it?" Nothol asked.

Dorl shook his head. "Don't know. One of the crew I think."

Nothol moved closer to peer over his friend's shoulder. The head was missing. "Looks like we'll never know for certain."

"Who would do this?" Dorl asked.

Rekka returned from the bow. Her face registered a mix of puzzlement and disappointment.

"No killer?" Nothol asked her.

Rekka shook her head and stared down at the corpse. "Not even a sign. This does not bode well."

The warning in her voice caused both to look up in unison. Her sword swung menacingly in a low guard.

Dorl held his hands up. "We didn't do this."

She didn't move. "We are all suspects until the killer is found. I do not trust you."

"Fair enough. We need to get Bahr," Nothol told them both.

Dorl looked to both. "Who goes? There's not a lot of love being spread around here."

"I go," Nothol suggested. "You two watch the area and try not to kill each other. One murderer is bad enough."

THIRTEEN

The Pell Darga

Mahn led Raste up a sloping path for a few hundred meters before bringing his horse to a stop. The younger scout gave him a confused look. Camp was clearly in the opposite direction. Mahn took a deep pull from his canteen and rolled some of the strain from his shoulders. He then dismounted to relieve himself. Raste could only watch in disbelief.

"What are you doing?" he asked as the older man returned and stretched.

Mahn smiled lightly. "Taking a break."

Raste made a show of looking around. "From what? I don't know about you, but I'd like to get back to camp and get some sleep. What are we doing?"

"We're being tracked."

Raste resisted the urge to draw a weapon. Doing so would only counter whatever Mahn had in mind. He might be young, but Raste was experienced enough to know better than to jeopardize their chances recklessly. That didn't change the fact he remained skeptical of Mahn's decision-making process.

"You said he was nothing to worry over and had run off."

Mahn hardened his gaze. "Don't make me beat you."

He shrugged. "You did say it."

"I thought he had. I was wrong."

"Do you think it's the same person?"

It was Mahn's turn to shrug. "More than likely. If it is someone new, he's almost as clumsy as the first one."

"Let me circle back around and finish him off. I'm tired."

"No. This is the same argument that we had before. I still think he's harmless," Mahn replied tersely.

Raste wasn't so sure. "Harmless enough to get under my skin and make us ride in the wrong direction. This is getting irritating, Mahn. There's no way we can lead him back to camp. Aurec would kill us if this guy doesn't first."

Mahn winced. He wished the boy had been smarter than to mention names. Their pursuit was almost close enough for the night to carry their conversation to him. He wanted to side with Raste but for a nagging feeling in the back of his mind. This wasn't right.

"We're not going to."

"Care to let me in on the plan?" Raste asked.

"If the maps are correct and we are in the right place we can trap him in the sharp draw just ahead."

Raste doubted their luck was so strong. "Sounds good, but how can you be sure he's going to follow us into the draw?"

"Not us, you. You're going to lead him in while I loop around to seal him in. Pin him down and find out why he's so interested in us."

Raste didn't like being the decoy, but there was little choice. The quicker they did this the less of threat the man posed. If he did mean them harm, he wouldn't last the night. Raste's only concern came from not knowing who this man was or how dangerous he might be.

"What if he decides not to cooperate?"

"I think he'll see things our way," Mahn said with a dark confidence.

Raste muttered, "I hope so."

"Get moving before he gets too close. About another two hundred meters and then turn on him. I'll be right behind you."

Raste rode off. He knew better than to argue. Mahn was the sort who didn't like to change his mind once it was set. He also hated having his orders questioned. The last thing Raste needed was to go on report for disobeying orders once they returned to Rogscroft. He hoped this spy was harmless, else he'd do his best to run his sword through the man.

The trail was used enough so he didn't need worry about obstacles. Heavy clouds peppered the sky, occasionally blocking the pale moonlight. Raste preferred it that way. This was the kind of work that needed doing at night. Regardless of

Mahn's opinion, Raste fully expected a fight. Raste casually picked his way down the trail, never once bothering to look over his shoulder. He knew their plan was working and the enemy had taken the bait.

"I have got to be crazy," he muttered under his breath.

Raste debated turning and riding the man down to beat a confession out. People generally responded well to pain, especially when it was unnecessary. Mahn would be furious when he found out, but he was willing to accept a berating for saving all their lives. This little game of cat-and-mouse was already getting on his last nerve. The sooner it ended the better. Then again, there was the off chance that this was what their spy had in mind. Lure them in with feigned ineptness and spring his own trap.

Wouldn't that be nice? Raste snickered. *Killed for being too clever.* He could just imagine the look on Aurec's face when he found out his two best scouts had been snookered and killed, if he ever found out at all. His rage would be legendary. Raste tried to shake the image. He was tired and it began to show. Fatigue did odd things to men. He rode on, trusting in the gods to protect him, but more importantly trusting in Mahn to bail him out when things turned sour. The young scout kept riding, fighting the urge to turn and finish this. He wanted a fight nearly as much as a soft bed. Finally he was rewarded with the crisp sound of footsteps breaking on the dried autumn leaves. It was time.

Mahn watched his younger partner ride off with a sense of satisfaction. Raste was a good lad with potential to go far in the army. He just needed to learn how to be a better follower. Mahn backed his horse into a thicket of pines and watched. Their stalker was still there, slowly moving closer. A crisp wind tousled Mahn's long hair, sending a chill down his back. Winter was coming quickly this year.

The wait proved shorter than expected. Raste had barely ridden off before their mysterious stalker came into view. The scout watched him closely, eager to see just who it was that had such an interest in them. Whoever it was moved with a new composure. His movements were fluid, rehearsed; definitely not the same fool they'd seen earlier. Mahn found odd familiarity in the man's movements. He watched the man slither over a boulder and stalk down the trail. The act wasn't so remarkable as much as the fact that he didn't leave a trace of his passing. Mahn's eyes narrowed as he suddenly remembered where he'd seen such behavior before. The Pell Darga. Mahn knew they were in trouble. Raste was moving into a trap.

"Damnation," he breathed.

The Pell were ruthless. He'd grown up listening to horror stories of trappers and hunters caught in the mountains. The bodies were never found again, but then they didn't need to be. Other travelers usually found the heads on menacing pikes to warn them off. Some said the Pell were cannibals. Regardless, the Pell were monsters that a sane man would do well to avoid.

Mahn only had a few moments to come to a decision. The Pell never moved alone. That meant others had to be close, just far enough out of range to come storming in when their scout gave the signal. Mahn had to move fast if they stood any chance of escaping this. Both he and Raste were dead otherwise. The Pell scout moved quickly, forcing Mahn to ride harder. He drew his short sword and hoped for the best.

The Pell took no time to close the gap between Raste and himself. Mahn's plan crumbled. He swore under his breath. The careful trap they'd set was about to backfire on them. Mahn's decision turned out to be easier than he thought. He kicked a heel into his horse and bolted down the trail. He couldn't let the Pell trap them in the gorge.

The Pell scout whirled at the sound of hoof beats. He dropped flat to avoid being trampled, but when Mahn looked down it was as if the Pell had simply disappeared. His horse jumped over where the man fell and veered right. Mahn caught a rising clamor behind him. The other Pell had arrived.

"Raste!" he shouted at the top of his voice. "Raste get out of here! It's a trap."

There was no way to know if his partner heard him or not, nor did he have the time to find out. Mahn looked back and felt his insides turn. Dozens of shadowy figures emerged from behind rock and tree. Clothes in dark furs and leathers, the Pell hunters took their time. They could afford to. This was their land. Mahn struggled to find the courage to sheath his short sword and drew his rapier. The act was more desperate defiance than courage. There was no way he was going to survive this. The Pell formed a circle around him and slowly drew it tighter.

Raste burst from the trees just as the Pell were in striking range for Mahn. There was no chance in breaking the circle. He was still a good hundred meters away. A look of hopelessness twisted his face. All his suspicions had been correct but now was not the time to say I told you so. He scanned the surroundings and felt his heart sink. The Pell Darga had chosen their ground wisely. They hardly noticed his arrival. Raste grimaced as a lone Pell advanced on Mahn.

"Come no closer," Mahn growled. He dropped his sword point towards the Pell.

The Pell halted.

Mahn found a small measure of courage. "I don't know who's going to die this night, but I promise you will be the first."

The Pell slowly raised his hands to remove the crude hood from his head. Mahn grimaced at the face staring back at him. Tattoos covered the flesh. When he smiled all Mahn could see were sharpened teeth and the dark emptiness of malevolent eyes staring back. He suddenly believed all the wives' tales.

The Pell spoke. "There is no need for talk of death, man of Rogscroft."

Mahn tried to conceal his shock. "Actions speak louder."

The Pell gestured to his men. "Look around. Do you see my men attack?"

Mahn took it all in. Not a single Pell had a weapon in hand. They all stood relaxed with hands exposed to avoid confusion. Was this part of the game?

"I don't believe you. What trickery have you for us? We know the stories of the Pell Darga," Mahn shakily said.

"Again you speak with your emotions. Your head should decide, not your heart. My people are not enemies. We come to aid you. Darkness is coming. Alliances must be forged."

Mahn was only slightly dismayed by the talk. This mountain savage was addressing him as a subordinate. Mahn suddenly felt uncomfortable. The tide had shifted. He quickly realized that there was no claimable advantage. Whatever the Pell wanted he was going to get. The Pell knew it as well.

"Tell me your name." It came out as more of a command than a request.

Mahn shifted uneasily.

"Let's just kill him and get it over with," Raste rumbled as others herded him into the center of the circle. His patience was gone, as was the will to fight.

Mahn shot him a withering glare. "Quiet."

The Pell grinned savagely. "I am not offended. He is young and does not know better. Now, your names."

"Don't do it," Raste cautioned.

Mahn ignored him. Besides, there was no point if the Pell were just going to kill them anyway. "I am called Mahn and this is Raste."

The Pell nodded thoughtfully, mouthing each name. "I am Cuul Ol. These are my hunters."

"Not exactly our pleasure," Mahn replied harsher than he intended. "What are you going to do with us?"

"We wish to speak to Prince Aurec."

Mahn felt sick. What could a Pell Darga hunter want with his prince? More importantly, how did he know the man to begin with?

"You'll have to go to Rogscroft for that. The prince is a busy man."

Cuul Ol shook his head. "I would prefer to be taken to your camp one league from here."

Damn, Mahn cursed. These Pell were better than he gave them credit for. He never felt as outmaneuvered as now.

Cuul enjoyed the shock on their faces. "You did not think that we are ignorant of what goes on in our own lands? These mountains have been our home since the dawn of the world."

"We will not betray our prince by leading you into his camp. Their heads won't end up on one of your damned pikes. You'll have to kill us first," Raste warned.

"Again with your fascination for death. Do all your people seek the cold earth so foolishly? How can you raise civilizations with that attitude?"

"Through our resolve," Raste replied. "We don't fear the likes of mountain savages like you."

A ripple of discontent went through the Pell. The insult demanded vengeance. Cuul silenced his men before they bayed for blood. He glared hotly at Raste but spoke to Mahn.

"The young one should know to bite his tongue."

"They're going to kill us anyway," he urged Mahn.

"I give my word there will be no killing. I might change my mind if you continue," Cuul snapped. He took a deep breath before continuing, "Your prince must know of the coming darkness."

"Why should we trust you?" Mahn countered. "The boy is right. Do what you are going to and be done with it."

"We could have killed you several times. Yet here we stand."

Mahn couldn't argue that. He decided to give in and at least hear the Pell out. There was no harm in living awhile longer. "You keep speaking of some darkness. What do you mean?"

"War, man of Rogscroft. A great, terrible war that will tear the soul from this world. No one will be spared. Only through new alliances can we survive."

Cuul was thankful Mahn chose reason over rashness. Otherwise, there was no way he'd be able to convince the scout of his sincerity. A lifetime of superstition was not easily overcome. Cuul took it as a good sign and chose to reveal his one secret.

"Prince Aurec and I are already known. We have had dealings before."

"Impossible."

"How else do you think you crossed our mountains so easily?" Cuul countered.

Mahn's mouth dropped open. He was confused. Part of him questioned how they'd achieved their goals so easily, but the Pell's explanation was too easy to accept. He refused to give blind trust to the dark-skinned savages, but also recognized a losing situation. Aurec's safety was paramount, nothing else mattered. Mahn and Raste were insignificant in the overall scheme of things.

Once again he had a difficult choice to make. He ran through all the scenarios in his mind and reluctantly picked the least violent. He exhaled sharply and looked down at Cuul Ol. "Tell me why I should believe you and we will take you to the prince."

FOURTEEN

Investigation

Bahr stood on the aft deck warily studying his passengers and crew. One of them was a murderer. Nearly forty years on the seas and he had never had such committed on his ship. The sheer audacity of it churned his stomach. Above all, Bahr wanted justice. A measure of vengeance wouldn't be so bad either. The only problem came from him not knowing where to begin.

Anienam Keiss counseled him as best he knew how, but it was little comfort. The old wizard's secrets were quite happy to remain hidden. That made Bahr less than happy, but aside from the threat of physical violence his options of inducing conversation were severely limited. Rekka answered all he asked and, though her answers were truthful, they did little to enlighten the situation. Dorl and Nothol weren't much better.

Winds drove the *Dragon's Bane* steady on, unheeding of the troubles on board. Normally Bahr enjoyed the sting of salt and wind on his face. There was no solace this night though. The men shuffled uncomfortably under his gaze. He pinched the bridge of his nose and winced. *Why me?* Boen stood ever behind him, massive arms folded across his barrel chest. Even at his age the Gaimosian was more daunting than ten men a third as young.

"Now what?" he asked when it became clear no one else would.

His stern gaze kept the crew and mercenaries from moving. No one was eager to gain the wrath of a Gaimosian, especially on such a close-quartered ship. Boen smiled to himself. His reputation was a powerful tool.

Bahr scowled. "I don't know. I've half a mind to put ashore and be done with the lot of them."

"That won't solve anything. We were hired to do a job," Ionascu eased forward to say. "We can't do that if you drop us ashore in the middle of nowhere."

Bahr leveled his gaze on the man. "I didn't hire you. This is my ship and I will cast you off wherever I see fit. Do we understand each other?"

"Oh I understand all right. You're putting your own safety above that of your kingdom!"

"How dare you!" Bahr exploded.

A sword pulled free. Then another.

Ionascu refused to back down. "You hide behind this wooden hull, coming out to get your hands dirty when it suits you. Look behind me. Every last one of these men would give their lives to Delranan without thought. We've bled and lived in the mud for the kingdom all our lives. When have you had to sacrifice so much?"

Bahr stepped closer, sword in hand.

"Mind your tongue, dog. I'll not be insulted by a gutter rat the likes of you!"

"Hold!"

The two men froze. Boen's mighty axe slammed into the deck between them. His poise and tone of voice made it clear he wasn't about to tolerate any more foolery. He waited long enough until both were staring at him rather than at each other.

"Both of you stand down. Think with a clear head. We've a killer to find and you two trade bandy words like old women."

Both men glared hotly at him. Bahr was the first to realize what almost happened. A simple murder nearly led to slaughter. Crew and mercenary would go at one another until the decks washed red and only ghosts remained to guide the ship. The look in Boen's eyes told him there was no give. It was the Gaimosian's way or none at all.

"Well?" Boen pressed.

Ionascu wisely backed down first. He sheathed his sword with the knowledge of how precarious his position had become. His eyes burned with festering anger that would soon evolve into great hate.

He bowed curtly. "This is the captain's boat. I will abide by his wish."

Satisfied, Boen turned on his friend. "And you?"

Muscles bulged. Bahr met Boen's glare with one of his own. It had been a long time since they had come to blows and he wasn't eager to journey back that way. He glanced down at the steel axe wedged in his decks. "You broke my ship."

Boen gave a toothy grin. "I can break more than that."

"I'm beginning to think you Gaimosians appreciate violence a bit too much. Very well, I'll stand down too."

"Good. I'd hate to rip the rest of this deck up. Now, the question remains. What do we do next?"

Bahr still hadn't a clue. "We could accuse them, make them feel guilty enough to come forward and admit it."

"That solves nothing. It could have been no more than a drunken brawl gone wrong," Ionascu criticized.

Bahr ignored him. "Someone killed that man."

"Thirmas. His name was Thirmas."

Boen ripped his axe free and slung it over his back. "You knew him?"

"Aye. He was one of our younger men. Too young to know what he was getting into, but a good lad all the same. I worked with his father some years ago," Ionascu admitted. There was genuine sorrow in his voice.

Boen nodded thoughtfully. "You can give his eulogy."

Ionascu walked off, clearly unhappy but unsure what else to do. Thirmas was one of his, handpicked for his intense dedication. His loss hurt. Ionascu felt guilty for the boy's death. He was one of the few house guards to have survived the night of blood in Chadra Keep only to die here on the *Dragon's Bane* leagues from home. The king's man cursed Harnin for sending them all on this task. Keeping secrets from Bahr and his Gaimosian goon was getting harder.

"That one is dangerous," Boen whispered as he watched Ionascu go. "He's the sort who puts a knife in a man's back."

Bahr agreed. "I've been watching him since he came on board. He's hiding something from us. That much is certain."

"Do you think he's the killer?"

He paused. At this point he wasn't willing to put anything past a single soul on his ship. "He's at the top of the list, but my gut tells me no."

"That might just make him our little spy," Boen suggested. "Ah, my friend, you certainly know how to give a man a good time."

Bahr shook his head ruefully. "You have an odd sense of humor. Have I ever told you that?"

He slapped Bahr's back hard and laughed. "Keeps me young. What do we do with the rest of these curs?"

Bahr shifted his gaze back to those assembled. He'd like nothing better than to interrogate the masses and be done with it. Unfortunately, his work was just beginning.

"Bring them to my cabin one at a time. Hopefully we can break one of them. Have the ones loyal to us scour the ship from aft to stern. If this bastard is hiding I want him found," he finally said.

Boen agreed and barked orders to Dorl and Nothol. "If he was smart he would have dumped the weapon and his clothes overboard already. Rekka Jel said she didn't find a blood trail either. Whoever did this is good. Assassin grade."

"That's all we need."

The prospect of an assassin made him sick. A single-trained assassin could easily kill them all before dawn. Soured, Bahr left the Gaimosian to oversee operations on deck. He was not a happy man but knew better than to lash out blindly. That solved nothing. Right now the crew was looking to him for guidance and leadership. His example depended on how well they struggled through this ordeal. Bahr did his best to calm down. His rage was enough to break necks. He stopped at the top of stairs with a thought.

"Boen, please send Rekka down to my cabin. I think she might be able to help."

Skuld remained oblivious to the tension on deck. Relegated to the galley, he had been peeling potatoes when the commotion broke out above. His hands were raw and pruned. His arms were tired. Torg, the ship's cook, was a brute of a man as unforgiving as the winter snows. Easily two hundred and fifty pounds of muscle and angst, Torg pushed his new charge with no sympathy.

Skuld listened to the noise above and stared at the growing pile of vegetables. He already questioned his decision to sneak aboard the *Bane*. Just as soon as the thought entered his mind he shoved it out. He spent his entire life being told he was never good enough or he'd never amount to more than a penniless beggar, a nameless corpse facedown in a back alley. Skuld took the criticism and used it to fuel his rage. He wanted to be able to spit back in the face of every man who said he was nothing. It made him more determined than ever to make his name, lest history pass him by. All the naysayers be damned for doubting him.

A potato rolled from the table, striking his boot. This was not the name he wanted to make for himself.

"Should have stayed in Chadra, boy," Torg grumbled in a deep, gravelly voice. "You ain't the warring type."

Skuld tossed the knife down. "What is that supposed to mean? I can fight."

Torg laughed in his face. Steam rising from the huge stew cauldron gave the cook an ethereal look. "It means this is no place for a boy. We ain't off to spar against some palace guard who fight with rules and honor. The Pell are cold-blooded killers who'd just as soon split your belly open than shake your hand."

"I'm not afraid of them," Skuld replied. His voice betrayed the false confidence he tried to project.

Torg laughed again, lighter this time. "You've got spirit boy, I'll give you that. But you're a damned fool like the rest of us. Anyone ever tell you how the Pell like to kill their prey?"

He shook his head.

"Them Pell like to catch you alive, see. They'll string you up like a gutted deer and slowly start to flay you. Ripping strips of flesh off and throwing them on the fire. Some folks say the Pell eat you like that. Just like a rasher of bacon."

Skuld swallowed hard.

"See boy, I told you you're not ready."

Skuld struggled to find a proper response but was saved by the sudden commotion on the stairs. Men shouting and the heavy stomp of boots echoed through the door moments before it swung open. He recognized them as Dorl and Nothol. Still, there was no friendliness in that recognition. Their look alone told him they were on the job and dangerous. Gone was the gentleness they'd shown earlier.

"Find out who it is?" Torg asked.

Dorl Theed shook his head. A hint of anger flashed in his eyes. "Not yet. Are you missing any knives or tools?"

The cook did a quick scan more for show than anything else. He knew exactly what he had and what he was missing. "Nah. Everything looks in order. It would take a mean knife to take a man's head."

"Agreed," Nothol said.

Dorl cleared his throat, clearly hesitant to ask the next question. "Has the boy been with you the entire time?"

"Most of it. I'm not his sitter. He has freedom to use the head or get some fresh air. That's fine by me. Aside from that he's been here."

Nothol Coll settled a disturbed gaze on the boy. "Have you seen anything?"

Skuld felt his face flush. He was both embarrassed and confused by the question. They should already know he wasn't a murderer. Sure, he was a stowaway, but that's where the crime ended. Skuld suddenly felt small.

"No," he answered. "I haven't left the galley."

"Didn't even hear a little bump in the night? Are you sure, Skuld?" Dorl pressed.

He frowned. "You peel potatoes for six hours and see how much energy you have left to pay attention to things."

Both smiled at him. Torg reach down and gently slapped the back of his head. "Mind yourself there boy. That ain't the way to be talking to your betters."

"Thanks, Torg. I didn't think he had anything to do with it, but we told the captain we'd ask everyone."

"No problem."

Skuld waited until the sell swords were long gone and Torg had lost interest. He shuffled over to a quiet corner and hung his head. If Torg noticed the tears he didn't mention them.

Rekka Jel stood patiently before Bahr's desk with her petite hands folded in front of her. Her light brown robes concealed most of her lithe curves, more so than the skintight clothes she's worn earlier in the night. He certainly appreciated the effort. Feminine distraction right now was the last thing he needed to worry about. Bahr yawned, wondering how she managed to remain so awake. His eyes were raw, almost burning. He had a headache and felt far too old to be looking for intrigue in the one place he should feel safe.

"What are you thinking?" she asked unexpectedly.

He looked at her appraisingly. "To be honest, I'm not sure what to think."

She cocked her head. "I do not understand. This is a serious issue and it must be dealt with as quickly as possible. Delay will not avail us."

"That much is clear to me."

"Why do we not confront this man and bring it all in the open? Ionascu is a cancer among the ranks," she advised.

Bahr offered a thin smile. "It's not as easy as that. Sure, we could out him in front of the rest of the crew, but that would only cause more problems. We do not have proof and therefore lack the teeth of conviction. Ionascu is our spy, or not the only one at the very least. Any number of those nineteen men might be in Harnin's pockets. This is a dangerous thought process and if we do it wrong we will look the fool. I will not risk a damned mutiny on my ship. Not yet."

Rekka thought for a moment. "If it becomes known that Ionascu is the spy then a potential partner would feel safer thinking that we will end the hunt, correct?"

"Precisely."

"You are a strange people, Captain Bahr. Your decisions confuse me. I am not used to this political strategy and intrigue."

Bahr wasn't so sure he was either. "Rekka, I need your eyes and ears. Most men regard a woman on board as an ill omen. That being said, they will be prone to tell the truth than risk the ire of the sea."

"You wish for me to try and detect lies and misdirection," she said, catching on.

He did. "Yes. I'd like you to hide behind that curtain if you don't mind. Between you and Anienam Keiss we should find our killer and our spy."

She bowed at the waist. "As you wish."

Bahr knew it wasn't going to be as easy as it sounded. It was a thin plan at best, but it was all he could come up with.

FIFTEEN

A Different Hunt

"That can't be right. You've made a mistake."

Anienam Keiss stared back at Bahr, his look impassive. "I can only speak of what I know. None of those men lied."

Bahr slammed a fist on the table. "I refuse to accept that one of my men had his head cut off by a ghost or some such. The killer has to be on this ship."

"But who?" Anienam countered. "We have spoken to everyone. The killer is simply not here."

Bahr wasn't convinced. He couldn't be. It didn't make sense. How would a killer just disappear in the middle of the ocean? Going overboard was suicide, besides which, no one was missing. "How can we be so sure? Can your magic be wrong?"

"Do not doubt my capabilities, captain. The foe you seek is not on the *Dragon's Bane*."

The Sea Wolf ran both meaty hands through his thick silver hair in frustration. "If what you say is true this killer can strike again at any time. There is no security for us."

Anienam nodded.

"What can we do?"

"Nothing," was the almost empty reply.

The implications were frightening. He didn't like the prospect of constantly looking over his shoulder for that silver blade coming for him. Old already, it was no stretch of the imagination to feel the icy fingers of death come reaching for him.

Bahr grimaced. "Not what I needed to hear right now."

Rekka Jel added, "The wizard is correct. We found no blood, no sign of struggle and no murder weapon. This is a confined area with limited room to hide. There should be clues."

Bahr eyed the tiny, foreign woman from the heart of the southern jungle with a new sense of appraisal. "I have sailed across the northern oceans and a dozen kingdoms in my time. I've seen strange things, from monsters to dancing Elves, but what the two of you are suggesting is impossible. We must be missing something."

Anienam asked, "Are they impossible because you choose to disbelieve them or because your mind cannot fathom the depths of mystery? The trappings of the unknown far exceed our mortal realm."

"Impossible because no one else is missing. Why would a man murder another and then abandon ship? Where would he go? The cold would kill him in minutes."

"Your line of questioning does you disservice," Rekka said. "There is no point to wondering if the rest of the passengers and crew are accounted for."

She had a point, he begrudgingly admitted. Then again, she also took an unwitting step towards defending his point of view.

"Precisely," he countered. The gleam in his eyes whispered mischief, like a hunter catching the scent of wounded prey. "The killer is still among us."

"If what you say is true that implies our killer is somehow able to mask himself from my powers, making him a..."

"Wizard," Bahr frowned.

"Impossible."

Bahr arched an eyebrow. "Is it?"

"I would have felt him the moment he boarded. Magic cannot be hidden from other users. He could conceal himself from those insensitive to the gift but I would have known."

"This takes us back to the beginning. The question remains, what do we do next? I am out of ideas and ill at ease," Bahr all but hissed.

He collapsed back into the cushioned chair. All this intrigue left him haggard, raw. He had half a mind to turn back to Chadra. Every moment wasted hunting this phantom killer stole from his niece's life. Above all else, her life was paramount. His thoughts never strayed from the softness of her face and the mirth in her laugh. Tears welled in the back of his eyes. It took every ounce of strength and dignity not to cry in front of his guests.

"We might ask them again but I fear it would end the same," Rekka suggested.

Bahr asked, "What do you propose? At this point I am willing to listen to any suggestion. Nothing we've done has worked yet."

"There is no need to argue," Anienam cautioned at the glint of rising anger in Bahr's voice. "Let me meditate first. Both of you go topside and try to keep the peace. The answer will present itself to me, of that I am convinced."

"Hopefully before another body turns up," Bahr added.

He left the wizard behind, cautiously wondering how the old man managed to turn the conversation and place himself in a position of power.

"He's done nothing but glower since the confrontation this morning," Dorl said after dropping his last card on the barrel.

Nothol snatched the card and laid down three of a kind. "He'll be all right. If not then we get to adjust his attitude."

Dorl eyed the card angrily. "Damn. I swear you're cheating. How much is that?"

"Sixty," Nothol smirked. "You can save some dignity and quit now."

"Not until I win my money back."

Nothol laughed. "We don't have that much time. Besides, you still owe me from the last three months. I'm waiting to see that."

"Stop taking my money and I'll be able to pay you off," he glowered.

"Let you win?" Nothol feigned astonishment. "You've got a better chance of me cutting my own leg off."

Dorl gave him a wounded look. "That hurts. Do you think I would do such a thing?"

"Shut up already and deal the cards."

The soft swoosh of Rekka's sword slicing intricate patterns through the air mimicked the pulse of the wave against the prow. She ignored the sell swords and their constant squabbling. Dressed in a simple dark brown bodysuit, Rekka was the perfect combination of beauty and lethality. Her hair was tied back in a long braid that whipped around her head and shoulders with each movement. The thin film of sweat gave her flesh a glossy sheen enough to make Dorl sigh.

"You're going to get yourself in trouble," Boen rumbled as he walked up behind them. He took a seat and admired Rekka going through her drill. "Still, she's a fine looking woman."

Dorl couldn't agree more. "That she is."

"Judging by the way she wields that pretty little sword, a very dangerous one. Be careful with that one lad."

"You're full of unusual cheer this morning," Dorl said. He shifted back to Rekka but it was too late. Boen had already spoiled the vision.

The Gaimosian shrugged off the comment.

Nothol set down the cards with a sharpened look. "Is the old man any closer to finding the killer?"

"No," Boen answered. "The old salt is spooked and good. That wizard is keeping secrets from us."

"Never trust a wizard. They've been the curse of Malweir for generations," Dorl spat.

Boen shot him a skeptical glance. Gaimosians had evolved to become some of the first mages. The order eventually rose to such heights that it tore itself, and most of the world, apart. Men and women of all races filled the ranks. A force for justice, they became corrupt with the taint of darkness and a great and terrible war erupted. Those that survived suffered the effects for thousands of years after. Few living remembered the true beginnings of the hatred of magic, but it had been ingrained in Boen from childhood. It was also his deepest dread. He hoped and prayed his blood lacked the desire to take himself beyond mortality. Malweir had hurt enough because of his kind.

"How much longer till we land?" he asked.

Nothol answered. "Should be this evening. The wind has been good to us."

"Good. I am tired of boats," Dorl yawned.

"Who says land is less dangerous?"

"How so?" Nothol asked.

"The killer is confined here, limited in what he can do. Once we get ashore he gets a host of options."

Dorl swallowed hard. He was a seasoned man, but the thought of being stalked by an assassin chilled his blood. He idly wondered how long it would be until others found his body with a knife in his back.

"I'm beginning not to like this," he mumbled, thoughts filled with desperation.

The *Dragon's Bane* sailed on, drawing ever closer to the port town of Dredl. Rekka Jel finished her exercises against the soft blue sky backdrop. Clouds smattered the skies like so many puffs of dreams from the gods. She casually wiped the sweat from her brow and gave them a peculiar glance. Dorl took it for what was: she knew exactly what they'd been talking about. Dorl Theed blushed for the first time in years.

Ionascu watched them from the corner of his eye. He hadn't been involved in any more conversations since Bahr went on his witch hunt for the killer. The dead body on deck had been disturbing, making his mission more difficult. Everywhere he went Ionascu felt eyes silently measuring him. Noting his every move. Accusations sat on each lip with a growing ache to be said. Ionascu struggled with maintaining a sense of calm and flashes of anger stewing in his core.

No one on board knew his true identity and it was a good thing considering recent developments. If they so much as guessed he was one of the king's captains he'd be drawn and quartered before dusk. Even the mercenaries would turn on him. No one liked a rat. He snorted. Rat. A lifetime of service devoted to Badron and Delranan had only managed to secure him the title of rat. His veins burned with rage.

"I don't be liking the way they think they be better than us," Lon, a gangly youth barely old enough to grow a beard said as he came up beside Ionascu.

The king's man feigned indifference. "How would you have them act? A man they didn't even get to meet was brutally murdered. There are nineteen of us left who don't fit in with the crew. Bahr doesn't want trouble, but he isn't willing to trust men he doesn't know. I don't think I'd act any differently. Besides, one of us is the killer."

"Wasn't me," Lon shook his head. "None of my boys neither. We're all good men signed on to help the princess."

"So are we all. It doesn't change the facts."

Lon wasn't buying in to it. "You're in good with the Cap'n. What do they be saying about us?"

A gust of wind tossed his stringy blonde hair across his face.

Be careful here, Ionascu cautioned himself. "Captain Bahr and the others are worried about us."

"Huh. Can't tell by me. I say we look at that brown skin girl, her being a foreigner and all. The way she be swinging that fancy sword of hers I got no doubt about her being able to hack a few heads off."

The boy had a point. He may have been some small village hick with a terrible accent, but he recognized the natural progression of dangerous thought. Ionascu almost smiled. Rekka Jel was the obvious choice for the assassin, which cancelled her out. He knew better than to go with the obvious choices. For all he knew Lon was the killer. Ionascu knew better than to trust anyone at this point.

"Go ahead and try her if you want. I'm sure King Badron will give a good stipend to your next of kin," he told the boy.

Lon gave it a quick thought. "I'm hungry. Come on, let's see if there's any of that stew left."

"You go ahead. I want to finish oiling my sword. We should be making landfall soon."

Lon grunted again. "Looks like you be expecting a war as soon as we land."

"It never hurts to be prepared. You'd do well to follow my example."

"Just cause those fools named you our leader don't mean we have. For all we know you killed that man. Can't trust nobody on this crate."

Ionascu bristled. He may be a spy, but he was no murderer. Lon's youthful ignorance needed a lesson; one he could ill afford to give with everyone's attention on him. Ionascu was still good enough to hack the man to pieces in a fair fight. He forced the thought from his mind and took a calming breath.

"If I am not your leader why do you keep looking to me for guidance?" he asked. Anger laced the words like poison.

Lon shot back, "Someone's got to talk to the Cap'n. Might as well be you. Me and the boys didn't come to do no talkin'. 'Sides, they always be asking for you. Looks like they found a leader of their own."

"Careful friend. I'm a patient man but I do have my limits," his voice was measured and warning.

Lon's face hardened. "If I didn't know better I'd say that be a threat."

"Think what you want. I'm one of you."

"We'll see," Lon said and walked off.

Ionascu frowned. His life suddenly got much more complicated, making his task damn near impossible.

"We'll see."

Skuld listened intently to the mercenaries argue. He fully expected an all-out brawl before the younger one stormed off. The gutter rat idly considered running to tell Captain Bahr what he'd heard. Being a stowaway was bad enough, but if the mercenaries got wind that he was spying for the captain he wouldn't last the night. Dorl Theed and Nothol Coll would stand for him, but even they wouldn't be able to watch him constantly. One of Lon's troop would slit his throat and drop the body in the waters.

Skuld shivered at the thought and paled as Ionascu turned and looked him dead in the eyes. Recognition flashed, though just a hint. The older man sheathed his sword and moved away, leaving the boy to wonder how much shorter his life just became. Skuld felt trapped. He desperately needed to be trusted. Turning in the mercenaries to Bahr would assure that much but it would make dire enemies out of men who lacked scruples. A jolt of fear ran down his spine. He was the least harmless on the boat. So why did he feel it all hinged on his actions? Skuld suddenly knew exactly what he had to do to preserve himself another day.

SIXTEEN

Dredl

"Land!"

The call echoed over the frosted decks of the *Dragon's Bane*. Most of the surviving mercenaries crowded the bow, eager to see the calming effects of the nearing shore. A singular sentiment echoed in them all. They wanted off the boat and the choice of disappearing completely if things went sour. No one wanted to be the next to die.

Bahr stomped on deck. He looked haggard from the lack of sleep the murder had produced. There'd been no breaks in solving the murder. Suspicions rose across the boat. Boen had been forced to put down three fights between passengers and crew. Tensions ran high and Bahr had no solutions. Rekka Jel and the wizard were proving to be of little worth in the matter. The greater part of Bahr wanted to put the mercenaries ashore and head back to Chadra.

Bahr gazed out towards the eastern shore. It took a moment of careful scanning but he was satisfied that the northern tip of the Murdes Mountains lay off to his starboard. They'd made land close enough to Dredl to make him happy. Better, they didn't have to worry about crossing into Pell Darga territory. Another hour or two and they'd make port. Delranan was far behind. The closest rule was that of the city-state of Rogscroft. He frowned. Rogscroft was a potential enemy. Bahr recognized the fact they needed to be careful from here on out.

"Dorl!" he called out. "Round up the others and have them meet me in my cabin."

Dorl obeyed, silently wondering what had sparked this new round of meetings.

Bahr waited for Boen to close the door behind him. He was the last to enter.

"Our focus changes once we hit land. Dredl is a neutral port but we will be under the constant scrutiny of Rogscroft.

We have no friends here, no allies. Do nothing to provoke any sort of attack or our lives are forfeit."

"We can handle ourselves well enough," Ionascu said for the men under him.

While Bahr approved of the man taking charge, he wasn't clear of the motive. Men like Ionascu almost always had a second angle of approach. He was still dangerous, even with some of the wind taken from his sail.

"I'm sure you can, though it is not the conduct of your mercenaries that concerns me. I've had suspicions King Badron is preparing Delranan for war. If that is true, Rogscroft is the only viable target. My….king has long envied the city. That makes our task all the more hazardous."

"What makes you think the army is coming here?" Ionascu asked. A tinge of nervousness hinted his words.

He regretted the comment immediately. Talk like that was the surest way of revealing his true reasons for being on board. *Just like Bahr nearly slipped by saying my king.* Ionascu idly wondered what that was all about. He needed to stay focused, especially now. The good captain had a secret he didn't want people to know. The spy smiled. He'd get to the bottom of that sooner or later and the game would shift back in his favor.

Bahr was hesitant to explain his reasons for what he knew. Doing so would just give the spy more time to panic and he needed calm heads all the way around.

"Some would claim an army has no use unless deployed to the field. The Wolfsreik is the strongest army in northern Malweir but they haven't been tested in nearly a decade. Their blades have grown rusty while lesser kingdoms' grow sharper," Bahr told them.

And I know Badron better than any man alive. He'll stop at nothing to expand his empire, no matter the cost. He'd even sacrifice his own flesh and blood to advance. An empire wouldn't be enough for him.

"Perhaps you know more than the rest of us," Ionascu slyly suggested.

Bahr didn't take the bait. "Perhaps I do. That doesn't change the obvious. If it is war ahead we need to avoid contact as much as possible."

"We'll be watched from the moment we touch ground," Boen put in. "Strangers are never accepted easily. If it is war, the leadership here should already know, in which case our problems will become simplified."

"Simplified?" Dorl exclaimed. "How do you figure that? We'll be wanted men the moment the harbor master logs the *Bane* in."

"Then stay on the boat," Rekka Jel said in her straightforward manner.

Nothol Coll stifled a laugh with the back of his hand.

Dorl's face reddened but he stayed quiet. The foul look he gave his best friend was enough.

"You could stay on the boat, but the *Bane* sails at dawn," Bahr told them all.

"What?"

Shock rippled through the cabin. No one could believe Bahr was willing to abandon them on hostile ground.

Ionascu exclaimed, "What is our plan for escape once we have the princess? You'll doom us all if this is done wrong."

The Sea Wolf waited long enough for the uproar to calm down before explaining. A sidelong glance told him that even Anienam Keiss was concerned. Good, Bahr thought, that ought to take out some of his smugness. Truth be told, Bahr felt trapped almost every time the wizard opened his mouth. A little humility went a long way.

"My helmsman has been given explicit instructions on where to meet us. Fear not, and do not concern yourself on this matter. The *Dragon's Bane* will be there."

"How can this not concern us? We're being dropped off in enemy territory to fend for ourselves! This is madness," Ionascu protested.

Anger flashed hotly in his eyes. He wasn't the only one thinking they'd been betrayed. Bahr noticed that same reluctant doubt in Dorl and Nothol. Even the stalwart Boen appeared taken back.

Rekka Jel bowed her head ever so slightly. "This is the captain's boat. He may do as he wishes. I will prepare."

She slipped through them and out the door before any could object.

Boen shifted suddenly. There was something about Bahr's speech that didn't sit right. He just couldn't put his finger on it. "Dredl won't be the problem. I've been here before. The folk are pleasant enough, after a fashion. It's the city guard and any garrison that will make things difficult. This should be fun."

His booming laugh echoed off the cramped walls even as he filed out to gather his meager belongings. The others all spoke their peace and left Bahr to carry out his final preparations. Their mission had suddenly become real and they needed to rely on each other if he expected to make it back to Chadra with Maleela. Bahr hoped he had collected the right people for the job.

Dorl and Nothol were the last to leave. Halfway out the door Dorl turned back and said, "At least we can get a proper mug of ale before we all get killed."

Bahr could only shake his head. He realized their chances of success were relatively small, even with a wizard pushing senility on board. The Sea Wolf sat back down and tried to get the images of his niece out of his head. *She might be dead by now*. He frowned. That kind of thinking would tear him up inside and steal from the mission. Distractions cost lives. Bahr already had more than enough deaths on his hands, making room for more would be difficult.

Anienam Keiss finally came out from hiding and took the opposite seat from Bahr. His eyes were cold, forbidding.

Bahr wasn't impressed. "What? No pearls of wisdom or sage advice to give before I commit us all?"

"What is there to tell a man who's already made up his mind?" he countered.

"I think I prefer when you speak in riddles."

Anienam flashed a thin, almost feral, smile. "I speak as I must."

"There's the crazy old man I know. What is that supposed to mean? I'm trying to decide if you are more of a hindrance than help."

"A bit of both I believe."

Bahr's eyes narrowed to thin slits. "You know something you're not telling us."

He stayed silent. The only sound was the gentle creaking of the hull against the tide.

They stared at each other for long minutes. Neither gave way nor flinched. Anienam sat in quiet confidence, as if he already knew how the future was going to play out. That possibility worked to unnerve Bahr. The future shouldn't be known by anyone; not him, not anyone. Destiny had a part to play and it was up to men to stumble into it. The wizard was an aberration to life.

"Very well. Keep your secrets. I have mine as well," Bahr finally said. "All I ask of you is that you do your part in keeping us alive until we get back to Chadra Keep. After that you can go as you please."

Anienam betrayed no emotion. "That has been my intent since seeking you out. Please keep this in mind: you have a great destiny to fulfill. Delranan and indeed all Malweir will have need of you, Bahr."

"So you keep reminding me."

Anienam bore a sad look. Could it be pity? "Right now you think only of yourself."

"How else am I supposed to think? This has not been a kind world to me, wizard. I make no illusions about Malweir owing me, but I also know that I owe Malweir nothing. Not one damned thing."

"Perhaps not. Perhaps I was wrong and found the wrong man."

Bahr waggled a menacing finger. "Oh no. I'm not about to play that game. You won't guilt me into feeling what you want."

"There is no intent for guilt, but you must be made to understand the severity of the situation."

Bahr grunted. "Funny how the situation is adapting to suit your needs, not mine. No one is even at war."

"Yet. You said it yourself, your brother is determined to expand his kingdom. You can't truly believe you will be safe when that happens?"

"I'll take my chances."

"And waste everything? Just get on your boat and sail off until the storm blows itself out? There will come a time when you will be forced to step out of the shadows, Bahr. Become the man you are meant to be. It is the only way."

The words weren't stinging, but they had enough conviction to give him pause. Right now all that mattered was rescuing Maleela alive. All else was a secondary concern. He could deal with his brother well enough once they returned home. He'd also be able to think more clearly once she was safe. Hang the rest of the world. Still, he couldn't abandon all his friends to such a dire fate. Either decision bore terrible implications. This was not an easy choice.

Anienam remained silent and let him think. He could see the wheels turning in Bahr's eyes. The captain was not the heartless man he portrayed. He was the sort whose natural aggression was a mask for kindness. The wizard was old enough to trust to fate. He had faith in the future. Malweir had survived hundreds of wars in his time. Numerous petty tyrants were come and gone. Elves, Dwarves, Trolls and Goblins alike, no race was immune to the madness of dictators.

Anienam Keiss was the last of the mages, older even than his sire Dakeb had been. Time had not been kind. Friendless, the wizard wandered the forests and deserts of Malweir always trying to prevent the dark gods from returning. He often felt that there was more to life. A life he envied in normal men. Men like Bahr.

"Very well," Bahr finally said. "I'll think on your words, though without promises. I don't like your portents."

"Fair enough. I ask only you make your decisions wisely."

Anienam didn't know how he was going to tell this proud northern man that his actions were going to decide the fate of the world. A dark time was fast approaching and no one was going to be safe. Anienam Keiss closed his eyes. How did one tell another that the dark gods had returned to wreak vengeance upon the world once again and he was the key to victory or doom?

Dredl was unlike anything Skuld had ever seen. Not that his experiences formed much of a basis of opinion. He knew the back streets and gutters of Chadra and the port, but he hadn't been anywhere else. The rest of the world was still a dream. He only knew hardship and dissatisfaction. Dredl offered the potential of unlimited possibilities. Skuld found it nearly impossible to focus on any one thing. The streets were clean, well, clean enough at least. There were no signs of riffraff or undesirables lurking in the shadows. For a moment Skuld saw himself staying here and making a new life.

"Come on boy," Boen growled from behind. "We've work to do before you go sightseeing."

Skuld almost snapped back but thought the better of it when he saw the giant Gaimosian stalking up on him. Instead he sighed and bit back his retort. He hefted his pack and waited. Other crew was busy securing the Bane to the dock. Still more had gone ahead to secure lodging for the night and to scout the town. The crew went about their work with mechanical precision. Skuld was most impressed but knew better than to comment by now. The last thing he needed was another thump to the back of his head.

Boen smirked. "I know what you're thinking."

Skuld did his best to hide his smile. "I don't even know what I am thinking. This is all so new to me."

"This is nothing, lad. I've seen cities with thousands of people in them. Towers that touch the heavens. Never been one to care for them either. Almost as bad as the Dwarves and their damned holes in the ground."

"You've seen Dwarves?"

Boen nodded. "Aye. Seen them and fought with a few here and there. Good sturdy folk but I hate their caves."

A thousand questions sprang forth. All Boen's experiences and adventures must have been exhausting. He doubted he had the same level of fortitude to put himself through half as much. He also found it hard to keep the daydreams from returning. Skuld briefly imagined himself a giant swordsman dashing from kingdom to kingdom in the name of honor and justice.

"Stop daydreaming, boy. What's the matter with you?"

Embarrassed, he replied, "I was just thinking is all."

"About?"

The Gaimosian dropped the two sacks he'd been carrying and headed back for more. He was a far better warrior than laborer but Bahr had wisely decided to disguise this trip as a trading venture. It would work well enough to give them enough time to pack up and leave town without too much notice. Otherwise, Rogscroft agents would be swarming them in no time.

Skuld watched Boen return with more heavy bags. "What I would give to have done some of the things you have."

Boen almost smiled. "My life has been one sad affair after another. Spare yourself the trouble and forget about what I do."

"I've only ever seen the gutters of Chadra. My life hasn't been much better."

The big man clamped a fatherly hand on the boy's shoulder. "Lad, I can see the fire in your eyes, but you have to know when to let it cool. I'm not a role model. Never had a family, never known love. All I know is pain and suffering. War is not the fancy images in your mind. It is demanding, brutal work. The weak die fast and those of us who manage to survive long enough grow bitter, callous. Go find yourself a good woman and an honest living."

Skuld listened but remained unconvinced. There had to be more to being a famous warrior than just misery and sad memories. Why were all the old tales centered around such men if that were true? Certainly Dorl and Nothol lived good lives. Neither seemed to want. They were professionals. Skuld paused to wonder how bad Boen's life had been to make him act so.

A spark of inspiration caught then. Skuld suddenly became determined to make more out of his life than what it was. He was convinced destiny held some measure of greatness. This was his chance to prove his worth, not only to himself but to those who held doubts. His thoughts wandered down split roads, some dark, some not. Bahr's sudden appearance on the dock made him abandon those dreams and focus on the task at hand. The Sea Wolf had every intention of leaving him here. Skuld needed to make his move soon before the opportunity was lost.

"Most of the supplies are offloaded," Boen told the captain.

Bahr nodded absently. "Have any of the local factors approached us yet?"

A small crowd of merchants and sailors crowded the docks, though none seemed overly interested in the Bane. Gulls squawked as they flew over. A random pelican sat on the stump of an old pier, sharp eyes piercing the blue for fish.

"Couldn't say. That's Rekka's area, not mine," the Gaimosian replied.

Bahr acted as if he didn't hear. "We need to sell the goods and get moving. I don't want to waste any more time than necessary."

Boen did a quick take on the pier. "Trouble?"

"Maybe. I've got a feeling that we are going to have company soon. If Badron has spies here, then Rogscroft has spies in Delranan."

"That means enemy soldiers."

Bahr smiled weakly. "Then the war begins tonight, with us."

Boen agreed. "I would not have come along if I didn't think there wasn't going to be at least a little blood spilled."

Dorl and Nothol came up to them. Both noticed the eagerness in Skuld's eyes but didn't ask the obvious. Their gait was measured and very controlled, suggesting they were being tracked.

"What news?" Bahr asked.

Dorl rolled his eyes to his friend. "You tell him."

"We've secured billets at the inn on the far side of town. You won't believe this, but the name is actually the Dragon's Bane. Seems you're famous, old man."

Boen snorted a chuckle.

"A small world," Bahr grimaced.

He hoped the inn lived up to his expectations of his ship. "Finish with the supplies and get us there. I want everything done by nightfall. Oh and Dorl, no one drinks tonight."

Dorl Theed frowned.

SEVENTEEN

The Wolfsreik

"Has there been any word on my daughter?"

Badron's eyes had grown hollow, dark circles aging him. They were shot through with tiny red streaks. It wasn't that he missed her, truth be told she could already be dead and he wouldn't lose any sleep. He wanted her back and under his control before she had the chance to give any secrets to his enemies.

Harnin One Eye shook his head. "The *Dragon's Bane* should have made port by now. If all goes well they will be moving on Rogscroft within the next few days."

"Not good enough."

"My lord, there is no possible way for us to know what exactly is happening. Bahr and your daughter could still be hundreds of leagues apart. There is no way to track the *Bane*."

Rage flashed through Badron's tired eyes. "What good is my senior advisor if he cannot predict the actions of his very own handpicked agents? You give excuses where I seek answers."

Harnin knew better than to respond. Anything said now would only serve to further enrage an already unstable king. The one eye began to ponder the question of a new king. The situation was dangerous enough. Harnin wasn't sure how to react. He had plans of his own and those didn't involve Badron.

"Are you certain that your man on that boat is reliable?" the king asked.

"He is. Ionascu is a dead giveaway, but one that Bahr shouldn't take much issue with once he finds out. After all, an agent of the king is required for a task so complicated."

Badron didn't fail to notice how Harnin managed to deflect accusations when speaking of his people. He knew then that Ionascu and all the others Harnin hired were going to have to die.

"How goes the mobilization of the Wolfsreik?" he asked in an attempt to prevent himself from reaching out and strangling Harnin unnecessarily.

"The army is close to half assembled. Training is already underway."

Not good enough. "I do not want to be caught here after the first snow. How much longer until we have enough to march?"

"We could deploy today if need be, but without much of the strength to sustain a major offensive," Harnin replied.

"We don't need a long offensive. All I need is to get the army to the walls of Rogscroft. The follow-on trains can bring in reinforcements and supplies."

"That would leave our supply trains exposed to attack from the Pell Darga and whatever forces are left outside of the city. They'd be picked off at will, leaving the rest of us cut off in the middle of winter."

"What then would you suggest? Send a friendly message with promises of good will and kindly asking for my daughter back? I will see that city razed to the ground before I grovel to Stelskor."

Harnin struggled to keep his anger from flowing over. "I am suggesting nothing of the sort. I merely point out that we need to march with the full strength of the army at our back. Fragmented, the Wolfsreik will not be strong enough."

"Perhaps," Badron said tentatively. "Go to the camp. Press General Rolnir into greater urgency. I want this campaign underway before the snows come."

Winter was just as much of an enemy as Rogscroft. Heavy snows were responsible for as many deaths as enemy arrows. Worse, the mountain passes would close, sealing them to their doom. Harnin had been part of such disaster before. That was how he lost his eye.

"Three weeks, Harnin. The Wolfsreik marches in three weeks, with or without the full muster. Do not fail me on this."

Harnin bowed and left.

Badron ignored the man. The door slammed shut behind him. The king of Delranan turned his attentions back to what he had planned for Rogscroft.

The encampment was a sprawling complex of men, weapons, and horses. Huge stacks of materials necessary for making siege weapons lay in random piles on the far side. Row upon row of soiled brown tents filled the plain in precision rows. Fires spotted the camp in wasted efforts toward keeping the men warm. Roasting meat and cauldrons of boiling stew filled the air with an almost pleasant aroma. Despite the surface tranquility, the camp had but one purpose. War.

Harnin rode in on a roan mare, impressed at how the mighty war machine could so easily be called to action. Life always had a way of seeming simpler amongst men when they readied to deploy. An outsider might view the actions as unorganized and chaotic though in truth it was anything but. Each soldier knew precisely what needed to be done. Sergeants barked orders while senior officers planned the campaign. Life or death was based on a soldier's level of preparation.

Companies of infantrymen drilled on the open plain. Harnin noted the grim severity in their eyes. It had been long since last they were called to fight. Each was a proven veteran ready to knock off the rust and march back into slaughter. He felt pride stir in his aging heart. It reminded him of his own days in the Wolfsreik and how much he loved his kingdom.

"Lord Harnin, we were not expecting you."

He looked down to see a familiar face staring back. Granite-like features dominated the man's face. His skin was weathered from long years of campaign. Thick muscles corded his arms and chest. He casually reached up and clasped Harnin's hand.

Harnin half smiled. "I did not have much of a choice. Rumors are circling that you'd been killed in bed with a young whore, General Rolnir."

"With a very large whore, no doubt," Rolnir laughed. "It is good to see you again, my friend."

For a moment Harnin missed his army days. Both he and Rolnir enlisted at the same time and passed the trials. Connections to Badron's father quickly pulled him from the ranks to palace guard. There were times when he regretted the decision.

"How go things in Chadra? We hear that the king is growing impatient," Rolnir said.

Harnin replied "You always were one to get straight to the point. Our lord wants you to deploy with half of your full strength. The rest can follow on."

"That's madness."

"A point I won't argue."

A gust of wind blew Rolnir's long locks of red hair. "There is a reason we have never been beaten. Our strength lies in our ability to fight as a cohesive unit. We are nothing at half strength. The king knows that he'd be sending us to our doom."

"I tried telling him, but he refuses to listen," Harnin calmly said. "How much longer before you can realistically march?"

Rolnir rubbed his chin. "We planned on at least three weeks. It will take that long just for all our units to report in. Forget about getting all the supplies collected and loaded for a sustained march."

"Three weeks takes us close to winter's edge."

"True, but we still have no deployment orders. What is our target?" Rolnir asked.

"The same as it has always been. Rogscroft."

The old soldier forced a smile. He saw no significant gain from conquering a kingdom on the far side of the Murdes Mountains. War was well and fine, but it needed to be done in a reasonable fashion. "Finally. I've been expecting this for a long time. Let us be done with that sad city and move on."

"Badron agrees. We must be across the mountains before winter. Otherwise there is no point for any of this." Harnin gestured to the field around them.

"Either way it will be dangerous. I'm more concerned about being cut off than fighting the Pell. Badron should have waited until spring."

Harnin couldn't argue. Badron was no tactician. That should have been left to the army. What Rolnir didn't know was the intricate details revolving around the king and Maleela, or even the reasons Delranan was going to war. Still, Harnin owed his friend if he expected the continued fealty of the Wolfsreik.

"The initial plan was to invade once the snows melted, but circumstances demand otherwise. Princess Maleela, as I am sure you know, was abducted the same night the prince was killed. Matters have progressed sharply since."

Rolnir's eyes widened. Of course rumors ran wild about that night, but none of the details had been confirmed to him until now. Harnin continued to explain the events of that long night in Chadra Keep and how the royal family was virtually wiped out in the span of a few moments. He naturally left out key details, all for the greater good of Delranan.

Rolnir took it in stride. This wasn't the first time he'd heard heart-stopping news. The royal family he'd been chartered with defending and blood sworn to protect was in ruins. The pain came from not being able to do much about it. He cursed his ill fortune for having been placed in such a dire situation.

"I do not envy you," Harnin added.

In truth he didn't. The Wolfsreik was trapped. They'd be destroyed if they moved too soon and damned if they moved too slowly to rescue the princess. Harnin debated telling his friend about the mission already underway but thought the better of it. There was always the slight chance of Rolnir not putting his heart into it if he knew that Bahr was taking a team by sea.

Rolnir was unperturbed. He folded his arms across his chest. "This wasn't the way I planned on ending my day. Tell the king we shall do everything we can to speed the process, though realistically we can only shave off a few days at the most."

"I understand."

"The enemy picked the right time of year to strike. One might even say the perfect time. They hold all the advantages," he added suspiciously.

"Rolnir, this is a difficult position for all of us. I will give your message to Badron and try to twist it so that it makes sense to him."

"Harnin, I understand his devotion to his blood, but I will not risk the lives of this army so casually. They are my priority. Delranan will be left open to invasion should the Wolfsreik fail."

Harnin shifted uneasily. "Badron might not see the same point of view."

Rolnir shrugged. "All the same."

"Very well. Do what you must. The Wolfsreik must be battle ready if we are to have a future. Good hunting, old friend."

Rolnir walked back to his command tent. An uneasy feeling gnawed at the pit of his stomach. He couldn't help but feel responsible for hurrying the certain death of the princess. On the same token, he wasn't going to risk ten thousand lives for the sake of one. The decision was more difficult than any he'd had to make, but one that needed to be made soon.

The pair of men rode into Chadra without a sound. Concealed beneath heavy wool cloaks the color of midnight, they eased past the sentries by the use of arcane and foul magic. Both were creatures of another time, another plain of existence. No one in Malweir remembered their truth. Exactly as they, and their masters, desired.

History named them demons. Shortsighted men who lacked the ability to know better scoffed at their mention and waved the notion off. Their origins remained a mystery to all but their masters. Both bore the guise of men and were anything but. Only in times of dire importance did they manifest a physical form. Two rode into Chadra, but a total of four roamed the world.

"Did you feel that?" asked the nearest guard after the non-men passed.

His partner, trying desperately to stay warm beneath his bearskin cloak asked, "What are you talking about?"

"The cold. I just felt a deep chill down to my bones."

He waived it off. "Shut up. You're imagining things."

Neither noticed the riders continue into the city. The shorter rider grimaced with disgust. Once clear, he turned to the taller one. "Why do you insist on dealing with these pathetic mortals?"

"They serve their uses."

"They are vermin, unworthy of cleaning the streets of horse dung."

"Kodan, we need them if there is to be any chance of success."

Kodan Bak wasn't so sure. He'd been alive for tens of thousands of years and had yet to find value in any species on Malweir. Perhaps it was a reminder of his own mortal days, before he'd become enslaved to the powers that now dominated his every thought and deed.

Amar Kit'han slowly shook his head, the movement barely noticeable under the heavy hood. He was older, if just slightly, and used to the rash judgments of his counterpart. Not equals, the elder took Bak's remarks with a grain of patience.

"Our success has always hinged on these pathetic creatures. As have our failures. They are nothing more than blight upon the world. I do not understand what you continue to see in them," Bak persisted.

"We were once mortal ourselves."

Kodan snarled. "Those days are hardly memories."

"We all need to remember our beginnings."

It was the same argument they'd had for millennia. Neither managed to see the other's point of view. Kodan Bak hated humanity, almost as much as he did every other mortal race on Malweir. He wished desperately to be able to finish his task so that he could return to the cold nothingness that managed to give him his only comforts. They'd spent far too long here already, despite feeling the long anticipated ending coming closer. He was the harbinger.

EIGHTEEN

Gathering

Tension filled the night. Cuul Ol and a circle of Pell Darga warriors surrounded young Prince Aurec of Rogscroft. Ancient hatreds threatened to boil over. It was only through the collected feelings of Cuul and Aurec that kept their men from tearing into each other as lightning danced across the distant mountaintops. Only the Pell war chief appeared calm. Aurec tried to match him, but knew he wasn't fooling anyone, least of all himself. He had never been so close to the mythic warriors. All their contact was done through men like Venten. Aurec watched the Pell closely. A combination of admiration and revulsion gripped him.

Cuul took the opportunity to break the silence. "You are uneasy by our presence."

"I am more uncomfortable with how easily you managed to capture my two scouts," he replied tersely.

Aurec purposefully left out the fact that they were also his best scouts. Mahn was still on his horse, shoulders slumped forward in stark embarrassment. Raste was the opposite. Rage consumed him. There was no defeat in the hard eyes staring down at the Pell. Both were eager for redemption. The weight of their failure would be long lived if things went ill.

Cuul ignored the barb. He hadn't come to trade insults or inflame a smoldering war.

"Not my concern, Prince of Rogscroft. I have come to you with grave tidings," he continued.

Aurec was unconvinced. "You didn't mention this in our way west. My men said you were more than amiable to us but nothing else. What has become so important now that we are on our way home?"

"New events. Prince Aurec, you stand on the cusp of eternal darkness. Certain enemies have returned to Malweir. Time is essential if they are to be defeated."

"Speak plainly please."

Cuul Ol stepped forward. Venten immediately drew back on his bow. Pell Darga hunters crouched, ready to attack each of the defenders. It was the cold, emotionless reaction that fueled their myth. There would be no pleasure in the killings. Only Mahn did not move. His eyes steeled against the possible threat as Raste drew his sword. The scout had been through worse and came out without a scratch. It was his example that inspired the others to stand down.

"Put down your sword, Raste," he said in a smooth voice.

Raste's eyes flew wide in disbelief. "Are you mad? I told you they wanted to kill us! And now you side with them?"

"No one is killing anyone," Mahn snapped back.

Dawn was breaking. A thunderstorm was moving on. He was exhausted and more than a little cold and hungry. The only chance this problem had of being solved was through direct confrontation.

"Sheath your sword," he repeated. "That goes for all you."

"They want to kill us, Mahn. That's what they have always wanted."

Mahn lost his patience and snapped, "Why haven't already? Answer me."

It was true. Raste looked around, surprised to see that only the Rogscroft men were prepared to fight with drawn steel. It didn't make sense. The Pell had been hunting them since the lowlands and now they had the prince at a disadvantage. There would never be a more perfect time.

Aurec's voice broke the silence. "Do as Mahn says. Everyone lower your weapons. There is no danger here. I wish to hear what Cuul Ol has to say."

Aurec raised his hands ever so slightly, palms open. Times had changed in northern Malweir. Ancient savages and civilized Man suddenly found common ground. The rustle of clothing scraped against a tent caught their attention and all eyes turned to see Maleela step outside. She had dark circles under her eyes and her normally lustrous dark hair showed signs of being ragged. Mild shock registered as her gaze went from Aurec to the dark-skinned man standing before him.

"Aurec, what…"

Cuul smiled genuinely. "Ah, Princess Maleela. It is an honor."

"Who are you?" she stammered despite the warmth in his voice.

He bowed and introduced himself. A thin hand went to her mouth. Pell Darga. Murdering savages who ate human flesh. She suddenly felt in more danger now than when she had been abducted. Her father's wrath would see the mountains brought down for this should he find out. Cuul Ol saw her consternation and attempted to assuage her doubts.

"Young Prince Aurec and I have business. No harm will come to you so long as you remain on our lands. You have my word."

She doubted that. "Can that stop my father's hatred once he finds out where I am?"

"We have met your Wolf soldiers in battle before. They do not frighten us. Their strength is on the open steppe, not our mountains. My people can hide you in places the world has forgotten. You are safe among us."

The words, well intentioned, had a hollow ring for a young woman fearful for her life. Maleela took no solace in them and silently contemplated the fate of yet another race. She felt responsible. Responsible for everything gone wrong. Perhaps it would have been better if she had died and her mother had lived. She scolded herself. This was not the behavior of a princess. She covered her doubts with a false smile and generously pulled the tent flap back.

"Perhaps you and the prince would care to continue this conversation over the warmth of a fire? I am not as young as I look and the cold saps the strength from my bones. Please, accept our hospitality," she said.

Cuul Ol rubbed his hands together over the softly cackling fire. The smile on his face showed the jagged rows of teeth, broken and yellowed. The smile was one of simple joy.

He was close to eighty summers old and felt it on nights such as this. The warmth of the fire was a pleasure he rarely partook in the field. His skin hung loose on his bones. Any fat he had long since burned away. What was once a full head of hair was now a mostly bald scalp complete with scars. He looked old. Worse, he felt it.

"Winter always seems colder than the year before," he said casually. His hard eyes never left the colors of the fire.

Dancing flames reflected in them and for a moment Maleela had a sinister feeling, as if he were already plotting against them. Aurec concurred. Ill feelings began to take root, festering in the depths of his soul. They didn't stem from being so close to the Pell chieftain, ancient enemy of a dozen races. They came from Cuul's initial statements. Evil wasn't that uncommon. He could find a small measure in any man if he looked hard enough. But the evil Cuul Ol hinted at came with unsurpassed dread.

"What evil did you speak of?" Aurec asked when he couldn't stand the idle banter any longer.

"It is a fell darkness come to steal the very soul of the world."

That didn't help him. "What could possibly be so bad? We have all fought our share of wars and battled evil in one manner or another before. What makes this special?"

Cuul Ol ran one of his leathered hands through the flames. "This story must be told from the beginning, back to a time before any of us were brought to live on Malweir. Back to a time of gods."

"We know this tale," Maleela chimed in. "There was a war between the gods that ended with them all leaving Malweir."

Cuul nodded softly. "A student of history. Very good. However, there are parts of the tale you do not know. There was indeed a war, great and terrible. One that stretched across the stars and lasted countless eons. Neither side could win, so they created a force that is eternal. Unstoppable."

"What force?" Maleela asked hesitantly.

The Pell chieftain's eyes hardened. "The Dae'shan. Gods from both sides met secretly to create the Order. The Dae'shan shifted the balance. They were souls taken from various races. They were twisted into un-things. Neither good nor evil, they served the will of the gods."

Aurec rubbed his face in disbelief. "I don't get it. Why have we never heard of them before? And if they aren't good or evil how can they be the cause of this vision of yours?"

A cold wind shuffled under the sides of the tent, infuriating the flames.

"The war of the gods ended with the dark gods banished. The victors maintained the fallacy of believing their victory complete. They left Malweir to the races already here. We were free to make our own destinies. Malweir no longer had the spark the gods once dreamed. Time passed. People came to forget the gods, forget their origins. That is when the dark gods found a way to come back."

"History is filled with times they nearly broke free of their prison and returned to Malweir. Each time they have been stopped, but they get closer to their goal. The last attempt they managed to send the Dae'shan back. With no other gods to serve, the Dae'shan were seduced into the service of evil."

"What does that have to do with us?" Maleela asked. The hairs on her arms were on end.

"The Dae'shan are corrupted. They serve the dark gods. With no balance, they have become evil. I have seen them in my dreams. Riders who offer ecstasy while only condemnation awaits."

Aurec began to put the full picture together, but there were too many holes. "If they have come to serve evil, why would they be concerned with us? Wouldn't the Dae'shan be trying to open the paths to release the dark gods?"

Cuul shook his head. "No. The time is not right. Only once in every thousand years are the paths between worlds open. There is still much to go before the next time. Malweir has only three known crossing points. None are in this part of the world. The Dae'shan have come for other purpose."

He fell silent, deep in thought. Until now the Dae'shan were but legend, much the same way his people were to the lowlanders. Cuul could not fathom why they had shown up here or now, despite the knowledge of their being. The fierce warrior had never been as afraid as now.

"Do you think they have come for us?" Maleela whispered.

Tension strained her voice. The idea of the Dae'shan was enough to chill her blood.

"I do not believe so, but it is hard to say. Who knows the will of the gods?"

Aurec squinted, lost in thought. Most races stopped believing in gods long ago. Left to their own devices, many found no need for such firm obedience to a race that had abandoned them. Mothers no longer passed the lore down to their children.

"How can you be certain they walk among us?" he asked.

Cuul Ol stared the prince in the eye. "There are many forms of magic still. We each have dark secrets to keep."

"So they could easily be after you," Maleela concluded.

The Pell scowled. "They would not have gone to Chadra if they sought the Pell."

Stark terror sunk in. Chadra. Delranan. "Father!"

"My heart tells me they have set the wheel in motion. Chadra is merely a beginning. A cog to their plans."

Truth be told, Cuul Ol was just as confused as they were. The return of the Dae'shan too conveniently timed with King Badron's war. Why now? Why here? Questions without answers. The veil of shadow was too thick to peer through. Cuul knew the Pell lacked the resources to learn the answers. There was another solution.

"Prince Aurec, it is said Rogscroft has one of the finest libraries in the north. Perhaps we may find the truth to this in your tomes."

"Yes. Ours is second only to the royal Averonian library in Paedwyn. I'm not so sure if the answers we seek are there or not. Up until now I had never even heard of these Dae'shan."

"You must go. My kind will be not accepted. Go to your great library and learn the truth. Only then will we be strong enough to combat them," Cuul instructed.

Aurec made a decision that would affect and haunt the rest of his life. "I will do what I can, but I cannot promise results."

"That is enough. We will do what we must on this side of the mountains. Tell your father that the Pell will stand with him against the Wolf soldiers, but we cannot fight the war for you. The enemy will make the crossing despite our best efforts. You must be prepared for siege."

"I understand," Aurec answered.

"Make no mistake, Prince of Rogscroft. Dark times are coming. We shall be in contact."

Cuul Ol slipped from the tent and moments later the Pell simply faded from the campsite. Venten blinked and didn't even see them go. The mountain shadows seemed to swallow them.

Mahn and Raste patrolled outside the tent; one was interested, the other angry. The older Mahn didn't understand the situation any more than the rest, but he had a feeling in his gut that this meeting was a good thing. His horse snorted from boredom, causing Mahn to reach up and pat his neck affectionately.

"I still don't like this," Raste snarled in a low voice.

Mahn rolled his eyes and fought off a yawn. "Are you ever satisfied? The Pell haven't shown any inclination to attack us. Don't be so eager to start a fight."

"They started it by capturing us."

"There has to be a valid reason for what they did. I will not be the one to ruin it now before the prince has his talk." He knew his words were lost on the youth. Perhaps the fateful battle that changed Raste's life was still too near the heart to let him rest.

Raste scowled harshly, thankful for the predawn lest Mahn take offense. "I don't care what you say. They're going to kill us all in our sleep the moment we let our guard down. And then where will we be? We should take that Ol hostage and escape."

"How do you propose to do that? We are outnumbered and deep in their territory. The Pell would cut us down without a second thought," Mahn mocked. "War is coming soon enough. Stop being in such a hurry to meet it."

The younger scout kept his tongue. Arguing served no purpose, especially when both were beyond exhaustion and starving. The indiscipline of it was enough to severely punish him should Mahn pursue the issue. Their discussion abruptly ended when Cuul Ol exited the tent and stalked off. The Pell faded away as if they'd never been. Aurec came out next and Mahn felt his mood darken. He saw trouble brooding on his prince's brow. Whatever he and the Pell talked about seemed enough to galvanize the prince into immediate action.

"Strike the camp," he called out more sharply than intended.

Venten tried unsuccessfully to hide his concern. "What is it, Aurec? Why rush now? The Pell have left and we are but a few days from home."

"Cuul Ol has brought certain news the king must know. I cannot explain it now, old friend, but I believe it is of grave importance."

That was enough for Venten. He trusted the word of father and son equally. He turned and echoed, "Strike camp!"

Aurec reluctantly turned to his scouts, knowing they were at their limits. "Mahn, Raste, lead the way. I want to be out of these mountains by dusk."

Three days later Mahn crested the last rise and gazed down upon the distant spires of the city of his birth for the first time in a month. Rogscroft. He was home though it didn't feel right. Events of the past few days left him with an empty feeling. Euphoria would be short lived.

NINETEEN

Rogscroft

King Stelskor stared longingly out the enormous windows of the throne chamber. A flight of snow geese soared past. He longed for that freedom. Castles and throne rooms were far too confining for any man's sanity and health. He needed to feel the wind in his hair and worn decks of a ship beneath his feet as he rode the open waves with only the far horizon for a friend. Sadly, those days were behind him. He was king and needed to act accordingly.

Delicate matters constantly demanded his attention. All Rogscroft was abuzz. Aurec and his band had returned a short while ago. News had already reached the king of the urgent matter his son bore. He sighed. Dreams of escape would have to wait. The aging king was a mix of emotions. He longed to see his son again yet was concerned over the severity of the message. He'd guided Rogscroft from one crisis to the next, through turmoil and war, but this felt different. A growing foreboding burrowed in the back of his mind. Stelskor wished he had a better feel for the storm rushing towards them.

The future felt dark. He smirked, more at himself than anything tomorrow might have in store. His dark grey robes reflected his mood. He should have known better than to expect anything good from agreeing to let his son carry out a raid on Chadra Keep. And because of that Stelskor felt the need to wear the crown for the first time in several months. Content to wait for his son to finish freshening up from the long journey, the king went back to his favorite chair in front of the fireplace. Times were coming when he would not be able to enjoy the simple luxury.

"A darkness you say. That seems vague," Stelskor said, absently stroking the stubble on his chin.

Aurec bowed his head, expecting such. "I know what it sounds like father, but Cuul Ol was adamant about this."

"What reasons have you to believe this savage?"

"The Pell are ruthless, and savage to all who have never had dealings with them. I did not once have reason to feel threatened by him. His tale of the Dae'shan bears merit. I wish to check the library as soon as possible."

Stelskor's gaze sharpened. "Don't be so quick to trust strangers who merely claim a fact. There is always a new crisis that needs dealing with, son. What you have told me thus far doesn't suggest anything special about to happen, Dae'shan or not."

"Father, both you and I have dealt with the Pell before. Yes, they are cruel and filled with a vengeance we will never know the origins of, but they have shown the potential to be staunch allies in the coming war."

The king exhaled a short breath. "War. That's a terrible premonition. The future does not need to lead us into war. It may yet be averted."

"You know we have no choice," Aurec replied coldly.

Rather than let his son's defiance inspire anger, Stelskor kept his emotions in check, or at least tried. "Badron would not be provoked into crossing the Murdes if you hadn't stolen his daughter. Your actions were reckless and potentially damning. Delranan will not hesitate to invade and our army is no match for the Wolfsreik."

"I did what I had to do, father. He was close to discovering the truth! Badron would have imprisoned Maleela or worse. He has no regard for his own flesh and blood."

"That is beside the point! The dealings of Delranan nobility are not our concern. You and I have a sworn duty to the future of this kingdom and our people. Nothing else."

Aurec was dumbfounded. "I love her."

His words stole some of the king's bite. Father laid a tender hand on Aurec's shoulder. "I know you do, son. That is what makes this situation so bad. You do not know Badron as I. He has long had his eye on Rogscroft. He knows that we are the key to him controlling a free trade route across the northern steppes and down south into Averon. Ever has he dreamed of unlimited power. That path will be open all the way down to Paedwyn once he finishes with us."

"How could you know all this?" The words haunted him. Memories of what Cuul Ol had said floated just out of reach of making sense.

Stelskor hung his head ever so slightly. "King Badron and I were once close friends. We met while students at the royal war college of Averon. A magnificent academy but built from necessity. They had forever been under the threat of attack from the wicked land of Gren. Badron and I were eager students. We wanted to learn the ways of war and thought nothing of the rest of the world.

"Little did I know Badron had other views. I knew from the beginning that I would be king one day. My first instinct was to defend Rogscroft, not turn it into a superpower. Badron wanted the world. He and I cut ties soon after our coronations. My father died peacefully one winter night. It has long been rumored the Badron had his henchman, Harnin, poison his. No one has been able to prove it, though it makes sense. The lure of power is more addicting than the charms of a good woman."

"I don't understand what that has to do with Badron wanting to harm his own daughter," Aurec cut in.

"That is something she needs to tell you personally. Enough of this. What makes you believe the Pell will actually fight for us?"

Aurec tried to ignore the prospect of confronting Maleela. "Cuul Ol has promised to position his clans along the passes. They will not fight the war for us, but they should be able to harry the Delranan supply trains enough to draw out their columns. Any troops they have to waste defending their supplies gives us that much more time to raise our army and form an adequate defense."

"You have never seen the Wolfsreik in the field," Stelskor replied solemnly. "They are the finest army in northern Malweir. Their soldiers are disciplined and well trained, much more so than any other force we might offer. No matter what we attempt by means of defense, the Wolfsreik will wait until they have massed their full strength and fall upon us like a hammer. We will not survive a head-on fight."

Aurec shook his head. "I think you lack faith in our men, father."

"I wish that were so. Our demise is already written. The army of the Wolf is coming and nothing we have is capable of stopping them."

"But the Pell…"

"You said it yourself. They will not fight a war. Nor would I ask them to. It is to our people we must look."

"Why do you argue we are already lost, father? I do not relish the prospect of having to go to war against a stronger, better-trained army, but I cannot abandon our kingdom so easily. The people deserve our best efforts, even should it result in failure."

"I agree. The people must come first. What then do you propose, prince of Rogscroft? What would you do before King Badron and the Wolfsreik howl at our gates?"

Aurec fell silent. Never had his father been so direct. The unspoken responsibility left the most astounding feeling. Could this mean his father felt he was finally ready to do what was best for the kingdom? No, he'd just been admonished for stealing Maleela. Still, Aurec was beaming on the inside. Nothing was more important than the love and respect of a father.

"It is clear that we are no match for the enemy. We must rely on guile and deceit to stop them," he answered carefully.

Stelskor gave him an approving look. "You have anticipated this?"

It was more statement than question. They'd spent countless hours working through scenarios and situations that might one day arise, a Delranan invasion among them. The threat was not new. Stelskor had spent his entire adult life under the threat of invasion. Only now in the autumn of his life were those fears realized. Rogscroft had never been very large, certainly not large enough to support a large army. The defenders would fight bravely, as all men in a death situation do, but that would only delay the inevitable. Rogscroft would fall. The only question left was how many were going to die first.

Aurec said, "Yes Father, I have. I think we have the opportunity to severely hurt the Wolfsreik before they reach the city."

He paused, eager for approval.

"Go on," Stelskor encouraged.

"The Pell agreed to waylay the supply trains. This will cause the Wolfsreik to divert combat troops to defend them. We can use that delay to our advantage by making fast strikes on the forward deployed units. Let me take two battalions and I will spread them out by platoons. From there we can begin a campaign of guerrilla attacks."

Stelskor found the idea intriguing. War was inevitable. He recognized this for truth. Badron's hunger had finally grown too much to control. The Wolfsreik campaign would be fast and brutal. Any delay Aurec might cause them prolonged the life of his beautiful city.

"Such actions would give me time to evacuate the civilians," he concluded. "Every life saved is a bonus. Your plan has merit, my son."

"Thank you, Father."

Aurec blushed at the sort of compliment he'd waited his whole life to hear. To hear them now filled him with pride and intent.

"Yes," Stelskor added. "This might work. It seems as though you have grown up without me realizing it. I caution you this, however. Do not throw away the lives of our men needlessly. Strike the enemy hard but wisely. Even should we lose the city the time will come when we will get revenge."

"I promise," Aurec answered.

Stelskor slapped Aurec's shoulder with pride. "I know you will. Now come, tell me of this princess of yours. I would like to know more about the woman who has managed to capture your heart."

The king of Rogscroft had much on his mind but welcomed any diversion.

Maleela hugged Aurec tightly as she wept on his shoulder.

"I'm scared, Aurec," she whispered between sobs.

He reluctantly admitted, "So am I. My people are on the edge of destruction and I am only one man. I am almost powerless to stop the enemy."

"Can we leave now and head south? Averon will not turn us away. We can make a new life and put this all behind us."

Aurec fought back his own tears. "My fate will be the same as my people."

"What?"

He pulled away, making sure to look deeply into her eyes. "Maleela, I will not abandon my kingdom. Would you do any less? Could you do any less?"

"I betrayed my people to help save yours! How dare you ask me that? What about us? Our life hasn't even begun. Tell me the point of stealing me from my home if it was for naught."

"Fate has not let me choose."

He cast his gaze down from shame.

Maleela caught his hesitation. "You're not telling me everything. There is more."

Aurec fought through momentary confusion. How could he tell her that he intended to destroy her father's army and sanction the killing of King Badron himself? The knowledge would be enough to break her heart and possibly turn her cold. Aurec decided not to chance it.

"Your father's army is coming. He will burn this city to the ground unless I can stop him. Let us not forget the portent of Cuul Ol. I feel deflated."

Maleela took a seat on the floral pattern bench at the foot of their bed. "The Wolfsreik has never been beaten. They do not know how to lose. There is no way you can stand against them in battle."

"I don't plan to. We have a plan in place that will buy my father time and hopefully save lives."

She listened intently as he explained the basis of the coming campaign. To her credit she did her best to put on a good face and ignore the fact that he plotted to kill her people. She'd come to accept that the war would not be stopped, but still had trouble adjusting to the fact that Aurec aimed to kill as many of her people as possible. The thought never strayed far from the front of her mind.

"I don't understand why it has to be you. There must be plenty of generals and competent commanders in Rogscroft who can lead the war. Why does it have to be you?"

His eyes welled. The emotion became too strong. "These are my people. I am the heir to the throne. What choice do I really have?"

She knew he was right, and suddenly felt very selfish for asking him to remain safe while others bled. That didn't assuage the heartache. Maleela dearly wanted to escape the nightmare her life had become and find the dreams that drove her through childhood. Life had other designs. Maleela was torn. The only thing she had in this world was her love for Aurec. She wouldn't be able to go on without him. More so, she wouldn't be able to leave his side. Ever.

"Do you love me?" Aurec asked unexpectedly.

"With all my heart."

He touched a finger gently to her cheek. "Then have faith in me. I will not leave you. Not now, not ever. The fate of our two kingdoms lies in the balance and I would see at least one come through this intact. I will return to you. I promise you with my every breath. We will be married, my love."

"Do you swear?" she timidly asked.

"I swear."

She wrapped herself around him, enveloping his strong body. There was desperate need in her actions. Months of pent up passion suddenly boiled over and, instead of fighting it, she gave in. She let the passion sweep her away. It was raw. Lustful. Maleela kissed him fiercely, hungrily driving her tongue into his warm mouth. Aurec responded, his own body betrayed.

"Make love to me," she whispered between frenzied kisses.

And he did. Aurec picked her up and carried her into their bed. They tore the clothes from each other and became one for the first time. Thoughts of war and death melted. There would be plenty of time for that in the future. Tonight belonged to love.

TWENTY

Ambushed

Skuld awoke to a heavy hand clamped tightly over his mouth. He shook the blur from his eyes and found Boen staring back at him. Danger laced his eyes.

The big Gaimosian placed a finger over his mouth in warning. "Shhh."

Skuld nodded understanding and was rewarded by being let go. Boen, sword already in hand, motioned for the boy to follow. Skuld didn't hesitate. Reaching for his own woeful dagger, he slid from the cot and slipped on his boots. Boen was at the door by the time he finished.

"Stay close behind me and do not get in my way. It would be a shame if I accidentally cut you down," Boen whispered.

"What's happening?"

"Keep your lips together and follow me."

Boen slipped into the shadow-darkened hallway. A lone lamp flickered weakly in the distance just before the turn of the stairwell. He moved menacingly, with a measure of stealth. Each step was lethal, leaving Skuld to wonder what exactly awaited them. Boen moved faster, reaching the stairs and easing his head around the corner. He gestured Skuld forward once he was satisfied the way was clear. They made it to the final steps when the front door creaked open. Three soldiers dressed in Rogscroft armor eased inside. Each was armed.

Moonlight glistened off their steel helms. Forest green capes flowed from their shoulders. Boen immediately saw them for the threat they were. They had come here with the specific intent on killing the Delrananians. Boen froze and met their gaze. The three moved as one. This was no accident. The enemy had been waiting.

"Halt right there," the sergeant barked.

Boen instantly dropped into a fighting stance. The stairwell reduced his range of motion but it also protected his rear. The enemy could only come at him from one direction. Their numbers meant nothing. He readied for attack, praying they failed to recognize him for what he was.

It was an attack that never came. Two shadows detached themselves from the darkness and fell on the soldiers with swift fury. A rope of blood flew. An arm dropped. A head was chopped. It was over in seconds. Skuld's mouth fell open at the sight of the dead men. Pure shock froze him. He'd never seen so many cut down so fast.

Boen sheathed his mighty sword and grunted. "You just ruined a bit of fun."

Dorl Theed's smiling face emerged from the shadows. "That's your problem. We saw them first."

The Gaimosian barked a quiet laugh. "He did all the hard work."

Nothol Coll shrugged, refocusing on wiping the ropes of drying blood from his blade. "It's what I do."

"How many more are there?" Boen asked.

Dorl answered grimly. "We're surrounded. I'd guess at least a company."

"Just a company? I'm insulted."

"Yeah well, that's more than enough for me. I'd like to make it back to at least get paid."

Boen shook his head playfully. "Not very patriotic."

"Says the man without a kingdom. My loyalties only stretch so far. Right now I just want to survive. How about we stop talking and get out of here before whoever is in command realizes he's missing a few men," Dorl suggested.

Boen led the way through the kitchen towards the back. His blood pounded in his head. Old tactics and strategies immediately took over his thoughts. Decades of warfare flowed through his veins. A company was a decent size force, decent enough to finish him off without much problem despite his earlier bolstering. Finesse and guile was needed if they were going to survive. He waited until Dorl and Nothol slipped into place beside him. They would do well enough. It was Skuld he was worried about. Clueless Skuld.

Boen snatched the lad by the nape and jerked him close. "Listen to me, lad. This is no game. No fanciful daydream. Men are going to die tonight. Perhaps one of us. Stay focused. Do not lose yourself in this battle. That is how men die."

The boy did his best to gulp down the rising terror inside him.

"That and a nasty slice from a sword," Dorl added glibly.

Nothol elbowed his partner. "The boy is about to wet his trousers. No need to help him."

Boen growled. "Enough. We move."

"Wait," Dorl hissed in warning.

All paused. Dorl was looking out the narrow window to their right. His face twisted with dismay. "I can count ten men on my side. We're trapped."

"We don't have much of a choice. Fight and die or stay and die," Boen said.

Dorl shook his head. "Bahr is waiting for us a few hundred meters in the forest."

"If we can make it," Boen added.

Nothol said, "Which you said we can't. I say we get this over with. The Gaimosian is right. Death stalks either choice."

Hefting his sword, Boen flashed a devilish grin. "Come then, let me show you what it means to be named a Vengeance Knight."

"We'll be right behind you," Nothol confirmed.

"What should I do?" Skuld squeaked. He was all but frozen with fear. His body refused to respond. All it wanted to do was find a safe place to hide and pray death passed him by.

Dorl snipped off a laugh. "Hope you don't get killed."

The Gaimosian had had enough. "Now," he barked.

He kicked the door with the strength of three men. Wood splintered, shattering on impact. Boen charged through as the soldiers ducked from the shrapnel. He lashed out with his sword. A head dropped, eyes wide open in shock. An arm was ripped away at the shoulder. Thick ropes of blood arced in the moonlight. A man screamed until he was silenced with a cold steel thrust to the heart. Boen moved like a whirlwind. His actions were well rehearsed, practiced on a hundred different battlefields.

The sell swords stormed out a few seconds behind, careful lest they be cut down by the Gaimosian's rage. Three seconds and Boen had already killed two men and crippled another. Dorl and Nothol fanned out on the flanks, killing another three with flawless precision. Only Skuld remained still. His mouth agape, the boy watched in horror as his companions systematically cut down every soldier unfortunate enough to come within range. Nowhere in his wildest dreams did he imagine the truly violent nature of combat. Skuld struggled not to throw up. A heavy knock off to his right shook him back to reality.

"Archers!" Nothol shouted.

Boen grunted in pain. A thick shaft pierced his right thigh. He slashed down as another soldier attacked. Sword bit deep into flesh and a gash opened from neck to groin. The remaining soldiers broke and ran. Boen recognized the greater danger before it became a substantial threat. Enemy archers were going to have a clear field of fire in a matter of seconds.

"Run now!" he bellowed.

Dorl jumped back and snatched Skuld out of the path of three more arrows. They ran. Boen pulled up the rear. Arrows whizzed by, the vibrations tickling their flesh. The smell of blood and carnage left them. Rogscroft soldiers rushed after. The Gaimosian thanked their impatience. There was no way he was going to outrun them with an arrow sticking out of his thigh. With the soldiers in the way, the archers were rendered useless. The sound of jostling armor grew louder behind him.

Dorl pushed them hard. The forest edged ever closer, but he feared it was not enough. Unarmored, they were no match for the lethal shafts of the archers. Sweat beaded on his brow. All they had to do was gain the safety of the trees. That and keep Skuld alive. He doubted either was possible. He looked over at the lagging Skuld. Keeping him alive might prove an obstacle. He was a good kid, but right now was nothing better than a target. Skuld was as lost as a sailor in the desert. Dorl grunted. Skuld was dead weight, only serving to slow them down.

Rogscroft's soldiers pushed just as hard. Pride clashed with rage and embarrassment. Too many of their friends lay dead in twisted ruins of flesh. Revenge demanded justice. Their blood was hot. Few bothered to think clearly as they hounded the enemy.

"Do not let them gain the forest!" their commander bellowed. "A month's wages for each head you fetch!"

The distance between them shriveled. It was just a little further for both groups. Boen didn't think they stood a chance. The sudden barrage of arrows coming at him from the forest almost stopped his heart. He cursed and felt foolish. Bahr had indeed been waiting. A second flight of arrows whipped by. Curiously, few of the pursuing soldiers were hit. Boen didn't care. The archers served their purpose. Men raced to take cover, both from the arrows and from the unknown threat in the wood line.

"Move your asses!" Bahr barked. The old Sea Wolf was in rare mood.

Dorl reached for the nearest tree and collapsed. His breath came in ragged hums. He looked up at Bahr in disbelief. "You could have killed us!"

Bahr grinned savagely. The sell sword pulled himself up enough to look back across the small courtyard they'd just crossed. Only a hundred meters, Dorl was shocked to find there was no cover whatsoever. They were lucky to have made it. Apparently so were the enemy soldiers.

"You do realize your archers didn't hit anything right?" he asked.

"Of course they didn't. We're not here to start a war," Bahr scoffed.

Boen gave a sidelong glance. "We did that for you. It won't be long before they figure out your little ruse."

"We don't need long. The horses are saddled and ready a few meters deeper into the wood."

Skuld doubled over without a sound and retched.

"No time for that, boy," Bahr scolded. "We've got to move now."

The tiny group hurried to find their mounts and escape.

Half the night went by before Bahr felt comfortable enough to call a halt. Each of them was exhausted from the flight, the horses most of all. Events in the port city had not gone as planned. Bahr checked out their surroundings. Lightly wooded with large boulders, it should provide enough cover to last the night. Frost-colored plumes of breath formed clouds in front of everyone. The night air suddenly grew cold. Soon their sweat would turn freezing. They needed a fire.

He caught Boen staring at the two empty saddles. "Hersch and Loem. They got killed when we saved the horses. Loem took a crossbow to the throat. Hersch was run through."

"You figured on something like this, didn't you?" Boen accused softly.

Bahr nodded. He took in the worn curve of leather, the way the bridle rested on the horse's back. "I did, though I didn't expect it. Rogscroft is normally peaceful. For them to attack us so soon bears bad tidings for the rest of our quest. They are clearly expecting an attack."

"There's no surprise in it. We've been watched from the moment we landed," Boen grunted. His face was blanched. They'd removed the arrow and patched his thigh as best they could, but he had lost a good amount of blood before and survived.

The Gaimosian was the most accustomed to such treatment. His kind had been ostracized and hunted for more than a thousand years. The centuries following the fall proud Gaimos were neither kind nor easy for the survivors. Aptly named Vengeance Knights by those who didn't know them, the Gaimosian bloodlines consistently struggled in the quest for redemption. Entire wars had been fought and won by their skill.

Boen chuckled softly. "I'm used to it by now."

"As am I, but we're a long way from finishing this mission. Rogscroft is two-day's ride from here. Add another three back and a week or so to Chadra. It appears our enemy isn't inclined to grant us the time we need."

"So much for diplomatic relations," Dorl snorted.

His cynicism bled through his words, prompting Boen to immediately grow suspicious. The words were meant as a jest, but it gave Boen reason for concern. He glanced over to Bahr.

"You know something you're not telling us. I would like to know it," he said.

Bahr knew it was pointless in trying to conceal it further, but he still wasn't sure exactly what he was keeping secret. "There are some things that need to remain unspoken."

An eyebrow arched. "Secrets? Secrets tend to kill men. I value my life, Sea Wolf. It is time to stop playing games."

"Yes, yes," came Anienam's thin voice. "Secrets. We all have them. You included, Gaimosian. We still don't know who killed that man on the boat, nor do we know who is feeding King Stelskor information of our whereabouts. The game is dangerous. There are many facets, far too many for us to control."

"Then we should abandon this quest?" Boen snapped. "I have no loyalty to Delranan or her king, but I have honor, wizard. Honor and I trust Bahr."

Bahr swallowed nervously.

The Gaimosian continued, "If I cannot trust him, I leave."

Bahr opened his mouth to speak. He suddenly found himself wanting to tell them all the hidden truths. Tell them how he and Badron were brothers and destined to do battle before the end. The wizard, however, had other ideas.

"I said we all have secrets, Boen of vanquished Gaimos. This man has dedicated his life to the service of a kingdom long unappreciative of him. The least you can do is lend him your loyalty until this matter is finished." The diminutive wizard snorted his disgust. "Men are too quick to turn on each other."

Boen visibly stiffened. "Speak your next words cautiously, old man. We Gaimosians do not suffer insults kindly."

Anienam waved his concerns off. "Perhaps you should be more cognizant of your surroundings. Bahr has done nothing but given you reason to trust him. Your focus, as should be all ours, needs to be on rescuing the princess."

"He's right," Nothol Coll said. "We'll have serious problems if she makes it to Rogscroft."

"Rogscroft poses its own challenges," Bahr finally said. He wasn't sure why, but he was glad he hadn't been given the opportunity to speak. The words he was ready to say would have been damning. What they needed was to refocus on Maleela. "It is the heart of our new enemies. We will need either great skill or strong magic to get inside the city walls."

"Best we catch her before they can get her inside," Anienam suggested. "Stelskor is a capable king. There is small chance we will be able to sneak inside his city."

Ionascu looked up from the empty saddles. "Ha! Many of us have been within Rogscroft. This should be no difficult feat."

"No doubt you've been in the royal chambers as well," Boen snickered.

Ionascu snarled. His right hand dropped perilously close to his sword. He'd had enough with this group and their damned quest. Truth be told, he didn't care one bit if they got Maleela back or not. It's not like Badron cared. Right now he wanted nothing more than to report back to Harnin and be done with this sad affair. His patience was worn thin. The motley assortment of would-be heroes sickened him with their constant bickering and small dreams. Compounding matters was the death of his man on the *Bane*. Now two more had fallen. Ionascu wanted to lash out but didn't know against whom.

It was entirely possible Harnin had another agent on board. Ionascu only knew a few of the men. Natural suspicions spread roots. He wondered how much he could trust Harnin. He scolded himself, realizing just how close he was to drawing his blade. Boen was a big man, forget the fact that he was Gaimosian. No man in his right mind dared challenge a Vengeance Knight in single combat.

Ionascu walked to the fire and sat down. He had much to think on if he was going to survive and learn the identity of the killer. He had suspicions, but they remained baseless. Instincts warned of the mysterious jungle girl. Rekka Jel was as dangerous as any man he'd met. Her skill with the sword rivaled even the most competent fighter. Ionascu had heard rumors of such tribes but dismissed them as fanciful stories. He knew better now. Women like Rekka should be avoided.

He looked up, noticing how the others still stared at him. He decided it was time to change the subject. "My men and I came here for the king. The princess is our one concern. Once she returns to King Badron we shall settle these differences."

The old wizard eyed him thoughtfully but stayed silent.

"He's right," Nothol said. "Princess Maleela needs to come first. All else can wait."

Skuld shook his head. The night's events had proven too much. No experience as a street thief compared to the sheer terror he'd witnessed. He finally understood what it meant to be a man and wasn't exactly sure he liked it. Skuld was thoroughly convinced all these men were crazed.

"The kidnappers could be anywhere, potentially already in the city," Bahr added. "Regardless, the attack tonight changes things. We will be hard pressed to move quickly if the enemy decides to continue to pursue us."

Nothol Coll stretched. "Dorl and I should range ahead. We need scouts now."

"Of course we will," Dorl scowled. He clearly did not enjoy the thought of being a scout in enemy territory. A single mistake and no one would ever know if they were killed. Worse, he shuddered at the thought of spending the rest of his life locked away in a dungeon.

Bahr nodded thoughtfully, rubbing warmth back into his hands. "It is settled. Rest now. We move again in an hour. Wizard, can you see to Boen's wound? He may be big and burly, but that hole is going to slow us down."

Anienam blanched under the Gaimosian's withering glare.

TWENTY-ONE

Stalked

The slender blade ripped clear of the man's stomach. Thick ropes of dark arterial blood preceded the drop of entrails. Rekka Jel instinctively dropped back into a fighting stance. Her long brown hair, tied neatly in a tail, hung lazily over her left shoulder. Sweat beaded across her brow. The dying man at her feet groaned, a rattled whisper. Rekka looked down and inched away from the spreading pool of blood.

Her breath was calm and measured. Her slightly pinched eyes narrowed. Five men already lay dead in her wake. She'd waited on the trail as Bahr and the others rushed off. Only the captain knew she'd stayed behind. Not that she cared. Stealth and secrecy were her closest friends. Friends that she sorely needed right now.

The soldiers of Rogscroft were not accustomed to the warrior ways of the south. Rekka almost smiled at how easily they fell under her blade. Granted, none of them had seen her coming. She had changed back into the form-fitting black clothes. The combination transformed her into the definition of lethality. She slipped unseen through the trees, doubling back on her unwitting prey. All it took after that was a single cut and she patiently waited for her next opponent.

Rekka jerked up at the sound of leaves crunching beneath a boot. The soft glow of torchlight told her it was time to move again.

"Captain, over here!"

She froze. The voice was much too close.

"Who is it?"

A pause. "Trent. His belly's been ripped out. Damned body is still warm."

"Spread out. The killer can't be far. Fan out. I want the bastard's head on a pike before dawn."

Rekka crouched and scanned the immediate area. She counted seven, maybe ten men still hunting her. Too many to fight at once. Rekka knew when she was outnumbered. It was pointless to risk her life so carelessly. It was a matter of time before the soldiers beat through her defenses and killed her. She had one hope. Go to ground and take cover.

"Think you can hide in the dark without us finding you, little bitch?" growled a deep voice in her ear.

Rekka's heart jumped. How had he managed to get so close without her sensing it? She cursed herself for being careless.

The man continued. Sheer violence dripped from his words. "You left five of my friends gutted out on the trail back there. Seems only right I do the same to you."

His voice was a low whisper, harsh and threatening. Rekka didn't move.

"Such a shame too. You're a pretty little thing. It's a waste to cut you up into tiny pieces."

A mistake. He was more focused on her looks and the way her clothes hugged her every curve. Amateur. Rekka flinched, wanting him to feel like he was in total control. He took advantage and leaned closer, inhaling deeply at her neck. A chill rippled across her exposed flesh. Her eyes widened. This man was more dangerous than she'd given him credit for. He laughed in response to her body tightening.

"Yes, pretty. I'm not like those others."

The sound of soldiers gradually faded until all that remained was the diminishing glow of torches. Soon even that was gone. They were alone in the dark.

Rekka decided to push him, praying he made a mistake. "What now? Do we lay here until dawn?"

"What's the rush?" he snapped. "In a hurry to meet the afterlife?"

"I want you to shut up and get it over with," she replied harshly.

He laughed and shoved her forward. Rekka stumbled, using it to her advantage. She dipped low and brought her sword around in one smooth motion. She caught only air. Rekka's pulse quickened. There was no sign of her attacker.

Gone, as if swallowed by the night. Panic threatened. She knew she was in trouble.

"Ah, weren't expecting me, were you?" he chided.

His voice was distant, off to the right. Rekka fought the urge to run. This man was obviously skilled and trained in one of the lost dark arts that she had no weapons to counter. Rekka Jel was worried. It had been a long time since she last faced such a challenge. The last time she barely escaped with her life. A troubling thought. Tonight might be her last.

"Where are you going to run?" His voice came from the left now. "You don't know where I am. I can smell your fear, see it in those lovely brown eyes. Yes. Fear rises. It paralyzes your thoughts, threatens you with atrophy. Every heartbeat is like ice flowing through your veins."

Rekka stepped left. Her footsteps were soft, like freshly blown sand dancing across glass.

"Which way to go. There is no answer," he mocked. "Does it frighten you? The knowledge that I can kill you at any moment? In a blink you might feel the stab of cold steel piercing your tender flesh."

Rekka held her ground. It was a struggle to keep her fears in check lest they render her useless. Her natural instincts told her to break and run as fast as she could. Reality was far crueler. Fleeing was an invitation to death. Rekka needed to tactically withdraw until she found a place in which to mount a defense. It was her only chance.

"Go now; run as far away from me as you can. I will still find you. No matter where you go or how fast you run I will find you. When I do it will be a moment of unspeakable horror. Run now, little girl. Run for false hope."

Rekka stood fast despite the icy malice threatening her. Dead or alive, she refused to play his mind games. Any sign of weakness now would only play into him. A single bead of sweat trickled down her right cheek before dropping onto her chest. The midnight air was thin and chill. She tightened the grip on her sword. The first few moments were critical to her future. Rekka drew three deep breathes and sprang into action.

She cut and slashed in a series of well-rehearsed moves, managing three complete circles before settling on a direction and sprinting off. She ran for all she was worth. When she finally stopped, her breath was ragged. Her chest burned. She struggled to catch any signs of her assailant. There was nothing but the stale breeze caressing dead leaves. Rekka felt sick.

She'd never been hunted before. Rekka was always the unflinching aggressor in this situation. To be caught in the opposite position was as infuriating as it was humiliating. She allowed herself a brief moment to imagine the nightmare she was about to unleash if she managed to catch him first. Puzzles raced through her mind as she ran. What was it about this man that made him more special than his fellow soldiers? She had a suspicion that he was far more than a mere soldier. His demeanor whispered assassin, or worse. Rekka scowled. She'd had run-ins with assassins and would-be murderers before and managed to escape with little effort. The jagged scar running between her breasts was a living reminder of those experiences.

The regular Rogscroft soldiers provided no challenge. The men of the north were renowned to be fierce fighters but were unaccustomed to her lightning style of combat. Her stalker proved the exception. It would be a long contest and she was unsure of the outcome. Rekka decided to sheath her sword and run. Sticking around in the dark wasn't much of an option. Nor was waiting for him to find her. She paused only long enough to make a conscious decision which way to run.

The last thing she wanted was to lead him back to Bahr and the others. She had no doubt they would give a good account of themselves, but the resulting battle would serve as a beacon for any Rogscroft soldiers in the area. Her only option was to trail after the foot patrol that had just passed. They were clumsy, undertrained, and young. Following them was no large task. Rekka moved as fast as she dared. The young warrior maiden from the south settled in for the long night. The assassin was close on her heels.

"Sure, we'll scout ahead," Dorl Theed mocked. "What were you thinking?"

Nothol remained taciturn. He knew his friend well enough to know when to stay quiet. His anger would soon wash away. After all, this wasn't the first time.

Dorl continued to shake his head. "Did I happen to mention its damned cold out and you volunteered us for this damned mission?"

Nothol yawned. "Who else was going to do it?"

"Send the Gaimosian. He's used to working alone and that damned arrow didn't so much as slow him down."

"He's too big, can't hide as well as we can."

"Just what are we expecting to hide from?" Dorl asked suspiciously.

The dark-haired sell sword shrugged.

Dorl pressed. "We are two men on horseback. That's not exactly an easy thing to conceal."

"Boen would be?"

"Don't turn this around on me. We shouldn't be out here. We don't even know where here is!"

Nothol pointed ahead. "Rogscroft proper is that way."

The entire kingdom was named after the main keep. Rogscroft wasn't unique in this. Several of the smaller northern kingdoms followed a similar model. First came a castle that grew into a village and eventually a kingdom as a lord's power and sphere of influence grew. Today Rogscroft was a large area with more than twenty villages and a standing army of three thousand men.

"Rogscroft is that way," Dorl muttered under his breath. "Did it happen to occur to you that neither of us has been here before and that Stelskor has an army between us and the city?"

"We're not trying to find the army, Dorl."

He blinked. "Then what are we scouting for? Goblins? Elves?"

"Signs of the princess." The answer was matter-of-fact, as if he couldn't believe Dorl didn't know.

Dorl paused to regain his composure. "You are a very infuriating man."

He missed Nothol's smile.

"How do we know they took the princess this way? They could be anywhere in this miserable country by now."

"Providing they have already cleared the Murdes Mountains," Nothol suggested.

"Which means they are in league with the Pell Darga."

A cold wind caught Dorl on the sliver between his neck and cloak, making him shiver violently. He knew, as Nothol must have guessed, that it was more than just the wind that froze his guts. No one in their right minds dealt with the Pell.

"I have a bad feeling about this," Dorl admitted.

Nothol nodded agreement. "The same bad one I've has since we agreed to join Bahr."

"Remind me again why we came."

"The same reason we always do."

"Because no one else is good enough to do the job," Dorl finished, "I'm getting tired of always being the right man for the job."

Nothol's dark eyes continued to sweep the area. Shadows diluted the pale moonlight. The landscape before them turned into a virtual nightmare. Enemy could be lurking everywhere.

"Bahr should have stayed on his ship like he told us," Nothol said quietly. "He has a vested interest in this princess that he is unwilling to tell us."

"It would be nice to know, but it doesn't matter. The old man has gotten us this far, let's hope he can deliver the rest of the way."

They continued in silence. The night drew colder. Dawn was close. The sell swords constantly checked over their shoulders, more in the comfort of knowing Bahr and the others were close behind than fear of ambush. Events hadn't gone as planned, Dorl reflected. Though to be fair they seldom did. Bahr had hoped to sneak in and make the castle undetected. King's agents had clearly been awaiting them. That knowledge meant Stelskor had a hand in abducting Maleela and killing her brother. Stelskor and his son were fools. Badron wanted blood for the death of his son. The Wolfsreik was strong enough to crush the entire northern lands in a wash of blood and destruction should they be unleashed. Total war would ensue.

Dorl didn't think for a minute that bringing the princess home was going to stop any of it from happening. The princess. What made her so special Bahr was willing to risk his life and all theirs? Ideas swirled around, the answer remaining just out of his grasp. There had to be some connection between the two. Otherwise this whole affair was sheer madness.

He glanced at Nothol. "You don't suppose the old man is some distant relative of hers, do you?"

"Makes sense, I guess."

"Think about it. Bahr was originally hired to take Ionascu and the others east. Instead he builds a team of his own and struck his own expedition. Why else risk his life? It doesn't add up, Nothol."

"Perhaps Badron sent him ahead to scout Rogscroft's defenses?"

Dorl didn't believe that for a second. "No. Badron hates Bahr and I think the feeling is mutual. Bahr's not working for Delranan anymore than we are. And don't give me that nonsense Skuld tried with the hordes of treasure lost in the mountains. He should have been slapped for bringing it up in the first place."

"You shouldn't be so hard on the boy. He's young and impressionable. There was nothing else for him back in Chadra. Besides, we had the same ideas."

"He belongs in Chadra. At least it's safer, and you didn't answer my question."

Nothol Coll stopped his horse. He turned on his best friend with a deadpan look. "I think you are asking dangerous questions neither of us is ready to answer. Like Anienam Keiss said, we all have secrets and some need to remain unspoken. Whatever Bahr's reasons are it is not our place to question. At least not while we are being paid."

"Do you have to be so pragmatic? I don't like doubt and right now I have too much of it."

"What do you really want?" Nothol asked with a curious hint in his voice.

Dorl Theed thought for a moment. "I want to know that we are doing this for the right reasons."

"Those being?"

"I don't know yet."

Nothol edged his horse forward. "Now who's the infuriating one?"

Dorl rode on ahead, eager to escape the inevitable argument. He often figured this was the real reason he'd never taken a wife. He hated arguments and was hardheaded enough to start a fight every day. Besides, he preferred the freedom of being a sell sword. The term mercenary was much too severe for his tastes. He was a simple man with simple tastes. He loved cold ale, warm women, and the opportunity to test his skills against a worthy opponent. Dorl decided to take the rest of the winter off and head south. With or without Nothol.

They'd worked together for the better part of a decade. Their meeting was accidental. Redundancies hired by the same man to do the same job in the event one failed. They were secretly instructed to kill each other upon completion of their task. After an in-depth conversation the pair turned on their employer and ensured he'd never stab another in the back. The bond they formed since then was unshakable. Both knew the other had his back in a bind, in good times and bad. Dorl Theed considered this a bad time. He silently made up his mind to confront Bahr once they reunited. He needed answers.

TWENTY-TWO

Night Visitors

Badron stirred awake with a feeling of dread. His bed chamber was cold, almost to the point of freezing. He squinted at the fire, the embers gently cackling. He shivered. It felt as if the fire had never been lit. The king was more concerned than angry. He shuffled out from the covers and donned a thick bear skin cloak. Then he noticed the sweat on his forehead. Ill suspicions formed in the dark corners of his mind. Nothing was right. Badron went for his sword, all the while wondering if this was but a dream.

He froze in midstride. The shadows behind his wardrobe were darker than normal, more malevolent. His eyes had to be playing tricks. For a moment he thought he saw one of the shadows move. His heart beat faster, louder.

"You have no need of that sword with us, King."

The voice was cold and raspy, capable of inspiring his deepest nightmares. Badron stumbled backwards. He tripped over a stool.

"Relax your mind, King. We only wish an audience."

The shadows split. Two distinct forms emerged from the darkness. Both were human in shape though he believed them demons from the pits. Pale eyes glared out to him. They twisted his stomach.

A vicious laugh, the sound of a blade slicing meat mocked him.

"No. This is no dream. We are very much real."

Badron fought back a whimper and summoned what courage remained.

"He whimpers as a frightened child. He is not the one," rasped the second figure. "We should kill him now and find another. He is not strong enough."

Badron's mind screamed. *I don't want to die!*

"The masters have chosen him. There is no time to find another."

Warm urine ran down his leg. Badron recognized the servants of death come to collect his soul. The gods had finally abandoned him to torment and despair.

"King, I would have you sit and listen, for we come on urgent business that must be concluded with you. Will you hear us out?"

There was urgency in the fell voice, an almost desperate need to fulfill some suppressed desire. Badron found the end of a glimmer of hope.

"Hope. Yes, there is much to hope for. For all of us," the shadow rasped.

How can these devils know my mind? Badron slumped onto the stool and found the will to speak. His words were weak, shaky. "Wh…what is it you want from me? Who are you?"

The larger shadow eased, almost glided, closer. "Ah, the king has a tongue after all."

"Yet it lacks strength. There is no fire in his soul," said the second.

The shadow turned his pale eyes on Badron. "He is what we are required to… recruit."

"Recruit?" Badron asked.

The second shadow ignored him. "He is but a shell of flesh. The soul is dead. As he should be."

"You forget your place, Kodan Bak. I am the voice of the masters."

Kodan Bak shrank back. "As you say."

Their argument bolstered Badron's confidence. His heart slowed. His eyes ceased to wander nervously. It was time to learn more of these beings while he had the chance. He might yet be able to meet the dawn with his life.

"Yes, recruit. Have you ever paused to wonder where the darkness in your heart, the blackness of your soul comes from? Why events happened as they did in your life?"

"Yes," he found himself stuttering back.

"Perhaps we can give you answers. We hold the truths to certain…. secrets."

Badron frowned. "Secrets? You speak in riddles."

"Finish him now before he becomes a greater liability," Kodan Bak hissed.

Shadows swirled around him in suggestive anger. Amar Kit'han was more dismissive of the building threat to Badron's life. It was that subtle confidence that sapped the warmth from the king's veins. He'd never been more afraid in his life.

"Unfortunately, such is a character flaw amongst our kind," Amar almost apologized. "Consider it a price for immortality, or servitude."

"What are you trying to recruit me for?"

"Your wife died in childbirth, an event you have reduced your daughter into tones of hatred from."

Kodan Bak added, "Were she to die tonight not a tear would be shed."

"Indeed. The horrors in your dreams would lessen. Perhaps assuage the guilt over the death of your son as well."

"Murder is more appropriate," Kodan corrected.

Badron easily became confused as they continued their game. His heart ached, but from love or the urge for revenge he wasn't sure.

"My son was everything to me after Rialla's death," he whispered.

"The fallen prince. Your dreams center on vengeance for blood spilled."

His eyes narrowed. "You know more than you should of the goings-on of my household. You speak with forked tongue while I do not even know what you are."

A laugh. It was a most horrible sound. "That is the limit of your request? A name?"

"Sorrows are often the definition of the man. This one knows great pain. It would be well in our interests to release him. Very well, King. A name. Though I caution you, names hold power. I am Amar Kit'han."

The shadows swirled, parting just enough for Badron to glimpse his confronter. Amar Kit'han had skin the sickest shade of grey, almost pale in its vileness. He had no lips or eyebrows. It was like looking into death's grim face. He could see the bones pressed against what little flesh remained. Badron wanted to run, for there was terror in those pale eyes.

"Perhaps you now understand a little more of our nature," Amar suggested as the shadows concealed him again. "I sense you have more questions aching to be answered. By all means, ask. I would not keep you from knowing the true depths of your soul."

"What manner of demon are you?" Badron asked.

The shadow rippled. "Demon? We are anything but. There is no vested interest in your prolonged suffering. Rather the opposite. I offer you the chance of a lifetime. End this pointless agony and rise above your fathers. Take this one opportunity the gods have decided to give you."

"The gods have long gone and whatever potential I had was squandered with the end of my bloodline. Do not think I am ignorant to the venom in your words. You seek to entice me with lofty dreams while you have yet to answer my questions."

Amar Kit'han held out his robed arms. "I was mortal once, just as you. Young and naïve as you are now. In fact, my story is much the same. I too lost everyone I loved and, for a time, wallowed selfishly in my own regret. I was lost and did not know which way to turn. I contemplated suicide. Then my masters found me and offered mercy to my pain. I became a new man; youthful and invigorated with new purpose. That is all I wanted."

Badron caught himself fanning the briefest flicker of a new dream. The dawn flared hotly in his imagination's eye. He stood upon the break of the wave as it drowned his enemies all in the name of holy vengeance. Rogscroft would be the beginning of his ascendency to the throne of the world. Badron the Invincible they would call him. Every citizen of that wretched town would be a slave to his whim. Stelskor and his kin would be wiped from the memory of Malweir.

Amar Kit'han flashed a fanged smile deep within the comforting shadows. "You begin to see the truth of my words."

"Yes," came Badron's whispered reply.

Kodan Bak remained unimpressed. "He is not what our masters seek. He does not have the strength to become one of us. There is weakness in his heart."

"Us? There are more of you?" Badron suddenly asked.

"We were once a large order, close to becoming an empire. But that was long ago. Time has been unkind to us."

Badron felt the veil of fear slowly dissolving. He had no desire to become one of these hideous manifestations, whatever they were, but saw there was opportunity here. A chance to fulfill the dreams once set for his son. He smiled. Anything to keep his legacy alive. Badron found new strength and rose. The greater part of his mind begged caution, but that voice was strained, distant. Curiosity edged closer. He had to know more. Desire tickled his veins.

The subtle transformation did not go unnoticed. Amar Kit'han watched with rapt fascination. He was amused at how easily the king had fallen under the sway of their arguments. To be fair, the outcome was never in doubt. Aging men like Badron tended to do anything to hold on to power for one more sunset. All it took was the proper sort of manipulation.

"All we ask is for a little of your time," Amar pressed.

"Time?" Badron asked skeptically. "What is time to a self-described immortal? I would think you immune to its trappings."

"We suffer from certain… limitations."

"Kill him now, Amar. Be done with this sad waste of flesh," Kodan bit. His patience was expired.

Amar Kit'han spun on him. The shadows swirled fiercely around him. Violent energy played dangerously off the walls, chipping paint and spreading cracks through the structure. Badron was forced to steady himself as the two ethereal monsters readied to battle. "Speak again and it will not be pretty."

Kodan Bak withdrew deeper into his shadows and retreated to the corner of the room. A low animal growl accompanied the glare of pale eyes.

Amar returned his attention to Badron. "The time has come for your decision. My masters need your answer."

Badron thought long. There were far too many variables for him to comprehend being put on the spot like this. His mind swirled. All his life he'd believed fate held something special for him. Was this to be the final catalyst? The king swallowed hard; his decision made.

"You speak of time. Time involves action. What is it you expect of me?" he asked.

"Only what you already desire. Attack the kingdom of Rogscroft. Raze the very walls to the ground," Amar replied smoothly. The Dae'shan drank in the power of the words. They were intoxicating, addictive.

Badron fought back a derisive snort. "There must be more. I am no fool."

"Indeed there is. It involved the men you sent to bring back your daughter."

"My daughter? She is nothing to me, a liability perhaps but no more. Those men are expendable."

"None the less, they pose a danger to your success. Among them is an agent who would bring about your ruin. Your brother incites them to rebellion."

Brother. Badron's heart lurched. There seemed no secret these devils could not discover. He began to find the truth in Kit'han's words. Sudden anger twisted his thoughts. Bahr. Why was that man such a nuisance? Badron decided it was long past time he dealt with his meddlesome brother. Amar Kit'han offered the means.

"What do you suggest I do?" he asked.

Amar smiled unseen. Thin tendrils swirled around the Dae'shan in tender embrace. "Detain them under the auspice of being traitors. Use it as a further cause for war. Execute them publicly and you will cement the validity of your actions."

The king shook his head. "Surely not all are traitors. Lord Harnin recruited them himself."

"Think clearly, King. Your brother has had weeks to subvert their minds. More than enough time to twist their thoughts until no shred of loyalty remains. Not one of them can be trusted."

Badron rubbed his chin thoughtfully. The future was his. He only needed to play it right to reap the benefits. Everything lay with Bahr. He regretted not killing his brother years ago.

"How can I contact you again?" he asked.

"One of our Order will find you when the time is right. Have no doubts to that."

He snorted again. "I take no comfort in your secrecy. How many are there of your kind?"

"Four, king of Delranan. Just four."

The shadows thickened and Badron suddenly found himself alone.

"Will he obey?" Kodan Bak asked before Amar had finished materializing from the darkness.

"I can foresee no reason otherwise. Damaged souls are always the easiest to manipulate." He paused. "You did well. He believes there to be division between us. That will drive him closer to our masters' will."

Kodan bowed. "I live to obey."

Amar Kit'han stared back at Chadra Keep. "We must move quickly. There is much to be done if King Badron is to be convinced properly."

"King," Kodan spat. "Ever these mortals cling to lofty titles well beyond their station. It is pathetic. We waste our time with them."

"The masters will end humanity's lethargy once they are freed."

"Much depends on this one man. Such tactics have been done before and have all failed. This is a dangerous game you have begun."

Amar agreed. "We are naught but the playthings of the gods in the end. It is they who decide fate, not us."

They walked on in silence, carefully avoiding a patrol or group of drunken townsfolk. Dark dreams haunted their every step. Some called them damned, others cursed. Neither living nor dead, the Dae'shan did as they always had. They scoured Malweir at their masters' bidding.

"What is our next move?" Kodan Bak asked.

"To Thrae. It is time to incite the Goblins to go to war."

"Against whom?" he asked.

Amar Kit'han enjoyed the fire of rage in his eyes. "The entire northern region. Only then will the masters be strong enough to break free."

"Then Malweir will burn."

Neither of them noticed the pale-faced man gaping at them from shadows of his own.

TWENTY-THREE

Argis

Lord Argis hurried past the Dae'shan without so much as a glance. His mind was focused. His chest was near bursting with information that needed to be told. A foreboding consumed him. He was more worried now than ever before. War was fast approaching, or worse. Argis felt himself slowly slipping into that foul place he often feared to go. Pulling his cloak tighter to fight off the cold wind, he hurried off into the city and to the ones who needed to know.

A pair of older men emerged from a side street. Covering down on both sides, they fell into step. Each wore haggard looks, as if they had done this too many times. Their clothes were poor cloth, boots ragged. A second pair, much younger and violent looking, fell in behind. The cold wooden handles of truncheons poked from beneath their heavy overcoats. They eyed Argis with undisguised contempt. Argis continued walking.

"Come with us," the man on his right said.

The air was chill. The first winter storm was already working down from the roof of the world. Soon it would expend fury on Delranan. Winter, however, had nothing to do with the icy fingers dancing down his spine. They moved with purpose, as eager to be by the warmth of a fire as they were to conduct the necessary business. Armed patrols continued throughout the city. Argis knew there wasn't much danger until a patrol decided that five odd and armed men were a potential threat. After that the entire garrison would be down upon them.

They finally arrived at a small cottage on the far side of town. The soft glow coming from the frosted window suggested warmth and hospitality. Argis welcomed the ideas, all the while knowing what awaited. Those he came to meet would be anything but happy. They would listen to his tale and take his words with a measure of cynicism. No one would be willing to accept him on face value. He was a valuable member of Badron's inner council. Just because he was here now did not mean much. A thousand soldiers might easily be awaiting his signal. Argis steeled himself for the scrutiny and followed the first man inside as the younger men took up guard positions near the door.

Four men and two women stood in a half circle around an old table. Layers of dust coated the aged pine. A broken mug rested beside a pile of melted candle wax. Argis looked down at the small black and yellow spider stalking across, oblivious of the greater importance going on around it. The rest of the cottage was bland, as empty of life as it was of a lived-in feel. This was one of the many safe houses established throughout Chadra by the Delranan underground movement.

He met the gazes of his judges without shame. They were farmers, peasants. None posed a significant threat to the king until they combined with the thousands of dissatisfied citizens across the kingdom. Each of those assembled thanked the Fates for the providence of having one of Badron's own in their council, for the king was a violent and unforgiving man. Death awaited them all should he learn of their identities. Fortunately, none of the safe houses had yet been discovered.

Argis stood before the informal council and bowed his greetings. Shadows and flickering firelight clashed across the background, alternating concealing parts of their faces and placing them in vivid view. None of that mattered to him. He didn't particularly care who these people were. Their lives were not as important as his. Separately they meant nothing. It was their combined presence that had the potential to change things.

The eldest of the council struck a metal-tipped staff on the dirty wooden floor three times in quick succession. The murmur circling the council died off. Silence gripped the room, as if emphasizing the ominous portent tomorrow held. They stared hard at Argis, judging him before he opened his mouth. Suspicious guilt played in their eyes. As a senior ranking leader of the kingdom, he was unused to such treatment. It comforted and chilled him. Here he was just another face, another asset in a growing struggle.

"No names shall be spoken," the elder announced.

His voice was dry and cracked as he spoke. The years had not been kind. His skin was old and wrinkled, dried from prolonged exposure to the harsh northern elements. Argis recognized him for the farmer he was. Surprisingly, this farmer commanded a power comparable to that of King Badron himself. If only Badron was able to surmise the goings-on under his very nose, Argis mused.

"There shall be no names," echoed the others, Argis included.

The soft cackle of burning wood was the only sound for a time. Argis felt as if he were being measured.

"What news do you bring this late in the night?" the elder asked once he was satisfied all was in proper order.

Argis cleared his throat. "I have come before you to warn of a grave danger."

The council murmured again. A look of latent concern spread across their aged faces.

A dark-haired female asked, "What possible danger? We know that the king assembles the Wolfsreik and prepares for war."

"His war is of minimal concern for us," said a redheaded man, one of the town smiths.

The woman agreed. "Badron will make his war. Nothing we do will influence it. Surely there must be more?"

Argis wished there weren't. "It is not Badron's war that need concern us. The danger I speak of is far more sinister. I have been witness to a new darkness this night."

"You speak in riddles," the elder stated. "These nights have all grown dark over the past few weeks. Speak plainly."

"I saw two creatures, not of Delranan, perhaps not of Malweir. They moved as if in water, more gliding than walking. I do not know what to make of them other than they had an ill presence and spoke in whispers of the end of the world."

"Perhaps they were shades of the dead," the redhead suggested.

"No," Argis argued. "I have seen shades before. They neither speak nor plot. These did both. I felt a great malice surging off of them, as if they were the definition of evil."

The council remained unconvinced.

"Danger you say. The only danger in Delranan is the will of the king," the elder replied. "It is that matter which has drawn us together in purpose and intent."

"You would discount my words so quickly without hearing me fully?"

Argis struggled to bite back on his rising anger. He was a senior councilor to the king and unaccustomed to being dismissed. Still, he needed these people if there was even the slightest chance of saving the kingdom from tearing itself apart in civil war. He let his humility take control and folded his hands over his belt.

The elder spread his hands in a futile gesture. "Very well. Tell us of these strange creatures that have you so spooked."

Argis drew a deep breath, still unsure exactly what he had seen. He did not know how to convey the sheer dread they inspired and was left with a sickly feeling in the marrow of his bones.

"They walked as men but were wreathed in shadow. I could see *through* them. Delranan is in grave danger. I overhead them speak of a private meeting with the king. They spoke of going to Thrae next to incite the Goblin clans. It is as if they are behind this war. I do not pretend to understand how this is so, but it was enough to spark terror in my heart. I fear for us all."

"If what you say is true our task to recover Princess Maleela must be considered secondary."

It was the woman's turn to disagree. "This conspiracy exists for the sake of the princess. She is our concern."

"Can't you people see? These creatures are using us to start a war. They whispered something of their *masters*. They are clearly working for some higher power. We must discover the truth in this and figure out a way to stop them before Badron dooms us to a course of action from which there is no return."

"But the princess?" the woman protested.

Argis slammed a fist into his palm. "She is beyond any of us! Our trust must fall to Prince Aurec now. Pray he and his father can keep her safe."

"From the Wolfsreik?" scoffed the redhead.

"They have never been beaten," the elder reminded.

Argis himself had once been a proud member of the vaunted army. He knew their strengths and weaknesses and was smart enough to realize that no level of insurrection could stay the killing blow once the campaign began.

"No, they haven't. Nor are we capable of doing such at this time," he said.

The elder blinked rapidly. "What then makes you assume the people of Rogscroft will stand a better chance?"

"They have an army," he replied, some of the hotness leaving him. "They have the ability to turn the war against the Wolfsreik. We would be slaughtered for the peasants we are in the span of a single night."

"Wouldn't this war be considered a good thing?" asked another man, a youth who had remained silent until now.

"In what way?" the elder asked.

"They won't think of looking for us if they are busy fighting a war. We can save the princess and finally overthrow Badron."

Argis grimaced. They were missing the point. All his talk of monsters and dark forces was wasted on limited minds.

The elder sensed this as well. "Forgive our young counterpart. I fear he still suffers from the delusions of youth. Regardless of the Wolfsreik, we are faced with a grave decision. If what you say is true, our enemies may have doubled. You are close to the king. We need you to watch for any significant changes. His actions over the next few days may give us a clue as to his intentions."

Argis knew he had already lost the argument. Clenching his teeth, he stood motionless. "Very well, but I leave you with caution. These dark *things* will be back and we are unprepared to stop them. I pray your inaction will not be the death of us all."

Argis drew his cloak about his shoulders and stormed from the cottage. The fools, he cursed. They were so preoccupied with their petty rebellion they weren't willing to see the bigger picture. Argis was sickened with premonitions of disaster. He was angry and seemingly alone. He'd made his decisions and was now forced to live with them. Unfortunately, he doubted anyone else was willing to see matters through. That left him stuck.

There was no going back to Harnin or Badron, although it would be easy to betray the rebellion and be labeled a hero. That didn't remove the fact that he had been the one to leave the secret passage open for Aurec to sneak inside Chadra Keep. Not only that, but he was the one who had slain Badron's son. That sin he would take to the grave. It also stood to reason that if Badron was in league with these monsters so too was Harnin. Argis scowled within the confines of his hood. Delranan was in jeopardy. His life was insignificant compared to that of his kingdom.

A cock crowed off in the dying night. It was time to return to the Keep and attend the king. Argis stalked off, eager to return before suspicions were raised.

King Badron awoke unexpectedly for the second time this night. His head was pounding, much like the nights he'd overindulged on wine with his captains. When he moved he found his entire body was sore. Perhaps it was the aftereffects of his meeting with the Dae'shan. The thought of them made him tremble.

"My lord, are you all right?"

He opened his eyes, shielding them from the sudden burn of sunlight. "Harnin?"

"Yes, my lord."

Badron groaned. "What time is it?"

"Three glasses past dawn, almost noon."

Noon? Damnation. "Why was I allowed to sleep so long?"

Harnin One Eye cleared his throat, giving Badron the feeling of apprehension. "The house jarl heard voices late in the night. We judged it best to let you sleep."

Voices in the night. Badron cursed himself. Fear made him careless and now another man knew he had received unexpected visitors. He almost panicked again. If word spread through the household it might prove disastrous for them all. Badron knew he must act quickly if he was going to be able to keep his dealings private. He did not have the luxury of waiting on the Dae'shan's return. He had to act now.

Badron motioned for water, which Harnin graciously supplied. The king drank deep as his eyes slowly adjusted to the sunlight. Harnin stood patiently at the foot of the bed with an expectant look in his eye. Greedy bastard, Badron thought as he set the mug down. *Very well, a secret I shall give him.*

"Lord Harnin, do I have your full trust and confidence?" he asked with a measured voice.

Harnin feigned momentary confusion for Badron's sake. "Unquestionably."

Badron gave him a stern look but did not speak his thoughts. Instead he said, "I have something you should know. Listen closely, for this affects the future of the kingdom. I did indeed have visitors last night. Two of them to be precise."

Harnin passed his first test and remained silent. He listened intently to a man he'd known for decades as he wove an impossible tale of creatures that could not exist. A small part of him recoiled at the telling. That part was much smaller than he expected. The one eye clung to every word. The horror was initially too much but then greed set in. He envisioned a new world of possibilities. A world where he might rise to be king himself. To become a terrible warlord of the frozen north. Harnin concealed the glee he felt inside.

"What do you think of my tale?" the king asked once he finished.

He studied Harnin closely, searching for any minute sign of betrayal.

Harnin blinked rapidly. He felt trapped. The next few moments needed to be handled carefully. "I do not know what to say. It hardly seems possible that such beings can exist."

"There are older beings in this world than man. Some we know, yet others remain hidden. Who can say what their motivations are?"

"So it must be with these Dae'shan," Harnin surmised. "That does not explain why they have come to Delranan."

Badron agreed. "No it doesn't. It is too convenient for these *Dae'shan* to arrive on the eve of our invasion. I feel that they are after much more than the kindly offering of their services. They want something and are unwilling to tell me yet."

"We have no incentive to trust them," Harnin added.

"Precisely my thought."

Harnin scratched his jaw. "Perhaps there is a chance to turn this into a great opportunity for our kingdom."

Finally. "How so?"

"If these creatures are as powerful as they claim, they will be useful in securing conquered territories. Think of it, sire. We would be invincible. I see why we should limit the fury of the Wolfsreik to a single kingdom."

The king pretended to think on this. In truth he already had everything worked out. He half smiled. "Why indeed. There is one problem, however."

Harnin narrowed his eye. "What would that be?"

"The house jarl."

He agreed, perhaps a bit too readily for Badron's taste. "He is a loose end. Do you wish me to deal with him?"

"Personally, if you don't mind. I do not yet know if we can trust everyone in this house, especially given our recent attack," Badron told him. He was surprised at how easy the order to kill a trusted man was to give.

Harnin bowed. "He will be taken care of today."

Badron's smile was deceptive. "Good. I knew that if I could trust anyone it was you, old friend."

"I have ever been at your side," One Eye admitted proudly.

His reply answered most of Badron's questions. "Now, tell me of the army's disposition. How close is General Rolnir to going to war?"

"He assures me that the first battalions will deploy before the next new moon."

"Under cover of darkness? Reckless of him. Isn't that dangerous, especially through the Murdes Mountains? I would think Rolnir would be looking forward to displaying our full military might to the world."

Harnin expected the reaction. "He feels that it is best for surprise. We do not know how prepared Stelskor is to repel our invasion or if the Pell Darga will bar the way."

"Stelskor would be a fool to come at us piecemeal," Badron grunted. "He knows his defenses are no match for us."

"Sire, the confines of the mountain passes will steal our strength of force. I am in agreement with Rolnir on this."

Badron remained skeptical but he had virtually no choice in trusting his top military commanders. They were the men who were going to win or lose this war.

A fisherman found the body washed upon the shore later that night. The tongue had been cut out and he'd been crippled before death. Every finger and toe was broken. The fisherman prayed for the man's soul and turned the body in to the harbor patrol. Not a question was asked.

TWENTY-FOUR

At the Walls

I can't believe I am going to do this, Bahr thought for the hundredth time as he gazed up at the near impregnable wall. Cold and tired, he was far too old to be playing at games like this. That didn't take from the fact that they'd made it all the way to Rogscroft without further incident. Bahr and Boen agreed to send out reconnaissance patrols in the city and around the castle. The Sea Wolf insisted on leading a team himself. No one questioned this.

Bahr let Ionascu take a six-man team around the east while his went west. He was becoming increasingly convinced that Ionascu either knew who the spy was or was the spy himself. Either way he didn't trust any of Harnin's handpicked men. He cursed again and heard Boen snort mockingly behind him. He must have read my mind, Bahr thought.

"What do you think?" he asked, trying to focus on the task at hand.

Boen stared hard at the walls. "Solid construction. Good walls. We'd need an army to break them down."

"We don't have to break them down, just get past them."

"Doesn't matter," Boen shrugged. "I'm sure the alert has already been sent to every guard station and outpost in the kingdom. Just because we lost them in the wild country doesn't mean we are safe."

"We should get back. This is not the place for a conversation and Ionascu should be headed back by now as well."

Boen agreed and led them back to the village. They'd been moving constantly since arriving the night prior. The journey to Rogscroft had not been dull. A raiding party caught up to them a day ago. The battle was vicious and bloody. Another of Ionascu's men was killed by a barbed pike. The loss was relatively minor in terms of mission success but it left a hollow feeling among the survivors.

A half hour later Boen pushed open the door to the abandoned hut they'd confiscated. Skuld eagerly awaited them.

"Miss us, lad?" Boen asked with a gruff laugh and tousled the boy's hair.

Skuld grinned wolfishly.

Bahr asked, "Has anyone else returned?"

"No sir. You are the first. I was starting to think something had gone wrong."

A twinkle entered Boen's eyes. "What could possibly go wrong? You've got me here, don't you?"

Bahr ignored the boast. He was never one to stand on arrogance and felt there was little room for it in this situation. He supposed it was a failing of Gaimosian bloodlines, seeing as how they'd been hunted and abused for generations. Most ordinary people would have given up and faded into history. Not the proud sons of Gaimos. They continued to struggle with sheer tenacity and indomitable will that had damned them for generations. Sometimes Bahr wondered if those responsible for the destruction of Gaimos ever understood what they had unleashed upon Malweir. All that aside, Bahr thought Boen needed to be more considerate of the attitude he was fostering in Skuld. He made a point to talk to the man later.

"What do we have to drink?" Bahr asked.

"Mint tea like you said."

The Sea Wolf nodded. "Good. This cold will be the death of me yet."

They closed the door behind them, only Skuld choosing to remain on guard outside.

"You shouldn't encourage him so much," Bahr chastised once he'd taken his gloves off and poured them both a mug of tea.

Boen's face tightened. "He needs a positive male role model. The boy's had no one his whole life. I give him hope."

"All I am saying is not to fill him with false hope. Skuld is young and impressionable. He's the one person capable of believing all the shit you talk," he replied with a laugh.

The Gaimosian shrugged. "I am nothing without an audience."

Nothol Coll and Dorl Theed arrived then. Their faces had a bluish tinge and they were out of breath.

Dorl spotted the mugs. "Drinking without us?"

"Tea," Bahr replied stiffly.

Nothol graciously accepted a mug and said, "It is getting colder out there. The first snows aren't far off. Could make trouble for us on the way out."

Bahr agreed. "Hopefully we can make it back to the *Bane* before the snow gets too deep and she doesn't get iced into the shore. That might be worse than being hounded by Stelskor's men all the way to the coast."

"You're planning something," Dorl suggested.

A calculating smile. "Naturally. Any captain worth his salt has some scheme cooked up just in case. You worry about the princess. I have the rest of it."

Others returned, each bearing a dejected look.

Dorl raised an eyebrow. "Seems getting in is going to be more of a trick than we had planned."

"You didn't seriously think we could just walk through the front door did you?" Bahr asked him.

The sell sword wisely chose to remain silent.

Bahr continued, "We wait for everyone to return before we jump to conclusions."

The wait proved shorter than expected. Ionascu and his team were the last to return, and then only by a few minutes. Everyone was at the point of exhaustion. Bahr watched them all, on edge from the dangerous glint in Ionascu's eyes. He sighed. They had been delaying the inevitable since leaving Stouds. The time for talk and plots was done. Action needed to be taken and the mercenaries were already prepared.

"What news?" Bahr asked.

Ionascu swallowed the last of his tea. "Nothing good. Seems the castle's been told about us. The whole place is on a war footing."

"Looks like they are gearing up for a major campaign," seconded another.

Bahr heard the concern in the man's voice but made no comment.

"It can't be about us," Boen chipped in. "We're just a handful of men. That doesn't make us much of a threat to national security."

"Nonetheless, what Oleg says is true. Rogscroft prepares for war," Ionascu reinforced.

Bahr thoughtfully chewed the side of his tongue. "What do you suggest?"

"Hard to say. The walls are solid and too well armed for us to climb unnoticed. The main gates have rotating shifts every four hours. That keeps the guards fresh and alert. We might just be wasting our time."

"We knew the risks when we accepted the job," Bahr told them.

Ionascu shrugged off the comment. "That doesn't change the fact that we simply cannot break in. My men found no weaknesses along the perimeter."

"How about we go in the front door?" Dorl suggested.

"What?" they shouted in unison.

Boen cracked a smile.

Dorl eased to the center of the room. "It's the one place they won't be expecting us."

Bahr waited for the murmuring to die down. There was some merit to what Dorl was saying, but he needed more to be convinced. "What's your plan?"

His cheeks flushed. "No one will be looking for men trying to break in. We don't need to be sneaky about it. Besides, they might easily be preparing for something Badron cooked up."

"A deception."

The sell sword nodded sharply. "We could pose as a trader caravan, maybe just a few merchants with guards."

"A trader caravan?" Ionascu laughed. "Just where do we come up with the costumes, goods, and animals?"

"We can buy what we need from local merchants. Princess Maleela will be in the most heavily guarded part of the castle. We wait until market day to get inside," Nothol came to his friend's defense.

Boen arched his eyebrows. "He has a point. They both do. We can afford it all, but they will be wary of strangers, especially ones with Delrananian accents."

"I didn't say it was much of a plan," Dorl admitted.

"All right, calm down!" Bahr growled. "It may not be perfect, but it is all we have to go on. Besides," he grinned, "we have enough cunning and guile amongst us to make it work."

"Our next move?" the Gaimosian asked.

"Find out when merchants are allowed in the castle, scout out what we can and get ready to fight."

Boen nodded. "Good. I'm tired of running and hiding. I need to knock the rust off my sword."

"Which leads me to my next point. No visiting the local taverns. No drinking. No whoring. We do this right or we all die."

Outside, ear pressed closely to the door, Skuld listened to every word. He began to see these hardened killers for what they were, madmen. He doubted his decision of sneaking aboard the *Dragon's Bane*. Pell Darga treasure. What was he thinking? All life's hardships conspired to send him to this very moment where death stretched out its icy fingers and reached for his throat.

The grip on his shoulder was enough. Strength left him and his legs went numb.

"Shhh," whispered a familiar female voice as he began to whimper.

Rekka Jel stepped out of the darkness and patiently waited for him to compose himself. Raw emotions could easily drive the boy mad and a knife in her gut was the last thing she needed.

Skuld's eyes went wide. "Rekka? We thought you'd been killed. Where were you?"

"Matters have turned against us," she whispered. "Where is Bahr?"

"Inside with the others."

She nodded. "I must see him now. I have much to tell."

Despite the urgency in her voice Skuld took the time to smile as he opened the door. "I'm glad you're back with us."

Rekka touched his cheek with the back of her hand and slipped inside. The conversation slowed to a quiet murmur as each took notice of her. Bahr pushed his way through them and came face to face with worry in his eyes. Rekka nodded in understanding.

"I bring ill tidings," she simply said.

Boen's deep voice rumbled from the hearth. "Quiet down lads, let the lady speak."

She waited for them to settle before beginning her tale. "I was covering the withdrawal like we'd agreed. I managed to slay five of their scouts without much trouble. Then I ran into something unexpected, something darker and threatening. I am not ashamed to admit this, but I knew fear. It spread from my very marrow and nearly consumed my mind. It has been many years since last I felt that sting."

"What could rattle your nerves so?" Nothol asked. His voice was cold, almost somber.

"They are known as the Dae'shan."

Anienam Keiss hissed, "Impossible!"

One by one they looked to the old man who, until now, had been no more than a steward. He winced, cursing his carelessness. That left him with just one choice.

"The Dae'shan are extinct. Naught but ghosts in the night. The last of their kind vanquished from the face of the world ages ago. You speak of the immaterial."

Rekka's eyes hardened. "I know of what I speak. The Dae'shan threat is real, wizard. This is not the first time I have encountered one."

"Rekka, what are these beings you speak of?" Bahr interrupted.

"Murderers. An ancient order intent on bringing the dark gods back to Malweir," Rekka explained. Her voice rippled with conviction.

"They are no more. I was there, Rekka Jel. I had a hand in ending their evil for eternity. The Dae'shan are dead."

Anienam Keiss bordered on vehement. He knew he was right. He must be. After all, it was his sword that slew the last one. That was the day his father, Dakeb, died. Four against two and only Anienam had walked away. The past drifted further away, but the nightmares continued to this day.

He quietly added, "This simply cannot be."

Boen, having traveled the face of Malweir many times over, gently asked, "What are these things and how do we kill them?"

The wizard relented, but only a little. "Some might call them demons. Certainly their powers are equal to the name. No one knows where they came from. They are the soulless servants of ancient evil. It is chronicled that they were the true power behind the war that destroyed Gaimos." Boen's face darkened. "They manipulated the kings of old and used them to wipe Gaimos out. That is not their only crime. They have done this throughout our known history."

"Why?" Boen asked in a dangerous growl.

"A prophecy. It is said that the sons of Gaimos would deliver the final blow and vanquish the dark gods forever. The Dae'shan are afraid of this and sought to end the threat once and for all. They ultimately failed. It was Gaimosian blood that first began the order of mages. Peace and prosperity reigned for a time, until the Dae'shan returned. They seduced Sidian, the Silver Mage, and began a new war that lasted almost five hundred years."

"When my father managed to kill Sidian in his fortress city of Aingaard he thought he had at last accomplished what our kind had been struggling against for so long. He was wrong. The Dae'shan returned to hiding, patiently waiting in the dark forgotten places of the world. If what Rekka says is true, they feel their time is here."

"Is it?" Bahr asked.

She nodded. "It appears so. This is a day my people have long feared. The Dae'shan are the ultimate evil. They have the power to destroy us all."

"You rely too much on your fears," Anienam scolded. "If what you say is true, if, why now? Why here? There is no path for the dark gods to step through in this part of the world. The nexuses have all been closed. The nearest one is more than a thousand leagues from here. You must be mistaken, Rekka."

"Perhaps they are on a different path," she offered.

"Hold on, what was all that about a nexus?" Dorl asked.

Anienam abruptly stopped pacing and looked up. "What? Oh. Nexus, yes. They are the gateways between worlds. A sort of portal if you will. Malweir is but one world in a host of hundreds, at least so far as the Mages at Ipn Shal were able to learn. To my knowledge no living being of any race has ever survived the journey."

"Making them the perfect prison in which to banish the dark gods," Rekka added.

He waved her statement off. "Naturally this is all very suggestive. The gods of light tried to kill their dark brothers by sending them through the nexus. They failed. After all, how do you kill a god?"

"Stop believing," Boen grumbled.

A twinkle in his eye, the wizard continued. "Exactly, and this was not done. Man, Elf, and Dwarf all continued to believe. The Goblins and Trolls go without question. Evil was allowed to remain. But back to the nexus. There are at least three that we know of. One lays at Ipn Shal where the Mages built their domain. The second is in the land of Gren and was destroyed when Sidian was finally killed. The third your country helped destroy, Boen. It was almost two thousand years ago that Kaven and Pirneon did battle in the ruins of Gessun Thune."

Boen's mood soured at the mention of Pirneon. That legend was passed down through the bloodlines for every Gaimosian to heed. Once the Knight Marshal of Gaimos, he turned his back on his people and succumbed to the dark powers. Kaven had been right to kill him.

Bahr asked, "There are no others? Just these three?"

"None that we know of. That is why it is a mystery. The Dae'shan have no reason to be in the north."

"Regardless, they are here and involved with us now," Rekka said.

"I must think on this. The news goes far beyond any we previously expected."

Anienam stole off to the far corner of the room. Most of the mercenaries were in complete surprise of his sudden revelations. A moment ago he had been a simple servant and now he was lecturing them on the history of Malweir. Bahr hid his smile lest they discover he'd been keeping this from them the whole time.

"Who is this old man?" Ionascu demanded. He was the most tired of games. The past week was taking a toll on him. The murder aboard the *Dragon's Bane* initially spooked him and he hadn't settled since. All he wanted now was to grab Maleela and be done with this miserable affair. His days as Harnin's spy were ending. The admissions of Anienam only compounded matters.

Bahr recovered quickly. He didn't think it was time to give up all his secrets. "Forget about him. We have more important things to worry about than one old man and ancient spirits. What we need is to focus on getting to the princess and infiltrating the kingdom before anything worse happens to us."

"What could possibly be worse than this?" Dorl asked.

Bahr turned on the young sell sword and replied, "The Wolfsreik."

Ionascu nearly choked. *How could they know?*

"Why would the Wolfsreik come here?"

Bahr shrugged. "Doesn't it make sense? Badron hates Stelskor and this can be his big chance."

Ionascu stewed in silence. Everything had changed.

TWENTY-FIVE

A Plan is Laid

Dawn broke without much fanfare. Nothol Coll pulled the last watch, welcoming the warmth of the morning sun. The night was always coldest before dawn and he was frozen to the bone. He stared off, mesmerized at how the golden sunlight broke through the veil of clouds. Little did he realize that he was the only one of the group who did not fear the future. He saw tomorrow for what it was: an opportunity. Nightmares had walked the land long before he was born and would long after he was dead. The hatred of the Dae'shan offered great challenge the opportunity to prove himself against a worthy foe.

Movement to the right drew his attention. "A quiet night. No need for two of us to stand watch."

"You sound disappointed," Rekka Jel replied. She had spent the night outside, waiting to see if her greatest fears were going to be realized.

"Unfulfilled is closer to the mark."

She was confused. "I do not understand."

Nothol yawned, shifting his focus on the small woman, silently measuring her worth. Finally, he said, "This stays between us."

"Of course." She sheathed her sword and folded her arms across her chest.

He paused, suddenly uncertain about sharing his most intimate moments with this strange woman. "I was cursed some ten odd years ago. A minor shaman caught me killing a man. Turns out it was one of his kin. I don't think I committed a crime. I was being paid to kill a murderer, so I did."

"A curse is no easy thing."

He nodded. "I agree, but it was what I did at the time. I was a fairly good assassin but his curse changed that. For my sins I am now forced to wander Malweir in search of an opponent capable of ending my life. That is the only way I will be set free. So I move through life in a constant battle. My soul knows no peace."

"That is why you have come."

"Yes."

Dull rays of sunlight washed over Rogscroft. A cock crowed off in the farmer's district. Soon the city would be alive with merchants and ordinary townsfolk going about their daily lives. It would not be safe for the tiny band from Delranan for much longer.

Rekka eased closer and gave him a knowing look with her deep brown eyes. "Perhaps you will find peace on this quest."

She pulled away but not until after he snatched her hand. "Please, do not tell this to the others. Not even Dorl knows the truth."

Rekka promised.

"It's not going to work," Dorl said between bites of something that looked like lamb but tasted a whole lot worse. It was hot and food, and better, it was cheap.

Nothol shook his head. "You keep saying that, but nothing ever changes. Tell me why it isn't going work this time?"

Dorl scowled. "Can't a man be pessimistic from time to time?"

"Define time to time."

"Shut up. You and I both know Bahr's plan is shaky. How are we supposed to get enough local coin to buy a wagon, horses, and enough goods to pull off being legitimate merchants?"

Nothol sipped his tea. "Skuld is an accomplished thief. If nothing else Bahr has faith in the boy to come through."

"Skuld is a liability at best. I admit, the boy has personality, but no experience. We're all in trouble if he gets caught."

"Enough already. You're making my food taste bad."

The sell sword rolled his eyes. "Bad would be an improvement. Don't go changing the subject. We are in over our heads."

"We have been there before and always managed to pull through. Why should this time be different?"

Dorl set his fork down, nearly choking on the food in his mouth. "You can't be serious. Did you not hear what Rekka had to say last night?"

"I did. It changes nothing. Like Bahr said, our priority is finding Maleela. We can leave after that."

"These are unenviable times," Nothol agreed.

It was a comment Dorl had no reply for. He preferred to keep his fears to himself regardless that Nothol was his best friend.

"Look," he said. "Here comes Skuld now."

The street thief sauntered towards them, sitting down like he belonged. He was clearly struggling to keep the smile from his face.

"Good news?" Nothol asked.

He nodded, tossing a bag on the table. "Enough. I haven't counted it but I think there is more than one thousand in here."

Dorl snatched it up before anyone might get suspicious and tucked it inside his leather jacket. "That's quite impressive for a morning's work."

"I have a lot of practice. How much more do you figure we need?" Skuld asked. He finally smiled as Dorl pushed the remnants of his lunch over.

"Not much. Bahr guesses fifteen hundred should be enough. Good job, lad. Looks like you're not just a stowaway anymore."

"Thanks."

Nothol grinned. "Good lad. Now go and see if you can get the rest so we can see if we can all get killed."

Skuld snatched up the rest of the meat and dashed back into the crowd.

"You shouldn't haze him so. He's a good boy," Nothol admonished.

Dorl shrugged. "I'm simply speaking the truth."

"From your point of view."

"There's no other like it. Come on, let's get this back to the captain. The sooner we do this the better."

The sell swords dropped enough coins to cover their meal and a small tip and headed back to the safe house. Neither noticed the gaunt man with crisscrossed scars on his right cheek get up and follow.

"These horses are a bit scraggly," Boen grunted.

He walked around the back side, checking the musculature and grooming. He'd seen better and would never be able to ride one, but all he had to do was buy them and walk alongside. Still, he wasn't used to such small animals. Gaimosians were larger than normal people, making the simple matters more difficult.

The stable master looked up at him indignantly. "They'll do their job well enough. What else do you need them for?"

"That's not what I am paying for," Boen replied.

"Fair enough. What else can I do you for?"

"A wagon would be nice. Something to go along with these damned small beasts of yours."

The stable master shook his head. "Can't help you with that. I only have the horses for sale. Old Sven might have what you need. How big you need?"

"Big enough to start hauling supplies."

"Ha! You and your boss are the damned fools. What sane man would start up a business on the eve of the invasion?"

Boen had two choices. He could either answer the question and give the stable master reason to sound the alarm or just go along with it. It didn't prove to be much of a choice.

"Smart ones. War means business. If you were smart, you'd be thinking of doing the same. Take advantage of the situation and you might find yourself a rich man."

The stable master already had similar thoughts. Visions of a fat purse sparkled behind his eyes. Rogscroft was about to succumb to chaos and a smart man would be there to recognize the potential for profit. Boen was right, wars made men rich.

"Sven you say?" he asked.

The stable master nodded. "Aye. Tell him I sent you and he should give you a good deal. Leastwise for what you want."

Boen dropped the money pouch into the horse man's outstretched palm. "Thank you for your time. Take care."

"You as well, big man. May the war find you well."

The wagon groaned as it ambled across the aged drawbridge. Bahr sat beside Anienam Keiss, handling the reins. He constantly scratched the skin where the fake beard was glued. The disguise was irritating but necessary.

"You shouldn't be messing with it so much," Anienam scolded.

Bahr frowned. "It doesn't stop itching. Isn't there something you can do about it? You are a wizard."

"Not now. We are too close to the enemy. Try thinking of a different moment. That might take your mind off the irritation," he suggested.

"And get us both killed before we even realize what happened. I still think we could have done without the beard."

"We have been over this. You look too much like your brother to go in without camouflage," Anienam replied.

Bahr had no choice but to accept it for truth. They'd already risked so much that any betrayal now was comparable to treason. An innocent woman's life depended on them. The weight was nigh unbearable. Bahr's dreams reflected the torture of losing his only niece and he vowed to keep that from happening. He loved her more than her father ever could.

"Wizard, Maleela is the only important factor on this trip," Bahr said. "All else is unimportant."

"Yes, I know." Anienam's voice sounded hollow. He too had his share of demons lurking in memory. The sudden reappearance of the Dae'shan proved his life a lie. Everything he and the other mages wasted their lives to destroy was now loose upon the world. He, like every mage before him, had failed.

"Perhaps we are approaching this from the wrong angle," Bahr offered suddenly.

Anienam glanced over, his eyes bright beneath his bushy brows. "In what manner of speaking?"

"Think about it. Why would Badron send his entire army here for a girl he doesn't care for? You've seen this kingdom. They are only now preparing for war. I would have expected them to have been waiting in the trenches already. None of this makes sense to me right now. I feel like we are missing an important key."

"Your thoughts suggest that the princess is in league with her kidnappers."

Bahr didn't think so. "Or in love with one."

"There is always the possibility that exists. We will not know for certain until she is safely away from this city."

Anienam fell silent, unwilling to ask those two most dreadful words in man's vocabulary: what if. Bahr was too close to the truth and not ready to learn it. Malweir was in dire straits. The future was grim, but still uncertain. Anienam had a moral responsibility to gather forces to stand in the path of the dark powers. The needs and emotions of one family were of small matter. Still, he was plagued with the empty visions of what Bahr's bloodlines might mean to the future. He wished he had more answers.

"What if she is in love?" Bahr asked.

"Matters would be sorely complicated."

"More so than now? That's not very reassuring."

Anienam flashed a thin smile. "It wasn't meant to be. Are you ready? We are coming up on their guards."

The Sea Wolf didn't know if he was ready or not. Love was both fickle and dangerous. It was the damnation of many a good man. If love were the culprit, there was no way Maleela would willingly leave Aurec. He couldn't blame her. There was a chance for her to have a normal life here in Rogscroft. Away from all the misery her father subjected her to. Here she might grow to be a queen. What if.

The sergeant of the guard held up a gloved hand, signaling the wagon to halt. He was a hawkish looking man, heavily muscled and clearly in the prime of his life.

"State your business in Rogscroft," he ordered. His voice was terse, angry at having to waste his time on a toll bridge when he'd best be used out in the field with the rest of the army.

Bahr offered a wave and a friendly smile. "We are bringing rare silks from the southern desert to appeal to the ladies of the court."

Clearly unimpressed, the sergeant gestured for his clerk. "Mark your name on the ledger and have your men stand aside so we can search the wagon."

"Yes sir," Bahr replied earnestly.

"That's sergeant," he corrected.

"Of course. My apologies, sergeant."

The sergeant scowled but said nothing more. Gathering his short staff, he rounded the side of the wagon and patiently waited for the rabble to climb down. They were an odd assortment but were altogether too familiar for his liking.

"Funny, you don't strike me as being from the southern deserts. Maybe except for the old man and the woman. In fact, if I didn't know better I'd say you were mostly from Delranan."

The accusation only slightly caught Bahr off guard. He'd been expecting to be called on it, just not so soon. The stakes rose. Time became more important. The sergeant's superiors would soon know of them and it would all be over. Bahr decided to use as much of the truth that wouldn't get them locked in shackles immediately.

"Some of us are. My sons and I have made many successful trips to the towns and villages of Rogscroft. There never was a finer land."

"Maybe so, but that was before your king decided to pick a fight," the sergeant snapped, unconvinced.

Bahr did his best to shrug it off. The knowledge that it was his own brother who was responsible haunted him again. "Kings do as they will. It is unfortunate that this war must come between our two peoples. There was much profit to be made between us."

The sergeant's eyes hardened. "Perhaps at one time. No more. Sell your wares and leave this city while you still can. Go."

Bahr bowed down and walked away before the man had a change of heart.

"That went well," Anienam said once they were back underway.

Bahr wanted to laugh. "Not well enough. He's going to go back and turn us in."

"Wouldn't you?" Anienam seconded.

"More than likely. We must be fast. Time is a bigger enemy to us than Rogscroft."

"Do not berate their choices, Sea Wolf. They are doing what they needed to save their kingdom, just as you would for Delranan. Ultimately we seldom have much choice in the matter."

The words stung, more so because it was his own family that had betrayed the peace in the north. It was almost too much for a single soul to bear.

"Let us be about our business and leave this place."

The wagon groaned past the growing crowds of peasants and merchants eager to make the best deal. The main keep of Rogscroft was a complete opposite from Chadra Keep. The city was vivid and proper. People filled the courtyards. Song and laughter rose to the skies, undaunted by the heavy winter just beyond reach. The streets were warmer, friendlier than Bahr remembered. They were clean and well taken care of. The wooden homes had been replaced with white stone long ago. Four towers rose high into the sky as monuments to the achievements of Man.

Bahr sensed pride surging from the people. The air was clean and Bahr saw not a piece of trash recklessly thrown about. Ditches ran alongside the roads allowing water to run off rather than flood the city. Chadra could use such innovations. He knew it would be a long time in coming. Badron meant to destroy this city to the ground. All they had struggled to accomplish over the years would be erased as if it had never been.

"Rest your mind, Bahr. This will not end as badly as you imagine," Anienam said once he noticed the look of consternation on Bahr's face. "All men go through dark times before the dawn. All you must do is weather the storm."

"I would seek encouragement from your words, though not for myself. Would that these were normal times."

Anienam smiled sadly. "It has never been for men like us to decide such matters. Not even my powers grant me such. Focus on Maleela. All else will fall into place."

Bahr took comfort in the wizard's words. There was strength in them he did not know he possessed. He focused on that strength, used it to bolster his waning confidence. He'd generally considered himself a practical man. Sadly, there was nothing practical about any of it. Bahr suddenly realized that he had lost the will to fight. They rode on in silence for a while longer, taking in the freedoms of Rogscroft. The way of life here was much better than in the depressed kingdom of Delranan.

"Something you said earlier bothers me," he finally said as they pulled into the merchant area.

Anienam waited patiently. "One thing? I must be losing my touch."

Bahr reined in the wagon team. "All right, there are probably a lot more things but there is one in particular."

"That being?"

"If all this is part of some elaborate plan for Maleela to escape her father we should assume that she is happy here and not a captive."

"You mean in love?"

Bahr nodded. The thoughts refused to go beyond that singular human emotion capable of building and breaking societies. If it was love, it was bound to be poked through with misery.

"I do not have an answer for that. All I can tell you is that we must not leave without her. Much hinges on your niece."

"Why not? She deserves the chance to be happy."

Anienam frowned. "Because your brother's men will hound us all and betray us when we least expect it. Your earlier suspicions are correct. Ionascu and his people belong entirely to Lord Harnin. This is a dangerous game we play."

"What then should we do?"

"Find the princess and the rest should fall into place."

TWENTY-SIX

Abduction

Aurec moaned softly and rolled over. The unfamiliar sounds and movements were enough to awaken Maleela. She yawned, stretched her lithe body to get comfortable again and fall back to sleep. Her slender hand snaked out to caress his bare chest. A smile warmed her face. This was how she had envisioned the rest of her life. Maleela closed her eyes, but sleep refused to come. It danced ever so carefully away each time she reached out to it, taunting her with unfulfilled dreams and peace. A chill ran down her arms. It came from the thin windowpane in the bed chamber. She made a note of having the housekeepers put curtains up in the morning. Winter was already coming.

The thought was oddly soothing. With winter so close and the snows that came with it, there was no way her father would march the Wolfsreik over the Murdes Mountains until spring. At least she hoped so. Rogscroft was not ready to fight a war, despite her lover's proclamations otherwise. Every day Badron was forced to delay was another fleeting spark of hope for the defenders. Dozens of villages had already been abandoned, the citizens moved further away to avoid the fighting.

A whisper of wind touched her exposed flesh and she drew the bear skin blanket higher. This winter promised to be cold. Maleela closed her eyes again, and again sleep did not come. Scowling, she slipped from the bed and threw her heavy cloak around her shoulders. She then bent down and kissed Aurec on the cheek. He stirred but did not awaken.

"I will be right back," she whispered and slipped from the room.

The door closed quietly behind her and she set off down the hallway. After relieving herself, Maleela decided to head down to the kitchens in the hopes that a bite to eat would help her fall asleep. The castle was alarmingly quiet, almost supernaturally so. She entered the massive kitchens, engulfed by the warmth of the ovens. Maleela quickly found a chunk of white cheese, some day old dark bread and a few strips of dried venison. She washed it down with a glass of spiced wine.

Maleela used the quiet to think about the direction her life had taken. She'd never done anything to earn her father's ire. Naturally, he would argue that. She was responsible for her mother's death, or so Badron believed. Yet even living under the watchful gaze of such hatred she managed to avoid temptation and not betray the love that should have been. She had been a loyal family member and citizen of Delranan until the day she learned of Badron's plans for Rogscroft.

She felt trapped. More so now than before she'd conspired to leave with Aurec. Her brother's death was the most regrettable part. She knew he would still be safe, probably leading a battalion of the Wolfsreik if only he'd have stayed in his room. But once again life proved to have bigger plans. Argis was left with no choice but to kill him. Part of her struggled to fight back the tears while the rest wondered why. She'd never done anything wrong. Not to herself. Not to her father and especially not to her brother. None of that stopped him from adopting his father's point of view.

Maleela scowled. The food did not have the desired effect and her own thoughts betrayed her need for sleep. She let out an exhaustive sigh and pulled her cloak tighter. It was time for a quick walk. She didn't know why, nor even where the thought came from, but her legs had a mind of their own. She found herself marching away before her brain could rationalize what was happening.

Empty halls stared back at her. Several guards who should have been awake and patrolling the corridors were asleep in chairs or sprawled on the floor. That alone should have been alarming but she only shrugged and kept walking. Her path took her out of the main building and into the stables. Why the stables? She'd always loved horses and took the time to pat one or two in passing. It was much colder here, making her wish for the warm cook fires of the kitchens. Maleela found herself whistling. She missed innocent nights like this. Nights when all her cares faded away and time had little meaning. She passed a pair of dogs, both asleep.

"It seems like everyone is asleep but me," she said to herself.

She rounded the last corner of the stables and darkness took her.

"Be ready. She is on her way," Anienam whispered.

Dorl and Nothol stared skeptically at one another. They felt uneasy. Magic was unnatural and they were now ankle deep in it. Unexplainable forces radiated around the wrinkled old wizard. He either didn't notice or didn't care for their concerns. Anienam Keiss focused on the web he'd painstakingly cast over the people inside the castle. The spell took total concentration. One misstep and all was lost. They'd be dead before they could remount.

None of that mattered to the sell swords. They'd grown up in a world without magic and much preferred to keep it that way. Popular belief was that all Malweir's problems stemmed from magic users. Seeing the strength with which Anienam wielded his craft frightened them. Dorl was the first to look away and was rewarded with his first glimpse of Maleela ambling around the corner and then collapsing.

"Go," Anienam hissed. "What are you waiting for?"

Startled into action, they rushed out and collected her unconscious form. Dorl checked for a pulse and breathed a sigh of relief. She was still alive, contrary to his initial fears.

"Come on, come on," Anienam urged.

Dorl and Nothol gently picked her up and moved as fast as they dared back to the wagon. She was much heavier as deadweight than they imagined. They hefted her up on the count of three where Boen waited with open arms. The Gaimosian snatched her up like a feather and placed her down on the cushions and silks not sold earlier in the day. He chuckled at the thought. They'd come here to steal a princess and wound up making money in the process. Rekka Jel stepped from around the front of the stables, sword in hand. Her eyes never stopped roaming.

"Anything?" Boen asked.

"No. The guards are all asleep."

Anienam groaned. "Doesn't anyone appreciate talent? The whole castle is asleep. They won't stay that way for long though. We need to be back across that drawbridge in a half a glass or it's the gallows for us all."

Boen nodded. "We're ready. Start moving."

The wagon inched forward. Rekka and the sell swords rushed off into the night. Each had a part to play in the escape. Their job was to hurry back and secure the drawbridge in the event the wizard's magic failed. Dirty work, but Bahr decided they were best suited for it. Killing seemed a small matter for those three.

The Sea Wolf looked over his shoulder to where Boen and Ionascu guarded the sleeping princess. "Will she be all right?"

"I don't see why not," Anienam answered. "I have used this spell many times before. She might have a headache when she awakens but will be fine."

"What exactly are you, Anienam Keiss?" he asked curiously.

The wizard snickered. "I would like to think that I have become a friend, but if not I will settle with being very old."

They shared a soft laugh. Neither seemed particularly interested in maintaining the moment. Each noise the wagon made was the sound of thunder in Bahr's ears. He knew the enemy was going to awaken at any moment and attack. Shadows danced in their path, teasing and tempting with a special brand of torment. Time was his foe now as much as any man ever was. One unsure step and it was all over. Bahr did not relish the thought of languishing in a Rogscroft dungeon for the rest of his life.

The main avenue was empty except for them. The wagon covered the ground swiftly, much faster than was realistically safe. Bahr relaxed, if just slightly, as they drove past a stretch of road lined with marble columns. A pair of statues stood sentinel at the end, flanking the road in eternal defiance. Swords in one hand and shields in the other, they faced the plaza just inside the walls. They were heroes of old, back from the days of the kingdom's founding. Bahr was impressed. Each statue was more than four times the size of a man and had deeply defined facial features. He felt guilty passing under their stern gaze.

Dorl and Nothol eased from the shadows, the latter fiercely waving them on. The unnatural silence was unnerving them and Bahr didn't blame them. His skin crawled at the thought of all the possibilities that might go wrong. He snapped the reins and the horses surged ahead. The sell swords jumped on the runners.

"Where is Rekka?"

Nothol pointed ahead. "She's already across the bridge."

"That wasn't part of the plan."

"She didn't say so but I suspect she's out hunting her Dae'shan," Nothol replied more tersely than intended.

Bahr cursed. Her private crusade was the last thing they needed.

Dorl felt the need to defend her actions. "She knows what she's doing."

"She is going to get us all killed," Boen growled.

Anienam said, "He's right. We must hurry."

"Fine. Back to the safe house. Rekka has one glass. After that we are gone," Bahr ordered.

The wagon rolled free of castle Rogscroft and back into the city proper.

Prince Aurec blinked twice, the first dull rays of sunlight tickling his eyelids. He smiled and rolled over.

"Have I ever told you how much I love you?"

There was no reply. The smile faded when he noticed the other side of the bed was empty. Aurec looked around the bed chambers. Her clothing was sitting right where they had left it but her housecoat was missing. He frowned. Maleela was the type of woman who took great pains to look elegant. She would never be caught roaming the castle in naught but bed clothes and a robe. Aurec sensed danger though couldn't tell why. Dressing quickly, the prince snatched up his sword belt and hurried off to find his father. He hoped King Stelskor had the answers he wanted. Aurec found the king in the throne room.

"Father!"

Stelskor looked up from the massive map painted out upon a table. He bore a look of concern. A pair of royal advisors fell silent as the prince approached.

Aurec stopped and bowed respectfully. "I must speak with you. Maleela is missing."

"I had figured as much," his father said with a sigh.

"You knew?"

The king's head dipped lower. "We were violated during the night. None of the night staff remembers anything and those merchants from Delranan who were supposed to have an audience with us this morning are missing."

"Delranan? Why would Badron send merchants on the eve of his invasion?"

One of the advisors stepped forward. "As near as we can tell the princess is the only thing missing."

"The only thing? Watch your tongue. She is not a thing and I will not tolerate such."

"I meant no offense, sire."

Stelskor struggled to contain his sorrow. He knew even if his son failed to that the balance of power was now irrevocably shifted. Badron had no reason to withhold his aggression. It would be an all-out blitz when the Wolfsreik arrived. Stelskor saw glimpses of his city burning in ruins, his citizens raped and murdered.

"I am sorry, my son."

Aurec heard the resignation in their voices but refused to give in so easily. "We must get her back before they make it back to Delranan. We cannot give Badron the upper hand."

Stelskor held a hand up. "Slow down, Aurec. Think this through."

"Every minute we delay lets her kidnappers get further away. I can't lose her."

"We are not going to let him have her," the king replied. "Aurec, you must know one thing. I have feared telling this to you because I know how deep your love is."

"I don't understand."

"Badron may have no love for his daughter but he is using her kidnapping as a call to arms. Our spies tell me that the bastard has twisted his people into a frenzy. Hatred for us is stronger than ever before. Word arrived just this morning. The Wolfsreik is coming."

Aurec was still confused. He knew all this.

"Badron will not let Maleela get back to Chadra Keep alive. He can't risk losing support for this war. He will kill her and blame us. Your love may well be the ruin of us."

Aurec staggered under the weight of the revelation. The love he and Maleela shared never intended such horror. All they wanted was a quiet life and the chance to make something better in this world. Aurec saw those visions fade away to darkness and it was all his doing. He felt betrayed by his emotions. Condemned to become the instrument of his own demise.

"What can we do?" he whispered through the pain.

Stelskor's voice hardened. Resolve strengthened in the old man. "We must take faith in our beliefs. Badron will attack regardless. It is time to gather our full strength and prepare for war."

"But I..."

"Hear me out. Badron is evil. His heart is consumed with greed and an undesirable thirst for power. We might be the first kingdom he unleashes his fury on, but we certainly won't be the last. He wants it all, a kingdom to rival the strength of Averon. Nothing can stop his coming."

"We still have the Pell Darga," Aurec protested.

"They will not be enough. That is not the issue. Right now I want you to take a company and head north."

"North? Father, the mountains lie west."

Stelskor smiled. He was ever proud of his son. Aurec would make a fine king someday. "Precisely why the Delrananians went north. It is the most direct path to the shore.

I believe these thieves have a boat anchored off the coast waiting to carry them home. Reports from Dredl mentioned a Delranan vessel docking a week ago. Rumor has it the vessel was none other than the *Dragon's Bane*."

"That is a risky ploy. We could have compounded the ship and crew."

"I agree, yet the fact remains. Badron is sending us a message. He will suffer no trespass when it comes to blood. Retribution is going to be severe. Assemble your men quickly and push hard. Cut these thieves off and bring Maleela home."

Home. "It shall be as you say, Father," Aurec announced. "I shall return as soon as possible."

"Farewell and be safe, my son."

Aurec wheeled around and stormed out with intent and a fire in his eyes. The most important piece of his life was marching straight into death and he was her only hope. Everything else could wait. Stelskor took a seat, suddenly cold and alone. The reality that he had just sent his only son off to his doom haunted him. These were the days he regretted being king. He looked to his advisors blankly.

"What?" he snapped once he noticed their stares. "I know what I am doing."

At least he hoped so.

The lone figure leaned against the base of a mighty oak that must have been at least two hundred years old. The tree had spawned a small forest and been witness to the birth of a small village that became a kingdom. None of that mattered to the watcher. He was old when the world was young. Some claimed he was a harbinger of darkness, but for himself he wasn't so sure. Good and evil were empty concepts. He simply was what he was.

He watched as first the wagon carrying the young woman he'd hunted through the forests rolled past. A first step in the right direction. Then came the angered and embarrassed princeling and his men at arms. Excellent. Everything was going exactly as Amar Kit'han had predicted. The war was coming and with it the key to unlocking the prison of the dark gods. Malweir was finally going to pay for past sins.

TWENTY-SEVEN

Pursuit

Bahr turned and frowned. The slender cloud of dust was getting bigger, and closer. He had hoped that the reaction to their deeds would take longer. Bahr snapped the reins again and kicked the horses into a faster gait.

"Not a good sign," Boen commented from the back.

Bahr wanted to remain optimistic. "Might just be a precautionary measure."

The big Gaimosian barked out a heartfelt laugh. "I like you, Sea Wolf. The enemy is wise to us. The coast is still too far away. You know what has to be done."

"I know, but I find myself not wanting to do it."

"Bahr, we can't trust Ionascu and his men. Send them back to delay the enemy."

They'd been over this more than once already. The conclusions were almost always the same. Trustworthy or not, Ionascu was still a man of Delranan. He did not deserve to be sacrificed so quickly on suspicion. Boen argued otherwise. This was the perfect opportunity to delay their pursuit and remove a problem.

"It needs to be done," he insisted. "I'll lead them myself if I have to."

Bahr was forced to make a decision; one he wasn't enthusiastic about. "No, I can't risk losing you. Stay with the wagon. I want to hear from Dorl and Nothol before we commit ourselves to murder."

Boen nodded. To him this was an inevitable action. He bore neither love nor animosity for Ionascu, but he also knew that good leaders were sometimes forced to make difficult decisions. Such was the moment. Besides, matters would improve once the spy was eliminated. It took another half a glass for the sell swords to catch up to the wagon. The looks on their faces confirmed Bahr's worst thoughts. He cursed silently. They were so close to the end of the journey.

"Well?"

Dorl spat and wiped his mouth with his sleeve. "A company, maybe less. Looks like the prince himself is leading them."

"Determined bastards, aren't they?" Boen smirked.

Bahr wished he could be as flippant. "The prince complicates things. I don't like this. We need to adjust tactics. If we kill him here Stelskor will make it a point to hunt us down at all costs."

"Don't stray from the path now," Boen cautioned.

Nothol Coll said, "They are under armored and lightly armed. Prince Aurec is leading a raiding party designed to cover great distances at speed. They won't be expecting a head-to-head fight."

Bahr had heard enough. He faced his brother's spy. "Can you do this without losing too many men?"

"Yes. My boys want a shot at revenge. This must be paid for. We have already lost two," he replied tersely. Anger tainted his eyes.

Bahr had sudden misgivings but remained true to his convictions, weak as they were.

"Don't engage them directly. We can't afford to lose you now."

Even Anienam was shocked by this.

"I know how to do my job, Captain. Keep the boat moored long enough for us to get on board," Ionascu snapped.

Boen instinctively reached for his sword, the spy's words were too stern for his liking.

For his part, Bahr kept his emotions in check. He promised, "We'll be there."

Satisfied, Ionascu nodded and rode off with his men. Bahr and the others watched them go. Only a few showed mild interest. Most were glad the mercenaries were gone. The tiny column broke into groups and disappeared into the forest.

Boen spoke first. "Bahr, we are wasting time here."

"I agree. We must get to the *Bane*. The princess will be awake soon and we had best be out to sea when she does," Anienam added.

He looked back over his shoulder to check on their cargo. Princess Maleela lay sleeping comfortably, if unnaturally, in the trance he'd placed her in.

"Ha!" Bahr snapped the reins and the tiny band resumed their long journey to the coast and freedom of the open seas beyond.

The thunder of horses grew increasingly louder. Ionascu struggled to keep his own mount from growing too excited. The last thing he needed was to be discovered so soon. His gaze flickered across to the four men riding with him. Each had their bow drawn and ready. Ionascu smiled, grim and unsure of the pending outcome. Fresh doubts and concern over why he'd volunteered to lead this mission arose. This wasn't his war, regardless of his loyalty to Harnin and the king. Harnin's orders had been precise. Ensure the princess returned safely and accuse Bahr of high treason. Instead, the aging captain manuevered him into an untenable situation. Ionascu knew from experience that it was more than likely going to end badly.

The plan was simple. He figured that the best way to keep too many things from going wrong. They'd split into four groups. He staggered their positions along a narrow deer trail running parallel to a small creek. The intent was for the first group to make contact and then draw the enemy into a twisting series of ambushes deeper into the forest. Strike and run. Cavalry was no good on enclosed terrain. With a little luck they'd be able to keep drawing the enemy in until they had enough wounded to make them quit the field. Ionascu was no fool though. He knew that his plan had only a marginal chance of success.

Thankfully the terrain was in his favor. Large boulders littered the forest. Each ranged in size but the largest could easily conceal several mounted men. The forest itself was old and filled with pine and oak. Scrub brush and saplings were just thick enough to keep a mounted force from charging in at full speed. Natural ditches and depressions turned the forest into a very large obstacle course.

"Ready yourselves," he told his group in a soft voice. "Remember the plan. Kill or wound as many as you can and ride north to the next group. Do not overextend yourselves. Two bolts and escape. If you fall here you will be lost forever. All I can tell you is do not let yourselves be taken alive."

They said nothing. They didn't need to. Each of them was a blooded warrior. Most knew Ionascu's legend on the battlefield and were comfortable with his leadership. He had a reputation as a hard, merciless man. Time disguised how many men he had killed over the years, though estimates whispered close to two hundred. Ionascu was content to let them wonder; he had seen his share of blood and was prepared to shed more, if for no other reason than self-preservation.

"They are almost on us. Aim true and ride hard."

He wheeled his horse to the edge of the boulder so he could get a clear shot. A downed oak tree lay across his front, further camouflaging his men. Prince Aurec rode at the head of his men. They were riding too fast to notice the brief glimpses of enemy archers hiding in the trees. Besides, there was no reason to believe that any of the Delrananians stayed behind to attack. Ionascu smiled. That was precisely the reason he and his men were spread throughout the forest.

The prince's company rode closer. Ionascu poked his head around the boulder and was rewarded with the soft glint of morning sunlight on a rider's steel helm. He saw Aurec for the first time. The man was proud, borderline arrogant. He was also hurt. The love of his life had been ripped from him. All that made him a dangerous man to face. It also made him predictable.

Ionascu drew back on the bow string. The feathers felt familiar to his cheek. The string was taut. He sighted his eyes from finger to bow. His breath came slow, measured. His aim centered on Aurec's chest. But he didn't fire. Dark visions of the future danced just beyond the grasp of his comprehension. He was no great thinker, nor was he of a strong military mind. He did know one thing, however: killing Aurec now would be the worst possible event since Maleela's brother died. His death would serve as a catalyst to set the people of Rogscroft on the paths to vengeance. Right now they were prepared to defend. Badron didn't need them taking up the offensive.

Ionascu shifted aim to the third rider and pushed out a soft breath. His fingers released. The friction of the string scraped against his face. The arrow sped. A cry went up. He delighted to see the rider's arm rise as the arrow struck the gap between neck and chest armor. Warm blood sprayed in a mist as the dying man fell from his saddle. Ionascu reached behind and put another arrow to the string. Three more arrows spit from his left and right. Two hit their targets. He fired again, catching his target in the thigh.

"Ambush!"

Aurec's eyes filled with rage. "Come about and ride them down. Don't let them shoot again!"

His second-in-command drew a mighty broadsword. "Kill them all!"

As one, the Rogscroft cavalry wheeled and charged. Pikes lowered; swords waived in the air. They'd already suffered three dead and two wounded without catching so much as a glimpse of their foe.

Ionascu decided it was time to go. "Fall back!"

His mercenaries broke and ran in an unorganized mass. What they had in courage and sheer tenacity they lacked in cohesion and discipline. Ionascu broke out in the lead, pushing his mount as hard as he dared. Aurec's men did not suffer the same prohibitions. They forced their way into the forest without regard. Vengeance filled their hearts. Blood lust rose. Ionascu practically felt the heat of their anger burning down his neck.

Aurec jerked his head back at the startled cry. He watched in shock as Tonas dropped dead, the black shaft piercing his neck killing him instantly. His horse continued to race. Aurec snarled, realizing the trap. This entire charade was designed to delay them enough to keep his prize from being recaptured. A fool's gambit and he had fallen into it.

"Come about and ride them down! Don't let them shoot again!" he bellowed at the top of his lungs.

Venten drew his broadsword and uncharacteristically cried, "Kill them all!"

The prince smiled grimly. He knew that his captain and closest friend was normally the voice of reason. Venten abandoned reason and let weeks of pent up frustration and the desire to avenge the embarrassment of failing his prince take control. The company charged.

"Mahn, Raste, provide a rear guard. I don't want anyone sneaking up behind us," Aurec ordered before losing himself to the charge.

The two scouts reluctantly obeyed.

Raste turned to his superior and asked, "How can he just ignore us like that now? After all we have done. He needs us!"

"Keep your lips shut and pay attention. This not the place or time," Mahn scolded as he struggled with his own heart's longing.

Aurec's blood stirred. The battle was different from his skulking assault on Chadra Keep. This was hard and fast. He tightened his grip and dug his heels a little harder. The enemy was close. He felt them. He smelled their horses, felt their special brand of excited fear as they desperately sought to escape. Aurec felt his battle rage build. He sorely wanted to punish these men.

"On the right!" Venten cried out.

Aurec watched as another of his men fell dead. He snarled. At this rate his forces would be rendered combat-ineffective by the time they reached the shore. *If we reach it.* The second band of ambushers broke from cover. The prince scowled at the level of efficiency his enemy showed. Suspecting another trap, Aurec changed tactics.

"Venten! Take half of the men and route out the rest of these damned ambushes. I suspect there are more."

Venten nodded. "What about you?"

"I'm going after this group. Try not to kill all them. We need a prisoner for questioning."

"Yes, my lord."

Venten gestured with his sword and half of the column broke off to attack the second group. He had deep reservations towards leaving his prince, but he was the kind of man who carried out every order to the best of his ability. Besides, he reasoned, Aurec was more than capable of taking care of himself.

The Delrananians were clearly taken by surprise by the shift in focus. They were slow to react and barely had the time to displace before Venten's riders crashed into them. Venten slashed at the nearest man, who successfully managed to duck back a fraction of a moment before losing his head. The next wasn't as fortunate. Blood splashed Venten's chest. The body toppled over, an agonized look permanently etched on the face.

Venten reined in for another pass, pausing long enough to briefly survey the battlefield. Two of the enemy lay dead or dying while a third lay slumped over his saddle with a short spear penetrating his back and chest. The fourth and final enemy was riding away at full speed.

"Hold!" Venten bellowed above the clamor of horse and man.

His men slowed and stopped. Fumes of hot breath steamed into the chill morning air. Crimson droplets stained the rocks and leaves underfoot. One of Venten's men suddenly pitched forward. His body landed on its back, cold dead eyes staring up into the grey morning. Venten nudged his horse closer. He made a note of who had died and how. The deep gash running across the man's thigh was enough. Venten's heart grew leaden. It was cold enough not to notice an injury and one like that would bleed a grown man out in less than five minutes.

"Check for wounds," Venten ordered.

He knew the cold was as much of an enemy as swords. He looked back down at the body. *That's how poor Ilmas died. He just didn't pay attention. At least he died quick.*

"We are all good," the senior sergeant reported.

He nodded absently. "I think we've given our foe enough time. Let's go."

The war party stormed off. Vengeance continued to demand.

Bahr let out a breath of relief when the bow of the *Dragon's Bane* came into view. He would never admit it, but he had doubts about it being in the right place. Of course, they could just as easily have missed the mark during the retreat.

"I am impressed," Boen announced from the wagon bed. "How did you know where to go?"

The Sea Wolf gave a devious grin. "I used to do a lot of coastal trading when I was younger. I'd use this cove to ride out bad storms."

The Gaimosian laughed. "You're a tricky old bastard."

"I do what works."

The wagon rambled on. He guessed they still had a little less than a glass before reaching the shore. That bothered him. He wanted to get on his boat and race away from Rogscroft as soon as possible. Bahr felt his troubles starting to get the better of him. He still hadn't mentioned his plans for stealing Maleela away to a safe house rather than give her back to Badron. He guessed the wizard suspected a trick like that but was smart enough to keep his mouth shut. Bahr idly wondered how the others would react.

"We must hurry. Put the princess in my cabin. Rekka, guard the door. No one enters. No one," he ordered.

Boen looked down at the sleeping girl. "I don't think we need to worry much about that. The girl won't be awake until we reach Stouds."

Bahr nodded absently. "Even so, I won't feel safe until we are away from here."

"You have one of those bad feelings, eh?"

"Yes. I think Rekka's Dae'shan is real. I've felt a threat growing in the back of my mind ever since we escaped the castle. It is like we are being constantly watched. I think these Dae'shan have more to do with us than we know. Might be he is responsible for the murder on our journey here as well."

Boen grimaced. He had much the same thoughts but didn't know why. "No one will get on the ship. I'll defend the gangway."

Bahr's nagging feelings grew progressively worse the closer they got to the shore. More than premonitions haunted him. They hadn't seen or heard from Ionascu and his men since Bahr had sent them off. He struggled with mixed emotions about sending them to their apparent deaths. They were men of Delranan after all.

Boen caught the sorrow in the corners of the Sea Wolf's eyes. "You did what you had to," he guessed. "Ionascu knew the risks. They all did. Don't think they rode off without knowing that they stood a good chance they might all die."

"Easy to say. What if they do all get killed?"

The Gaimosian shrugged, indifferent. "So be it. Do not forget they were as much of a threat as the enemy. This was the easiest way, Bahr. Your hands are clean of blood."

Anienam Keiss listened to the conversation. He was amused that neither man seemed squeamish about spilling a little blood to accomplish their tasks and yet here they were arguing about sending bad men to their demise. Still, the wizard kept his mouth shut. He too had premonitions about the Dae'shan. Their return was the coming of a dark storm on the horizon. He felt lost, blind to their actions. A cold wind blew. Anienam Keiss shuddered at the portent.

TWENTY-EIGHT

Reunion

Cold winds howled across the barren plains in stark contrast to the blazing inferno raging unchecked all around. The ground was split in a thousand places. Fissures gaped like leprous lesions. Death ruled here, hidden amongst the broken boulders and dead tree stumps. Ash and grit swirled in small funnels. The very ground bled in pain and eternal suffering. Acidic rain fell from black clouds so thick they blocked out the sun.

Maleela awoke to the flash of lightning. Her head pounded. She was dehydrated and aching from head to toe. Her clothes were torn, burned through in some places. Small cuts crossed her palms and the soles of her feet. Maleela forced herself to get up. She had to find some way out of this nightmare. But every time she tried she wound up back in this same position. A series of nearby low growls forced her to move.

"Run Maleela. This way. Come to me."

She paused. The voice was new. The tone was laden with urgency, despair. It was also soft and kindly. It wants the best for me, she reasoned without knowing why. Maleela reluctantly placed her trust in the voice and ran.

"Quickly, my dear. They are coming for you."

A pair of demons burst from one of the larger fissures. Their bodies were enormous, covered in ripped flesh and boils. Both had overdeveloped muscles practically ripping from their bodies. They were the worst possible thing she could imagine, almost beyond accurate description. They were creatures of torment and pain. Tufts of black hair spouted across their ragged bodies. Glistening swords replaced hands. Neither had eyes or a mouth.

The larger of the two turned his head towards Maleela and pointed. She'd been spotted. The princess ran for her life. The ground trembled under the demon's gait. Her heart quickened. This was the end. There was no way her legs could move fast enough to outdistance these monsters.

"Hurry child!"

Maleela pushed herself harder. Her only thoughts were of Aurec and the comfort of his embrace. Instincts made her look up. Her heart buoyed in hope. A figure stood upon a hill beckoning her. The source of the voice. The man raised his arms and the world blurred by in slow motion. Dark blue glowed from his fingertips. The glow built and shot outward in a series of jagged bolts. They raced past her head, wild strands of hair singed away. The first bolt struck the lead demon full in the chest, bursting it apart with raw power. Flesh and bone flew everywhere.

Maleela reached the feet of the stranger just as he unleashed his fury into the second demon. She collapsed from exhaustion. Darkness took her while the stranger began to glow a blinding white.

"You are safe now," was the last thing she heard.

Kodan Bak screamed in agony as his illusions were defeated. He hadn't expected such powerful counter magic. Up until now none of them believed there were any Mages left in Malweir. It was a gross underestimation changing everything. He had to get back and tell Amar Kit'han of this new twist. All their many long years of plot and toil now stood in jeopardy. The future was no longer certain.

Steam burned off his black robes. What was left of his body was a mass of burns. The lightning had been real. He could have killed a lesser wizard outright. Kodan glanced over his surroundings, wary that his foe might somehow be near. Nothing. Satisfied that he was safe, Kodan Bak stalked off. A familiar tickle itched at the corners of his mind. He smiled. It was the woman from the forest. The one he'd spent the night hunting. She was back aboard their ship. The Dae'shan paused. She was a worthy opponent, but not the main target. If the woman was aboard so too must be the princess and the wizard. Informing Amar Kit'han would have to wait.

Kodan Bak wrapped himself in his shadows and disappeared.

"Welcome back to the land of the living."

Maleela slowly blinked the sleep away. The voice in her head was the same as from her dreams. She opened her eyes and waited for them to focus.

"Are you all right?" he asked.

She groaned. Her body a mass of pain. "Where am I?"

He smiled kindly. "Quite safe, I can assure you."

"You didn't answer my question," she snapped.

Silence. She caught the faint shuffling of feet outside the door. The subtle caress of water sloshing against the hull. She was on a boat. But where?

"You can trust him, Maleela."

She turned her head, eyes wide in shock and disbelief. "Uncle?"

Bahr smiled tightly. The moment was bittersweet. He'd wanted her to be safe, the sole reason for agreeing to Harnin's mad quest. Now he looked into her brown eyes and found that he had merely succeeded in stealing the love from her.

"Yes. It is me."

She ignored the sadness in his voice.

"I don't understand. Why am I here? What are you doing in Rogscroft?"

Anienam Keiss picked out the pleas in her voice and selfishly thanked the gods that he was not Bahr.

"I'm afraid the answers are complicated."

"Please, Uncle."

The Sea Wolf sighed. "You are aboard the *Dragon's Bane*. Your father hired us to rescue you. I took my crew and sailed to Dredl to come and get you. Had I known of Badron's plan beforehand I would not have agreed."

She frowned. "My father wants to take over Rogscroft. He'd been planning a secret invasion. That is why I came up with the idea to kidnap myself."

"I am afraid it goes far beyond just that," Anienam added.

She considered the old man. "You are the one from my dreams."

He bowed. "I am. Anienam Keiss is my name and the pleasure is all mine."

She forgot her situation for the moment. "What were those things chasing me?"

"Very powerful demons summoned from the void. If they had killed you in your dreams you would be damned to wander that world for eternity. I had to save your soul, child."

"My soul?"

Anienam cleared his throat. He'd forgotten that the old beliefs had fallen into the rotting pages of distant memory. The gods and all associated with them weren't even childhood stories anymore. Of course she didn't know about her soul.

"Ah yes. Your soul is the eternal essence of your being. A sense of moral conscience if you will. Each of us has one and we possess inherent traits that either lean towards good or evil. Those demons understood that killing you there would doom you forever. I did what I had to."

Her confusion deepened, almost to the point where she forgot about her second kidnapping. She'd never heard of such a concept. The fact that there was some mystical eternal spark inside her wasn't comforting. Her world grew that much smaller while opening a new theme in her mind's eye. Worse, she now had demons stalking her.

"I have done nothing. Why would these creatures want me dead?" she asked.

"A question I have no plausible answer for. Nor is this the place for such conversations. I shall leave you with your uncle." He laid a soothing hand on her knee. "We will talk later."

The wizard bowed again and excused himself from the cabin. Uncle and niece stood in awkward silence. They were not especially close, much to Bahr's regret. He loved her as his own daughter and would make any sacrifice to ensure her safety and she had not a clue. Badron had done his best to keep them apart, denying him a family. He reminded himself of that and hung his head.

She sensed his sorrow. "Uncle, you have to take me back to Rogscroft. They need my help."

"I am sorry, but it is too late to turn back. Fate has not been kind to either of us."

"It is not too late. We can still save them," she protested. "You know my father is not a good man. Help me, Uncle Bahr. Help me slay him before more lives are lost."

"More?"

She forced down the lump in her throat. Memories of blood and violence drifted up to mock her innocence. She saw her brother lying in a growing pool of his own blood. "The night Aurec came and took me away was a nightmare. They were forced to fight. He didn't want to, but my brother gave him no choice. There was so much blood. I can still smell the death. Every time I close my eyes I can see it. I must go back, Uncle. I have to help him prepare for my father's wrath."

Bahr's heart wept. The answers she so desperately wanted were not within his power to give. "I fear your father's madness goes well beyond vengeance for the prince. The Wolfsreik has been mustered. Badron means to come and take Rogscroft by force."

"Using me as the reason."

"I am afraid so."

She choked out a laugh. "The people will believe him. He's managed to keep his hatred for me a family secret. This is all my fault."

"I don't know why my brother wants Rogscroft so badly. He has lusted after it since we were in our youth. Though I am loath to admit it, Badron has a black heart. The Wolfsreik will not stop until the leadership of Rogscroft is dead and her people on their knees."

She refused to acknowledge the easy defeat. "We must find a way to stop them. The people here have done nothing wrong."

"Perhaps," he admitted, "but there isn't much we can do from here. Our best chance is to get you home and show the people of Delranan that you are safe and there is no justified cause to go to war."

"But Aurec…" she protested.

"Must fend for himself. Maleela, I am sorry, this is the only way."

She struggled to rise but her body hurt too much. She'd lost too much strength thanks to the wizard's spell. Maleela fell back on the soft bed and whispered, "I hate him."

Bahr replied, "I know. Rest now. I'll have Skuld bring you some food. At least that way you can regain your strength."

He excused himself, allowing the totality of what was about to happen sink in. It was the only way he knew how to get her to understand. Maleela struggled to fight back the wave of tears threatening to consume her. She failed.

A brisk wind washed over the decks, pushing new life into the *Dragon's Bane*. Bahr breathed in the sea air. He'd just done an unenviable task and was rewarded with an ache in his stomach. It was quickly becoming clear that he had underestimated the depravity of his brother's intentions. That frightened him. Too many had already died in this mad scheme. Bahr feared for the future of both kingdoms. Unspoken frustrations dominated his conscience. He knew of his brother's dark hunger when they were still children. Knew and did nothing about. Bahr almost blamed himself.

The notion was foolish of course. He was no more to blame than King Stelskor or the fickle hand of chance. Pain and perpetual suffering seemed the course of life here in the frozen north. He idly wondered if there was such turmoil in the south. Surely Averon did not suffer from the same. He could have wished for a different life, but that would be a waste of time. Bahr accepted his life for what it was and vowed to make it better for himself and for his niece.

"You look like a man with too much on his mind."

He looked up to see Boen studying him. "Have you ever felt like the world was crumbling around you and nothing you did mattered?"

The words came out more as a sigh than significant question.

Boen leaned against the rail and stared off into the ocean. "I'm Gaimosian. The world has always been against me."

"I just told my niece that her father wants to destroy everything she knows. Somehow I envisioned my life turning out a little differently."

"Few of us get choices and the ones we do get we don't like. Life is hard, Bahr. We struggle and fight from the moment we're born until the day we die. Be strong. The hour is yet early. This will get better."

"I hope so. She deserves a better life."

Boen laughed. "Don't we all?"

"Yeah," Bahr roguishly admitted. "I suppose we do."

"Good. Now you understand that we have a decision to make. We can't wait forever for Ionascu to return."

The Sea Wolf sighed again. "I know. I figure we can't stay past midday. Who knows how many troops Aurec will be able to bring down on us by then."

"I agree. I also believe that they aren't coming back. He's a quick man. There would have been a runner by now."

Bahr wasn't so sure. "I still don't like the idea of abandoning my countrymen."

"You pointed out that they all belong to Badron and his one-eyed flunky. Don't make the mistake of thinking any one of them wouldn't hesitate leaving you behind."

They both knew the answer. A man like Ionascu would have already set sail. Bahr, however, chose to live his life with a sense of pride. Using that quality as his gauge, he made his decision.

"Midday we sail."

Boen merely nodded. This wasn't his ship or his mission. His singular purpose was to keep Bahr alive. It didn't mean he approved of the call, but it was never his to make.

"Riders approaching!" Dorl Theed shouted.

All heads on deck snapped around to see the haggard forms of four riders coming at them hard. Bahr spotted

Ionascu. The look on his face was pure terror. Bahr cursed. Four out of eighteen. That was all that returned. Even more blood had been spilled because of a madman's dream.

TWENTY-NINE

A Long Debate

Venten threw the wounded man down to his knees and lowered his sword to the base of the man's neck to ensure he didn't make any sudden moves. The prisoner winced at the flash of pain. A deep gash ran down his right thigh. Venten slapped a hasty bandage over the wound lest the man bleed out before being questioned.

"I don't have need of another corpse," Aurec told his best friend as the other half of the raiding company arrived.

Venten spat. "Of course, my lord, though it's no big loss."

Aurec squeezed out a strained smile. "Your opinion is well known. Can he still walk?"

"Not well. He definitely needs a horse to get him back to the city."

Aurec reined back his horse and slid from the saddle. He grimaced at the sight of the prisoner's mangled thigh, reminded of his own pain. The battle had not been a kind one. He allowed his hardened eyes to meet his prisoner's.

"What is your name?" he asked.

The mercenary looked down and remained silent.

"There is no harm in a name. All your friends are dead and you'll be joining them soon if we don't get that wound treated."

"I'm not telling you nothing," the mercenary ground out.

Venten backhanded him across the side of his face. "That's a prince you're speaking to, scum."

"Not my prince," he replied. Dark malevolence lined his eyes.

Venten drew back to strike again. "Mercenary filth."

"That's enough, Venten," Aurec cautioned. He knelt in front of the mercenary. "My friend does not have the same tolerances that I do. Now, your name."

Laughter mocked him.

Aurec leaned in closer. "I'm not asking again."

"There is nothing you can do to me. I know that I am already dead."

"No, you only think you are," Aurec stunned him. "The way I see it you have two choices. You can either cooperate and tell me what I need to know about the coming invasion or I make you feel so much pain you'll beg for death."

The mercenary didn't even blink. His arrogance forced Aurec to smirk. "Are you sure this is the way you want to do this?"

"The only way that makes sense to me. Do your worst, little princeling."

The prince smiled darkly and spun away. "Venten, put a tourniquet on that wound and bind his hands. I want him in the dungeons by nightfall."

"What about the others?"

"We left a few alive in the hopes they'll lead us back to their camp."

Venten scratched the corner of his mouth. "I doubt there is a camp. We are too close to the sea. Common sense says they have a ship nearby."

"More than likely," Aurec agreed. "But we have a duty to find out. Take your half of the men and return home. I'll scout the shoreline."

Venten started to protest. "I'm not going to go back and explain to your father why I left you out here."

"No buts, my friend. Your group did all the fighting. The men deserve a break. I will be fine."

"As you wish," Venten conceded. "Hurry back. The king will be anxious for your report."

"We'll be back as soon as we can."

The gentle sounds of waves lapping against the shore greeted Aurec and his men like an old friend. Advance scouts had already returned with negative reports. The beaches were empty. Still, Aurec led them on. He was tired. They all felt it. They'd spent the better part of the day fighting and hunting the

Delrananian mercenaries. Each man knew they were successful, but a sense of emptiness hung over them like a pall. The mission remained a failure until they had proof that the entire enemy had been destroyed.

"Anything useful to tell me?" Aurec asked.

Mahn shook his head. "Nothing but a few blood trails. There's a broken sword but not much else."

"They had a boat."

"It looks that way. We saw tracks from a long boat."

Tears welled in the corners of his eyes. Aurec couldn't bring himself to say it. Maleela was gone. Emotion was the last thing he needed. He still had a duty to his men.

"We'll get her back," Mahn whispered.

Aurec forced a smile. "Form up behind us. We're going home. I'm sure Venten is fuming right now with me gone."

He led the column back, confident that the danger had passed. Aurec's mind was on everything except for what he was doing. Kidnapping Maleela was the spark responsible for igniting this building storm. All the kingdoms in the north knew of Badron's propensity for spontaneous violence. His wrath was legendary, even amongst the Dwarf clans. There was no doubt as to his reactions. The king of Delranan had been embarrassed, and worse. His bloodline was destroyed.

Aurec regretted the killing of his counterpart, but the man gave him no choice. He frowned at the memory. No one was supposed to have died. He made that specifically clear to Maleela and Lord Argis both when they'd come to him at the behest of the underground movement. One death and all their carefully crafted plans were in danger of being undone. Aurec realized one future truth: there was no way Rogscroft could survive, even with the aid of the Pell Darga. Worse, he didn't know what to do to stop that end from happening.

"Our scouts in the lowlands report the Wolf soldiers are moving," Sint Ag told the war leader.

Cuul Ol's heart darkened at the news. This was a war he'd long dreaded. He looked to his fellow warriors. All bore the same concerned look. For that he was glad. Distressing times demanded strong will.

"How many?" he finally asked.

"Many. We cannot fight them and win."

Cuul Ol stood abruptly and walked away from the warmth of the fire. The warmth of darkness consoled him. Winter threatened to be bad this year. He gazed up at the veiled stars and prayed the snows came early. Wisps of clouds marred an otherwise perfect night. His people held strength, but there was no amount available to oppose the will of the Wolf soldiers. The Pell Darga were familiar with these soldiers, clashing numerous times over the course of their long histories.

Sint Ag continued, "They come fully armed. Their horses are well armored. This is no skirmishing force."

"No. They come for war. This time will be different."

Murmurs swept through those assembled.

"We will fight nonetheless," growled a large man of too many summers.

Cuul Ol sighed. "Yes. We will fight, but not the way in which you think, Durgas."

"What do you mean?" Sint asked.

"The Wolf soldiers do not come to make war on us. They go to attack Rogscroft. This is our advantage."

Durgas stood. His skin was dark and leathered. His face bore the creases of a great veteran. "Then the Wolf soldiers are not our problem. Let the lowlanders kill each other."

"We will not abandon our allies, Durgas."

Durgas shrugged. "It is their destiny. They bring war upon themselves. Why should Pell Darga die for any of them?"

"We sealed a pact with the blood son of Stelskor. The tribes of the Pell Darga owe him a debt. This is our way, Durgas. To go back on our word means dishonor. I will not be named so."

Durgas snarled at Cuul Ol and addressed the others. "You all know me. I am no coward, nor am I shamed by my words. Let the lowlanders fight each other. We have suffered enough at their hands. This is not our war."

"Your words make sense to all of us," Cuul Ol surprised him by saying. "But there comes a time when every people must look beyond themselves. That hour has at last fallen on the Pell. Brothers, I have given our pledge of support to Prince Aurec. The tribes will meet this foe, but on our own ground."

Sint Ag added, "We do not have the strength to face them."

"I have no intentions of it. The enemy is strong. Their weapons and armor will slow them down where our own warriors can move freely. We can strike more often and melt back into the mountains. Our pact is to strike their supply lines and reinforcement columns. No tribe or war party is to attack a large unit. This is the only way."

Cuul Ol fell silent with the knowledge that the others would differ to his logic. They were fierce warriors and smart enough to know when victory was next to impossible. Striking the supply lines would prove difficult and equally rewarding to the war effort. His warriors were up to the challenge. Even should the main army try to corner them and counterattack there was no real danger. The Pell would disappear back into their mountain shadows.

"What of the horse soldiers about to gain the passes?" Durgas finally asked in quasi defeat.

The war chief gave him a toothy grin. "Let them pass. Aurec and his army will be waiting. Each of you should go and ready your warriors. The enemy will soon be here."

"Has he said anything yet?"

Venten shook his head. "No, my lord. He remains defiant."

Stelskor watched the prisoner with great interest. "Perhaps he knows nothing of importance to us."

"There is little doubt the man is a mercenary, but he has to know more than he lets on."

For his part, the mercenary ignored them. He focused on any sign of weakness that might lead to his escape from this prison. The prince scared him, surprisingly enough. The king and his henchman were plain, inexperienced in this sort of business but the prince showed almost too much restraint.

Stelskor moved close enough to the bars to make his guards flinch. "Do you know who I am?"

"That little brat princeling's father."

"I am the king of Rogscroft. Even a mercenary should know better when addressing such," he admonished.

The mercenary sneered but was otherwise unfazed. Death was already a conclusion. "My apologies, king, but a man in chains doesn't much feel like entertaining customs."

Stelskor backed away a step. "Perhaps some time here in our dungeons will cool your temper. I look forward to your stay."

Silence. The king and his men spun and headed towards the ironbound entrance door. Stelskor was the last to leave. He cast a withering glance over his shoulder, silently offering one final chance. "You are the kind of man who is worth the coin paid you. I appreciate that. How much has Badron paid you?"

"Why?"

The word bounced off the slime-slickened walls. It was more accusation than question.

"I can use men such as you in the future. You are a mercenary after all."

The door slammed shut leaving the prisoner shackled in near perfect darkness with misery his sole companion.

"He will be a tough one to break," Stelskor told Venten halfway down the hall.

"All men have two things, sire. A price and a breaking point. If one does not work we will try the other. He will fold, we just need to try harder."

"Will he be of any use when he breaks?"

Venten shrugged nonchalantly. "He is mercenary scum. I would put no faith in him."

"Anyone can be bought, Venten, as you have so thoughtfully reminded me."

"All the more reason not to trust him. He is of Delranan blood. No matter what happens, he is the enemy."

Stelskor disagreed. "He is a prisoner of war. Perhaps you are right. Break him, but do not treat him so bad as to give fuel to Badron's rage. I want to know everything he knows. Troop strengths, timetables. All it. Our position has grown perilous if Badron's killers can sneak inside our castle and steal with impudence."

Venten didn't add the obvious fact that they were the ones who had precipitated this action by doing the very same thing less than a month ago. Curiously, the invaders had killed no one during their raid.

"He will break," Venten confirmed.

The king gently gripped his arm. "Do what must be done."

Venten waited until the king and his retinue were gone before letting a wicked smile crease his face. He quickly summoned the jailor. He was going to enjoy this.

Prince Aurec rode with a mixture of sorrow and disappointment. Not even the sight of the castle his great grandfather had built offered solace from the misery consuming him. Maleela was gone. The enemy was sending their entire army. His people were not ready. He had failed. The only thing he couldn't figure out was what had gone wrong. He'd gone to Delranan to save the woman he loved from a horrible life and succeeded in bringing war to both kingdoms.

The idea that he alone was responsible for the calamity befalling the northern kingdoms was ridiculous. Badron needed no encouragement to unleash his hatred upon the world. The fact that the vaunted Wolfsreik had been so easily assembled and deployed was testament enough. Aurec's guilt should have been absolved, but he felt worse. He failed and his people would suffer for it. Aurec couldn't decide which was worse, the guilt or the pain. Loud cheers brought him out of his self-induced misery. Aurec looked up in surprise at the hundreds of people lining the main avenue cheering his return.

He stared in disbelief as the people of Rogscroft, his people, celebrated what they believed to be a triumphant return. He wasn't a hero, and he certainly didn't deserve such praise. What he didn't know was that word of his victory had spread through the city. It gave them hope, a fire to keep them warm before the coming storms. He had no choice. Aurec reluctantly smiled and waved back.

"This is incredible," one of the younger soldiers said to his friend.

Aurec genuinely smiled at that. "Enjoy this moment, trooper. We've won our first victory in what promises to be a long war."

Another great cheer erupted through the crowds. The people had hope.

THIRTY

The Noose Draws Tighter

"Do you believe my father cares whether I live or die, Uncle?" Maleela snapped.

She was wrapped in a heavy bearskin robe. The autumn wind was harsh, lashing specks of ice across the *Dragon's Bane*. The prow broke the waves as a small flock of gulls floated off the port side. The waters were capped in white froth.

Bahr kept his gaze on the darkening horizon. It was the same argument they'd been having since setting sail. "You know how I feel about your father."

"Why do you insist on returning me to him?"

Her voice strained from the hours spent crying. She cringed at the thought of the horrors her father was capable of unleashing. Ever she'd been a thorn in his side. He sought conquest and fortune while she desired only peace and the chance to live life like her mother would have wanted. All that was lost now.

Bahr wasn't sure how to respond this time. He loved Maleela like a daughter, making it harder to do what must be done. He suffered, felt her pain. Worse, he didn't know what to tell her to calm her down.

"Nothing has gone right since I accepted Harnin's offer," he finally said. "All I wanted was to save you from your kidnappers. I never dared to dream that you had fallen in love with young Aurec. The whole mess is a disaster."

She reached out to touch his hand. "He's given me everything my father never found it in his heart to do."

"Everything except a father's love."

Maleela forced a smile. "You've done that."

"Ah lass, if only you'd been born mine."

"Uncle, you and I both know there is no point in wondering what if."

He gave her an approving look. "You've grown into a fine woman. Your mother would have been proud."

A small tear escaped the corner of her eye. "Don't take me back. I cannot live with that man. His hate gnaws away at my resolve."

"I'm sorry Maleela, but I just can't see the alternative. Returning you back to Badron can end this nightmare before it begins."

"There is another way," she carefully said.

"How do you mean?"

She cleared her throat and met the questions in his eyes. "More people are opposed to my father's rule than you might think. A movement is underway to remove him from the throne and repair our kingdom."

"That's treason!" Bahr blurted out.

He never thought he'd see the day when his niece would advocate overthrowing her own father. Worse, he hadn't even heard so much as a whisper of this movement until now. Bahr suddenly felt as if the wind was knocked out of him.

"What are you talking about?" He struggled to keep the rest of the crew from hearing the shock in his voice.

Maleela stole a glance around the deck. All it took was the wrong person finding out and it was all over. "Please keep your voice down. I do not know who I can trust yet."

"At least you're smart enough to recognize that much. Harnin has at least one agent aboard." He left out the part about the murder at the beginning of the voyage.

"Harnin is almost as much of a threat as my father. He wants the throne for himself."

"He's been your father's closest supporter for years," Bahr reasoned. "I can't believe such."

"He agrees with everything my father says and does but I have seen the secret longing in his eyes. He wishes to make his own name. Harnin would sell out in a heartbeat and steal the throne."

"How do you know of this?"

"One of the council of lords has joined us. It was he who helped Aurec to get inside Chadra Keep. He's grown tired of the subtle tyranny my father represents. And no Uncle, I am not going to give you his name. Not yet at any rate. Let it suffice to know that the underground is growing and we have friends."

"All this means nothing now, I am afraid. The Wolfsreik should be ready to march by now. Harnin gave us a timeline and we're already past due."

The color drained from her face. She whispered, "Then it is already too late."

"I'm afraid so. The wizard tells me that Badron has already set the wheels in motion," Bahr said in a voice laden with regret.

He naturally assumed a hefty portion of the blame. Bahr understood his brother's appetites more than anyone and had done nothing to stop them.

"We can still take the kingdom and deny my father the resources he needs," she quickly replied.

He shook his head. "You're going to kill a lot of your countrymen by doing so. The soldiers are our people too, regardless of how you view them. They fight because they must. I'd be willing to bet almost none of them know Badron's true intentions. We cannot abandon them so far from home and in hostile territory. Think this through."

"I have. We need to move now and stop my father from destroying both kingdoms. Aurec and his father are kind. Once the Wolfsreik surrenders they will be allowed to return home," she stated tersely.

Bahr scowled at his niece. She'd grown much since the innocent child he fondly recalled. Life had been unkind to her and it showed in her actions. "How do you plan on stopping this without destroying our own home?"

"I don't know yet."

Ionascu threw the empty bottle against the bulkhead and reached for another. Drunk, he only wanted to get drunker. Sleep beckoned, but every time he closed his eyes he watched the slaughter of his men. They glared accusingly. Ghosts demanded to know why he still lived and they didn't. Ionascu drank deeply and fought back the tears. Dead. They were all dead.

"For what?" he shouted.

Footsteps came from behind.

"What are you talking about?"

Ionascu spun to find Dorl Theed near. He swung his head sorrowfully. "We didn't even kill the prince."

Dorl noticed the half-empty bottle in his hands and the stench of alcohol. He sighed and slouched down against his better judgment. "I didn't know the prince was chasing us."

"The boy led the attack. We killed a few, but the rest slaughtered my men. I should have died with them, Dorl."

Dorl Theed didn't really have the time to worry about a man who only felt sorry for himself and was a confirmed spy. Still, his heart ached at the thought of the agony Ionascu suffered.

"We did what had to be done," Dorl told him. "We all knew the risks from the very beginning. The princess is safe and we'll be back in Chadra soon."

Ionascu glared at him. "Easy for you to say. I didn't see any of your friends dead in the forest."

"I didn't see any of your men inside the castle when we sprang the princess. You need to put that bottle down and get some sleep," Dorl snapped.

"Get away from me and mind your own business."

They sat in silence for a moment. Both men were on the verge of coming to blows. It was Dorl who finally gave in. He rose and stalked away. Ionascu took another long drink.

"What was all that about?" Nothol Coll asked his friend once he was back on deck.

Dorl cast an angry glance back down the stairs. "Nothing. I figured he needed to get the pain off his chest."

"And?"

"Guess I was wrong. What's going on up here?"

Nothol said, "Bahr wants us to meet him in his cabin. He claims to have some new information to share with us."

"Did he say about what?"

"No, and he's being too secretive about it for my liking."

The sell sword looked unexpectedly at his friend. "That doesn't sound like you. You're supposed to be the sensible one."

"Come on, we're already late," Nothol replied.

Last to enter, Dorl frowned when he realized there were no more seats. His legs were sore and he still wasn't used to the rock and sway of the ocean. Damned boats, he cursed for the hundredth time that day. Folding his arms across his chest, Dorl leaned against the nearest wall and looked around. There were no smiles. The princess fidgeted in her chair. Bahr drummed calloused fingers on the table. He felt like a tiny island on the edge of a hurricane.

"Close the door," Bahr instructed.

Anienam Keiss waited for the cedar door to snap shut before whispering the words of a concealment spell. He gave Bahr the go-ahead once he was satisfied their words were shielded.

"I'm going to get straight to the point. Matters have changed drastically for us."

"In one day?" Dorl asked skeptically.

"Yes. In one day. Princess Maleela has informed me that her father has always intended on going to war with Rogscroft. What we did holds no bearing whatsoever. Further complicating matters is a group of growing dissidents who want Badron removed from the throne."

"How close is this to civil war?" Boen asked. His loyalties to Bahr only stretched so far.

"I don't know but the outcome will be disastrous if it comes to that. Badron will tear Delranan apart to regain total control."

Rekka Jel added in a quiet voice, "It is the people who will suffer."

Bahr agreed. "I can't allow him to do this for that reason. A rebellion must not take place."

Maleela stifled a gasp from the corner she sat in.

"What do you need from us?" Nothol asked.

"Your help. We land in Delranan in two days. Princess Maleela will take me to the leaders of the underground where I will try to talk them out of their decisions."

"Uncle, you can't!" she blurted out.

Collective shock rippled through them. Bahr felt his carefully crafted deception crumble around him. Mouths dropped open. Eyes opened wide.

Dorl was the first to react. "Did she just…?"

Bahr was left with no choice but to confront. "Yes. Badron is my brother."

The sell sword blinked twice. "Whoa."

"My brother and I have never liked one another. We came to an agreement long ago. He stays out of my way and I leave him alone. He rules Delranan and I have the seas. It's been that way for almost thirty years."

"Who is the older brother?" Boen guessed.

"I am."

The admission would carry potential repercussions for months to come if it left the ship. Even Nothol Coll's eyes widened in surprise.

"So… you should be king," he stammered.

Bahr offered a sad smile. "My father did not see it so, and his decision is one I feel perfectly fine with. I have never wanted to be king. It is not in my nature."

Maleela, suddenly weighted with guilt, stood. "Uncle Bahr, I apologize for what I said but you have a chance to put an end to this madness. You are the heir to the throne, not my father."

"It is an empty throne. I would not take it even if there was no other choice," he argued perhaps a little too harshly.

Anienam Keiss added, "It appears to me that there is no other choice. The future of Delranan may well rest in your hands."

"I said I don't want it. I may not have much love or respect for my brother, but I will not be branded a traitor."

"If Badron tears his kingdom apart and you do nothing to stop it, won't that make you a traitor to your people?" the wizard pressed. "There comes a time in all our lives when we must look beyond the borders of our own constraints. It is for the greater good."

Anienam paused to look at each of them. "The captain's secret is now on the table, but there are many yet to be revealed. The Dae'shan have indeed returned to Malweir and all life is in jeopardy. It is no accident that I have come to Delranan during this time. I must get back to the ancient temple of Athonos. It is the only way we have a chance of winning before the shroud of darkness falls."

"Winning what?" Dorl asked. "There is nothing that we need to win. The princess is safe and our jobs are done."

Boen added, "I agree. We did what we came to do. My contract with Bahr is fulfilled."

Bahr felt the wind go out of him. He suddenly lost the urge to fight. All this had become too much to bear. It was the old fears he had been running from his entire life. Memories of his father's chastisement came rushing back. Nothing he did was ever good enough. His dreams were naught but childhood fancy. All his life he struggled to find acceptance in his father's eyes but there was only lingering disappointment. No matter what he did, Bahr could never be as good as his brother.

The Sea Wolf slipped from his tormented memories enough to realize what was happening around him.

"Don't you understand? Badron must be stopped if the Dae'shan are to be defeated!" Anienam fumed.

"How do we know what you tell us is true? You have more secrets than all of us combined," Nothol fired back.

Rekka Jel slammed a tiny fist onto the aged wooden table and shouted, "What hunted me in the forest? What killed the man on this boat? Ghosts? I do not believe in ghosts. But I have seen the Dae'shan. Them I believe in."

The comment snapped Dorl's mouth shut before he could comment. He shot her a wry look but otherwise remained quiet.

"Enough of this!"

They quieted and glared at the captain. His voice was strong and authoritative, echoing from the corners of the cabin.

He had had all he could take. Decades of pent up aggressions and wasted opportunities finally won free. Bahr stepped from his family's shadow for the first time.

"Delranan is my kingdom. I have given everything in her name and asked little in return. My fate is sealed. I will go back and meet with this underground. The decent people of the land deserve no less. Like you said, Anienam, there comes a time when we must look past our own selfish interests."

Maleela let a bright smile sprawl across her face.

"I hold none of you accountable. You are free to go as you see fit once we dock," he continued.

He took no comfort from their surprise. Each was now forced to come to terms with their own inner demons and decide what was more important: themselves or an entire population.

THIRTY-ONE

A King Falls

"I had wondered when you planned on returning to me," Badron calmly said as the ethereal figure of the Dae'shan materialized.

Amar Kit'han made no move. He had evolved beyond the simple whim of kings. Disdain poured from him. The Dae'shan glared back at the king, arms folded within his billowed robes.

"Am I supposed to guess what you want?" Badron asked once he grew bored. His initial fear of these supernatural beings was subsided, though lingering deep within. Having decided to accept their offer, he found this new strength empowering.

"Badron King, matters have changed beyond our sphere of control. Your daughter is now on her way home," he replied tersely.

Badron leaned forward. His mind raged silently. "You are not Kit'han. Who are you and why have you come to me unbidden?"

Pelthit Re nodded approvingly. *This one just might hold potential.* "Very astute of you, king. My name is Pelthit Re. Amar Kit'han is my," a treacherous pause, "brother, for lack of a better term."

Badron snorted. He was in no mood for foolishness. "Another one. I do not approve of these games your kind insists on playing. One might think you a blight against humanity."

"Take heed with your tone, king. I am not my brother. I have no grievance with ending your life prematurely."

Darkness swarmed out from his bony form. Badron ducked backward as waves of pain lashed into him. Fingers of fire lanced into his muscles, penetrating down through the marrow of his bones. He cried out but the Dae'shan had shielded the room with magic. He only stopped when Badron raised a weak hand in surrender.

"Enough," he gasped. Smoke burned from his flesh.

Pelthit Re folded his arms back over his chest and waited for Badron to rise. "Do not doubt me again."

Anger flashed behind his eyes. "What is it you expect of me?"

"Your people must not be allowed to see her alive. She is a danger to all you have planned. There is but one way to solve this situation."

A small sense of horror sprang to life deep inside. "You want me to kill my own daughter?"

"You have spent your life with nothing but hatred for this girl. Killing her is your best hope for the continued success of your plans."

Badron felt insulted at the coldness in his tone. "What you ask I am unable to give. I may hate her, but I will not raise my blade against her. She is my own flesh and blood and I will not willingly strike her down."

Pelthit Re slumped his shoulders. "Then we have already lost. Her princeling lover readies his people for your war. Your invasion will suffer greatly."

Anger finally boiled over. Badron smashed his fist into the wall. "That royal bastard is the reason war comes to them in the first place! He broke into my home and killed my son. For that I vow to kill every man, woman, and child in Rogscroft. My revenge will be absolute."

"Not if your daughter returns alive."

Badron narrowed his eyes. "You already know my answer."

Pelthit Re paused, rehearsed and manicured. "There is another way."

"I'm listening."

Badron turned his gaze to the window as the Dae'shan outlined his nefarious plan. The first hint of sunlight cracked the far horizon. There was a small measure of comfort in the rising sun. Once, long ago, he enjoyed this time of day. But that was before his beloved wife had been killed. *Ah Rialla, why did you have to leave me?*

Pelthit Re finished and studied the king's facial movements with mild interest. He recognized fear and uncertainty, but there was more. Longing? Perhaps a sense of emptiness dating back years? The Dae'shan ignored it. He'd done what was necessary to propel the future. With a little luck, Amar Kit'han would never know of his involvement. Pelthit Re knew he was taking a big chance in forcing Badron to act so rashly.

"I cannot afford to keep prisoners at Chadra Keep. It is too dangerous. None of those men are loyal to the throne," Badron finally concluded.

"Every man has a price, king. All you have to do is discover what that price is."

Badron shook his head. "No. There are too many variables. It would be best to accuse them of treason and be done with it."

"The final decision is yours, of course, though I must caution you on one matter. The army must march before your brother and daughter return."

"To what purpose? Your argument is flawed. There is no need for haste if I am going to condemn my brother."

Pelthit Re already knew this and it didn't fit into their plans. "The Wolfsreik is the issue, not your blood. Every delay is a day wasted. Your enemies are preparing for you. Do not hesitate. Give them what they want. Send in your armies and raze that city to the ground. It is the only way to ensure success."

"Time is now my enemy as well," Badron mused. "The list grows longer."

"Ever is the way of mortal life."

King Badron summoned up the courage to stare down the Dae'shan. It took every ounce of his strength to meet those cold, pale eyes. His knees went weak. Doubt flickered in his thoughts.

"I do not trust you, Pelthit Re. You would wield me like a sword with one hand and then cast me down as soon as I am no longer needed. Why me? Why now?"

Resisting the urge to lash out and crush the spark from Badron's heart, Pelthit Re simply replied, "Because you are the one. My masters have seen your potential and know that you can be the instrument of their freedom. There are things I do not take upon myself to question."

"Leave me now if you will. I have much to think on," Badron said weakly.

Pelthit Re bowed. "Do not think too long. Time flees from your grasp even as you struggle to understand."

He wrapped the shadows around himself and disappeared.

"Damnation," Badron scowled. "What have I gotten myself into?"

Only the gentle sounds of the winds kissing his ancient Keep answered him. Badron felt truly lost, and not for the first time. His lust for power was being checked by prudence. These Dae'shan frightened him almost to the point of abandoning his plans. The king of Delranan sighed his frustrations and went in search of Harnin, and answers.

"Inform the general that I will be there personally to oversee the first units deploy," Harnin told Argis.

Argis asked, "Who rides with them? There should be a strong command presence from the king's circle."

"That is for the king to decide. He has yet to let me know."

Argis shifted uncomfortably.

"Is there anything else, Lord Argis?" Harnin accused.

"We have heard no word of the mission to rescue the princess. Does the plan to invade still stand if she is rescued?"

Harnin frowned suspiciously. "Whatever the king decides is his business. He is the ruler of this kingdom. It is for us to obey his commands."

"I am not debating that legitimacy. I merely think the men have a right to know before they go into battle."

"What exactly should they know, Argis?" came Badron's booming voice.

Both captains turned and bowed to their king.

Harnin cleared his throat. "Lord Argis and I were debating if the army needs to know about the quest to rescue Princess Maleela before they deploy."

"I do not think we should worry about matters that do not concern them. The coming campaign is going to take all their strength and martial prowess. Let them concentrate on the fight. We can worry about those other matters."

"Yes, sire," they answered in unison.

Badron said nothing more on the matter, but his suspicions were already raised. He knew Harnin was as deep in this mess as himself. Murdering the house jarl went a long way in securing his silence. Argis was another matter. He could easily turn into a dangerous liability. The king stared once at his trusted captain. The time was fast approaching when those he deemed unreliable would have to be culled.

He turned slowly, fixing his gaze on Harnin. "What is the status of my army? Are they ready to begin the march?"

"Enough of them are."

"Meaning what exactly?" Badron asked.

"Sire, General Rolnir says he is close to seventy-five percent strength right now. He believes, as do I, that we are strong enough to secure a foothold in Rogscroft and begin combat operations before winter sets in."

"The sooner we attack the better. I am tired of being mocked by those lesser sons," the king hissed. "Does the general give an estimate on how soon the rest of the army can deploy?"

"He is confident that they can be underway within the month."

"That is unacceptable. The Wolfsreik's strength lies in a full-combat contingent, not scraps of units." Badron struggled to keep his anger checked.

"Delranan is a large kingdom. It takes time to assemble so large a force with arms and supplies," Harnin protested.

"I would have thought the supplies had been collected from the first muster. Are you telling me that my best commanders and advisors are incompetent?"

Harnin offered no answer. He knew Badron well enough that there was no point in arguing.

"Inform General Rolnir I will be riding with the main body and I expect him to have his army in order before we leave."

"Sire," Harnin nodded.

"And Harnin, I fully expect to be moving before sunset."

Badron stalked off, leaving both men to wonder what had turned his mood so foul.

Rolnir crumbled the message and threw it angrily to the ground. His adjutant, Piper Joach, looked up expectantly.

"The bloody king has decided to join the main army group," Rolnir scowled.

Piper laughed. "He must have great confidence in us."

"That's not the problem, Piper. You and I both know he's only going to be in the way. I might as well hand over command to him and stay home." Rolnir snatched his canteen and drank deeply. "Still, better him than that idiot son of his. We'd never make it beyond the border with him in charge."

"Not all us are born to lead men into battle."

The general found reason to laugh. "Neither one of them have much martial potential. Badron might prove to be an issue. I think I am going to need you to run interference once we cross the mountains."

Piper shrugged nonchalantly. "That shouldn't prove a problem. Stelskor's pickets and scouts are going to give us a handful until we can get enough combat power on line for the advance."

A company of light cavalry rode by. The looks on their faces whispered an amused tale. All the rhetoric of king and kingdom was past. They were heading for the front lines, expecting to be the first in combat. Young men and old, they were carried a mixture of bravery and fear. Dread anticipation filled the recruits as veterans idly wondered who was going to live and die.

"That will be the most dangerous time. You have to hold until I can get the first infantry battalions deployed," Rolnir explained.

It wasn't necessary. Piper was the second most competent man in the army. He was one of the best of the new generation. He was also the heir to the army.

"We'll hold," Piper answered confidently.

Rolnir smiled. "I have no doubts, my friend."

He laid a reassuring hand on Piper's shoulder. "You'd best get out of here. The king will arrive shortly and I'd just as soon have your vanguard as far ahead as possible."

Piper nodded. "Sir, I will see you in Rogscroft."

Rolnir saluted even while questioning if they would. Wars were never easy. Nor was placing your friends in harm's way ahead of you. Rolnir trusted in their training and discipline to see them through.

"All right people, fall in!" Piper barked to his command. "Sergeant Major, get the ranks in order. We leave now."

Soldiers scrambled. Horses neighed and pranced in tune with their master's urgency. An excitement settled over them all. Weeks of preparation had come down to this one moment. The vengeance of the Wolfsreik was finally set to be released. The army was going to war. Corporals and sergeants barked orders as the company formed up.

"The company is formed, sir," Sergeant Major Bors announced proudly.

The playfulness of the encampment was gone. One hundred and twenty light cavalrymen sat in ranks of ten. Sunlight gleamed from the polished silver helms and breastplates. Barbed pikes rested in stirrups, dressed through the ranks. Every last man in the company bore serious looks. Many struggled with the fact that not all would return. Such was the eternal debate of the soldier. The uncertainty should have bothered them, yet it was the furthest thing from their minds. Gone were thoughts of family and friends. All that mattered was the man to the left and right.

"Gentlemen, my brave soldiers. Today we embark on the grand quest. Rogscroft has stolen the sole remaining heir to the throne. The king, your king, has declared war! We are marching to the enemy lands to make them pay for their crimes," Piper paused to look as many of them in the eye as possible. "The honor of first blood belongs to you!"

A great cheer arose.

"Sergeant Major!"

Bors edged forward. "Company….attention! By platoon, forward…. march!"

Piper and Bors rode at the head of the column as the vanguard of the Wolfsreik finally marched to battle and the promise of glory.

THIRTY-TWO

Spoiled Homecoming

Bahr wasn't the sort who believed in luck. Fate left too many open ends. Tonight it was different. The Sea Wolf decided that at least bad luck was real. It surely must be so to bring the *Dragon's Bane* sailing back to her home port under cover of darkness. He swept his gaze over the docks. A nervous feeling gnawed the pit of his stomach. There wasn't a soul in sight. It might have been nothing, but his instincts warned otherwise.

Standing beside him, the Gaimosian said, "Not good. Do you think we are expected?"

"Seems like it."

"As I thought. Your orders?" Boen asked.

Bahr replied, "Let's just wait and see. I don't want to make any wrong moves now. Not this close to the end."

"Or the beginning," Boen chided. "The men are ready should it come to a fight. I will be below."

"It just might."

The *Dragon's Bane* sailed into her berth. Deck hands jumped ashore to secure the mooring lines. The gangway dropped and both sell swords led the way off ship. Their hands stayed dangerously close to their swords. Boen came next, followed closely by Rekka. Bahr and Maleela went after, their boots barely touching the aged wooden pier before the trap was sprung. Dozens of heavily armed soldiers poured out from the surrounding buildings.

"Easy," Bahr warned his men as tensions rose. "Don't make any rash movements. We're all on the same side here."

"Excellent counsel," soothed Harnin One Eye as he slipped into the light. He too was girded for battle.

"Lord Harnin, we weren't expecting a reception," Bahr began.

Harnin stared blankly. "The king leaves nothing to chance. The kingdom is under my stewardship until he returns from the front. He wanted to thank you for doing a grand service for Delranan. Now if you will, please hand over the princess so you may cash in on your contract."

Bahr's neck hair bristled. "I'll hand over Maleela to her father personally, not a half-blind lackey with limited ambition."

Harnin tensed. "I'd advise against that. King Badron has no desire to meet with you or your…people."

"My people? These men and women risked their lives to save royal blood," Bahr growled.

He caught movement out of the corner of his eye. Ionascu and what was left of his men marched down to the docks. This is about to get interesting, Bahr thought. There was no way he could have prepared himself for what happened next.

Harnin stepped forward, ensuring his men had a clear field of fire. "This is the last time I say this, lesser son of kings. Hand over the princess."

"I said no."

Bahr's words sealed his fate before his mouth closed. A single bead of sweat broke free and trickled down his right cheek. He watched Harnin's face flush crimson. Both sides tensed in anticipation of a battle none wanted. A sharp wind gusted through. The piercing cry of gulls broke the silence. Harnin moved first.

"Archers!"

Windows in every building burst open. More than fifty bowmen nocked and took aim at the meager band of sailors and mercenaries. Dorl Theed felt his heart jump into his throat.

"The princess comes with me. If you or any of your men wish to contest this by all means, do so. Give me a reason to kill you," Harnin gloated.

There was frenzy in his eye. Bahr almost cringed from the intensity. He had no doubt that Harnin had gone mad.

"What is this? He is the king's brother, not some common dock rat!" Maleela sputtered.

"Princess, I take orders from your father, not you. This man has no favor in the eyes of the court. Come quietly and we can forget all this and go to bed," Harnin replied.

"If I refuse?"

He smiled, cruel and calculating. "What makes you believe you have a choice? Get over here now or your friends pay for your insolence."

Her eyes widened with the realization that Harnin meant what he said. "You wouldn't dare."

Ionascu came forward. "Let the girl go with her uncle, you one-eyed bastard. She deserves that much."

"Keep your mouth shut. I expected better from you, Ionascu."

Bahr, surprised by Ionascu's endorsement, tried to take advantage of the situation. "Let the others go, Harnin. They did what I asked of them. If anything I am the one you need to hold accountable."

Harnin made to reply when Ionascu suddenly pitched over in a drunken stupor. He smiled and made his move.

"Fire!"

Bow strings thrummed. Arrows whistled through the air. Three of Ionascu's men fell dead in a spray of blood and screams. Ionascu's own shout was lost amid their startled cries. A maniacal laugh burst from Harnin's throat as three score heavy infantry surged forward with sword and pike.

"Don't go for your weapons," Bahr shouted to his friends.

The last thing he wanted was to die now. Fingers of dark blood crept toward his boots. He held his hands up and waited for the soldiers to place him in cold metal shackles. Even the formidable Gaimosian went without a fight, though the implacable rage threatened to consume him.

"Captain Bahr, you and your confederates are hereby accused of heresy and treason against the king. I sentence you to life in confinement and I hope you rot in the darkest dungeons." Venom dripped from Harnin's voice. He eased close to Bahr. "I have been looking forward to this for a very long time. Take them away!"

THIRTY-THREE

Imprisoned

"That went well," Dorl mocked.

Nothol Coll rolled his eyes. "Knock it off, Dorl. We all could have ended up like those mercenaries. Bahr did the only thing he could to keep us alive."

Dorl Theed raised his arms and shook the chains for effect. "This is alive?"

"We're not dead yet," Skuld chipped in.

"We might as well be. No one has seen Bahr since we got thrown in here. Harnin's not going to let us leave here alive. He can't."

They hadn't put up a fight when Harnin ordered them arrested and the decision still didn't sit well. The guards took turns beating them along the way, Ionascu especially. Battered and chained to his knees in a cell across the hall, the former spy wailed his misery. He was the last of his men and deemed a traitor for helping Bahr. Harnin hadn't even bothered with an explanation before turning his back on the former captain.

Once their eyes adjusted to the murk they found the cells beyond disgusting. Human filth stained the floor and lower walls. Soiled straw lay scattered around them. Bones and dead rats were everywhere. Dorl Theed knew he was a dead man as soon as he was thrown into the cell. This was the sort of place where men went to die. They quickly lost track of time. No windows, no fresh air, the cell was buried far underground. Night and day were obscure concepts. They still hadn't been fed and were given just one bucket of fetid water.

An agonized groan stopped their conversation. The cell door opened to allow a squad of guards carrying Boen's unconscious form. His face was cut and bruised. The Gaimosian moaned as he hit the floor.

"Take that one next," the sergeant of the guard leered after scanning the cell.

Rough hands snatched at Skuld. He screamed and struggled, kicking one of the guards in the groin before being punched in the side of the head.

"Leave him alone, you bastard! He's just a boy," Dorl lashed out.

The sergeant laughed. "You wait your turn, pretty boy. Lord Harnin has something special for you and your friend."

Dorl struggled helplessly against his bonds. Skuld was dragged away. The door slammed shut. Anger and misery charged the air. Never had any of them felt so utterly helpless.

"Boen," Dorl called.

Anienam Keiss answered, "He'll be fine."

Oddly, the old man was the only one who had not been beaten. None of the others could explain it, Anienam, for his part, concealed his powers while struggling to keep his rage in check. He could have waved his hand and incinerated Harnin's men with ease. That would have given his presence away to the Dae'shan. It was much too early in the game for that.

Boen stirred, spitting blood.

Dorl exclaimed, "Boen!"

"Lower your voice," he grimaced. The Gaimosian slowly pushed himself up from the pool of filth. Anienam whispered a minor healing spell.

"Thank you," he whispered once he figured out what the wizard had done. Raw power flowed into his muscles, sealing cuts and reducing bruises.

The wizard nodded secretively.

"What did they ask you?" Nothol wanted to know.

Boen had been the first to undergo the guard's cruelty. It made sense. Break the biggest man and the others would lose hope.

"Nothing. They accused me of being a traitor and tried to make me confess to working for Rogscroft. The bastard even accused me of killing the prince," he smirked.

"That's ridiculous," Dorl protested. "This is all wrong. There has to be more going on here than we know."

"I don't think that matters much," Boen said as he tried to stretch out some of the soreness. "Harnin seems crazy. He has a vile taint to him."

"It is the influence of the Dae'shan," Anienam said. "I can feel them nearby. They have already gotten to the king. Our cause might already be lost."

"What cause? We only signed on to rescue the princess," Dorl's protested echoed off the slimed walls.

"Ah but we haven't yet, have we? She's in more danger now than she ever was in Rogscroft. Her situation is much worse."

The wizard's words were harsh yet filled with truth. All of them were in a much worse way with no foreseeable exit.

"Nothing we have done thus far has made a positive impact on the situation, despite our intentions. It is time we stood together and fought back," Boen told them.

"That's easy for you to say," Dorl replied. "This isn't your kingdom. You can leave any time you wish and there's not a soul who can stop you."

Anienam laughed. "Perhaps, but you really do not understand. We must all stay here in Delranan or the world as we know it will end. Cities will burn. People will be slaughtered by the thousands. Malweir will simply cease to exist."

Silence crept in. They sat shackled in shock. This was the most brutally honest the conversation had gotten since they'd first left port. Anienam whispered a small spell that enabled him to see each of their faces. Dark realization settled over the group. *At last. They finally understand the severity of the moment.* Not surprisingly, Boen spoke first.

"What do you require of us?" The Gaimosian was now completely loyal to the wizard thanks in large part to the healing spell.

Anienam paused. "We must be patient. There are hidden allies here in the castle. Princess Maleela is not in as much danger as Harnin would make us believe."

"Wizard, even if that is true, I cannot see us escaping these dungeons unscathed. The enemy is too strong, too competent. They have been burned once and are not prone to be taken again. There will be bloodshed no matter what happens next," Nothol said.

"The murder of the mercenaries makes no sense to me," Anienam told them, his mind already beyond their conversation.

Dorl asked, "I thought Ionascu was the king's man? Why would Harnin do that to his own people?"

"We could have been wrong. Perhaps Ionascu was just another puppet," Boen suggested.

Political intrigue and subterfuge raised his hackles. Gaimosians were born to live open, honest, and honorable lives. Delranan was a hive of the exact opposite. Any ruler willing to casually shed the lives of so many of his own people whispered of madness. Boen would have left already if not for Bahr and now the wizard.

Anienam shook his head. "I do not think so. The feeling is all wrong. Ionascu was not expecting Harnin's betrayal. He might have been the king's man at one point but he clearly outlived his usefulness according to Harnin."

"Are Harnin and Badron still working together or are there conflicting interests?" Nothol Coll asked.

"I'm not sure."

Boen asked, "Conflicting interests? To what ends? That doesn't make sense."

Dorl bit off a laugh. "Not much does."

"I have to agree with Dorl," Anienam said.

"Finally."

A lonely, agonized scream echoed throughout the dungeons. The sell sword felt his heart drop. Skuld. Even Boen twitched. Memories of his own torture were still too fresh in his mind. Anger washed through him. He knew, deep down, that it was time for him to live up to the full potential of his people's fearsome nickname. Vengeance Knight. Boen wanted revenge.

"The boy does not deserve this," he growled through a clenched jaw.

Anienam shook his head sorrowfully. "No. None of us do."

"We need to escape."

A menacing laugh came from the other side of the door. Creaking open, the sergeant of the guard stalked in, much like a predator on the hunt. He clapped loudly before stepping into the middle of the chamber. Wild amusement danced in his eyes.

"Yes, you do," he told them.

Dorl replied, "I'm glad we agree."

The sergeant stalked closer and punched him hard in the stomach. "Not a damned one of you will ever see the light of day again. I promise you that. This is where you die."

He walked back out. Rough hands shoved Skuld inside. The boy collapsed, weeping his pain away. His body trembled uncontrollably. Spasms wracked him.

"Next!" the sergeant called.

THIRTY-FOUR

The Temptation of Harnin One Eye

Harnin drank deeply from his crystal goblet. His eye was much darker than Maleela remembered. She smelled the wine, an obnoxious flavor that crinkled her nose. Danger pulsed from the steward. She was suddenly afraid. Here was not the simple man she'd grown up with. Her mind screamed. She needed to find a way out, a desperate path to freedom. She couldn't fathom what was happening to her beloved kingdom. It was as if her father had whipped them all into some bizarre frenzy of hatred and revenge.

"Why the long face, princess?" he sneered, clearly enjoying her discomfort.

She remained silent, unwilling to give him the satisfaction. He laughed at her. Bits of chewed meat flew from his mouth.

"Your father should have had you strangled at birth. Princess, bah! You've been nothing but trouble your whole life."

Maleela looked him dead in his cold eyes and said, "I don't know what dark powers you've gotten hold of, Harnin One Eye, but I promise you everything you are trying to build will fall apart."

"Truly?" He leaned menacingly closer. "What makes you think that? Your friends are confined in my dungeons. None will live much longer. Your own father denies your existence and I alone hold the keys to the future. What do you possibly have that can stop me?"

"I have faith."

"Misplaced, no doubt." He finished his wine. "Do you truly believe this upstart rebellion of yours has a chance of keeping Delranan from achieving dominance of the entire north?" Harnin smirked at the shock on her face. "Oh yes. We know of your pathetic group of friends. They will be dealt with soon enough. No dungeons or shackles for them though. Each and every one shall be hung publicly."

"You can't!" she shouted. A bitter combination of fear and rage clashed within her. Maleela felt sick to her stomach.

"Please princess, explain to me why not? They are traitors and enemies of the state. A quick death is more than they deserve."

"My father will not agree to this," she protested.

Harnin slammed his fist on the table, making her jump back. "Your father is not here. He's gone off to make a name for himself and his kingdom."

Maleela was defeated. Everything she'd risked her life for and fought so hard to achieve had just fallen apart. Her carefully constructed plans meant nothing. Harnin was too many steps ahead.

"This is madness," she whispered without conviction.

His smile was nauseating. "Gloriously so. It is a shame that there is no place in this new world for you. I can assure you this, however: you will be the last to die. I want you to witness every agonizing death, starting with your uncle. You deserve that much."

The horror kept her mouth shut. Her throat was dry. Her palms were slick with sweat. A dark scream stole her attention.

"The young always respond so well to a little torture, wouldn't you agree?" Harnin teased once he noticed her attention.

Skuld. "You bastard. He's just a boy."

"Who is engaged in treason. Perhaps if he'd remained a common street thief he might have gone unnoticed."

Maleela pleaded for his life. "Let him go, Harnin. He's done nothing wrong."

"Wrong is a relative state of mind. Don't blame me for this. I am acting in Delranan's best interests. Blame your uncle for involving the boy. You cannot hope to change my mind. Our course is set. The executions begin tomorrow."

Harnin One Eye motioned for the guards to take her away and went back to his meal. A chorus of screams echoing down the hallway accompanied her on the way back to her cell.

Bahr closed his eyes, trying to drown out Skuld's screams. He couldn't help but blame himself. He never should have let the boy stay on the Bane. Misery racked his conscience. It was all his fault. He'd led them to the horrible fate's waiting. Worse, all that they had struggled through had been a lie. Maleela didn't need rescuing. She was safer in Rogscroft than she could ever be at home. Bahr cursed his brother, wondering how long he'd been planning this war.

Nothing was as it appeared anymore. There was no way of knowing exactly what to believe. The world was crumbling around him. All his long life had been spent in search of a peace and quiet that could never be possible. He never held high aspirations, more content on being a simple sea captain than with entertaining ideations of the throne. Only now did he realize it was not enough. Fate demanded more.

The Sea Wolf stared down at the plate of dried venison and old cheese and wondered if this was a trick. The others were being mercilessly tortured, possibly even murdered in the dungeons while he sat in a lavish guest room with an impressive view of the ocean. He'd been alone since capture. Not even Harnin had come to gloat. Bahr had doubts as to who was really in charge. The soft click of his door lock finished his thoughts. He turned and faced the door.

Two guards entered, neither willing to meet his accusing gaze.

"Just sit tight, old man," the bigger guard ordered.

Bahr did as instructed. There was no point in doing anything else. The odds were stacked against him. Too many armed men lay between him and freedom and he lacked the strength to wage war against his own people. Bahr bite into a strip of venison and waited. Seeing Rekka Jel shoved into the room was the last thing he expected.

"Rekka?" he questioned.

The guard gave her a final shove. "Save your strength, pretty. Lord Harnin has promised you to the boys once he's had his fun."

Her eyes narrowed to thin slits. The door closed.

"Captain Bahr, are you all right?" she asked once they were alone.

"Well enough. You're the first person I have seen since we got here. I…started to believe you were all being killed."

She offered a sad smile. "I have heard the screams. Do you know why they are doing this?"

How could he possibly explain any of this? "Harnin is looking for something, but I don't know what. Common sense says they should have killed us all on the docks."

"You are the brother of the king," she said. "Surely you should be better thought of than this. We rescued the princess. Civilized lands would recognize us as heroes."

"Delranan is less civilized than I remember. I do not understand what fell power has caused this to happen in such a short time."

Showing less reservation than he, Rekka snatched a wedge of yellow cheese. "Perhaps it was always there, just waiting to be exposed? You should at least eat. We will need our strength if we are to escape."

"Escape?"

He admired her directness. Bahr continued being impressed with her deeds and actions.

"The princess was only a small part of the story. Anienam Keiss told us already. The return of the Dae'shan has sparked this war. Malweir stands on the border of destruction if Badron is victorious. We must escape. Much work is left to be done," she told him.

He understood but didn't see how it was possible. Bahr held out his empty hands. "I'm no hero. The only reason I went to Rogscroft was for her. Otherwise I might never have come back to port."

She laid a gentle hand on his forearm. "You are stronger than you know, Captain. The hour may be dark, but your men still need you."

"What can I do? I'm only a man."

The helplessness in his voice frustrated her.

"A time will come for self-pity, but it is not now. Each second we delay gives our enemies time to further their cause," she admonished.

"Perhaps you are right," he begrudgingly admitted.

Rekka smiled. "Good. What is our plan?"

Harnin One Eye finished the last of his flagon of wine, using his sleeve to wipe the stain from his lips. Dark thoughts plagued his dreams of late. He'd done what the shadow man had wanted. The *Dae'shan* as King Badron named them. They warned him of a serious threat growing against the throne and he had become a hero in the process of eliminating that threat. Why then was his mind troubled so? His thoughts turned dark. All he wanted to do was inflict pain. Hurt others. Harnin flung his goblet aside angrily.

"What is happening to me!" he cried.

Faint echoes of a desperate plea answered him. He should have been content with his role but he wasn't. He wanted more. Given this first taste of power, his cravings only increased to the point they threatened to overwhelm him. Unknown desires plagued his dreams. Badron was gone, leaving him the undisputed authority to rule Delranan as he saw fit. Harnin decided it was time to recreate the kingdom in his own image. Sudden dreams of empire emerged. Badron wanted Rogscroft, but why settle? Harnin saw the opportunity to conquer all the north. Delranan would be remade strong, malevolent, and feared across the face of the world.

Darkness swirled around him. Harnin cringed in the shell of his newfound arrogance. He relaxed slightly when the shadows coalesced into a now familiar form.

Pelthit Re stood before him, arms folded within the comfort of his robes.

"You come uninvited," Harnin slurred through the wine.

The Dae'shan sneered. "There is no mortal on all Malweir that may command me. Perhaps it is time for a further demonstration of my power?"

Harnin paled. "No."

Pelthit released the raw power gathering around him. Killing the one eye would only work against his greater vision. "Have you done as I commanded?"

"Yes. The mercenaries are dead and the rest are secure in the dungeon. They will be dead soon."

"Has word been sent to Badron yet? Holding the king's brother might prove dangerous. It may yet become necessary to kill him sooner."

Harnin nodded. "I sent a messenger yesterday. He should reach the army in three days."

Pelthit Re began to pace. He had to time his ploy near perfectly if he had any hope of unlocking the powers the dark gods promised him. His masters required the blood of a thousand sacrifices in order to transfer their foul power to the Dae'shan and begin the reclamation of Malweir.

"I have further need of you," he suddenly said. "Is there a place in Delranan where a temple might be constructed?"

"A temple? For what? My people do not worship any gods," Harnin replied.

Soon they will. Pelthit Re smiled. "Build me a temple and all your darkest fantasies will come true."

Harnin pretended to think, though in truth his mind was already committed to the ravishing of his own kingdom.

Battalions of squat, grey-bodied Goblins marched out from their underground kingdom. Their leather armor and helms were blackened. Their swords sharpened. Wicked looking pikes were barbed and poisoned. Each bore a bone shield on his back. Sergeants moved up and down the ranks barking orders and calling cadence. Overseers lashed their whips to keep the army moving.

Unbridled anger and pride choked the air. No more than five feet tall, Goblins were notoriously strong. Thick, corded muscles covered their arms and legs. Their faces were flat with coal black eyes and tufts of black hair. Tusks protruded from upper and lower jaws giving them a fearsome appearance. Most bore too many scars and all thrilled at the chance for combat.

The Goblin nation had once stretched from ocean to ocean. Their days of glory were over, plundered from history books by a combined campaign of men, Elves, Dwarves, and countless others. The Goblins were all but forgotten now, a blight upon Malweir that many chose to disbelieve. Today the army marched back to war, back to a time of dominance long since lost.

Grugnak, the Goblin king, stood atop a jagged rock outcropping and watched his hordes. He was barely discernible from the dull gray rock and the blackening sky. No vegetation grew upon the open plain. It was a sea of moving bodies, armored and hungry for war. He stared down upon his army with pride. Grugnak believed in destiny. Now was his hour, his time to lead his people back to the forefront of Malweir's future. The two shadowed Dae'shan standing behind him were here to ensure it. Pale moonlight made them almost ethereal.

"Your army is a magnificent sight," Amar Kit'han encouraged softly.

Grugnak grunted.

The Dae'shan exchanged knowing looks. They both remembered the days of Goblin dominance and it was an ugly memory. They were, however, necessary to affect the coming of the dark gods. Amar was confident that the stage had finally been set. All the pieces were in place. He folded darkness around him and left the Goblin king to his dreams of glory.

THIRTY-FIVE

The War Begins

Piper Joach wiped the sweat from his face. Dust and soot stained his skin a charcoal color. Blood trickled down the right side of his neck. A cold wind whipped his hair wildly. Smoke went down his lungs, choking him. He reached out and grabbed Sergeant Major Bors.

"Bring second platoon up and flank these bastards," he shouted above the crackle of fires raging around them.

"Sir!"

Piper turned, not bothering to see his orders carried out. Fires raged in a semi-circle around his company. The Rogscroft defenders had been waiting for them and were well organized. They fired the surrounding forest at the first sign of his scouts. Rumors that Prince Aurec himself led the defense reached Piper. He watched two soldiers drag another body back and lay it beside the seven others. Piper cursed harshly. Eight dead and he had nothing to show for it.

Sergeant Malleck rode up in hurry. "Sir, there is enemy cavalry moving up on the right."

Piper couldn't see through the smoke. Another damned distraction. "How many?"

"A company plus," Malleck replied.

"Damnation. Who's holding that flank?"

"Fensin. He's got a handful of wounded but is holding. Sir, when that cavalry strikes he won't be able to stand."

Three arrows zipped past their heads.

Piper had had enough. "Clear out those archers!"

A reserve squad unbuckled their shields and charged towards where the fire had come from.

"Sir," Sergeant Major Bors said after joining them. "General Rolnir is coming fast. We can't afford to let the army get trapped in those damned mountains. We have to push forward now."

Piper knew every man in his command had the same feelings. One hundred and twenty men against who knew how many enemies was not a tactically sound position to be in. He'd already sent a rider back to Rolnir explaining the situation. No matter how long it took for Rolnir's main body to arrive, Piper knew it would be too late to help. Bors was right. They had to act now if he expected to preserve at least some of his command.

"Sergeant Major, I want first and fourth platoons formed up on me at the double. Double-wedge formation."

Bors smiled. Sergeant Malleck looked questioningly at him. "Sir?"

"I mean to attack them."

It took mere moments for seventy riders to form up behind him. The only chance they had was to meet the enemy head on before Aurec could seal the trap. There was the chance that many of his men would be killed, but it was a chance he had to force. Piper climbed into his saddle. Malleck and Bors rode at the head of their respective wedges and nodded to their commander.

"Forward!" Piper drew a deep breath and gave the order before he realized he might very well be committing suicide.

The mounted force surged forward. A handful of arrows went by harmlessly. Piper suddenly decided that he hated archers. The horses started at a slow cant, carefully picking up the pace as the undergrowth thinned. One man fell from the saddle, an arrow in his side. The smoke cleared ahead, giving him the opportunity to see what awaited. He blanched. There had to have been over two hundred enemy cavalry riding in to meet him.

Piper struggled to keep his mouth closed. He'd never gone up against such massive odds. Death seemed a foregone conclusion. Resigning himself to apparent destiny, Piper gave the signal to charge. He prayed his men managed to do enough damage to Aurec that Rolnir and the main body would be able to smash through.

His men roared as they surge forward. The thunder of hooves boomed across the blackened field. The charged thundered closer. Another hundred meters and the lines would clash. Piper noticed the most unusual sight occur.

Prince Aurec lowered his visor and broke forward into a gallop. Piper felt deflated. Overwhelming numbers meant little in melee combat. The hammer stroke would be the hardest. Man and horse would die horribly. Aurec answered the blood pounding in his veins. Fifty meters.

Piper Joach watched his enemy launch their counter charge and felt his hopes dash. His meager forces stood little chance of success, much less survival. Dead men, they showed no signs of fear. The very thought of dying in defeat shamed him. Piper dug his spurs in harder. The battle lines closed. Piper became aware of every minute detail. Sweat flew from his horse. The wind whirled the dust and ash into small funnels. He listened to his heartbeat, smooth and steady. Piper wondered if this was what death felt like. Ten more meters and he was going to find out.

The lines clashed. Chaos erupted across the battle space. Men and horses screamed. Ropes of blood danced acrobatically through the air. Steel met steel in harsh clangs. Piper crashed into a foe, the impact jarring deep in his spine. He heard the snap of a horse's neck. Blood sprayed onto the ashes. Piper watched Malleck go down. A spear struck from his horse's head. He pushed the thought as far away as possible. Malleck would have to wait. Piper ducked to avoid a decapitating slice. He lashed out with his own, the blade biting into his enemy's throat. Blood splashed across his face. He ignored it and brought his blade up in time to guard against another blow.

Piper looked around. He was surrounded, cut off from the rest of his men in mere seconds. The battle had degenerated into a series of individual contests. Occasionally a knight got lucky and found himself in a favorable position, but that was rare. The men of Rogscroft fought with a desperate need. Piper knew his enemies had no choice but to win. Their combat reflected that attitude.

More of his men fell. Desperation took Piper. Dead and wounded littered the ground amidst growing pools of dark blood. There was no way he could win. Aurec was too strong. Piper hacked downward, taking off an arm at the elbow. Another rider charged by, knocking Piper's horse sideways. The move, accidental as it was, saved Piper's life. Searing pain lanced across his right shoulder blade as another rider slashed at his neck and missed. Piper stabbed and was rewarded with a deep grunt.

Sergeant Malleck struggled out from under his dead horse. His left leg was broken from the knee down. He used a shattered lance to push himself forward. A spear caught him in his chest, punching out his back in a bone crunching noise. His blue eyes rolled back in his head and a final gasp escaped his lungs. He was dead before he hit the ground.

Horns bleated down from the nearby mountain pass. The Wolfsreik had come. Piper Joach suddenly felt a small measure of relief. The battle paused, mercifully, as knights from both sides turned to see the first ranks of heavy infantry pouring down onto the open plains.

The defenders retreated in an organized mass. Piper's sorely beaten company was left to consolidate and lick their wounds. Seventy men had ridden out. Less than forty lived. Piper surveyed the battlefield. Bodies lay everywhere. All butchered in the name of duty. The sight of so much death made him wince. He felt like a failure. So much death and nothing to show for it. Rolnir would slap his back and congratulate them for securing the pass. The dead would be forgotten and the war would continue. He sighed and wiped the blood and sweat from his face. His eyes watered as they picked out Malleck.

Massed ranks of infantry formed up and pushed past the devastation of the flames. Battalions of cavalry followed. Among them rode General Rolnir. Not the man to shed tears after a battle, Rolnir couldn't help himself. The sight of so many of his men butchered was sheer horror.

Rolnir found Piper standing over Malleck's body. The general struggled to keep his emotions in check.

Piper looked up at him with a blank glaze. "We held."

"What happened?"

The adjutant could only shake his head. He idly rubbed a spot of blood from his cheek. "They were waiting for us. Fired the trees once we were fully committed. Aurec's a wily son of a bitch. He hit us with archers and light skirmishers. It would have been a rout if I didn't order a charge."

Rolnir scanned the area. There were over a hundred bodies just in the immediate vicinity. "How many troops do you think they had?"

"We squared off on about two hundred cavalry here."

Piper's voice was hollow. His eyes grew more distant, glassy.

"I'm proud of you, Piper. Your men did good."

Piper Joach found it hard to look at his commanding officer and friend. "General, I don't feel much like we won. I've got too many dead and nothing to show for it."

"You secured the lowlands for the rest of the army. Your men did well, Piper. To think otherwise is a grave disservice to their sacrifice. Honor your men tonight. It is the least we can do," Rolnir told him.

"Yes sir."

The general turned to leave. "Piper, have your men stand down. The rest of the army will set up the encampment. Get some hot food and some rest. We're not going anywhere for a while yet."

"What about the king?"

Rolnir forced a terse laugh. "I'll give him the report. He's about an hour behind us the last I knew. Go on now. I don't want to see your battalion again until I call for you."

Piper Joach hung his head, offered a half salute and went to find Sergeant Major Bors. They'd be glad for the respite but smarting from their losses. Rolnir watched him go. His heart wept for the man, but this was war. Death was a large part of it. All in all, Rolnir considered this a good start to the campaign. He spun about and began issuing orders. He wanted to get as much done before Badron arrived, just to keep the king quiet.

Prince Aurec slid his viewing glass shut and let out a long, slow breath. All that he'd heard of the vaunted Wolfsreik fell short from seeing them in action for the first time. The victory he won was hollow, almost tainted by so many losses. His position was already perilous and had grown decidedly worse now. His father had entrusted him with a host of five hundred men to try and delay the enemy for as long as possible. Based on the sheer strength of the army marching down from the mountains Aurec doubted that delay was going to be very long.

"They are still coming," Venten said from slightly behind.

"Ten thousand strong."

Venten looked at the prince, silently checking the measure of his will. "That number is a little less now."

"As is our own," Aurec countered. "Has there been any sign of King Badron yet?"

"No, though a large portion of his pavilion has already been erected by the tree line on the far side of the field. What are you thinking?"

"Cut off the head and see if the beast dies."

Venten shook his head. "That will be tricky. Who are you planning on sending in to accomplish that?"

"I'm not sure yet. Tonight will be our only chance. We need to strike while they are still unprepared."

"A suicide mission," Venten suggested.

Aurec reluctantly nodded. "More than likely. I'm thinking of leading it."

"I won't allow it. This is not the main army. We don't have the luxury to throw our lives away so foolishly. Least of all our commander and prince."

"You and I both know that if I wanted to go you wouldn't stop me."

Venten struggled to refrain from speaking his mind. "How your father managed to put up with you this long is beyond me. What is your back-up plan?"

Aurec hadn't made it that far. "I'm still working that out, who do we have that can sneak in there and bring me Badron's head? Literally."

"I'm sure Mahn and Raste would appreciate the opportunity."

He snorted. "Raste more so. But no, I have something else in mind for them. Come on. I want Shirsez and his men to meet us in one hour."

They stalked away, leaving the Wolfsreik in command of the field.

"Are there any questions?" Aurec asked.

He'd finished briefing what his expectations were for the mission. Fully one-fifth of his forces were going to be committed and that worried him. Venten stood by his side, ever the stalwart companion and mentor.

Shirsez rubbed his chin thoughtfully. This wasn't his first choice of assignment but he was fully prepared to do his duty for the kingdom. "My lord, my men will do their job. We can handle it."

"Don't do anything brash. I don't want one of my best getting killed this early in the war. You can do that later if you want," Aurec joked.

Shirsez grinned and went to gather his men.

Aurec turned to Venten. "Do you think he can do it?"

"I hope so."

Not the vote of confidence he was looking for. "And if not?"

The prince remained silent.

THIRTY-SIX

A Desperate Strike

Badron awoke to a chorus of shouts. The king threw on his heavy cloak, grabbed his sword and dashed outside. What he saw enraged him. It was if the underworld had erupted in his camp. Flames spread from tent to tent. Soldiers ran everywhere using anything they could to try and douse the flames.

"What is going on here?" Badron roared.

An armed guard stepped from the shadows. His sword had fresh blood dripping from it. "Sire, get back inside. It is not safe out..."

A flaming arrow punched out the front of his throat in midsentence. The guard frothed blood and dropped dead at Badron's feet. His flesh sizzled as the flames extinguished. The king looked past the corpse as flight after flight of fire arrows whistled overhead.

"King Badron," Rolnir shouted from nearby. "Get back in your tent. You are only in the way out here."

Badron seethed at being told what to do. "Do not assume to command me."

Rolnir closed the distance in a blink and snatched the king by his collar. "*You* are in *my* way. I give the orders here, not you. Now, back inside, sire. Let me do my job or go find someone better."

He shoved Badron off and stormed back into the inferno. The king stood alone in his shock as the battle raged.

Dawn was not kind. Rolnir, going off only two hours of sleep, sat brooding outside of the command tent as the coffee brewed. Just one day in enemy territory and he had lost more than a hundred men. Doubt gnawed away. *What am I doing wrong?* Yes, this was war, but he had been prepared for it. *Hadn't I?* Worse, he was now expected to go before his king with answers he simply did not have.

"It wouldn't do for the men to see their commanding general having such deep moments with himself. They'll start to talk, you know."

Rolnir kicked out a stool for Piper to sit on. He couldn't help but smile. "Didn't I order you to stand down?"

Piper rolled his eyes mockingly. "I tried, it didn't work for me. Besides, last night was kind of busy."

"I'm glad to see you in better spirits."

Piper tried to smile but it came out strained and false. The faraway look still lingered behind his pupils. "It's amazing what a little sleep can do."

The general let the obvious question go unasked. He didn't see how anyone could sleep through last night's raid. Soldiers were already busy doing their best to erase any sign of damage. Burned tents were torn down and replaced with what little the advance units were able to bring. The first supply train wasn't due for another few days. Rolnir hated the eternal issue of logistics more than combat. Getting supplies to an army in the field was a nightmare.

"Most of the commanders are inside," he told Piper. "Are you sure you feel up to this?"

"I never am but that hasn't stopped me yet."

Rolnir smiled and rose. Best not delay any longer. Besides, the king must be furious by now. That made him smile more. He wasn't exactly sure what he told Badron last night but the king's reaction had been priceless. Having the king underfoot was only going to end badly. The worst part was he had no one to voice his frustrations to. Any one of his most trusted men might be more interested in the crown than loyalty. Taking a calming breath, Rolnir entered the tent.

"On your feet!"

As one, his commanders and senior staff rose from their field chairs and came to attention. It was a custom Rolnir had always appreciated. It showed the proper amount of respect and discipline.

"Please, carry on," he told them.

He waited for them to settle before beginning. "First order of business, what happened last night?"

"Sir, as best as we can tell the enemy used archers to distract us, allowing a small band of assassins to enter the camp. Their target was obviously the king."

Unacceptable. "How did they know the king was here?"

The same man, lean and hawkish, replied, "They have scouts hidden throughout this valley. It is possible they spotted his column coming down from the Murdes."

"Meaning our security is that lax?" Rolnir cautioned.

"I wouldn't go so far as that, but it is also possible the Pell Darga are allied with Rogscroft," he continued.

Piper disagreed. "We saw no evidence of such on our way through the mountains."

"Doesn't mean they aren't in league, Piper," Colonel Herger said. He set down his long stem pipe. "They may just be biding their time."

"We still would have seen some trace of them. Our scouts found nothing."

"What were they looking for?" asked a dark voice from the far corner.

They turned to the sound of the newcomer. Rolnir responded first.

"The king."

Again the war council rose, only this time Badron left them standing. This war, his war, had gotten off to a dismal beginning and the men to blame for it were all standing before him. His glare cut into them.

"Has everyone suddenly forgotten how to speak?" he demanded.

Piper Joach swallowed hard. "Signs of the Pell Darga, my lord."

Badron's face darkened. The Pell Darga. His son's murderers. "It is a pity that we did not run in to them. I would have liked to kill a few myself."

Rolnir sidled through them to stand before the king. "My initial assumption on the ease of our passage through the mountains seems correct. It is entirely possible the Pell are working with Rogscroft. The enemy remains a step ahead of us, sire. I do not believe the Pell Darga should be our primary focus."

"Agreed. Tightening your defenses is a good place to start." His eyes narrowed to slits. "From what I understand your men have had their asses handed to them since they arrived in this godforsaken valley."

Rolnir struggled to contain the fury building. *The bastard is taunting me.* Rolnir didn't rise to the insult. He knew what his strategy was and he was bound to adhere to it until it proved fatal. "Sire, our defenses are improving. Intelligence reports say we are facing a small enemy host. I do not believe they are a heavy combat unit, more likely they've been sent out to harass us and slow the advance."

Badron's fist clenched. "My death would most certainly accomplish that, would it not? I am sorely disappointed in you, general. Do not make me find a more suitable replacement."

"We shall double our efforts," Rolnir managed to stammer. He was stunned, as were all his officers. He felt his grasp on the army slip.

"I should hope so, for your sake," Badron continued. "All Delranan is reliant on the success of the Wolfsreik. You hold the fate of the kingdom in your hands. Do not fail."

Badron stalked back to the door. "General Rolnir, I expect you in my quarters as soon as you are finished here."

Rolnir swallowed his pride lest the worst happened now. "Of course, sire."

The general waited until Badron was gone and everyone had the chance to calm down before continuing. Now was the most critical time. Any misstep here and he was in jeopardy of losing the respect of his commanders. Rolnir cursed the king for putting him in this situation. All the king had to do was let him command the army like he knew how.

Badron normally left military affairs alone. That made Rolnir instantly suspicious. The king was not acting like himself. He had a darker air about him of late. It was almost as if he were dancing to another's song. Rolnir made the instant decision that he could not trust the king any longer. He also recognized that victory was going to come from the men assembled in this tent, not from a spastic king who had an ulterior motive.

He tried to pick up where he they had left off. "The enemy assault on the camp notwithstanding, how soon can we expect the engineers to begin building the siege machines?"

Colonel Ulaf, master of engineers, thought for a moment and answered. "The first supply wagons should already be arriving. My boys will be up and running by the evening."

Rolnir cast Piper a glance. "I want the guard doubled in their area. Those machines will become a top priority for the enemy to destroy once we move."

"Yes sir."

"Gentlemen, the last twenty-four hours have tested our mettle. Right now we have been found wanting. The enemy is not going to sit back and let us march up to the gates of Rogscroft and plant our banner on their ramparts. This is going to be a hard fight. I expect every soldier in the Wolfsreik to give his all. We can relax when the war is over. Are there questions?"

No one spoke.

Rolnir nodded, satisfied. "Good. Go and prepare your troops. We march in two days."

He returned their salutes and motioned for Piper to stand fast after the others had left. Once they were alone he said, "Take the wagons scheduled to arrive later today and load the dead. I'm not going to bury a single one of our men in this damned kingdom. They fought as heroes and deserve to be buried with their loved ones."

"I'll make it happen," Piper solemnly confirmed.

"Piper, are you fit enough to return to the line?" He quickly changed subjects.

"Fit enough I suppose. My shoulder is killing me though."

"That's not what I meant, and you know it."

Piper let his eyes shut. "Sir, you and I have both lost men in the field before. Each death stays with me, but I use them to give me strength. This time will be no different. You can depend on my men to do their job to the last."

"That's all I wanted to know. Thank you, Piper. I truly do not know what I would do without you. Dismissed."

Alone, Rolnir stared down at the map of Rogscroft. He had a feeling that his troubles were only beginning.

The walk to Badron's tent was much longer than it should have been. He took the time to visit with the line units. Morale was still high. In truth there wasn't much reason for it not to be. Only a handful of units had been affected by the raid. He swung by the field hospital to check on the wounded. Most of them voiced their concern and volunteered to hurry back to the fight. He applauded their courage and told them in due time. That was good. Soldiers needed to get back into a scrape after a loss.

Rolnir swung by the growing engineer camp. All of them were busy unloading wagons or fashioning heavy bolts for the ballista. Smiths were also being erected. Wagon masters drove in huge loads of coke for the fires. Soon those forges would be able to repair or replace any battle loss. That part was important. Swords dulled; shields cracked.

Picket lines had already gone out along the obvious avenues of approach. The leaders of the Wolfsreik were determined not to get caught short again. Rolnir took great pride in all. The strength of his army was not in any one man, but in all. At last he made it to the king's pavilion. Guards, already expecting him, waved him past. He smiled politely and made small talk while wondering if he was going to take a knife to the back. Blood stained the ground beneath his feet. Badron's previous guard had been killed by the assassin squad. Rolnir tensed, prepared for the worst, and stepped past.

The king sat in the center of the central chamber, expectantly waiting on a makeshift throne. Plush carpets and oversized pillows were thrown across the ground. A fire crackled in the background. The darkness bothered Rolnir. Badron steeped his hands in front of his face, further concealing his intentions. The general was bothered by barely seeing his king's eyes.

"General Rolnir, please come forward," he said in a slow, measured voice.

Rolnir hesitated. This was not the same man who had been so belligerent back in the command tent.

"Sire," he nodded curtly and moved forward.

Badron watched his general. "How goes the rest of the deployment?"

What are you getting at? "Fairly well. The engineers are already working and I have most of the infantry battalions occupying positions along the front. Skirmishers will be sent out before dawn."

"Our enemy will be emboldened after yesterday's victories."

"I agree."

"Further proof that they have been prepared for our arrival. Security has been horrendous, General."

Rolnir didn't see it that way. They were doing what any normal man in the same situation would. Defending your home certainly wasn't a crime. The men of Rogscroft were no different from his men in that regard.

Badron leaned menacingly close. "I want them destroyed. Every last one of them. They murdered my son, kidnapped my daughter, and embarrassed my army. Stelskor's treachery insults our entire kingdom."

"The men will do their job, sire. I can assure you."

The king snapped a nod. "Good. Keep me apprised of the situation. I expect regular reports once the advance begins."

"Of course, sire." *Lovely, just lovely.*

Badron dismissed him with a nonchalant wave of the hand. "You may go now, and Rolnir, never speak to me in the manner in which you did last night again. I have no qualms about having you gutted in front of your army."

General Rolnir left more confused. The war had but begun and events were already spiraling out of control. Badron was bordering on insane and was obviously going to be an issue in the days to come. He decided to put his faith in the strength of the Wolfsreik and hope for the best.

THIRTY-SEVEN

Escape

"Ha! I finally remember."

Head slowly turned to the wizard with careful anticipation.

Anienam only bothered to look up when no one replied. "Is no one curious?"

"I think we've all been beaten up a little too much to be excited about a simple exclamation," Dorl Theed replied. His lips were dry, cracked in a dozen places. His throat hurt from a particularly nasty chop courtesy of his torturer.

Anienam was doing his best to heal them but he had limits to what he could do. Rather than apologizing, he remained focused on his own thoughts. "The Dae'shan have nearly unlimited power. There are nigh invincible but they do have an exploitable weakness."

Boen raised his weary head. "That being?"

"The legends are all vague on the name, but there is an ancient artifact that was once wielded to defeat them."

"Why weren't they destroyed?" Nothol asked. Curiosity peaked now.

The wizard paused. He wasn't sure how much to say here, how much Harnin's men might overhear. "Perhaps it was not used properly. I don't know exactly. What I remember is that this is the only key to defeating the Dae'shan and saving Malweir."

Dorl snorted. "That's all well and fine, but we need to get out of here first."

"I can assist with that, but my spell will only free our bonds."

"I'll worry about the rest after I get circulation back in my limbs."

Boen wasn't in the mood for the negativity. Instead he focused on Anienam's revelation. "What does this item look like?"

"A hammer."

"That's it? A hammer?"

He nodded. "A war hammer to be certain. Legends call it the Blud Hamr, or Blood Hammer. I recall a tale about explorers being able to hear the sound of hammers in the wind. This is our key to victory, my friends."

Dorl Theed hung his head again. He wanted to cry. The nadir of his life had finally arrived. Hopelessness stretched out from the darkness to lay claim upon the shadows of his soul and this damned wizard was yakking about some mythical hammer. How much more ridiculous could this get?

"Does the legend mention where we can find this mythical hammer?" Boen pressed.

"It does, but I do not know."

"Your words are not exactly forthcoming," Boen carefully said.

Anienam ignored him. "Patience is required. It is true that our enemies are many but hope is still to be had. Even now forces are moving in opposition to our foe. Victory is still attainable."

"That's easy enough for you to say. You're the only one who hasn't been taken and beaten repeatedly," Dorl snapped off from his misery.

Nothol Coll passed his friend a cross glare.

The wizard sat quietly. True, he hadn't been tortured, but he also devoted most of his energy towards healing his friends and working through the paths of his memory. He'd lost his grasp on sympathy long ago. Anienam believed that everything happened for a reason. There was no cause to lament bad times. Every life had dark hours. Matters generally sorted themselves out. Only this time he wasn't so sure of the direction matters were headed.

Maleela jumped at the booming sounds coming from the other side of the door. Her heart inched a little higher. She wasn't sure but it sounded like a fight. Her initial fear was that Harnin had finally come for her neck. She scrambled, desperately searching for something, anything she could use as a weapon. Her hopes sank. She didn't even have a glass of water. Maleela delved deep for what courage remained and prepared for the end.

The noises stopped. The lock clicked and the door slowly opened. Maleela instinctively tensed. She decided to attack. If she was going to die it might as well be with some measure of dignity. A shadow fell across the room. She let out a bitter scream and launched into an attack. Strong arms blocked her wild swings and easily wrapped her up.

"Whoa now, princess," said a familiar voice.

Maleela's senses swirled. Confusion slipped in. She looked up into the oddly familiar eyes of Lord Argis.

"What is this?" she stammered.

"It is me, Argis. I am taking you out of here. You have friends in the city. They will ensure your safety," Argis told her.

Her confusion only deepened. "My safety? I don't understand."

"I am a member of the underground," he whispered.

That was it. No long drawn-out speech. Just a simple admission. Argis looked almost guilty for how easy it had been. Admitting his traitorous actions, even to the princess, was almost overwhelming. His palms began to sweat.

She instantly wondered if he was in league with Aurec. Maleela's eyes opened wide. "You are one of my father's closest friends. How can you do this?"

"King Badron is not the man he once was. He is consumed by this dream of creating an empire. Your brother's death was the final act. He wants blood, Maleela. More than I am willing to give him."

The older man lowered his eyes in shame. Maleela was quick to correct him. "You have nothing to be ashamed of, Lord Argis. Brave men stand out in dark times."

He thought for a moment. "Perhaps history will judge me kindly, though I believe Harnin and Badron will have my head. Come, there is no time to spare. I merely knocked the guard unconscious."

Her ruthlessness stunned him. "You should have killed him. They will be able to identify you now."

"Enough have died because of me. I do not wish for more blood on my hands," he replied. "Princess, we have to go now."

She placed her hands on her hips as a stubborn child would. "Not without Bahr and the others."

"There is no time," he insisted.

"Then we make time. I will not abandon my friends to die by Harnin's hand."

Argis scowled darkly and cast a glance at the guards. "Very well, your uncle is closest. I hope you know what you are doing, princess."

Argis stuck his head into the empty hall and called her forward. The way was clear, though for how long he couldn't promise. The pair moved as fast as he felt they could safely. Argis rounded the corner and nearly bowled over an unsuspecting guard coming down a stairwell. Argis smashed the hilt of his sword into the guard's temple, knocking him unconscious.

"Hurry," he whispered to Maleela.

They fled down the stairs. The movement reopened terrible memories of her first escape from Chadra Keep. The screams. The blood. The heavy iron smells clinging to the air. Maleela tried to suppress her shaky nerves. The memory was still too strong, too powerful for her to accept without consequence. She focused on freedom. It was the only way she was going to have a chance to redeem her past sins.

"Here," Argis called. "Your uncle is behind this door."

Maleela struggled with suspicion. "Why no guards?"

"Harnin knew that by holding you he could keep your uncle immobilized. He did not see the danger of escape from the old man."

The former captain of Delranan wedged the tip of his sword into the lock and twisted. He heard the soft metallic click and smiled. Argis quickly re-sheathed his sword and turned the knob. Maleela rushed past him and into her uncle's waiting arms. She ignored the fact that both he and Rekka Jel were poised for a fight. The smaller woman stood with a knowing look, as if she'd been expecting this moment.

"Princess, hurry," Argis hissed from the doorway.

Bahr gently eased his niece away and looked at her. "Did they hurt you?"

"Not yet. Harnin would hardly look me in the eye, much less touch me."

Her voice dripped with disgust.

The Sea Wolf absently nodded. He turned to Argis. "Where is the snake? I'd like to borrow your sword and finish this while I am here."

"Now is not the time," Argis insisted.

Bahr narrowed his eyes, the kind of look he got right before he jumped into a fight. "I asked you where he is."

Argis changed tactics. "He went down to the docks. I think he means to burn your ship."

"What?" Bahr raged.

The time for secrets was over. Delranan already bordered on the brink of civil war. This one desperate act could very well serve as the catalyst to start the fire. "You have to know that Harnin wants to kill you all. You especially. He sees you as a viable threat to his plans. There is nowhere safe in the kingdom for you, Bahr."

Rekka broke her silence. "Captain, there will be a chance for revenge, but we must look to the princess now. She must live if the underground is to have a chance."

"My boat. My crew. Where does this treachery end? I want that man's head," Bahr snarled. His muscles bunched, strained under his tunic. The hatred was building, threatening to consume him and Bahr was content with letting it go.

Argis tried to make him see reason. "Captain Bahr, there is no time! You have no friends. I am the only man in the Keep involved with the underground movement. My life is in just as much forfeit as yours. We must leave now or Harnin wins."

Bahr eyes him suspiciously. "You've been a strong supporter of my brother for years. Why the change? I don't trust you."

"It's true, Uncle. Argis opened the door that allowed Aurec and his men inside," Maleela told him. She recognized the signs. Two men used to being in charge were close to coming to blows.

Something in her words stopped Bahr short. "What door?"

"The same one we are using to escape," Argis told him.

"Bahr, you shall have your revenge by a different path," Rekka prophetically said.

"Let's go," was all he said.

They decided to split up. Argis and Rekka went down to the nearest arms room to gather enough weapons for the others while uncle and niece hurried to the dungeons. The escape went relatively smooth. The handful of jailors fled upon seeing Bahr strike the head from their sergeant. Bahr snatched the keys from the dead man and unlocked the cages. His heart ached at how they limped and moved slowly. Their suffering only served to further enrage him. Only Boen passed him a glance, weary and prideful.

Anienam stopped Bahr before they left. "We must take Ionascu."

"Why? He's one of Harnin's men," Bahr protested. There was no point in taking one of their enemies.

"I feel that he has a significant role to play in our future," the wizard smiled thinly.

Bahr wasn't convinced. "I don't trust him, but it's your call."

Anienam bowed graciously.

"Dorl, you and Nothol go unlock him," Bahr ordered.

Dorl Theed caught the keys and begrudgingly went about his task. Bahr watched them, refraining from asking the obvious questions. Time would make things better. He shifted his focus back to the wizard who shook his head with caution. The message was clear. Now was not the time.

"Some of the guards got away. We're going to have company soon if we don't hurry," the Sea Wolf told the others.

Boen rubbed his sore wrists. "I am ready for a fight. The dogs don't deserve to live."

"We've got a long way to go before we'll be alive. Do you have enough left to make it out of here?"

Boen smiled. "I am Gaimosian. I can outlast anyone," the big man confirmed.

"Good, because we're going after Harnin."

Bahr tossed him the single sword he managed to take from the dead sergeant just as the sell swords returned with Ionascu's limp form. The man was babbling incoherently.

"He won't make it," Dorl insisted. "The man is deadweight."

Anienam sent a surge of strength into them both. There wasn't time for any extensive healing. He gave Bahr a nod once finished. The Sea Wolf led them out through one of the lesser-used passages. The old man pushed his battered group as hard as he thought they could go. Boen brought up the rear. Their route was so obscure that they made it to the door Argis and Rekka had secured without incident. Argis waited impatiently by the door. The last time he had been here was with a blade pressed to his throat by the members of the underground. This time he held the keys. He passed a glance outside and motioned for them to follow him into the forest.

Harnin took the honor of throwing the first torch. He delighted in seeing the *Dragon's Bane* catch fire. His men had spent hours filling the hull with whale oil and kindling. He had every intention of watching this damned ship burn to the ashes. The flames reflected hatred in his eyes. Bahr was the sole remaining obstacle to his grand designs for the future. The vice lord of Delranan watched gleefully as the flames licked higher.

A warm smile creased his face. The heat felt good in the cool autumn night. This was the beginning of his dream. It was a dream he had never internalized until that fateful night the Dae'shan came to call. No longer would he stand in the shadows of the lesser brother. Clouds of black smoke billowed as the oil caught fire. The *Dragon's Bane* had been an icon on the northern seas for almost three decades. Bahr's legend had grown partially because of his ship, making him a symbol of strength and respect. He was a hero to the common man, and Harnin wanted him destroyed.

"This is a glorious day for all Delranan," he addressed his men. "The stigma of the old days is ended. The people of this kingdom have lived under a lie for far too long. Tonight we find freedom and the path ahead to a greater destiny!"

His soldiers cheered above the crackle of flames. Each was loyal, totally subservient to Harnin. He praised their loyalties, for it was these men who were going to help him seize power and keep it. Harnin tried to imagine the look on Badron's face when he finally ran his sword through the king's stomach.

"Lord Harnin!"

The call shattered his illusions. He frowned at the angst in the voice. Something was wrong. The runner stopped and knelt at his master's feet. His breath was ragged. Small drops of blood stained his jerkin.

"Speak," Harnin ordered.

"My lord, the king's brother has escaped."

Harnin reeled. *Impossible*. He drew his short sword and killed the messenger. His men stared in muted disbelief.

"Back to the Keep," Harnin barked. Blood ran down the length of his blade. "I want Bahr found, dead or alive. Move!"

One Eye fumed while men scrambled to obey. He was so close to completing his long awaited revenge and now all his carefully laid plans were unraveling. Despite holding the throne Harnin felt powerless. Too much was happening too fast. Badron's wrath would be furious should he discover his brother had not only escaped but what Harnin was planning for the kingdom.

He watched the reflection of the flames on the water and slowly made up his mind. He had to act quickly if everything was to be saved. The alternatives were too bad to contemplate.

End of Book One

BOOK II OF THE NORTHERN CRUSADE
TIDES OF BLOOD AND STEEL
CHRISTIAN WARREN FREED

Excerpt from Tides of Blood and Steel:
Book Two of the Northern Crusade.

ONE

Anienam Keiss whispered a few words and the inside of the temple sprang to life under a pale blue glow. Together he and Skuld wormed their way around the piles of broken rock and marble that littered the floor, past rows of near petrified benches.

"What do you know of magic, young Skuld?"

The street thief was taken off guard. Truth be told, he never bothered to think about it. Magic was another of those things in life that didn't matter. "Nothing, sir. I don't see what this has to do with anything though."

Anienam smiled. "Consider it an old man's fancy."

They continued. Anienam was impressed with the scope of the building. At one point it must have been the largest building in the north. Ages old cobwebs hung from every corner. The air was more stale here than in the outer chamber. Skuld found his breathing grow harder with each step forward. A loud snap stole his attention, forcing him to look down. Two skeletons lay stretched out. Tatters of dark robes clung in strips to the dust-covered bones. The street thief wanted nothing more than to leave this house of death. He was no stranger to the tunnels, but this went beyond the depths of his courage.

"How will we know what we're looking for?" he asked. His voice was desperate to take his mind off of the present.

"Patience, my young friend. The way will be shown to us."

Skuld stared at the old man's back. He couldn't begin to fathom the sarcasm his elders constantly displayed. He shook his head and continued. The sooner they finished the better.

"Please hurry," he whispered. The walls closed in on him.

Anienam offered a compassionate glance. "We are almost done. A few more moments and we can leave."

Casting another spell, Anienam focused his attention on the far end of the ruin. It took a moment for anything to happen. Then the air heated, grew damper. A steady thumping noise haunted the shadows. It reminded Skuld of a heartbeat. The farther the duo went the louder the sound became. Skuld struggled to maintain what little courage remained.

"What is that?"

The answer drained the warmth from him.

"I don't know." Anienam gathered his power, just in case. "Keep a sharp eye. We are looking for a bright green light."

The thief did as he was told, hoping and praying to find the key to unlock the next stage of their journey. The ruins groaned. He felt tired eyes watching him, but no matter where he looked, they remained just out of reach. Shadows transformed into eerie hands creeping forward to snatch him away to some distant catacomb, never to be heard from again. His heart weakened and only found strength when Anienam spied the faint trim of green light.

"There Skuld! Quickly, go and grab the book!"

The thief climbed over a broken table and found a massive tome alone on a marble pedestal. He hesitated. The book looked new, as if waiting for his coming. Better judgment warned him not to proceed. Nothing good was going to come from this. *Could it be a trap?* He doubted the wizard's ability to protect them. A strange new energy seeped into him, his muscles and his resolve. Skuld reached out and ran his fingertips over the ancient volume. He suddenly realized how wrong he had been.

"Did you feel that?" Argis asked.

Dorl swallowed hard and clenched his sword that much tighter. It wouldn't mean much if they were attacked, but it helped sooth his frayed nerves. He shivered slightly. All the warmth left him. His breath turned to vapors.

"What in the…"

Dorl never got the chance to finish. The ground trembled and shook, throwing them violently down. Dust rained down so thick he could barely make out the others. The torches snapped and hissed. Dorl struggled back to his feet and immediately began searching for the source of danger. The far wall exploded outwards as dozens of skeletal hands shot out, clutching desperately at Maleela. Still on her knees, she barely rolled away in time.

Dorl Theed swore to himself. The skeletons pulled and clawed their way free of their eternal tombs. Nothol dropped into a low guard and waited. His eyes hardened. Of the many foes he'd faced over the years, this was a first. The undead continued to break free around them. Dorl managed to overcome his fright and pull Maleela to the relative safety their group offered. Nothol grinned savagely. He didn't know what it was going to take to kill a skeleton but he decided not to wait to find out. He attacked. With the confined space only one man was able to wield a sword effectively. Dorl and Argis fell back to protect the princess.

Nothol Coll's first strike ripped a broken skull from the neck a moment before he kicked the remains to dust. The skeleton collapsed in a ragged heap, taking three more with it. This might not be so bad after all. He swung again, this time splitting one at the waist. More came. And more. The skeletons numbered more than fifty. Even with Nothol Coll hacking and slashing the dead soldiers continued to break free. Bones piled around them.

Dorl Theed watched the situation worsen. He desperately wanted to help but there simply wasn't enough space for both men to maneuver without cutting each other. Frustration made him tremble.

"We have to help him," he told Argis.

The former captain stood with his mouth agape. Shock immobilized him. Never in his wildest thoughts could he imagine and army of the dead. His knees were weak. His mind refused to obey his body. Twice he almost dropped his sword.

Dorl snarled and slapped the man on his back. "Damn it Argis snap out of it! We're going to die down here if we don't act."

Recognition flashed in the back of his pale eyes. "What can we do against this?"

At least he still has his tongue, Dorl frowned. "Send them back to the underworld and hope for the best."

Dorl Theed took a small step forward and was violently jerked backwards. The force made him drop his sword. Bony fingers gripped him tightly, trying to rip him apart. He let out a strangled cry as they took him to the ground. Dorl struggled with all his might. He punched and kicked. A bone arm ripped away and became his only weapon. Dorl used the arm to lash out at his attackers.

The sudden attack finally forced Argis into action. His resolve strengthened, the old man clenched his sword and attacked. Dust and bones flew wildly about the small chamber. The Delranan noble fought like never before. Vague ideations of what would happen to him should he fail pushed him harder. His muscles soon screamed and began to ache. The old man didn't have much left.

Dorl managed to break free. The sell sword managed to find his sword through the mayhem and unleashed his pent up fury. Every beating and taunt from Harnin's guards came back now. Hatred, agony, embarrassment, and fear burst from the inner well of his soul. Dorl attacked, and attacked, with sword, fist and boot. He didn't stop until Argis placed a weary hand upon his shoulder.

Dorl looked around. His breath was ragged, clogged with dust and bone matter. The battle was over. All the skeletons were destroyed, sent back to the decay of their eternal death. Argis dropped to a knee. He was much the worse of the two. Maleela sat huddled in the corner. Even with all she had been through she couldn't bring herself to accept a battle against the dead.

"What just happened?" Argis asked through strained breaths.

Nothol sheathed his sword. "This place is cursed."

"Should we go and get the wizard?" Dorl asked hesitantly. The rage was gone, leaving a numb sensation in its place. He had had enough of magic and having Anienam around made him queasy.

The ground trembled and shook violently. Huge chunks of ceiling crashed down. The walls shattered and started to collapse.

"Cave in!" Nothol shouted.

Argis forced himself back to his feet. "We must flee!"

Dorl passed a desperate look to the empty doorway. There was no sign of Skuld or the damned wizard. Duty and honor urged him to go and look for them. Reality screamed otherwise. The very walls were coming down around them. Waiting was not an option.

"Run!" he tried to shout above the roar.

He pushed Argis ahead and ran for his life. Dorl Theed gave a last thought to the others and kept running before they all died.

THE FRACTURED UNIVERSE I
DREAMS OF WINTER
CHRISTIAN
WARREN FREED

It is a troubled time, for the old gods are returning and they want the universe back…

Under the rigid guidance of the Conclave, the seven hundred known worlds carve out a new empire with the compassion and wisdom the gods once offered. But a terrible secret, known only to the most powerful, threatens to undo three millennia of progress. The gods are not dead at all. They merely sleep. And they are being hunted.

Senior Inquisitor Tolde Breed is sent to the planet Crimeat to investigate the escape of one of the deadliest beings in the history of the universe: Amongeratix, one of the fabled THREE, sons of the god-king. Tolde arrives on a world where heresy breeds insurrection and war is only a matter of time. Aided by Sister Abigail of the Order of Blood Witches, and a company of Prekhauten Guards, Tolde hurries to find Amongeratix and return him to Conclave custody before he can restart his reign of terror.

What he doesn't know is that the Three are already operating on Crimeat.

Read Dreams of Winter now and begin your journey into the realm of the Forgotten Gods.

Law of the Heretic

Immortality Shattered Book 1

CHRISTIAN WARREN FREED

The Staff of Life has been lost for a thousand years. Imbued with the powers to dominate all life, the Staff can save or ruin the Free Lands. Many have sought out the Staff. All failed. Until now.

Aron Kryte has served the Hierarchy for years. Honorable. Duty-driven, the young man has risen through the ranks of the venerable Golden Warriors. Born into this life, Aron patrols the Free Lands, maintaining the long peace. Little could he know that the world he knows is built upon lies. His quiet summer days are shattered when he is led into an ambush by the man whose brother he once killed.

Imelin is the last of his order. A powerful wizard and member of the High Council, he has ever harbored the secret desire for power. Darkness dwells in his heart. He defects from the Council and heads to the forsaken land of Suroc Tol, where an army of darklings await his command. With the creatures of legend under heel, Imelin can at last embark upon his quest to discover the Staff of Life and begin a war of attrition that will bring the Free Lands to their knees.

Events are set in motion that will change the Free Lands forever. War brews. The ancient elven fortress of Dol'ir is overrun by a timeless enemy, the survivors forced to flee. Traitors rise. Armies gather. Only a handful of men and women stand against the coming storm. It begins in Galdea, where an aging king is slowly losing control.

THE CHILDREN of NEVER

A War Priests of Andrak Saga

CHRISTIAN WARREN FREED

The war priests of Andrak have protected the world from the encroaching darkness for generations. Stewards of the Purifying Flame, the priests stand upon their castle walls each year for 100 days. Along with the best fighters, soldiers, and adventurers from across the lands, they repulse the Omegri invasions.

But their strength wanes and evil spreads.

Lizette awakens to a nightmare, for her daughter has been stolen during the night. When she goes to the Baron to petition aid, she learns that similar incidents are occurring across the duchy. Her daughter was just the beginning. Baron Einos of Fent is left with no choice but to summon the war priests.

Brother Quinlan is a haunted man. Last survivor of Castle Bendris, he now serves Andrak. Despite his flaws, the Lord General recognizes Quinlan as one of the best he has. Sending him to Fent is his best chance for finding the missing children and restoring order. Quinlan begins a quest that will tax his strength and threaten the foundations of his soul.

The Grey Wanderer stalks the lands, and where he goes, bad things follow. The dead rise and the Omegri launch a plan to stop time and overrun the world. The duchy of Fent is just the beginning.

The follow up to the L Ron Hubbard Writers of the Future award winning short: The Purifying Flame, the Children of Never is an all-new novel set in a world of raw imagination. Get your copy today!

BIO

Christian W. Freed was born in Buffalo, N.Y. more years ago than he would like to remember. After spending more than 20 years in the active duty US Army he has turned his talents to writing. Since retiring, he has gone on to publish more than 20 science fiction and fantasy novels as well as his combat memoirs from his time in Iraq and Afghanistan. His first book, Hammers in the Wind, has been the #1 free book on Kindle 4 times and he holds a fancy certificate from the L Ron Hubbard Writers of the Future Contest.

Passionate about history, he combines his knowledge of the past with modern military tactics to create an engaging, quasi-realistic world for the readers. He graduated from Campbell University with a degree in history and a Masters of Arts degree in Digital Communications from the University of North Carolina at Chapel Hill. He currently lives outside of Raleigh, N.C. and devotes his time to writing, his family, and their two Bernese Mountain Dogs. If you drive by you might just find him on the porch with a cigar in one hand and a pen in the other. You can find out more about his work by clicking on any one of the social media icons listed below. You can find out more about his work by following him on:

Facebook: @https://www.facebook.com/ChristianFreed
Twitter: @ChristianWFreed
Instagram: @ christianwarrenfreed

Like what you read? Let him know with an email or review.

warfighterbooks@gmail.com

www.ingramcontent.com/pod-product-compliance
Lightning Source LLC
Chambersburg PA
CBHW031621100726
47898CB00006B/1887